Praise for the *New York Times* bestseller
MEG: A Novel of Deep Terror

"Nonstop excitement."   —*Library Journal*

"An adrenaline-pumping thriller!"   —*New York Post*

"Hellishly riveting . . . an utterly amazing climax."
                                         —*Kirkus Reviews*

Praise for the *New York Times* bestseller *The Trench*

"A heart-stopping thriller!"   —*Ingram*

"An entertaining tale of gripping nonstop horror."
                                         —*Midwest Book Review*

"A fast-paced thriller with many plot twists."
                                         —*Booklist*

"Alten can still write a mean prehistoric shark scene."
                                         —*Publishers Weekly*

Novels by Steve Alten

▼

*Published by Tom Doherty Associates

MEG
PRIMAL
WATERS

A TOM DOHERTY ASSOCIATES BOOK
NEW YORK

This is a work of fiction. All of the characters, organizations, and events portrayed in this novel are either products of the author's imagination or are used fictitiously.

MEG: PRIMAL WATER

Copyright © 2004 by Alten Entertainment of Boca Raton, Inc.

All rights reserved.

A Forge Book
Published by Tom Doherty Associates
175 Fifth Avenue
New York, NY 10010

www.tor-forge.com

Forge® is a registered trademark of Macmillan Publishing Group, LLC.

ISBN 978-1-2504-4282-6

Our books may be purchased in bulk for promotional, educational, or business use. Please contact your local bookseller or the Macmillan Corporate and Premium Sales Department at 1-800-221-7945, extension 5442, or by e-mail at MacmillanSpecialMarkets@macmillan.com..

First Edition: July 2004
First Mass Market Edition: May 2005

P1

ACKNOWLEDGMENTS

It is with great pride and appreciation that I acknowledge those who contributed to the completion of *MEG: Primal Waters*.

First and foremost, thanks to my literary manager and friend, Ken Atchity, and his team at Atchity Entertainment International, for their hard work and perseverance in bringing the entire Meg series to print and (fingers crossed) screen. Thanks also to Danny Baror of Baror International, and attorneys Joel McKuin and Robert Goldman of Colden, McKuin & Frankel.

My sincerest appreciation to Tom Doherty and the great people at Tor/Forge Books, especially Senior Editor Bob Gleason, Nicole Kalian, and Eric Raab.

Special thanks to Bill Raby, for his invaluable input regarding the lifestyle of a "daredevil," and to Dr. Lowell Krawitz, for his expertise in meteorology.

Heartfelt thanks to Leisa Cotner-Cobbs, for her talent and expertise in updating the www.SteveAlten.com Web site as well as all her work in the Adopt-An-Author program, and to Erik Hollander, whose graphic artistry continues to amaze.

To my wife and partner, Kim, for all her support, to my parents, Larry and Barbara, for always being there, and last—to my readers: Thank you for your correspondence and contributions. Your comments are always a welcome treat, your input means so much, and you remain this author's greatest asset.

To personally contact the author or learn
more about his novels,
click on www.SteveAlten.com

MEG: Primal Waters is part of
Steve Alten's Adopt-An-Author
Program aimed at assisting junior high and
high school students and teachers.
For more information, click on www.SteveAlten.com

The immortality of my youth,
Lacked all direction, avoided truth,
Hustling through my middle age,
I burnt through years lost in a haze,
The bells now toll from Father Time,
Fortunes fade, and so do mine . . .

—JONAS TAYLOR,
  excerpt from *Memoirs*

What a drag it is getting old.

—ROLLING STONES,
  "Mother's Little Helper"

PROLOGUE

And an Ice Age once again dominated the Earth . . . .

Officially it had begun some 1.6 million years earlier, ushering in a series of harsh glacial events, each of which lasted tens of thousands of years. Sandwiched between these cold spells were inter-glacial warming periods, the most recent coming to an abrupt end 74,000 years ago when the Toba caldera, a crater formed by a collapsed volcano on Samosir Island, Indonesia, erupted in one·of the largest volcanic explosions the planet had ever experienced. This catastrophic detonation released 1,700 cubic miles of debris into the atmosphere, enveloping the globe in a dense blanket of volcanic smog which trapped the Earth's heat, triggering a runaway greenhouse effect. (In contrast, the Mount St. Helen's eruption of 1980 yielded a mere 1.5 cubic miles.)

As global temperatures rose, great sections of polar ice from Greenland and the Arctic Ocean began melting. This deluge of freshwater inundated the Gulf Stream's North Atlantic Current, the conveyor belt of warm water that transfers heat to Europe and the Northern Hemisphere. The massive influx of freshwater diluted salt redistribution, preventing the process of down-welling, which, in turn, stifled the current's flow.

The combined effects of the Toba explosion and the cessation of the North Atlantic Current produced cataclysmic results. Temperatures plunged as much as one hundred degrees in a matter of hours, freezing animals in their tracks. Mountains of snow blanketed the Northern Hemisphere, wiping out food supplies. Large segments of human and animal populations starved, the few survivors forced to relocate.

Once more, the ice had reclaimed our planet.

Over the next 50,000 years, glaciers would continue to advance from the poles, with some of these continents of ice towering 13,000 feet. In North America, the Wisconsinian ice sheet would extend as far south as Pennsylvania, Indiana, Ohio, and Illinois, and as far east as Long Island. In Europe, the Eurasian ice sheet covered Scandinavia all the way to the Barents Sea.

With much of the water now locked up as ice, sea levels dropped over four hundred feet, drastically altering migration patterns. A land bridge formed in the Bering Strait, connecting the Eastern Hemisphere with the West, enticing prehistoric man and beast to cross over Asia into North America.

The Pleistocene Ice Age became a period of great transition. While some species evolved, most perished, unable to adapt. Among the primates, Neanderthal man yielded to Cro-Magnon, eventually giving way to the ascension of a new species—Homo sapiens—modern man.

In the oceans, the expansion of the ice-caps around the poles created ideal breeding areas for plankton and krill, which, in turn, lured fish to the colder regions. It wasn't long before this sudden abundance of food began attracting whales. This shift in the food chain influenced the whales to make dramatic changes in their own migrational patterns, and the polar region became their new summer feeding grounds.

Autumn's chill and the return of the ice flows signaled the whales' retreat to the tropics, where an ancient enemy lurked in their breeding grounds, its own kind struggling to adapt to the cooling planet.

Rhincodon typus moves just beneath the surface of the Pacific Ocean, its striking brownish-gray hide strewn with white dots and a grid of stripes. At thirty-two feet and 29,000 pounds, the juvenile male whale shark will grow another fifteen feet and add five tons to its girth by the time it reaches maturity. Despite its prodigious size, the creature is a docile giant and not a predator, its diet consisting of plankton, krill, squid, and sardines.

Gliding beneath the swarm of krill, the whale shark circles back suddenly, charging the surface with its flat, broad head. The wide slit of its lower jaw yawns open, creating a suction that forces large volumes of krill and seawater against the brushlike gill rakers located in the back of the shark's pharyngeal cavity. As these bristles strain food from the sea, hundreds of file-like teeth gnash the mouthful of planktonic organisms into pulp. The soup-like morsels are then flushed down the whale shark's tight gullet, the seawater diverted out its five-slitted gills.

Slapping its heavy tail along the surface, the speckled shark turns to feed again, unaware that, like the krill, it too is being stalked by a far larger adversary.

The monster glides east through depths cloaked in perpetual darkness, guided by its primordial senses. The shark, gargantuan predecessor of the modern-day Great White, is the most fearsome creature ever to inhabit the sea. At fifty-seven feet and 64,000 pounds, *Carcharodon megalodon* easily dwarfs its benign cousin, the whale shark.

Endowed with size, power, and senses that would put a nuclear submarine to shame, Megalodon has ruled the planet's oceans for tens of millions of years. It has survived the cataclysms that wiped out the dinosaurs and adapted to climate changes that devastated other prehistoric marine species. Intelligent as it is formidable, the brain of the elasmobranch is large and complex, controlling a plethora of organs that can see, feel, taste, and hear its underwater environment. A rogue hunter, the apex predator of all time is challenged only by members of its own kind.

But this latest Ice Age has done far more than simply cool the oceans, it has caused massive eustasis—a process that freezes titanic volumes of water. As a result, sea levels have dropped, creating land bridges that have cut off tropical currents to vital Megalodon nursery sites. Sheer size, combined with a unique internal heat-exchange system powered by the Meg's swimming muscles, protects the adults against even the most frigid seas, but the smaller anatomies of the Megalodon young have succumbed to the cold.

Mortality rates among the newborns have reached critical levels. Evolution's most savage creation has begun to die out.

The monster that stalks the whale shark is a female, and she is pregnant, nearly to term. Nestled within her swollen oviduct are live young, each four to seven feet long, weighing upwards of twelve hundred pounds. Undernourished, with their bloated mother struggling to find food, the surviving pups have been forced to turn to cannibalism, the larger infants feeding upon their smaller, less fortunate siblings.

What was once a litter of thirteen has dwindled to eight.

A thin current of ocean sweeps inside the female's slack-jawed mouth, frozen in its demonic grin. Concealed behind this mask of complacency are scalpel-sharp triangular teeth, the edges all finely serrated, like a steak knife. The upper front rows are largest, six to seven inches in length, four inches wide along the root. Behind each nightmarish fang, folded back along the gum-line, are columns of replacement teeth, each row ready to rotate into place, supplanting a damaged or lost member. Twenty-four rows of teeth span the upper two quadrants of the jaw, twenty-two rows occupying the lower, in a bite so wide and devastating it could engulf, crush, and swallow a small elephant.

The huntress glides with snake-like movements, her artillery-shell-shaped skull perpetually turning. As the Meg swims, water flows through its nostrils and across an olfactory organ designed to detect a multitude of chemical extracts in water. So keen is the predator's sense of smell that it can locate one speck of blood or urine in a lake-size volume of ocean.

Sensory cells situated along the animal's lateral line were designed to detect fluctuations in the sea over great distances. Internal ears can hear vibrations of sound originating miles away. Its eyes, black and cold, can focus in even the murkiest surroundings.

Then there is the creature's "electrical" sense.

Peppered along the underside of the female's snout are the ampullae of Lorenzini—dark jelly-filled capsules attuned to electrical discharges in saltwater. As if seeing, hearing, smelling, and feeling its prey were not enough, Nature has endowed the Megalodon with the ability to detect the faint electrical discharges generated by the whale shark's heart and moving muscles as it thrashes along the surface miles away.

To the starving female and her unborn pups, the beating heart is a dinner bell.

Closing quickly, the Megalodon streaks just below the surface, her dorsal fin towering six feet out of the water, cutting the sea like a blade. Her mouth widens, her prominent snout pushing upward, drawing out her cantilevered upper jaw, exposing row upon row of hideous teeth.

And then the female suddenly breaks away, her primordial senses on fire.

Rising directly beneath the whale shark is the male. Nearly a third smaller than the mature female and not nearly as broad, the adolescent is nevertheless a swifter and far more aggressive hunter, and his presence in these waters is a definite threat to the lumbering female and her unborn pups.

Sensing the challenge, the agitated male pumps its tail harder and charges the surface. Its mouth yawns open as it rises, thrusting forward its upper jaw, exposing rows of narrow triangular teeth.

Soulless ebony eyes roll back an instant before—

Wa-boosh!

The sea erupts, the stunned whale shark exploding clear out of the surf, its impaled belly bursting open in a ring of crimson geysers, its broken body entrapped within its killer's puncturing jowls.

For a heart-stopping moment, the male's upper torso seems to hang in midair, and then both predator and prey fall sideways into the sea, the whale shark convulsing in spasms as it struggles to free itself.

Refusing to release its prey, the Megalodon whips its conical head to and fro like a rabid dog. The serrations of its upper fangs saw through the whale shark's thick denticle-covered skin, tearing away a thousand-pound hunk of flesh.

The adolescent male moves off, circling below to swallow as it waits for its prey to die.

The pregnant female keeps her distance. Grapefruit-size nostrils inhale the pungent sea, her hunger gnawing at her insides as she impatiently awaits the scraps.

Sections of the whale shark's intestines drift by, only to be engulfed by swarms of surgeonfish and mackerel, the scavengers feasting on a blizzard of flesh and tissue, cartilage and gore.

Hours pass. Night falls, but the satiated male refuses to abandon its kill.

The pregnant female leaves just before dawn. For two days and nights she will trek east, devouring nothing larger than a tortoise as she continues to expend masses of energy in search of food.

On the afternoon of the third day, the famished goliath, close to death, arrives at the outer rise of a tropical island atoll . . .

CHAPTER

1

The engine powered off and I knew I was in trouble. I kicked at the battery . . . nothing. The heavy Lexan nose cone of the Abyss Glider sank, bobbing upside-down along the surface like a cork. Staring into the depths of the Monterey Bay Canyon, I saw the female's conical head appear from the shadows, her ghostly albino glow paralyzing me in fear as she charged.

Her hideous mouth yawned open, anticipating her next meal—me!

The thought of this enraged me. Reaching forward, I grabbed the emergency lever and turned it counterclockwise, then yanked it back, igniting the mini-sub's fuel. Instantly, my body was slammed backward within the pod's safety harness as the mini-sub rocketed downward like a torpedo into the awaiting gullet of my worst nightmare—

The telephone rings, shattering his concentration. Jonas Taylor grabs the cursed instrument off its cradle, strangling the receiver in his grip. "What?"

"Uh . . . Mr. Taylor?"

"Speaking."

"Sir, this is Ross Colombo."

"I don't know any Ross Colombo."

"With American Express. We spoke last week."

Christ . . .

"Sir, we still haven't received the payment, the one you assured me you had mailed."

Jonas's blood pressure ticks a few notches higher. "Look, Russ—"

"Ross. Sir, did you send the check?"

"Sure, I sent it. Can't believe you haven't gotten it yet. Tell you what, call me next week if it still hasn't arrived."

"Could you tell me the check number?"

"My wife handles all that stuff and she's not home. Why don't you call her next week."

Jonas slams the phone on its receiver, causing the taser-like star pattern of his screen saver to evaporate back into text. *Damn bill collectors . . .*

He takes a deep breath. Stares at his computer monitor.

Writing his memoirs had been Terry's idea. To Jonas, it seemed like a waste of time, a last desperate attempt to regain lost years of fame. Still, he had to make a living, and his once overflowing well of requests for speaking engagements had run dry long ago.

Face it, Jonas, you're a has-been—yesterday's news. You were never a real scientist and you're way too old to be a submersible pilot. At your age, with your limited background, you'd be lucky to get a job as an assistant manager in a fast-food joint.

"Shut-up!"

He commands himself to reread the last passage on screen, but the text refuses to sink in.

Reviewing his life on paper had forced Jonas to come to grips with the shortcomings of his existence. Almost sixty-four, he was at an age when most men were thinking about retirement, yet here he was, still struggling to make ends meet.

He glances at the stack of bills, becoming more depressed.

Snap out of it, you big baby. So you're over the hill, at least you're still near the summit. So what if you've grayed a bit, so what if your lower back feels like somebody ran over it with a pickup truck and every joint is wracked with arthritis. And who really cares if you can't run or keep up with the younger guys on the basketball court or pump as much iron? Hey, at least you're still active. Most guys my age would—

He stops himself.

You're not old, Jonas . . . you're just not young anymore.

The truth was, the more Jonas wrote, the older he felt, and the more he came to realize how much of his life was based on illusions.

The illusion of fame, of being important.

The illusion of being a good provider.

Jonas twists his head from one side to the other, his neck crackling like gravel beneath a tire. Health insurance, car insurance, mortgage payments, phone bills, electric bills . . . every month the mountain of debt gets higher, every waking moment dominated by stress. He has borrowed against the house, maxed out his credit cards, dipped into the kids' college funds . . . and still the mountain grows, along with his pessimism about the future and his constant fear of poverty.

Jonas Taylor can't remember the last time he has laughed out loud. Or even smiled.

His eyes focus upon the top statement in the stack, his annual life insurance bill—the irony of his life. *Bankrupt in life, rich in death. At least you married a younger woman. Yep, Terry will be well taken care of after you croak.*

"Shut-up!"

He tosses the bill aside, then massages his temples, praying the spot in his vision is just the sun's glare on his monitor and not another migraine.

Stay focused. Finish the book. Terry will sell it, and the rest will take care of itself.

He returns to the keyboard.

Darkness rushed at me, but before I could comprehend the consequences of my actions, I was jolted into unconsciousness. When I awoke, I was startled to be alive. The pod, miraculously, was still intact, but was now rolling in horrible darkness, the nose cone's exterior light occasionally illuminating refuse from the monster's last meal. A dolphin. Molten blubber. The upper torso of my former Naval commander—

The heavy bass of gangsta rap pounds through the ceiling above his head.

Jonas stops typing. Looks up.

"Dani?"

No response.

"Crap."

Jonas gets up from his desk. Walks to the staircase. "Danielle Kaye Taylor!"

No response.

Jonas's blood pressure creeps up another notch. Cursing beneath his breath, he climbs the worn beige-carpeted steps two at a time, turns right at the landing, then trudges down the hall to his daughter's room. Tries the handle. *Locked, of course.* Pounds on the door. Pounds again.

The door opens.

"What?" The blond-haired seventeen-year-old stares back at her father, her indigo-blue eyes furious.

"I'm trying to work."

"So? I live here, too."

"Can you just turn it down a bit?"

She lowers the volume, just enough so Jonas can comprehend the lyrics. "Geez, Dani, do you have to listen to that crap?"

"Dad, don't start—"

"A song about three brothers gang-raping their mother?"

"It's just a song."

"Well I don't like it. Turn it off."

"Excuse me, but you can't tell me what to listen to. This happens to be a free country."

"The only thing free is what you're paying in rent. As long as you're living under my roof, you'll listen. Now turn it off."

She slaps at the CD player, shutting it off. "Another seven weeks and I'll turn eighteen, then I am so out of here."

"Better hope financial aid comes through, or you'll be commuting."

"News flash: I'm not going to college."

His blood pressure tweaks again, his daughter's expression fueling his rage. "And exactly what're you going to do to make a living? Waitress? Flip burgers?"

"Maybe I'll write my memoirs!" She slams the door in her father's face.

Okay, good comeback. He pauses. Hears her crying. *So much for my Father-of-the-Year Award . . .*

Seeking absolution, he turns and knocks on his son's door. Opens it.

The fourteen-year-old with the mop of brownish-red hair poking out from beneath the Philadelphia Phillies baseball cap never looks up, too absorbed in his video game.

"David?"

"I already did my homework."

He kneels beside his son. Watches the boy's hands adeptly work the controls—a replica of his old mini-sub.

On screen, the blunt ivory nose of the Megalodon rises, its jaws chomping down upon the fluke of a fleeing Killer Whale. Crimson blood pours from the wound, dispersing across the animation like smoke from a chimney.

ORCA. MORTAL WOUND: 250 POINTS. CONTINUE FEEDING.

"Why do you always control the Meg? Why not the mini-sub?"

"Angel's more fun."

The image of a torpedo-shaped mini-sub soars by. David manipulates the controls, sending the Megalodon after it.

"You like stalking your old man, huh?"

"It's a thousand points."

"A thousand points. Be sure to engrave that on my tombstone, will you?"

"Shh!"

Jonas ignores the impulse to shut off the cursed video game, a reminder of a life that could have been. *Endorsements, merchandising . . . all gone.*

Gone with his youth.

He turns and leaves. Pauses again at Dani's door. Hears her talking on the phone, complaining about her life in some adolescent code.

The illusion of parenthood . . .

The front door opens. "Jonas?"

He heads downstairs. Greets his wife with, "Where have you been? I've been trying to get you on your cell phone for hours."

"I told you, the phone company disconnected me yesterday." Terry Taylor's long onyx hair is pulled up in a tight bun, accenting her Asian features. In her mid-forties, she is still quite the beauty. "How come you're not working?"

"I can't work in this house, all I get is constant interruptions."

"Since you're not working, can you get the groceries out of the car?"

Jonas sighs. Heads outside to the SUV in his stocking feet. Gathers as many plastic bags from the open rear hatch as he can handle, then glances at the car parked next to his wife's.

Notices the dent in the hood.

Registers the twinge in his left arm.

Jonas drops the groceries and examines the hood, which no longer seals shut.

Just keeps getting better and better.

"Terry!"

She pokes her head out the front door. "What're you screaming about?"

"Did you see the hood of the Chrysler?"

"I saw it. She said it happened last night while she was parked."

"Where did she park? A demolition derby? Damn car costs us two-fifty a month, plus another three grand a year for insurance. You'd think she could be a little more careful—"

"Jonas, calm down."

"A little appreciation, a little respect, that's all I ask." Blood boiling, he opens the front door of his daughter's car. Snarls at the heavy scent of tobacco. Reaches down to pop the hood and spots the bag of marijuana, hidden beneath the seat.

"Terry!"

—as the migraine squeezes tighter behind his eyeball.

TANAKA OCEANOGRAPHIC INSTITUTE
MONTEREY, CALIFORNIA

The deep blue hill of water rolls toward shore, its weight rumbling over the shoals as it crests, its bulk split in two as it kisses the submerged concrete walls of the man-made canal. Half the wave crashes into foam and races to a quick death upon the beach, the other half rushes into the channel, picking up speed as it is redirected into the main tank of the Tanaka Lagoon.

The old man's almond eyes follow another wave in, his soul soothed by its crushing thunder, his mind as restless as the undulating splashes that echo throughout the deserted arena like crackling paper. From his vantage—a cold alu-

minum bench in the upper deck of the western bleachers—
he can see everything: the incoming Pacific, the ocean-
access canal, the lake-size man-made aquarium, the western
horizon's dying afternoon sun.

Eighty-two-year-old Masao Tanaka fixes his collar
against the harsh ocean breeze that howls inside his empty
concrete fish bowl. Weathered eyes squint against reflections
coming off the lagoon's surface. The once azure waters have
stagnated olive-green, algae growth surpassing maintenance.
The once-shiny A-frame, perched at the southern end of the
arena like a giant steel scarecrow, is caked with layers of
rust, as are the bleachers, the rest rooms, food court, and
souvenir stands.

Masao shakes his head at the irony of his existence. The
lagoon had been more than the marine biologist's dream, it
had been his life, and now he is dying with it. Thirty years
have passed since he first designed the facility and risked
everything to build it. He had depleted his family's estate
and mortgaged his children's future, and when those funds
ran dry, he had accepted a high-risk contract with the Japanese Marine Science Technology Center, selling JAMSTEC
twenty-five of the Institute's Unmanned Nautical Information Submersibles. The UNIS drones were to be part of
Japan's Early Warning Earthquake Detection System. The
catch: Masao's team would be responsible for deploying the
array seven miles down in the Mariana Trench, the deepest,
most unexplored realm on the planet.

Masao's son, D.J., had escorted each UNIS into position,
piloting an Abyss Glider-II, the Institute's one-man deep-sea
submersible. For weeks the detection system worked flaw-
lessly, and then one by one, the drones stopped transmitting
data. With the Japanese threatening to hold back payment,
Masao had been forced to call in a favor from an old friend.

Jonas Taylor had been the best deep-sea submersible pilot
ever to wear the Navy uniform—until something happened
to him on his last dive in the Mariana Trench. Working in

33,000 feet of water, Jonas had suddenly panicked, launching his vessel into an emergency ascent. The duress of the maneuver had caused a malfunction in the sub's pressurization system and the two scientists on board had died. Diagnosed with psychosis of the deep, Jonas had been forced to spend three months in a psychiatric ward. His naval career over, his confidence shot, Jonas reinvented himself, going back to school to study paleobiology, intent on convincing the world that he was not crazy, that the unexplored seven-mile-deep gorge was inhabited by sixty-foot prehistoric sharks, long thought extinct.

Masao cared little about Jonas's theories; what he needed was a second deep-sea pilot to accompany his son on a salvage operation. Jonas accepted the old man's invitation, more focused on locating an unfossilized Megalodon tooth, proof that the creatures were still alive.

What he found instead was his own personal Hell.

Jonas Taylor was right, members of the Megalodon species had survived extinction in the hydrothermally-warmed bottom layer of the trench.

Upon entering the abyss, the two mini-subs' engines had attracted a male. D.J. was attacked and devoured, the Meg entwining itself in his sub's cable. As Masao's surface ship unwittingly hauled the entrapped beast topside, a larger female attacked the male, following it to the surface.

Having summoned the devil from its purgatory, it was left to Jonas and his team to stop it.

More death would follow as the Tanaka Institute attempted to capture the female, which birthed three pups in the deep waters off Monterey, California. Jonas was eventually forced to kill the creature, with the lone surviving pup captured and raised in Masao's whale lagoon.

Come see Angel: the Angel of Death. Two shows daily.

The captive female would attract millions of visitors and even more dollars. But a series of devastating lawsuits would cripple the Institute, forcing Masao to sell the majority of his company to energy mogul Benedict Singer. Losing control of his beloved Institute was bad enough, the undue stress on his family even worse. Terry's first pregnancy was stillborn, and Jonas was not there for her, too preoccupied with his concerns over keeping Angel secured in the lagoon. Eventually the female did escape, nearly taking the lives of Masao's daughter and son-in-law in the process.

Benedict Singer's demise would return the Institute to its rightful owner. Three years after Angel's escape, the lagoon's new canal doors were reopened, this time for the advancement of cetacean science, as had always been intended.

Masao had a new lease on life. Each winter day, as tens of thousands of the behemoths migrated south from the Bering Sea, the biologist would wait by the open canal doors, hoping to lure a pregnant cow into his protected cove to birth her young.

"Spooked" by the Megalodon's lingering presence, the whales refused to enter.

Hoping to remove Angel's "scent," Masao accepted a huge loan from his son-in-law to drain and scrub the main tank . . . all to no avail.

Deep in debt, Masao finally agreed to lease the facility to Sea World. A half dozen orcas, all born in captivity, were transported from their cramped tanks to the much larger ocean-accessible lagoon. Immediately upon entering the water, the Killer Whales panicked, circling the tank in a frenzied state. With nowhere to beach, they began bashing their heads against the canal doors, desperate to get out.

Two of the animals died, along with the Sea World contract.

As time passed, so too did the public's interest in Jonas Taylor. His speaking career over, Jonas was forced to sell his home in California and move his family to Tampa, where he accepted a public relations job at a new marine park. Masao stayed behind, hiring Jonas's best friend, Mac, to maintain the facility while he attempted to sell it.

The eventual collapse of the stock market wiped out Masao's pension and the savings of several potential buyers, sealing the old man's fate. The lagoon was his albatross, and, like it or not, he was stuck with it.

Masao stretches, his arthritic joints creaking with the effort. Across the lagoon, his eyes catch movement.

Atti . . . The old man waves.

Athena Holman waves back, then continues sweeping the empty eastern bleachers. Cerebral palsy has affected the young African-American woman's right hand and legs, causing her to walk with a heavy gait. Despite her challenges, the nineteen-year-old has been the Institute's hardest worker, her dark brown eyes and quick wit stealing Masao's heart years ago, making it impossible for him to let her go with the rest of his maintenance workers.

The arena turns gold, the sun setting at his back. It is the old man's favorite time of day, yet all he feels is remorse. Once the driving force behind his family's business, life's mishaps have reduced him to a shadow of his former self, a burden to his children.

He waits until the horizon bleeds scarlet and magenta, then stands, his back and knees aching. Like his facility, Masao is breaking down, yet his soul is still too restless to move on.

He hobbles down the bleachers to the concrete walkway.

Two men step out of the shadows, both in their late thirties, well-built, wearing lumberjack shirts and worn jeans.

The older of the two flashes a false smile. "Afternoon, Mr. Tanaka. You remember my younger brother, Devin."

The second man, dark-haired and ponytailed, offers a cold stare.

Masao nods uncomfortably. "I assume you received the reply from my attorney?"

Drew Dietsch gazes at the lagoon. "Received it in triplicate. Can't say I was happy with it, but I guess you already know that, seeing as how you haven't returned any of our calls."

"I'm sorry."

"Sorry?" Devin's green eyes squint in anger. "Listen, old man, we sank over half a million in site surveys and soil samples, not to mention the money it cost us to grease the zoning commissioner's office. And that personal loan."

"Easy, Devin." Drew steps in between his younger brother and the old man. "Let's keep everything civil . . . for now. Mr. Tanaka, I'm sure you can understand why my brother and I are a little upset about the way things played out."

"*Hai*. The money I borrowed will be paid back with interest, you have my word."

"We're not a bank," Devin spits.

"My brother's right. We had a deal to turn this entire beachfront area and lagoon into million-dollar condos and a high-end shopping marina."

"We had a deal in principle only. Your final offer was too low. Not enough cash up front."

"We had an agreement, Tanaka, which is why we agreed to that personal loan. You'd receive your share of the profits on the back-end with the rest of our investors."

"Profits based on trust. I don't trust you. Neither does my attorney. Too many loopholes. Put more money up front and we'll talk, otherwise I think I'll wait. Dietsch Brothers is not the only fish in the sea, you know."

Masao pushes past them and hobbles for the exit.

Devin goes after him.

Drew grabs his brother by the arm. "Okay, Tanaka, hey, if that's the way you want to play it, fine by us. Our lawyers are on retainer, how about yours? Can you afford to keep paying a mouthpiece to prevent us from getting a judgment? I doubt it. And what about your daughter and her loser husband?"

Masao slows.

"Yeah, I hear Terry and Jonas are hurting for money, just like you. Bad investment them sinking their life savings into this zoo, huh? Face it, old man, pennies on the dollar is the best you're ever gonna see. So why don't we settle this like men, before the judge does it for us."

"A better offer, gentlemen," Masao grimaces, "preferably before I die."

CHAPTER

2

The Pacific Ocean: Occupying sixty million square miles, it is the largest body of water on Earth and the deepest, possessing an average depth of 14,000 feet. Covering nearly half the globe, it separates the Americas from Asia and Australia and encompasses the titanic Pacific Plate, the most seismically active region in the world.

Descend beneath the chaos of waves, past the upper layer of light until the deep blue sea turns black and you arrive in a vast mid-water habitat, the largest living space on the planet. In this permanent realm of darkness mysteries abound, for despite man's curiosity and seemingly limitless know-how we have only managed to explore a mere five percent of this alien realm. It is here, where the sun's rays never reach, that Nature has provided its life-forms with the ability to produce their own light, endowing them with special chemicals—luciferins—or luminous bacteria that inhabit their bodies.

In this unexplored world of gelatinous species, the hundred-foot eel-like body of the siphonophore illuminates in a symphony of color that blinds would-be predators. An-

glerfish dangle luminescent bulbs before their open mouths,
luring unsuspecting prey. Hatchetfish use light-producing
organs as camouflage.

In the silent blackness of liquid space, light has become
the preferred form of communication and survival.

As we move deeper still, we enter the abyss, where the
enormous weight of the water causes pressures to magnify
beyond the range of air-breathers. Pressure is the ultimate
barrier to man, the primary challenge to scientific exploration, the reason we know more about distant galaxies than
the most populated region on our own planet.

Dominating the sea floor of the mighty Pacific is the Pacific Plate. Constantly colliding with other oceanic plates
and continents, the outer rim of the Pacific Plate forms a
network of volcanically active island chains and volcanoes, known as the Ring of Fire. This 30,000-mile-long
subduction zone snakes north along the Asian coastline to
Kamchatka Peninsula, follows the Aleutian Islands east
toward Alaska, then moves south along California's San
Andreas Fault through Mexico and clear down to the western tip of South America.

Subduction creates trenches, the deepest locations on the
planet. A series of these gorges shadow the Ring of Fire, the
deepest being the Mariana Trench, an arcing 1,580 mile long
depression, averaging forty-three miles in width.

At 35,827 feet below sea level, the Challenger Deep is the
lowest point on Earth, located at the southeastern tip of the
Mariana Trench. Follow this canyon north around the volcanic Mariana Island chain and the gorge flows into the
Kuril Trench, an immense depression that runs past Japan all
the way up to the Kamchatka Peninsula. From here, the Pacific Plate runs east, its subduction activity creating the
Aleutian Islands and Aleutian Trench, the latter stretching
clear across the Northern Pacific to the coast of Oregon.

Life requires energy. Terrestrial ecosystems and the creatures of the shallows derive their fuel directly from sunlight through the process of photosynthesis.

Occupying a world of perpetual darkness, the inhabitants of the abyss must rely on a different source of energy, one supplied directly by the Earth's inner heat. As cold sea water flows along the boundaries of separating tectonic plates, it seeps into deep fractures, bringing it in contact with molten rock. Superheated to temperatures exceeding 700 degrees Fahrenheit, the seawater dissolves manganese, iron, silicon, and other minerals before dispersing upward from the ocean floor through hydrothermal vents. Debris spewed from these vents piles high to form mineral chimneys, or black smokers, each volcanic stack in itself an oasis of life.

Microbes feast off these sulfurous compounds and oxidize them, creating nourishment for clusters of *Riftia*—ghostly-white tube worms, the tips of their seven-foot stalks dipped vermillion. Swarms of shrimp, mollusks, and other deep sea limpets feed off this Riftia forest, which in turn supply nourishment to bizarre species of albino crabs and fish in a chemosynthetic food chain that dates back to the beginning of time.

Miles from the surface, beyond the reach of man, life not only exists, it flourishes.

As in all successful habitats, there are always those exceptional life forms that occupy the very top of the food chain—a perch reserved for Nature's apex carnivores.

The monster glides in a primal world of silence and perpetual darkness, its movement relentless. Pigment-less ivory skin, as pale as death, seems to radiate against the pitch blackness, while its gray-blue eyes remain soulless and unblinking. The slack jaw quivers against the steady stream of seawater, its gill slits, arranged like six vertical blinds along each flank, ruffling gently as it breathes.

The Megalodon, an adolescent male, is an absolute brute, sixty-one feet from the tip of its snout to the point of its crescent tail, its weight exceeding 67,000 pounds. Birthed almost two decades ago, the Meg and its sibling, a smaller male, have survived the ravages of their dominant mother by inhabiting the Mariana Island Basin, a vast underwater valley located west of the main trench, separated by the Northern Mariana Island rise and trough.

Battle scars blemish the albino's alabaster hide. A semicircular scar along the top of its right pectoral fin marks a failed attempt at copulation with an unwilling female. The still-healing gouge behind its left gill slit is more serious, the wound inflicted by the big male's smaller sibling in a territorial dispute years earlier. In the end, the larger male had triumphed, biting off nearly a third of its rival's dorsal fin in the process, leaving its crippled adversary to die.

Nature endows its creatures with a simple genetic plan— survive and procreate, extinction being the penalty for failure. Once a flourishing species that preferred the shallows to mid-waters, the Megalodons of the abyss have become a dying breed. Dwindling numbers yield fewer opportunities for procreative encounters. Females that reach sexual maturity require extra nourishment that their unborn young need to grow large, a process that, in the abyss, can take upwards of seven years.

Upon entering an estrus cycle, an ovulating female Megalodon secretes a powerful pheromone trail, the lingering scent designed to entice males from hundreds of miles away. Should a mature male locate a female in heat, the chances of a successful conception are still quite poor. Subduing a larger female can be quite dangerous, and it can take an inexperienced male a dozen or more attempts before copulation is finally achieved.

Driven by its overabundant level of testosterone, the adolescent had become restless. Since its birth, the big male had inhabited the depths surrounding the Mariana Island chain, its languid metabolism subsisting on a diet of squid. bottom feeders, and exotic life forms that date back to the Jurassic Age. With no adult females within range of its senses, the male had abandoned its hard-fought territory, moving north into what had been an unexplored section of the Mariana Trench.

Within days it had detected the powerful scent of an ovulating female. That this female was, in fact, the big male's biological birth mother had no bearing on its intended course of action.

The quest to copulate had begun.

To the older, ovulating female, the presence of a large, aggressive male within her territory became an immediate threat. Abandoning the primal waters of her ancestors, the female trekked farther north until she reached the Kuroshio current—retracing a route she had journeyed through in her youth.

Distant memories returned . . . memories of surface water teeming with prey.

For unlike the few remaining members of her species, this particular female had been born in the shallows, off the coast of California. Held in captivity for nearly five years, the giantess had eventually escaped her human captors to return to the abyss to breed.

Angel, the "Angel of Death," once the star attraction of the Tanaka Oceanographic Institute, is now a fully mature adult, and, at seventy-four feet and thirty-eight tons, she is the biggest and most dangerous predatory fish of all time.

Like a giant salmon coming home to spawn, she had instinctively followed the Kuroshio current, a fast-moving river of water that flowed past Japan into the colder Oyashio stream until it eventually bled into the North Pacific Current. For weeks she remained in this easterly conveyor belt of water, guided across the Northern Pacific by her brain's biomagnetite compass. Arriving in Alaskan waters, she had continued south, stalking Grey whales and their calves off the coast of Oregon until finally arriving in the familiar waters off California.

Eighteen years and three months after fleeing captivity to inhabit the Mariana Trench, Angel had found her way back to the waters of her birth . . .

—leaving a pheromone trail in her wake that spanned half an ocean.

The big male enters the North Pacific Current, its senses searching for any lingering traces of its would-be mate. For the adolescent, this is the farthest it has ever strayed from the abyss. Accustomed to the pressures of the deep, it has never hunted in the mid-water region before, and the higher oxygen content is burning away its bottom-dwelling induced lethargy, increasing its appetite.

The cold does not bother the Meg. Sheer size allows the male to maintain a constant high body temperature, its thirty-four-ton bulk insulating its core from the colder environment. To further elevate body temperature, oxygenated blood from the Meg's gills is directed through a series of specialized arteries that bring it in contact with the creature's massive swimming muscles. This unique "internal combustion system" effectively makes the gargantuan prehistoric cousin of the Great White a warm-blooded fish.

While the higher oxygen content of the mid-level waters has increased the Meg's visceral temperature, it has also accelerated its digestive process.

Hunger is now a constant companion.

The big male slows, suddenly alert. Sensory cells situated along its mid-lateral flanks have detected two distinct vibrations up ahead, one a source of food, the other a direct threat.

The Megalodon alters its course, establishing a deeper,

stealthier approach as it homes in on the source of the disturbances.

The squadron of *Magnapinnidae*, a ten-tentacled species of giant squid, move as one through the mid-water depths of the Northern Pacific. Reaching lengths of twenty-eight feet, the docile giants possess two enormous fins resembling elephant ears, which help propel them through the sea.

Having risen to feed, the giant squid have caught the attention of not one, but two formidable adversaries.

Descending into these deepwater feeding grounds is the bull Sperm whale. At sixty-two feet and 82,000 pounds, the cetacean is the largest predator in these waters. A lone hunter, the male is the only mammal, with the exception of man, capable of descending into these near-freezing depths.

The bull, young for a rogue adult, has been deep diving in darkness for forty minutes. Its heart rate has slowed to one-third, its blood supply diverted to its brain and spermaceti organ. Weighing several tons, the spermaceti is a large fatty deposit, harbored in the whale's braincase, which focuses short, broad-spectrum burst-pulses, or clicks as a directional beam. As this beam of sound strikes objects in its path, it reflects echoes back to another fatty deposit located in the cetacean's lower jaw, which passes the information on to the whale's middle ear and brain for processing.

It is this sense of echolocation that now guides the giant predator toward a feast it cannot see but knows is there.

Thirty-one hundred feet . . . its target a mere three hundred feet away.

Excited, the young bull thrashes its great fluke harder, giving away its presence to the squadron of squid, who instinctively dive deep.

The Sperm whale alters its course accordingly. Accelerating into the fleeing wall of flesh, its narrow lower jaw chomps on the moving wall of fat. Severed tentacles swirl in the inky maelstrom as the whale's gargantuan rectangular head pushes through the debris, engulfing the cephalopod remains.

Preoccupied with feeding, the cetacean fails to heed its echolocation.

The ghostly white blur impacts the Sperm whale's flank with the driving force of a freight train striking a tractor-trailer.

Dagger-like lower teeth thrust deep into the mammal's hide. Serrated upper fangs saw through fat, gristle, and bone, excising a six-hundred-pound hunk of blubber and sinew before the larger whale rolls, shaking the Meg loose.

The Megalodon darts away, leaving its prey in a state of paroxysm.

Wounded and vulnerable, having expended precious air, the Sperm whale pummels the ocean with its muscular fluke, propelling its forty-one-ton bulk topside in a hasty retreat.

The Megalodon remains below. Huge jaws snap open and shut like a bear trap, its teeth gnashing the tough whale hide into digestible balls of fat, its jowl muscles causing ripples of flesh to gyrate down its ghostly belly.

As the predator swallows, its senses become intoxicated. Adrenaline levels soar. Nostrils flare, snorting up gobs of hot blood through its olfactory troughs.

The male has never fed like this before. In a state of frenzy, it relocates its fleeing prey and ascends after it, a dozen rapid sweeps of its two-story-high tail needed to overcome its slightly negative buoyancy.

Sensing the closing Meg, the injured whale thrashes harder, its blunt rectangular head undulating to and fro with the effort.

The Megalodon homes in on the telltale reverberations, its open mouth swallowing a bloody trail of seawater. Moving within striking distance of the whale's flapping tail, the

Meg hyperextends its jaws, preparing to deliver another devastating bite.

And then, suddenly, the male turns away.

Curtains of gray sunlight have filtered into the battlefield, stinging the deepwater shark's sensitive nocturnal eyes.

Avoiding the painful light, the male circles below and waits.

The wounded whale surfaces, expelling a bloodied burst of compressed air from its blowhole. Struggling to swim, the beast remains close to the surface, attempting to distance itself from the predator lurking fourteen hundred feet in the darkness below.

Painful hours pass. The sun dips beneath the horizon, beckoning the night.

A thousand nocturnal predators have assembled for the feast, all waiting for the young prince to strike the death blow.

Still, the Megalodon waits.

Another hour passes.

Barely moving now, the sperm whale moans its death cry at the dying light. A final *thumpa-thumpa-thumpa* and the Volkswagen-size heart stops beating.

The dead beast rolls belly-up like an enormous log.

Darkness takes the Pacific.

The albino killer rises majestically through the black sea, its scarred snout lifting, its mouth hyperextending open—

—*Whomp!*

The Sperm whale's lifeless carcass heaves with the impact as the 67,000 pound Megalodon tears into the cetacean's vertebral column.

Smaller predators move in, collecting the scraps. Within minutes the Pacific is frothing with life.

By dawn of the third day the bloated carcass will begin to sink. The downward spiral into the depths will last for hours, feeding the creatures of· the mid-waters. Eventually the whale will tumble to its final resting place on the seafloor, providing nourishment to thousands of bottom-feeders.

A full year will pass before the bones are stripped clean.

Nothing goes to waste in the ocean, such is Nature's way.

The big male descends well before sunrise, returning to the more familiar pressures of the mid-waters. Its hunger momentarily satiated, its senses quickly pick up the ovulating female's trail.

Hours later, the creature slips inside the North Pacific Current, allowing the warm river of water to carry it east toward the coastal waters of British Columbia.

CHAPTER

3

VENICE BEACH, FLORIDA

The Venice Beach Shark Tooth Festival, held at Caspersen Beach, Florida, just south of the Venice commuter airport, is an annual weekend gathering featuring live entertainment, arts and crafts activities, seafood vendors, and sand and ice sculptures. Most of all, the event promotes the city's unofficial title as "Shark Tooth Capital of the World." On these windswept Gulf Coast beaches are found tens of thousands of prehistoric shark teeth, some as small as dimes, others exceeding six inches in length. Each year, under the main tent, several dozen vendors arrive from all over the world to display their wares, the majority of their fossilized specimens belonging to *Carcharodon megalodon*.

Jonas Taylor grinds his teeth, his fingers tapping impatiently against the steering wheel. There is only one road leading to the fairgrounds, and, as usual, it is clogged in bumper-to-bumper traffic. "This is ridiculous. What time am I supposed to speak?"

Terry is in the passenger seat, her eyes closed behind tinted sunglasses. As always, she is the eye of the Taylor storm. "Today you speak at one and three, tomorrow noon and two."

"I knew we should have left earlier, you know I hate being late."

"They can't start without you. Try to relax."

"Did you tell them we want a cashier's check? Last year it took a week for their funds to clear."

"It's handled."

Jonas glances at the rearview mirror. David has fallen asleep beneath his headphones. In the seat next to him is Danielle, still staring out her window, angry at the world. Terry has grounded the girl for a month, forcing the teen to cancel this weekend's planned romp at a schoolmate's beach house.

Jonas grips the steering wheel tighter. What he had really wanted was to sell Dani's car and use the money to send his daughter to boarding school. Terry had, of course, dismissed his rants. *"She's a teenager, Jonas. Didn't you ever experiment with pot when you were her age?"*

"Hell, no. And if I had, my old man would have beaten the tar out of me."

"Dani knows the rules, now she'll pay the price."

"And how do you expect me to get any writing done while she's up in her room, grounded for a month? It's me you're punishing, not her."

A horn sounds, snapping Jonas from his thoughts. He creeps forward another fifteen feet.

God . . . here I am again, back in Venice Beach, playing up another illusion . . . the prehistoric shark expert. Where do the years go? Why does time seem to fly by so fast when you get older?

The parking lot attendant waves him ahead. "Eight bucks."

Jonas flashes his V.I.P. parking card.

"Professor Taylor? Sorry, didn't recognize you. Few more gray hairs, huh?"

Terry snickers as her husband drives off without a response.

————

The main tent is a beehive of flesh and perspiration, all nestled beneath a red and white tarpaulin that seals in the heat and dust. The crowd moves along a central corridor created by two rows of vendor's tables running the length of the open-ended marketplace. A procession of locals in cut-off jeans and sweat-stained tee-shirts mingle with sunburned tourists, all filtering past assortments of cardboard boxes filled with chipped shark teeth, glass cases of prehistoric artifacts, Megalodon tee-shirts, shark-tooth jewelry and posters. Fossilized shark teeth, ranging from $50 to more than $6,000, are propped up on clear plastic holders like tiny lead-gray stalagmites.

"Yo, doc, how's it goin'?" Vito Bertucci waves at Jonas and his wife from within his ten-foot-high set of polyurethane Megalodon jaws that he has matched with real fossilized teeth.

"Same old same old, Vito."

"Hey, Jonas, Terry, check this out." Pat McCarthy, another fossil tooth hunter, holds up a six-and-a-half-inch Meg tooth, stained a deep reddish-brown. "Found this beauty last month in the Cooper River. Nice, huh?"

"Still diving with the alligators? You're crazy, Pat."

"Gotta make a living. And you're one to talk."

"Not me. I'm just living on a reputation."

"And he's late." Terry leads Jonas to a sign that reads: J & S FOSSILS.

Sue Pendergraft waves them over. "Hey guys, we were getting worried you weren't going to make it. Big crowd this year." She greets Terry with a hug.

Jim Pendergraft counts change for a customer. "Knew you'd be here. Got your table set up right next to us. Sorry we missed you at the Phoenix show. Hey, where're the kids?"

"Carrying the boxes." Jonas notices a long stretch of people lined up at the far end of the tent. "What's going on over there?"

Jim wipes perspiration from the gray hairs of his goatee.

"Some feller from California bought himself a white Megalodon tooth. Everyone wants to get a photo."

"One of Angel's teeth?"

"Nope, this one belonged to a male. Figured he must'a bought it from that collection you sold to the Smithsonian a while back."

The Meg that killed Terry's brother . . . Jonas glances at his wife, who is busy setting up their booth. Masao Tanaka had sold the dead male's remains to the Smithsonian Institution to help pay for the D.J. Tanaka Memorial Lagoon.

That was twenty-two years ago . . . is that possible?

"Doc, there you are!" JoAnne Favre greets Jonas with a quick hug. "We're running late, are you ready?" Without waiting for a reply, the suntanned events coordinator switches on her microphone. "Ladies and gentlemen, gather 'round, we have a special treat for you. As always, one of the highlights of our annual Shark Tooth Festival is to welcome a man who knows more about *Carcharodon megalodon* than anyone else alive. In fact, you might say he knows these sharks *inside out.*"

The brunette pauses for a smattering of applause and laughter.

"Please help me welcome Professor Jonas Taylor."

Outside, Danielle and David walk around the back of the tent, each one carrying a cardboard box filled with old photos of Angel leaping from her tank.

Dani rolls her eyes. "Listen to them applaud. Bunch of geeks."

"What's your problem? Is it like your period or something? You've been grouchy all week."

"My problem is this family. I can't wait 'til I'm out of here."

"Where you gonna go?"

"I don't know. Maybe I'll move in with a friend."

"What about college?"

"Fuck college, I need to get on with my life." She slips inside the tent behind the J & S Fossils booth, then ceremoniously drops the box of photos on top of the folding table. "Later."

Terry grabs her arm. "Where do you think you're going?"

"For a walk, maybe to get something to eat. Is that okay?"

"It'd be nice if you stayed and listened to your father."

"You've got to be kidding."

"I want you back here in an hour to relieve your brother. And don't make me have to go looking for you."

"Fine." Danielle disappears into the crowd.

Jonas scans the group, recognizing a few faces from years past. "Are there any other questions?"

An African-American man raises his hand, his free arm draped around his teenage son's shoulder. "My wife and I saw Angel a month before she escaped. Greatest show on Earth."

"Yes she was."

"My question is, why hasn't anyone tried to recapture her?"

"Angel returned to the deep eighteen years ago. No one's seen her since. Even if we could relocate her, I doubt anyone would have the means of capturing her. If you remember, she was seventy-two feet when she escaped. God knows how large she's grown since."

A heavyset woman in a wheelchair asks, "Professor, any chance of you going back down into that trench? You know, just to do a little exploring?"

"Not in this lifetime," mumbles Terry, a bit too loud.

Jonas shrugs. "My wife's right. It's way too dangerous. Any other questions? No? Well then, we still have a few limited edition souvenir photos of Angel leaping from the Tanaka Lagoon. Only $12.99. Be happy to sign it for you as well." He hands the microphone back to JoAnne, then takes his place at the table beside a stack of photos.

Danielle threads her silky blond ponytail through the back of her Yankees baseball cap, then gathers her shirttails around her midriff, tying them high around her taut belly. Adjusts her sunglasses. Searches her purse for the pack of Marlboros. "Damn."

Leaving the main tent, she heads off into the hot April sun to stalk the fairgrounds, hoping to bum a cigarette. She strolls past the food court booths and gags at the heavy scent of barbecued beef and fried onions. Stops to purchase a bottled water, then follows the music to a small outdoor sound stage. Radio DJs are handing out free CDs. A local film crew is setting up.

A sign reads: MEET THE DAREDEVILS. ALL NEW SEASON COMING SOON.

A small crowd is seeking autographs from an Australian man in his early twenties. Danielle can make out mouse-brown hair with blond highlights. A skintight tank top and shorts reveal hairless bronze skin rippling with muscle—exactly the stereotype she and her friends have programmed themselves to hate.

She moves closer to investigate.

The Daredevil poses for a picture, then turns to Dani. "How 'bout it beautiful?"

"Excuse me?"

"Did ya want a photo or were you just oglin' the merchandise?"

"Not in this lifetime."

"What? Not a fan of the show?"

"God, no. Reality TV is so artificial. Just a bunch of wannabe actors playing up for the camera so they can extend their fifteen minutes of fame on *Oprah* or *Letterman*."

"Ouch. You're as cross as a frog in a sock."

She struggles not to smile.

"Ah, there's progress. Like I always say, life's too short to be cranky. The name's Ferguson. Wayne John Ferguson. Most of my friends call me Fergie."

"Dani Taylor."

"Taylor? As in Professor Jonas?"

"He's my father. The one who put the frog in my sock."

"Hey Fergie, it's time." A woman in a scarlet skintight bodysuit approaches. Shoulder length brown hair, late twenties, dripping with attitude and nipples.

"Dani Taylor, meet 'Jedi' Jennie Arnos, stunt pilot extraordinaire and wannabe teammate. Jennie and I was just about to engage in a little daredeviltry for the mob. Should be a ripper."

Jennie gives her a female to female once-over. "A little young for you, isn't she Fergie?"

Dani's eyes flash anger. "Excuse me?"

"And feisty. Think you can handle a little airplane ride?"

"Excellent idea, Jennie."

"Sorry, I can't. I, uh . . . have to help out my folks."

"Aw, that's sweet," Jennie chides. "Do you always do everything Mommy and Daddy tell you?"

"Look; *nipples,* I'm already grounded, and I don't need any more shit from my parents, let alone you."

"She's scared, I knew it." Jennie flings her arm across Fergie's shoulders. "C'mon, we're running late."

"Hold on." Fergie pulls Danielle aside. "Look, it's just a little ride." He points to the four-seat Cessna warming up on an adjacent airstrip. "We'll have you back on terra firma in thirty minutes tops."

Jonas finishes small talking with an elderly couple, thanks them for coming, then grimaces behind their backs after they decline to purchase a signed photo. "So? How'd we do?"

"Not great," Terry replies, counting the cash. "Just shy of three hundred dollars."

"It's a different crowd this year. I think we should cancel the hotel and—"

"Professor Taylor?"

Jonas and Terry look up.

The man is in his mid-thirties, six feet tall and stocky, with a receding hairline. His animated face is partially obscured behind a dirty-blond goatee.

In his right hand is the white Megalodon tooth.

"So you're the mysterious collector?"

"Erik Hollander, at your service, though I'm not what you'd call a collector. The tooth was actually a gift from an old college buddy."

"Nice gift. Authentic white Megalodon teeth sell from sixty to eighty thousand dollars. May I?"

"Please." Erik hands him the three-pound inverted Y-shaped object. "Measures six and a quarter inches from tip to root. Thing's hard as titanium, as sharp as any knife I've ever owned."

Jonas examines the tooth. "Yes, Meg teeth are amazing products of evolution. Each tooth is composed of apatite crystals enclosed in a surrounding mass of protein and spongy dentine, rendering it one of the hardest substances ever wrought by Nature. And yes, this one is quite authentic."

"For a while I wondered. The tooth seems narrower than some of the fossilized teeth I've seen on display."

"That's because it's a lower front tooth, from a male." Jonas eyes Erik suspiciously. "The only modern-day male Megalodon teeth came from the dead shark hauled topside by the *Kiku* twenty-two years ago."

Terry's expression darkens. "The Meg that killed my brother . . ."

Erik pales. "God, I'm so sorry, Mrs. Taylor, I had no idea."

"There's no code number engraved into the root. Every tooth was encoded before it was sold off or donated to museums."

"Really?" Erik takes back the tooth. Looks it over. "Apparently one of its owners must have had it touched up. Again, Mrs. Taylor, I'm so sorry. How embarrassing—"

"It's okay." She clears her throat. "So, Mr. Hollander, what brings you to the shark tooth festival?"

"Your husband, actually." Erik returns the tooth to its padded satchel. "My company, Hollander-Gelet Entertainment, produces the *Daredevils* reality series."

"I've seen that show," David says. "They do all sorts of wild stunts. Contestants get hurt all the time. One lady even got killed."

Erik nods. "Diana Hoag, third episode. Terrible tragedy, but a television first."

David turns to his father, his eyes animating. "This woman, real pretty, wearing this sexy bikini, drives a motorcycle right out of a cargo plane. Anyway, she's spinning and doing stunts, then she pulls the parachute, only the bike gets all tangled in the canopy, then the reserve chute deploys into the whole mess and there's nothing she can do, all you can see is her flailing away, and you're thinking, nah, she's gotta make it, I mean, this is television. Took her something like twenty seconds before she hit, then *wham*—her head busts open like a watermelon and her legs and arms fly off in all directions . . . man, it was so cool."

"David, enough!" Terry eyeballs the producer. "Is this the kind of influence you had hoped to have on America's youth?"

"Accidents happen, Mrs. Taylor, and yes, this was a bad one, but that's what *Daredevils* is, it's extreme stunts . . . true reality TV, and death is part of that reality. That's what makes it so intriguing to our viewers."

"Intriguing? It sounds disgusting."

"Maybe, but is it any worse than watching mindless sitcoms loaded with sexual innuendo? Or do you prefer the new wave of mob dramas?"

Jonas cuts off his wife's retort. "You said you came here to see me?"

"Yes, sir. Our Daredevils, well, they really look up to you. Practically worship the ground you walk on."

"Is that right? Hear that, honey, I'm a teen idol."

Terry rolls her eyes.

"More like a living legend. You're the man who committed the ultimate Daredevil stunt and lived to tell about it. When it comes to spitting in death's face, you raised the bar."

"You don't honestly think I intended to get swallowed by a thirty-ton shark, do you?"

"Maybe you never intended it, but when push came to shove and you were forced to stare death in the face, you didn't just curl up and die, you tore out its heart—literally! These kids live for that stuff, they eat it for breakfast. To them, you're Superman."

"These days, I feel more like Clark Kent."

"Ah, I don't believe that. You look great. You must work out."

"I pump a little iron, still, I'm sixty-three years old."

"And in the prime of your life."

"Excuse me, Mr. Hollander, I don't mean to interrupt my husband's ass-kissing session, but exactly what is it you want with old Superman here?"

"Erik, call me Erik. And what I want is to hire your husband to join us on our next season of *Daredevils*. Theme is the seven seas, right up his alley. Filming begins in ten days, the entire cruise should last about six weeks. We leased a replica of a Spanish galleon, the one used on the set of Roman Polanski's *Pirates,* an amazing vessel. We've got some wild things planned, everything taking place while we're out to sea and far away from civilization."

"What sort of wild things?" Terry asks.

"Swimming with sharks, stunts with Sperm whales, diving with schools of Man 'O Wars, that sort of nonsense. If there's danger attached to it, we'll be filming it."

Jonas offers his hand. "Appreciate you thinking of me, but I think I'll pass."

Erik ignores the brush-off. "Before you say no—"

"He already did," Terry interjects.

"At least think about it, Professor? A hundred and fifty gees is a lot of money."

Jonas smirks. "You want to pay me a hundred and fifty thousand dollars to go swimming with sharks?"

"Hell, no, that's for the crazies. I want to hire you to play guest host, sort of a color commentator. Mentor these kids on camera, pretend to advise them on a few stunts. When it comes to the real action, you'll be safe on the boat, while two teams of skimpily-clad thrill-seekers risk their necks for a two-million-dollar payday."

"A hundred and fifty grand and Jonas does nothing? What's the catch?"

"The catch, Mrs. Taylor, is ratings. Last season *Daredevils* battled for the number-one slot on television, and we can't afford the sophomore jinx. Mention the word 'voyage' and viewers think cruise. Add the name 'Jonas Taylor' to the mix and suddenly you're thinking blood and death. It's all hype and illusion, mind you, but illusion sells."

"That woman's death was no illusion," Terry says.

Erik reflects, the pause well-rehearsed. "Adrenaline junkies . . . some of them really push the envelope. Parachute stunts are dangerous; still, people pay good money every year doing it off planes and mountains and bridges. I'm not justifying what happened, mind you, but eliminate our show and they'd still be doing it. The difference with us is, if a Daredevil dies on our set, their contracted heir receives a million-dollar settlement."

"How wonderful of you," Terry says, the sarcasm dripping.

"Terry—"

"Fame and fortune, Mrs. Taylor. Everything comes with a price. I know it's hard to understand, but if you knew how these kids think—"

"My brother was one of those kids," Terry says, "a pure adrenaline junkie. To a lesser extent, I was too. It wasn't un-

til years after his death that I realized how foolish we'd been.
Your kind of show only glorifies their ignorance, while de-
sensitizing millions of viewers to these sorts of dangerous
activities."

"To us, it's dangerous; to these kids, it's a chosen
lifestyle." He pauses as a small plane passes overhead, momentarily drowning them out. "There's two of our Daredevils now. Come on, I'll show you what kind of mentality
you're dealing with."

Jonas follows him outside.

Terry instructs David to stay at the booth, then joins them,
wondering what happened to her daughter.

Erik leads them to a sound stage where several thousand
onlookers have gathered to view a promotional reel of
Daredevils: Season II.

High overhead, a single-engine plane circles.

Danielle Taylor is seated on the floor of the modified
Cessna, Jennie buckled up in the lone pilot's seat in front of
her. Fergie is stretched out next to Dani, confined in a tight
blue jumpsuit. Canary-yellow wings stretch from each wrist
down to his waist. A third wing is situated between his legs,
from his inseam down to his ankles.

Dani shouts, "that supposed to make you fly like Superman?"

"Oh yeah, absolutely. It's called a Birdman suit. Dangerous buggers. First seventy-five blokes using the prototype
ended up dead. Design's changed a bit since, but it's still unstable as hell. If you're not perfectly symmetrical on the
throw out, you go into a spin. Parachute lines wrap around
you as it opens and you die."

"My God—"

"Heck, that's nothing. The real bitch is the burble."

"What's burble?"

"Burble's the vacuum of dead air created as you plunge

back to earth. The suit's wings really slow you down, so you have to rely on your forward speed to open the chute." He points to a ball dangling from a spandex pouch at the bottom of his parachute container. "Ball's connected to the pilot chute. Wind catches the pilot chute and yanks out the parachute. Problem is, the Birdman suit creates a rather large burble. If the ball gets caught in the dead air, the pilot chute sort of just sticks to your back and stays there. At two hundred miles an hour, well, the impact is like a bug smashing a windshield. Splat."

From the pilot's seat, Jennie calls out, "We're at ten thousand feet. Time to flirt with the big guy."

"Right." He stands, then leans over Dani. "You know, technically speaking, this might be the last time I see you. How 'bout a kiss for good luck?"

She hesitates, then reaches up and gives him a quick kiss.

"That's it? Sweet Jesus, I'm as good as dead."

Dani blushes. Reaching up, she pulls him toward her and buries her tongue in his mouth. "There. Now you can land safely."

"No worries, my love." He turns to the pilot. "Play nice with my friend, Jedi Jennie. No technicolor yawns."

"Stop givin' orders and get outta my plane." She turns the wheel, pitching the cabin sideways.

Dani's head thumps painfully against the wall. *Bitch* . . . She scrambles to hold on as they level out.

Jennie activates a switch and the side door unlocks and swings open, revealing white clouds and the azure waters of the Gulf of Mexico.

Dani stares at the sea, her heart beating like a timpani drum.

The Australian Daredevil checks the smoke cannister strapped to his left ankle, pounds his chest with his right, then crosses himself.

"Wait!" Dani waves to get his attention. "How many times have you done this sort of thing?"

"What?"

"The Birdman suit," she shouts. "You have used it before, right?"

"Nah, this'd be my first time," he lies. He offers her a condemned man's wàve good-bye, then presses his arms to his side and steps to the edge of the cargo hatch like a baby bird about to leave the nest. Puffs of white clouds race below, adding depth perception to the precarious altitude.

Fergie clicks his heels together, activating the smoke cannister, and jumps.

He falls away from the plane like a plunging flesh missile, wind battering his body, waves of adrenaline stabbing his blood vessels with a million pins and needles, every nerve ending firing, every muscle contracting.

Looking up through a trailing crimson cloud of smoke, he confirms he has cleared the plane, then spreads his arms and legs wide—

—the wind punching his wings, pile-driving him higher with the suddenness of a tornado.

What a bugger! Come and catch me if you can, God, I can taste you in my belly.

Wind screams in his ears as his jump-accelerates forward, soaring through a cloud bank in excess of 160 miles-an-hour. Hunched forward, he de-arches his back, registering the strain in his abdominal and leg muscles as he gradually slows his descent to a mere 18 miles-an-hour.

Oh yes, oh yes, oh yes. Have no fear, Superman is here . . .

The dark blue of the Gulf shallows to teal. The beach appears, followed by the fairground greens and the vehicle-clogged parking lots.

The airport. A golf course . . .

Oops. Too far, lad—

He turns his torso, his muscles straining to remain uniform as his wings circle him back in a semi-controlled plunge. The Gulf reappears, reflecting silver. The sun warms his back.

He checks his altimeter.

Okay, crow-eater, time to release the brakes.

Symmetrically, he brings his arms to his sides, collapsing the webbing, increasing the speed of his descent. His right hand gropes along his back. Feels for the ball of the pilot chute. Grips it.

Ready . . . steady . . . throw!

Simultaneously, he launches both arms out to his sides, releasing the pilot chute,

—its bridle strap hopelessly wrapping around his wrist before he can react.

And suddenly time stands still, each adrenaline-enhanced heartbeat pounding in Fergie's skull, his entire existence caught in a vacuum, void of all thought other than survival as he struggles to get the pilot chute off him and free his main chute from the 'horseshoe' malfunction, one of the most dangerous foul-ups in skydiving.

Two attempts, then cutaway!

The first attempt fails at three thousand feet . . . the ground still racing closer to pulverize his existence.

Second attempt . . . twenty-two hundred feet . . . gravity intent on blotting his existence into mother earth.

Come on . . . come on . . . no good! Cut away and pray!

Two thousand feet . . . fifteen hundred—

Reaching across his chest, he pulls the cutaway handle on the left side of his body, disconnecting the risers from his harness, causing him to fall away from the main parachute. He grabs the reserve handle on his right with his opposite hand, pulling the reserve parachute's ripcord.

An image flashes across his mind's eye . . . his former fiancée and fellow Daredevil, Diana, the drop-dead gorgeous brunette flailing as she fell from 14,000 feet.

Fergie shudders. *No! It's not my time . . . not my time . . . not my time . . .*

A sudden jerk scatters the mantra as the reserve chute blossoms, slowing his descent.

Not my time . . . thanks, Di.

He strikes the ground seconds later, his legs and spinal

column taking the brunt of the bone-jarring contact. For several moments he lies on the tarmac, holding his breath against the pain, then he rolls over and sits up, smiling for the onrushing crowd, the bridle pilot chute and tangled main chute still hanging from his wrist.

Danielle presses her face to the window, unable to see anything. "Think he made it?"

"Maybe. Okay, jailbait, ready for some real fun?"

Before she can protest, Jennie Arnos pushes the plane into a near vertical descent, the Cessna wing-over-wing as it plunges back to earth.

Dani tumbles sideways, her existence reduced to forty seconds of unbearable nausea and fright, her screams suffocated by globs of vomit that splatter 360 degrees within the rolling cabin.

Jonas squints against the late afternoon sun, his eyes focused on the stunt plane, now looping downward in a stomach-churning descent before leveling out to buzz the fairgrounds.

"That's our Jennie," comments Erik. "Quite the wild woman."

Jonas feels queasy just watching. "Sort of reminds me of the first time Terry took me up in one of those puddle jumpers."

She laughs. "Your Superman lost his breakfast all over my cockpit."

"Daredevils are human, Mrs. Taylor. That's why the public loves 'em, they know they're not infallible."

"Or immortal."

The producer ignores the comment. "What hotel are you folks staying at?"

"It's, uh, sort of a small bed and breakfast off Interstate Forty-one. But we haven't checked in yet."

"Don't. I'm at the Sandbar Beach Resort, right on the Gulf. We're occupying all the suites. There's a room reserved in your name. Don't thank me, the network's paying for everything. Check in, relax, then meet me for dinner in the lobby around nine. We'll have a few drinks, stuff ourselves like pigs, then I'll fill you in on all the details of the gig. Sound good?"

"Sounds great."

"Uh, Jonas, can I speak with you a minute?" Terry drags him aside. "You're not actually considering this?"

"A hundred and fifty grand? I'm way past considering it."

"So you're planning on living on a boat for God knows how many weeks while I stay home with the kids? I don't think so."

"Terry, we need the money."

"Your book will sell."

"And what if it doesn't? We can't just walk away from this one, Tee."

"Well, I don't trust him. Something's just wrong about this whole thing."

An eavesdropping Erik intervenes. "Mrs. Taylor . . . may I call you Terry? Good. Terry, I know this whole thing is hitting you out of the blue, but that's the way these things happen. As for the money, when it comes to sustaining a Top Ten hit, a hundred and fifty gees is a drop in the bucket. If your husband's presence helps us maintain our ratings, or better yet, capture the number-one spot, then he more than pays for himself."

"It's not the money," Jonas interjects. "My wife and I . . . we've been through a lot over the last few years and—"

"And you've been screwed before, I completely understand. Trust is such a rare commodity these days, hell, it's virtually extinct in Hollywood." The producer waits for the stunt plane to touch down in an adjacent field, then opens the satchel draped over his shoulder. He removes the white Megalodon tooth, pauses for effect, then hands it to Jonas. "I want you to have this, Professor. Consider it a gift—no strings attached."

"I can't accept this."

"Sure you can. Keep it or sell it, it's up to you. All I ask in return is for you and your wife to join me tonight for dinner with an open mind." He glances at his Patek Phillipe watch. "Oh, there *is* one other thing. Your friend, Mackreides . . . the two of you still keep in contact?"

"Uh, sure. Mac's back in California, he works for Terry's father."

"Good. The network wants him too. Same deal as you."

"Why Mac?" Terry asks.

"Jonas and Mac are a team, at least that's how the public sees them. We want to play up on that. Is there a problem?"

"Only if you like your cohosts shit-faced drunk."

"Terry—" Jonas shrugs an apology at the producer. "I can't speak for Mac, but I'll talk to him."

"Hope he recognizes your voice."

Jonas turns to his wife, his expression screaming: *Enough!*

Erik smiles. "Terry, half our sponsors are beer companies, and believe me, all they care about are ratings and demographics. The network, on the other hand, wants both Jonas and Mackreides, or technically they could rescind the offer." He checks his watch again. "Oops, gotta fly, but we'll finish this tonight, okay?" Without waiting for a reply, he flags down his circling stretch limousine and climbs in back.

Jonas watches the car drive away, wondering what just happened.

Terry turns to her husband. "I hate this, I hate this whole damn thing."

"We need the money."

"Do I even have a choice here, or am I just supposed to let you go off on some singles cruise with a bunch of 'wild women' and that drunk ex-friend of yours?"

"It's not a singles cruise, and Mac's still my friend."

"Well I don't trust him, not anymore. Dad says his drinking's gotten worse and—"

"Enough already. Let's hear what the man has to say and then argue about it later." Jonas glances over his wife's shoulder. "Speaking of trust, here comes our daughter, late as usual."

Danielle staggers toward them from the parking lot. The teen's complexion is pale, her blouse undone and dripping wet.

"You're over an hour late," Jonas barks. "Where've you been?"

"Puking my brains out, if you must know."

"Were you drinking?"

"It's a female thing, Dad, but hey, thanks for the compassion. Want to ground me for another month?"

"Maybe I ought to get a urine sample—"

"Jonas, stop." Terry slips a motherly arm around Danielle's shoulder. "Your father and I were just worried. Come on, we'll finish up, check into our hotel, and order some room service."

"Mom, that dump we're staying at doesn't even have a kitchen."

"Change of plans." She shoots Jonas a look of her own. "Tonight we're staying at a hotel on the beach."

CHAPTER

4

The Monterey Bay National Marine Sanctuary encompasses 5,300-square miles of protected waterways, stretching from the northern coastline of San Francisco clear south to the shores of Cambria. Centrally located within this nutrient-rich habitat is Monterey Bay, a half-moon-shaped body of water, twenty-three miles long, curving inland from Santa Cruz to Monterey.

A diversity of marine life inhabits Monterey Bay. Depending on the season, one can observe pods of Grey Whales, Humpbacks, Northern Right Whales, Orca, Minke, Beaked, and even the magnificent Blue, the largest creature in the sea. Dolphin and porpoise also proliferate these waters, along with elephant seals, the favorite cuisine of the Great White shark.

But look beyond this waterway made famous by John Steinbeck, beyond its eateries and shops and fishing boats and tourists, and one finds an anomaly of underwater geology that is unique in all the world. Hidden beneath the deep blue surface is a near-shore underwater chasm of immense proportions, possessing a complex system of tides, currents, and upwellings that provide nutrients to the entire Monterey Bay ecosystem. This is the Monterey Submarine Canyon, a 15-million-year-old dynamic incision of geography that rivals the size and shape of the Grand Canyon.

Most of the planet's continents are bordered by gently sloping shelves whose depths, after several miles, may reach a few hundred feet. Not so the Monterey Canyon. Leap off the old pier at Moss Landing and you are treading water above a submerged gash of rock that can descend a half-mile, dropping as deep as 12,000 feet.

The Monterey Submarine Canyon is not merely a habitat for marine animals, it is a living gorge, oscillating with ebbs and flows. Originally located in the vicinity of Santa Barbara, the entire Monterey Bay region was pushed ninety miles northward over millions of years, carried along the San Andreas fault zone on a section of granite rock, known as the Salinian Block. The canyon itself is a confluence of varying formations; steep and narrow in some places, as wide as a Himalayan valley in others. Sheer vertical walls can drop two miles to a sediment-buried seafloor that dates back to the Pleistocene Age. Closer to shore, twisting

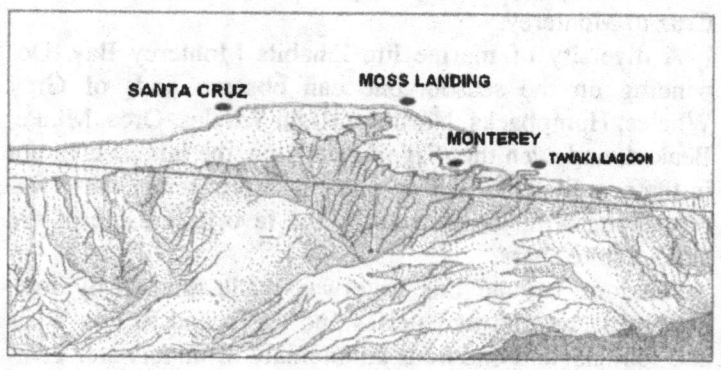

chasms, some as deep as 6,000 feet, reach out from the main artery of the crevice like fingers of a groping hand.

While these deepwater channels can be found from Santa Cruz down the coastline to Cambria, nowhere are they closer to land than along a C-shaped section of ravine that begins just off the coastline of Moss Landing. It is at this point that a mere thirty feet of seafloor separates beach from submarine gorge, sunbathers from the nocturnal creatures of the deep.

The 32-foot Albemarle sport fishing boat, *Angel-II* follows the Monterey Bay shoreline north, cruising at ten knots.

Former Naval pilot James "Mac" Mackreides cuts his speed in half, then wraps two more ice cubes in a paper towel, pressing them against his throbbing left temple. More annoying than the whine and choking exhaust coming from the twin engines is the constant rise and fall of the two-foot swells.

Up and down, up and down . . .

Mac hunches his two-hundred-pound frame over the wheel, grinding his teeth as he stares at his hawkish pale reflection in the console's chrome finish. Gone is the boyish twinkle that usually animates his hazel-gray irises, replaced by dark circles beneath bloodshot eyes and a hangover the size of Mount Rushmore.

Look at you. Older than dirt and twice as ugly.

Mac groans as the dreaded rumbling builds again in his belly.

"Oh, Christ—"

Mac shuts down the engines and hurries below to the head. Dropping down on his knees, he leans over the toilet and retches.

The boat drifts, the swells rocking the vessel beneath him. His equilibrium swimming, he vomits more lava, his inflamed throat on fire, the pain intensifying behind his pounding eyes.

Just take me, God. Stomp out this miserable existence and take me . . .

He gags out the last bit of refuse. Flushes. Reaches over to the sink. Manages to cup a handful of water. Spits, swallows, then lays his aching head against the cool porcelain bowl and passes out.

Angel moves through the pitch-black mid-waters of the Monterey Submarine Canyon, following the steep walls of the C-shaped crevasse.

Millions of years ago, this same California coastline had been a favorite habitat of the Megalodon's ancestors . . . until the seas had turned cold and the whales had altered their migration pattern. Having lost the staple of their diet, the apex predators eventually disappeared, "starved into extinction," according to the so-called experts.

Like their modern-day cousins, the Great White, Megalodon inhabited all the oceans of the world, proliferating in all depths and in a wide range of temperatures. As big-bodied animals, the monstrous sharks were endowed with the metabolism of a warm-blooded fish. Possessing six gills, the creatures could also ventilate at slower speeds or function in even the most poorly oxygenated waters. A reduction of calcification in the Meg's cartilage and the addition of more water in their muscles allowed for a more positive buoyancy, further reducing energy expenditures.

If ever there was a species designed to adapt and survive, it was *Carcharodon megalodon.*

Angel follows the contours of the Monterey Canyon's vertical walls, her torpedo-shaped body gliding with slow, snake-like movements. This distinct rhythm is perpetrated by the shark's powerful swimming muscles, attached internally to her cartilaginous vertebral column and externally to her thick skin, the latter providing a firm sheath to compress against. As these flank muscles contract, the Megalodon's caudal fin and aft portion pulls in rhythmic, undulating motions, propelling the shark forward. The immense half-moon-shaped tail provides maximum thrust with minimal drag, the fin's caudal notch, located in the upper lobe, further streamlining water flow.

Stabilizing the Megalodon's forward thrust are her fins, the enormous dorsal, situated atop her back like a seven-foot sail, and her pair of broad pectoral fins, which provide lift and balance like the wings of a passenger airliner. A smaller pair of pelvic fins, a second dorsal, and a tiny anal fin round out the complement.

Moving effortlessly more than a mile below the surface, Angel maneuvers along the contours of a canyon wall otherwise invisible to the naked eye. And yet the predator can "see" everything, her primordial senses tuned to the magnetic variations in the geography, the currents moving along the seabed, and the minute vibrations coming from above. Although she has no external ears, the big female can "hear" sound waves as they strike groups of sensory hair cells located in her inner ear. Carried by the auditory nerve, these "signals" not only alert the creature to variations within her environment, but allow her to track the precise direction the disturbance originates from.

To the south, Angel "feels" low, percussion-like *thumpa-thumpas* and a whisper of *swishes*—the reverberations marking the beating hearts and moving muscles of a distancing pod of Grey whales. Closer to shore, a cacophony of surface disturbances magnify into the distinct splashing sounds of dozens of Pacific White-sided dolphins. The alien hum of an outboard motor passes overhead, its electrical field momentarily drawing her attention before she refocuses on the high-pitched clicks coming from a family of Orca.

But it is a series of rapid vibrations—moving closer—that captures her attention.

Hitching a ride on an upwelling of cold nutrient-rich water, the gargantuan female ascends, her hunger building.

Darkness yields to gray. Shadows of movement dance along the edge of her field of vision. Reverberations and the scent of feces taunt her appetite.

Leveling out, she glides over the canyon wall and enters the shallows of the kelp forest—a tiger stalking prey in high grassland.

Harbor seals dart in and out of the kelp curtains, unaware of the female's presence.

Angel accelerates, her crescent tail lashing strands of vegetation in a flurry of movement, shredding them like a weed-whacker. Gray-blue eyes roll back, her humongous jaws spreading open—

—slamming shut upon curtains of plants . . . and a fleeing adult mother seal and her pup.

A dull *pop*—the adult's skull exploding inside her crushing jowls. Lower teeth buzz-saw the blubbery torso into a sweet fleshy pulp, even as the squealing pup, still alive, slides backward down her tightening gullet like a watermelon seed.

Suddenly alert, the rest of the seals race toward shore, skimming through the sea toward land like miniature torpedoes.

Angel swallows the morsel of fat, then pushes through the kelp forest in pursuit.

Moss Landing is more blue-collar fishing village than tourist attraction, cluttered with piers and boats, crowded parking lots and warehouses.

Thirty-nine-year-old Patricia Pedrazzoli walks along the shoreline, squinting against the late afternoon haze as she scans the gray horizon. The blue-eyed mortgage broker with the dirty-blond hair checks her watch for the sixth time in the last hour, cursing under her breath. *Dammit, Mac, are you ever on time?*

Her cousin, Kenneth Hoefer, joins her at the water's edge, handing her a Styrofoam cup of tea. "Diner was out of coffee, can you believe that." He pulls the collar of his windbreaker up past his cheeks. "Face it, cuz, he blew you off again. Why do you put up with this guy?"

"Don't start."

"How long have you and Mac been dating? Two years?"

"Drop it."

"All I'm saying is you deserve better. Unless you're afraid to break up with him."

"Meaning?"

"Knowing Rodney Cotner, I figured he must have threatened you not to upset any applecarts with the Tanaka clan until after Jericho closes the Dietsch Brothers' deal."

"You're sick, you know that. Give me a little credit."

"Fine, shoot the messenger, but I'm not the one who was supposed to meet you here two hours ago."

"Mac probably just got hung up at the Institute."

"More like hung over. Wake up and smell the vodka, Patricia, the guy's a loser."

"Not that it's any of your business, *Kenneth*, but Mac's had a rough childhood."

"Who hasn't?"

"Mac's father committed suicide on his tenth birthday. Uncle Johnny ever pull that number on you?"

Ken half-shrugs an apology. "Look, it's not like I don't like the guy, I'm just looking out for your best . . ." He pauses, his eyes searching the horizon. "Hey, isn't that Mac's boat?"

The *Angel-II* drifts north, seventy-five yards off shore.

"Mac!"

"He'll never hear you with his head in the toilet."

"Shut up." Patricia strips off her sweat suit, revealing her black string bikini.

"What are you doing? You're not swimming out to him?"

"The boat's drifting, he could be in trouble."

"Relax. He's probably just drunk."

Ignoring him, she wades in up to her knees, acclimating to the cool water.

Ken calls after her, "While you're at it, why don't you bring him lunch too?"

She washes handfuls of water over her shoulders. "Hey, Mackreides, get your ass out on deck!"

Still no response.

Maybe he really is hurt? Making up her mind, she dives beneath an incoming wave, then pauses in chest-deep water to reposition her bikini top. Head out of the water, she begins swimming.

Ken watches her, shaking his head. "I really have to fix her up with someone." He collects her clothes and heads back to the pier.

A strong swimmer, Patricia is now beyond the breaking waves, a good forty yards off shore. *Halfway there . . . keep going—*

A dark object passes beneath her, then another. She stops swimming and looks down, her heart racing.

Seals? Wow, I must be out pretty deep.

A wave of adrenaline courses through her body, followed by a cold shudder.

Maybe you should go back?

She looks up at the *Angel-II*. The boat has drifted closer to shore, its bobbing transom tantalizingly close.

She starts swimming again.

A dozen more seals dart past her underwater and surface, their honking calls of warning fading behind her back.

Plunging her head beneath the surf, she sprints the last thirty yards, then, huffing and puffing, treads water by the dormant twin engines, pausing to urinate.

Attracted by Patricia's churning legs and rapid pulse, Angel breaks off from the seals and circles back. Two hundred feet below the surface, the Meg glides silently beneath the hull of the boat, inhaling the pungent scent of urine, her senses locking on to her intended prey.

Patricia lets out an "ohh" as a swirling undercurrent spins her away from the stern. Stroking back toward the boat, she pulls herself up the aluminum ladder—

—as the *Angel-II*'s stern suddenly lifts three feet out of the water, sending Tricia sprawling face first across the tilting deck.

The boat slams back against the sea with a resounding *splat*.

"What the hell?" Patricia regains her feet and looks out over the rail.

A fishing trawler chugs past the *Angel-II*, unleashing its six-foot wakes. "Damn fishermen."

She pulls her hair back, squeezes out the excess water, then heads inside to find Mac—

—never seeing the surfacing ivory-white glow, or the mouth that briefly wraps around the outboard motor, tasting its faint electrical field.

Chemical detectors within the Megalodon's mouth confirm the surfaced animal is not edible. Sensory-cell hairs embedded in Angel's lateral line report the seals have fled the killing field.

With no other prey close by, the big female moves into deeper water, but continues to circle back at the strange yet familiar object . . . her hunger building.

TANAKA LAGOON
MONTEREY BAY, CALIFORNIA

The aquarium's subterranean viewing area is a dark, enclosed chamber located two stories below the main level at the southernmost end of the tank.

Masao Tanaka enters the watertight area, his face illuminated green as he gazes out the fifteen-foot-high, six-inch-thick Lexan bay windows. In this private viewing room he has entertained two U.S. presidents, a Chinese premier, dozens of senators, six California congressmen, a governor, countless Hollywood stars, and reporters and photographers from almost every major publication in the United States and abroad. All had experienced the same shortness of breath, tingling bladders, racing pulses, and wide-eyed expressions of fright and delight as they witnessed his captive thirty-five-ton monster devour her daily sides of beef.

Masao gazes into the underwater pen, the chamber's air heavy with mildew, its silence interrupted by the occasional echo of dripping. The once azure-clear tank is tinged olive green, the viewing window heavily blotched with algae.

Drains must be clogged again.

Masao checks the clock on his beeper. The Operations Manager at the Monterey Bay Aquarium will arrive for a preliminary visit in twelve hours, and the place looks like Hell.

Of all time for Mac to be off. He contemplates calling him on his cell phone, then decides against it. *Haven't paid the man in three months. Better handle this myself.*

Masao leaves the viewing area, then follows the subterranean corridor a quarter of the way around until he reaches the Mechanical Room. Keying the bolt, he tugs open the rusted steel door with both hands and enters, his senses immediately greeted by the heavy scent of chlorine and the ear-throbbing *hum* pulsating from several giant generators tucked behind a maze of corroded pipes.

Been years since I've been in here . . . what a mess. Should have never relied on Mac to maintain things. Be lucky to sell this equipment for scrap.

He locates the control panel and searches for the switches that power the lagoon's filtration system. Flips a switch.

Nothing.

His memory failing, he tries a half-dozen more switches until he happens upon the right one. The twin generators chortle as they shut down, choking off the filtration system.

The deep humming stops, replaced by a chorus of drips.

Masao leaves the Mechanical Room and heads for the equipment shack. He strips down, then removes a medium-size wet suit from a hook and pulls it on. Selects an air tank from a rack. Verifies it is full. Secures the tank within a buoyancy control vest, then grabs fins, a mask, weight belt, and an underwater catch-bag, which resembles a tightly meshed fishnet.

He hoists the tank and vest over his shoulder—

"—ughhh . . ." The stabbing chest pain forces him down on one knee.

Reaching for his pile of clothing, he fumbles inside a pant pocket, retrieving the bottle of white pills.

Struggles to free the child-proof cap. Hurriedly slips a saccharine-sized nitroglycerin tablet beneath his tongue.

The chest pain eases.

Stay calm. Probably just indigestion.

He rests another ten minutes, then feeling better, grabs his gear, unaware that a blood clot has formed on top of the plaque lining one of his coronary arteries.

The old man lumbers up two flights of concrete steps to the arena . . . and that's when he hears it, the unmistakable sound of voodoo drums, the baritone pounding coming from a dozen of the lagoon's underwater speakers.

Old fool. Must've hit Angel's dinner bells by mistake.

Annoyed at himself, he scans the gray, late afternoon

horizon, contemplating his next move. *Ah, just leave it on.
Have to go back downstairs to turn the filters on again later
anyway.*

He twists open the air tank valve, checks his regulator,
then begins pulling on gear.

"Mac?"

Patricia heads below, bypassing the guest quarters for
Mac's cabin. She finds him inside, leaning over the sink,
pale and unshaven. The room reeks of vomited alcohol.

"Mac?"

"Tricia . . . Christ, how did you—"

"I've been waiting for you for two hours. What the hell
happened to you?"

"Don't know. Long night, I guess. Give me a few minutes,
okay."

"I'll make some coffee."

"Yeah, coffee. Just pour it into my eyes."

She leaves him. Heads to the tiny galley—

—and confronts the girl.

Drop-dead gorgeous. Long, wavy, peroxide-blond hair
down to her tailbone. Pierced belly button. Tattoo of a Hammerhead shark around her ankle.

Stark naked.

"Hi. I bet you're Tricia. Mac mumbled your name last
night. I thought it was sweet."

Patricia stares at her, openmouthed, the blood draining
from her face. "And who the hell are you?"

"Tameka Miller. Mac and I met last night at a surfing
competition. Don't worry, I'm not into that whole dating
thing. It was just casual sex."

"How lucky for me."

Mac stumbles into the corridor, dead-man-walking.
"Oh . . . shit—"

"Yeah, oh shit." Patricia's right fist strikes his left eye in mid-sentence.

Mac falls backward, knocking over the coffeepot. "Oww, dammit Trish, if you'd let me explain—"

"Bastard! I've wasted two years of my life on you."

He rubs his eye, his brain still clicking on half-cylinders. "Look, I'm sorry. You deserve better, okay. It's just . . . I'm not ready to get hitched."

"So you slept with Miss Teenage California?"

"For your information, I'll be twenty-two in March."

"Shut up." Patricia leaves, stalking out on deck.

"Trish, wait!" Mac pulls himself up the steps into the blinding daylight. "Can we please talk about this?"

"Go to hell." She steps onto the transom and dives overboard, the beach a quarter mile away.

Masao climbs over the five foot concrete seawall and down a portable aluminum ladder into the lagoon, balancing against the lower rungs while he secures the diving mask to his face. Fixing the regulator in his mouth, he sucks in a few breaths, grabs the handle of the fishnet garbage bag in his left hand, then kicks away.

Filled with air, the buoyancy vest keeps him bobbing along the surface. Looking up, he sees Atti hosing down the ten-foot-high Plexiglas panels positioned above the lagoon's southern seawall. Despite poor wages and the challenges of cerebral palsy, the girl dutifully washes the glass every Tuesday, Friday, and Sunday, sweeping sand out of the arena on Mondays and Thursdays. Wednesdays and Saturdays are reserved for physical therapy, or Atti would be at the Institute all week long.

Masao returns her wave, then reaches for the length of hose running out of the BC vest, feeling for the exhaust valve. Pressing the deflator button, he releases a burst of air, the action sending him sinking feet-first into the olive green waters of the man-made lagoon.

The sound of drums pulsates in his ears. Ignoring the impulse to climb out and shut off the speakers, he continues sinking, pinching his nose to pressurize as he plummets seventy feet to the murky bottom.

The steel grating that marks the main drain is twenty feet wide, running the entire width of the tank. Masao hovers above the grate, now choked with kelp, dead fish, and garbage. The carcass of a sea turtle floats in the periphery, one of its claws caught in the drain.

The baritone thumping pounds his bones, his pulse dancing in rhythm to the beat. He looks around nervously, then smiles at his own paranoia. *She's long gone, old man. Ghosts can't hurt you.*

Holding the refuse bag in his left hand, he begins pulling clumps of kelp away from the grating with his right, shoving the debris deep into the netting.

Maintaining her head above water, Patricia Pedrazzoli strokes harder, her seething anger powering her muscles through the surf, the cold Pacific no longer a second thought.

Bastard . . . Kenneth was right. I should've dumped his ass long ago—

She never notices the glow that shadows her eighty feet beneath the surface, a glow that turns the royal blue sea jade green, but she does register the annoying disturbance to her right.

"Tricia—shark! Shark, Trish . . . it's a Meg!"

She stops swimming, her heart pounding in her chest. Panting, she treads water as she looks around.

The *Angel-II* putters in neutral twenty feet to her right. Mac leans over the rail, shielding his eyes against the water's reflective glare, failing to hide his boyish smile. "Sorry, I, uh, I just needed to get your attention."

"Asshole."

"I am an asshole, but hey, I'm a sorry asshole. At least let me take you in. You can blacken my other eye if you'd like."

"I'd rather swim with the Megs." She ducks her head and continues swimming.

Angel circles below, inhaling the sea, her brain processing detailed chemical information about the amino acids in Patricia's urine, the oil on her skin, the scent of her recent menstrual cycle . . .

The fish rises to feed.

And then the Megalodon detects another stimulus, a distinct baritone pulsating reverberation that tantalizes the female's primordial senses and stabs at her brain.

Thumpa . . . thumpa . . . thumpa . . . thumpa . . .

Angel shakes her head from side to side, unable to block out the vibrations.

Unlike most fish, large predatory sharks like *Carcharodon megalodon* possess complex brains—control centers for the most elaborate sensory system Nature ever devised. Auditory, visual, olfactory, chemical, and electro-sensory input are processed by the animal's midbrain, cerebellum, and hindbrain, as well as ten percent of the forebrain. The rest of the enormous cerebrum is devoted to learning and memory.

It was memory that guided Angel back to the waters of her birth. Now, it is the memory of a behavior learned long ago that forces her to refocus her senses.

Thumpa . . . thumpa . . . thumpa . . . thumpa . . .

Ignoring Patricia, Angel returns to the depths of the canyon, the vibrations intensifying as she glides closer to the face of the canyon. She follows the deepwater ravine to the south, chasing after the familiar stimulus like a 40-ton Pavlovian dog.

Thumpa . . . thumpa . . . thumpa . . . thumpa . . .

A branch of the gorge twists to the east. The monster follows it, her pulse pounding in rhythm to the voodoo drums, the dinner bells of her youth delivering her through the submerged concrete walls and into the Tanaka Lagoon's ocean-access canal.

Masao avoids touching the dead sea turtle as he shoves another handful of kelp into the net-bag, now filled to capacity. He checks his air gauge, then looks back at the thin trail he has cleared through the muck. *This could take all night.* Tightening the bag's ties, he reaches for the buoyancy control device to surface—

—then freezes, his chest suddenly constricting, his breath cut short as his eyes focus on the ghostly conical head moving toward him from out of the olive mist.

The awful peppered snout.

The mouth, parted in a devil's slit of a smile.

The streamline form. The incredible girth—so massive it creates its own current as it moves.

Angel . . .

Masao's skin itches until it burns, his muscles tensing as if electrified. He bites through his regulator and squeezes his tingling bladder tighter but does not move, despite the internal vise rapidly tightening around his chest cavity.

Angel looks through him with her gray hole of a right eye, then moves effortlessly past him, dwarfing him like a blimp. Enormous gill slits flutter in Masao's vision, followed by the right pectoral fin, which sweeps by like the wing of a 737 airliner.

The flow of water generated by the creature's mass lifts Masao away from the bottom, flipping him head over fins and around again. The monster's caudal fin, two stories high, swats him sideways and out of its wake like a bug.

The turtle drifts free, its shell smacking him in the face mask. He pushes the dead animal aside and stares, wide-eyed and petrified, as Angel approaches the southern end of the tank and the underwater viewing area.

The Meg rises, poking her colossal head topside to look around.

The drums . . . she thinks it's feeding time.

Another wave of pain grips his chest, doubling him over.

Atti Holman hoses down another salt-stained section of Plexiglas, then squeegees the surface using her good left hand, guiding it with her helper right.

And suddenly she is stumbling backward, falling against the concrete base of the rusted steel A-frame as an abominable alabaster head rises from out of the olive green water on the other side of the partition.

Her body rigid in fear, Atti can only gasp at the brute, its parted lower jaw opening and closing as if talking, revealing the tips of its gruesome seven-inch teeth.

The girl stays on her back, too petrified to move.

Masao remains curled up in a ball, fifty feet from the surface, a million miles from safety. Intense pain rakes his body, his chest feeling as if an elephant is sitting on it. The ache radiates into his back and neck, down his arms and into his jaw. He struggles to gasp air from his regulator as his ischemic heart, deprived of oxygen from the clot, stifles the flow of blood through his coronary artery. The rhythm of the organ has become irregular, the ventricular fibrillation causing his heart to quiver, preventing the muscle from pumping blood to his brain.

Through his agony he sees the behemoth prehistoric Great White sink beneath the surface and turn, her immense nostrils inspecting the waters of the tank.

The Megalodon's sensory array feeds her new information. The fish moves slowly toward Masao, seeing him as if for the first time.

A thousand daggers seem to prick the old man's flesh, his wounded heart convulsing in agony as he prays to die faster.

Angel's lower jaw unhinges as she moves closer . . . closer—

Splash!

The metal bucket strikes the surface along the opposite side of the tank, the sound startling the creature. She turns her head, then glides to her right, homing in on the source of the disturbance.

Masao's chest has become a tightening vise. He cannot move. He cannot breathe.

The empty bucket skims past Angel's snout, generating no interest.

The predator turns back to her prey.

Her senses search the south end of the tank, but the electrical stimulus has ceased.

Confused, the leviathan circles twice—

—then visually relocates her prey, her meal floating just above the murky tank bottom.

The devil's vacuous mouth opens, its gums and upper rows of teeth lurching forward—

Chomp!

Angel engulfs the rancid turtle, crushing its shell like a walnut—

—never noticing the old man's body, hovering facedown along the debris-covered grating.

Still hungry, the creature makes her way out of the lagoon and through the ocean-access canal. Pushing past the open doors, she returns to the sanctuary of the Monterey Submarine Canyon.

The old man's body convulses one last time within the entanglement of kelp.

Masao Tanaka is dead.

CHAPTER

5

VENICE BEACH, FLORIDA

Danielle Taylor lies back in the twin-size bed, feigning fatigue, as her parents enter from the adjoining room of the suite.

She inhales her mother's perfume seconds before the kiss on her forehead. "Still feeling queasy?"

"A little."

"Your brother's out on the balcony, playing video games. Try to get some rest."

"I will. Have fun at dinner."

Jonas waves from the doorway. "Night, Dani. Remember, you're still grounded. That means you don't leave this room."

"Do I look like I'm going anywhere?" She rolls over, exaggerating her annoyance.

Jonas starts to say something. Decides against it.

The outer door double clicks shut. Danielle waits five minutes, then heads outside to the balcony where her brother is spread-eagled on a lounge chair, absorbed in a video combat game.

"Hey, Poindexter, I'm going for a soda run. Want anything?"

"Don't lie. If you really wanted a soda, you'd be ordering room service. You're sneaking out."

"Okay, how much to buy your silence?"

"Ten bucks."

"Five."

She heads back inside. Removes a $5 bill from her purse. Crumples it up and tosses it at her brother. Returning to her bedroom she slips an unbecoming gray flannel jogging suit over her hip-huggers and see-through blouse, then applies makeup, doubling up on the eyeliner.

Danielle pockets one of the card keys to the room and leaves the suite. Avoiding the elevator, she takes the staircase five floors down to the lobby, pushes open the metal fire door, and peeks into the corridor.

Restaurant and lounge to the left, the hallway leading to the pool and beach to the right.

Keeping her head down, she turns right, following the carpeted corridor past the ice machine, then exits out to the pool deck and beach club.

It's after nine, the pool area closed for the evening. Leaving the fenced-in area, she heads for the beach.

The Gulf is calm and soothing, the night air warm, the sky a mixture of stars concealed behind whiffs of white clouds. She strips off the sweat suit, fixes her hair, then heads for the group of people gathered around a small campfire along a dark stretch of beach.

The aroma of beer and pot cut through the salty air, the pulse of rap music overpowering the sound of the surf. Couples are making out along the darkened periphery. Approaching the campfire, she stumbles over a sleeping bag, the naked couple inside barely noticing.

Several dozen people sit around a campfire, now burned down to charred logs and glowing embers. Dani sees faces in the shadows—teens, mostly female groupies, mingling with members of the Daredevil troupe.

Look at them . . . swooning all over these guys. How pathetic.

She turns to leave, then hears Wayne Ferguson's voice. "No

worries. Plenty of time to cut away. You do what you gotta do."

He is seated on a log at the edge of the campfire, dressed in a "Surf the Wild West Coast" sweatshirt.

Dani takes a seat behind two heavily tattooed bikers, uncertain if the one on the left is a man or woman.

Fergie takes a long swig of beer, draining it. "Yep, Lady Di was lookin' out for me today."

"Hey, Fergie, tell 'em the story about Blackfellas."

"Nah, they don't want to hear that again. Besides, Adam'll just interrupt, won't you mate?"

"Only when you get it wrong." Adam Potter is lying on his back, his head in the lap of a bikini-topped platinum blonde. Short and athletically built, the computer executive and part-time Daredevil manager has short-cropped copper-brown hair and a reddish-blond goatee. Dani notices the tattoo of an Indian on the man's right shoulder peeking out beneath his cut-off sweatshirt.

Catcalls of persuasion.

"All right, all right. Someone toss me another coldie and I'll spill my guts."

A bottle of beer is fished from a bucket of ice and passed to Fergie.

Shushes. The crowd quiets.

"Happened ten months ago, right Adam?"

"Eleven."

"Eleven, right. It was just after Diana left us. Anyway, Adam and me were hired by a surfing magazine out of Elliston to take underwater shots of surfers. First stop naturally was Blackfellas, our name for Blacks Point, a somewhat empty expanse of Australian sea located at the entrance to Anxious Bay."

"It's on the southside of Australia," Adam adds, "a wild surfing spot. As the waves hit the submerged rock shelf, they create immense left-handed breaks—perfect for filming."

"Am I telling this or you?"

"Sorry."

"Right. Anyway, I'm working below the waves while Adam's on the wave-runner, changing film and posing for the Sheilas, when one of the Yanks . . . what was his name?"

"Christopher Laubin."

"Right. Well, old Chris catches a beaut, and yours truly is bobbing right in the tube, camera pointed, clicking away like a battler, when all of a sudden, this enormous shark comes poking her head right out from under and bites poor Christopher below the left knee, surfboard and all."

Whispers of awe.

Dani feels her blood run cold.

"The wave takes Chris under, and I duck too, 'cept I'm rushing to let the air out of my vest, thinking maybe I don't wanna be on the surface about now, 'specially with all that blood in the water. So I'm sinking like a rock, and all I can see is pink foam, and then I spot the shark. It was a White Pointer, a real nasty bitch, what you Yanks call a Great White, and she was a big one, too, maybe seven meters from snout to tail, and she's circling poor Christopher, but I mean really circling, very fast, like she intends to finish him off. Chris's on the surface now and he's got hold of what's left of his board and he's paddlin' toward the cliff face, but I can see there's no way he's going to make it. Then I hear the wave-runner."

"I was circling, looking for him," Adam says. "I saw a little blood in the water, but I just assumed he cut himself on the coral. So I pulled up next to him and asked him if he needed a ride in. He looked pale, but calm, and he said, 'It bit me, Adam.' And that's when I noticed all the blood, it was just gushing out of him. So I grabbed him under the arm to hoist him on the wave-runner—"

"—and the shark struck again . . . wham!" Fergie smashes his balled fist into his other palm. "Grabbed Christopher around the torso and shook him like a ragdoll."

"About jerked my arm out of its socket," continues Adam. "That shark and I had a real tug-of-war. Big wave's bearing down on us and Chris's screaming, 'Go-go-go,' as he grabs hold of the side of the wave-runner, so I hit the throttle and yanked him out of that shark's mouth." Adam pauses, fighting his emotions. "It was brutal. He pulled clear but left half his lower torso behind . . . damn shark just mangled the hell out of him. Bled to death before we reached the cliff face."

Fergie nods. "Now it's me and the pointer, and she's mighty pissed because Adam just stole the rest of her meal. Before I know what's happening, she's charging me, driving her ugly snout clear into my gut."

"Oh my God, what did you do?" A tall redhead in a dental-floss bikini covers her mouth.

Feeding off the crowd, Fergie stands, pacing around the campfire. "Did the only thing I could—I held on. Pushed down on the top of her snout with both hands, preventing her from getting those nasty ivories on me. She's snapping and snapping, but her eyes are rolled back, see, so she's not quite sure where to bite. Meanwhile, I'm kicking and kneeing her, but it's like hitting a pickup truck. Finally off she swims, only she doesn't leave, she just circles above me, just like she did with Chris. Me, I'm staying close to the bottom, moving from one coral reef to the next, hoping she'll lose interest and go away—

"—but she didn't."

Fergie drains his beer, then tosses the bottle in a trash bag. "Charged me seven more times . . . seven. Enough to make a man go insane. Fourth time she knocked my mask off . . . now that was really scary. Could barely see her as she drove me into the reef. Feelin' around, I stuck my thumb in the white of her right eye. She didn't like that and spun away, giving me a chance to retrieve my mask."

"Wow. How long were you down there?" asks another groupie.

"Felt like hours, but my dive computer said it was only twenty minutes."

"How'd you get away?" the redhead asks.

"Coast Guard finally came by. I waited until the pointer

moved off a bit, then made a mad dash for the surface. Those were the worst moments . . . not seeing her, knowing she was coming around from below. But I made it. Two days later we finished shooting and that's all I have to say about that."

"Are you nuts?" Dani yells out, suddenly realizing she is standing. "I mean . . . why would you go back after that?"

Fergie smiles. "Had to go back. Can't let some guppie dictate how I make my living."

"Sharks aren't after people anyway." Michael Coffey enters the ring of listeners. Salt and pepper hair, built like a rugby player, the older Daredevil's presence is clearly meant as a challenge to Fergie's hold on the group.

"You're wrong there, mate. This shark tasted human flesh and wanted more."

"Bullcrap. The shark obviously mistook the surfer for a seal. It only went after you because there was blood in the water and it became aroused."

"Yeah, its hunger for human flesh was aroused."

"You know nothing about these creatures. I've swum with Great Whites in the open water, I'll be doing it again this winter in South Africa. The sharks have no interest in humans as food. Trust me, bee stings kill more people every year than these fish."

"Bee stings? You're daft, Coffey. Bee stings don't gut a man. And I don't agree with your theory about seals. Every year, shark tour operators dump more and more chum into Aussie waters, luring the whites closer to their dive cages so greenies like you can snap photos and act all macho. These Whites are smart, and we're training them to associate humans with food. Damn cage-dive operators. Their brochures should read: 'Man: The Other White Meat.'"

Scattered laughter.

Coffey is not amused. "And what would you do? Slaughter these magnificent animals because they happen to inhabit the same waters as surfers?"

"Sharks are like people, mate, there's docile ones, and

ones that have tasted human flesh. You get one that associates man with food and you'd better kill it, or close the beaches."

"More *Jaws* bullcrap. It's stories like yours that endanger the entire species."

"Only species I care about is my own."

Adam chimes in. "No one wants to kill a White Shark, but Fergie's got a point, Michael. If you'd been there, if you had seen this shark, you wouldn't be so quick to defend her. Lions that taste human blood have to be hunted down or else villagers die. Once a predator acquires a taste, it's kill or be killed."

Coffey shakes his head. "Live and let live, that's my creed." He eyes Fergie. "Besides, if I could choose how I'd go, I'd rather my meat be used to feed a godly creature like a Great White than waste my flesh by dropping it from fourteen thousand feet."

Fergie's balled fist slams into Coffey's mouth, and then both men are on the ground, punching and rolling. Adam and several other Daredevils jump into the fray, pulling the bigger American off the Aussie.

Coffey smiles, his mouth bleeding. "What's wrong, birdman? Can't take a little joke?"

Fergie is a raging volcano. "Eat me, you bloody drongo. This ain't over. We'll settle this at sea."

"Fine by me." Coffey spits blood and a front tooth into his hand, then tosses it at Fergie. "Here, give this to the tooth fairy."

Fergie pushes Adam's grip from his forearm and storms off into the shadows, his damaged ego kicking at the sand.

Dani waits a moment, then chases after him. She catches up by the water's edge. "Hey—"

Fergie ignores her.

"You okay?"

"Guy's a dill. Big hotshot. Thinks his piss don't stink just because he won last season's Daredevil."

"He sure knows how to push your buttons."

"Part of his mind games, and I fall for it every time." He tosses a shell at an incoming wave.

"Who's Di?"

Fergie looks out to sea. "She was my fiancée. Died during last year's show."

"I'm sorry." She waits out of respect. "Fergie—"

"You want to know why I do it. Why I risk my arse."

"You almost died this afternoon, but it doesn't seem to faze you in the least. Do you have a death wish?"

"You wouldn't understand."

"Try me."

Fergie turns to her. "Look, it may seem like I seek out life and death scenarios, but it has nothing to do with a desire to die, it has to do with a desire to live."

"You're right. I don't understand."

"Every person dies, Dani, but few of us ever truly live. Most people waste their lives working nine-to-five in some job they hate like poison, worrying about stupid deadlines, while greedy CEOs steal from their pension fund. My father, he used to work in a medical ward, a place they send the living dead to rot while their children haggle over the inheritance. During summers, I used to work for him, cleaning bed pans, massaging pockets of flesh that hadn't seen circulation in years. The stuff of nightmares is what it was. Old people who are clinically dead, sucking on breathing tubes, feeding off morphine. The loved ones insist on keepin' 'em alive. I've seen things, terrible things I wished I'd never seen. Deteriorating flesh. Exposed spinal columns. One old guy even had maggots growing in his throat. The flies sometimes get in through the tubes—"

"Stop, you're making me sick."

"Made me sick, too. But that's life, the uglier side no one hears about. Me, I had my fill. I quit school and left home, setting out to experience the thrill of living."

"And nearly dying gives you that?"

"I know it's hard to fathom, but when that parachute

failed, part of me was loving it. There I was . . . right on the
edge of living and dying, and I'm the only one who could
save me. That's living on the edge, and it's an amazing feeling. No fear . . . there's no time for it. At that moment, you're
totally focused on survival. Adrenaline goes into overdrive,
time seems to stand still. When the reserve chute opens and
you know you're going to live, you have so much energy you
feel like you're going to burst. It's still running through me,
it'll keep me up all night. That's what life's about, Dani, taking risks, putting yourself on the edge. In some ways, I'm
like that White Pointer, the one who killed Christopher.
Once you get that taste in your mouth, that taste for adventure, it never goes away. Diana's dead, but she lived a good
life, lived the way she wanted to, all the bullshit stripped
away. I miss her, but in a way, I'm happy for her too."

Danielle leans against him. "My life . . . it's such a bore
compared to yours. And my father—he's so uptight, sometimes I think his brain's going to burst. He drives me crazy
with all his stupid rules, and my mother—she's afraid to try
anything new. All she cares about is keeping the family safe.
She's so afraid, it's no wonder she goes to therapy. My
brother's nose is always buried in a book, he's a sci-fi
dweeb, and my so-called friends—all they're into is competing for guys. I have no freedom, and my parents already
have the next five years of my life planned. I hate it."

"Then do something about it. It's your life, Dani, take
control. Live every day like it was your last."

"I wish I could. I wish I could just come with you, live the
way you do . . . tell them all to just fuck themselves."

"Do it."

"I can't . . . I can't do the things you do. I'm too chicken."

"No one's sayin' you should jump from planes, just let
yourself go. You're immortal 'til you die."

She reaches into her pocket. Takes out a joint. "Want to
get high?"

"I don't do drugs. Drug highs are artificial, followed by

nasty lows. I get high on adrenaline. I get high on trying new things, by putting myself out there." He takes the joint from her, tossing it into the sea.

"Hey—"

Fergie's lips stifle her objection. Any thought of resistance disappears as she turns to Jello in his arms. He pulls her down to the wet sand, his touch electric velvet as he peels off her clothes, sending jolts of excitement through her groin.

"Let go, Dani Taylor. It's time to live."

It is after midnight by the time Jonas and Terry return to their suite. Jonas guides his room key into the card slot, cursing as the door fails to unlock.

"You're doing it backward. Give it to me."

"I can handle it, thank you." He flips the card around. Fails again.

Terry takes it from him and opens the door. "Men. So helpless."

"I'll remind you of that the next time you drag me off the couch to kill a spider." He kicks off his shoes, collapsing on the bed.

"Are we going to discuss this or not?"

"We've been discussing it all night. Bottom line: We need the money."

"So that's it? You're definitely going?" She yanks open the sliding glass door to the balcony and steps outside, letting in a gust of tropical air.

So much for sex. Jonas pries himself off the bed. He joins her on the balcony, putting his arms around her.

"Don't touch me."

"Come on, Tee, it's not that long."

"Open your eyes, Jonas. Dani turns eighteen soon. This is probably her last summer at home—assuming she doesn't take off after her birthday. Meanwhile, my father's health is deteriorating, David's on the traveling team for Little

League, and you're going on some Hollywood singles cruise
roaming the South Pacific for seven weeks."

"Working, Terry, I'll be working—bringing in money this
family desperately needs."

"Leaving me to hold this family together! I won't go
through this again, Jonas, I won't."

"Go through what? What are you so afraid of?"

She shakes her head, the tears of frustration causing silky
strands of ebony hair to stick to her cheeks. "I was eleven
when my mother died. My father—he didn't know what to
do, didn't know how he could raise a family and still earn a
living as a marine biologist. D.J. and I were too young to
take on ocean voyages, so my father hired a woman to stay
with us while he traveled. He'd leave us for months at a time.
The nanny cooked and cleaned, but she wasn't there for us
emotionally. That was my role, I was left to be D.J.'s parent.
Holidays, birthdays . . . it was all up to me. And each time
my father would pack his bags to leave us again, he'd put me
on his lap and say, 'Terry, you know I have to do this to support our family, so I'm counting on you to keep everything
together while I'm gone.' Thirty years later, D.J.'s dead, and
my father's still pretending he's doing everything for the
family . . . and now, so are you. Our children are growing up,
Jonas, and you're missing out on it."

"Tell that to our bank, Terry, when they move to foreclose
on our home. Tell that to the auto mechanic when our car
breaks down like it did last month, or the HMO who gouges
us every month for medical insurance. Tell it to the electric
and water company, next time they shut us off, or better yet,
tell it to Dani, God forbid she should actually want to go to
college next fall. I don't agree with what your father did, but
I understand his motives. As far as this stupid TV show is
concerned, it's a one-time thing, and I can't afford to let it
slip by because you're . . . well, you know."

"No, I don't know." She turns to face him, her almond
eyes full of rage. "Say it."

"Your therapist said it best. You're still haunted by memories of what happened to you eighteen years ago. You haven't been the same since the experience on the *Benthos*. It's left you overprotective, refusing to allow you or any of us to take any kind of risk."

"Fine. You want to leave us for two months, do it, I don't care anymore. And yes, maybe I do have some issues to deal with, but so do you. You can't blame all our financial difficulties on me. You had plenty of good job offers over the last fifteen years, but you refused to take them."

"I can't sit behind a desk all day."

"Why not? Other husbands do."

"Yeah, well, it's just not me."

"But you're jumping at this offer, aren't you? Another call to adventure, another chance to convince yourself that you're still some macho warrior capable of fighting the good fight, whatever the hell that means."

"I've been hired to emcee some stupid televison show. I'm not a contestant."

"Not yet, but you will be. I can hear it in Erik's words as he sings praises to your ego and I can see it in your eyes. I know you, Jonas Taylor. You can't wait to show the world what you've still got left in your tank. So go off and play, go sail your last soldier's hurrah while you deny your own male menopause, but don't feed me anymore of this bullshit about earning a living, because we both know that's a lie."

The ring of the telephone cuts off his rebuttal.

"Hello." Jonas watches as Terry's expression changes, her eyes saddening, her lower lip quivering. "Okay . . . okay . . . No, I can handle it. Thank you for calling." She hangs up.

"What happened? What's wrong?"

She looks up at him, a lost child. "My father . . . he's dead."

CHAPTER

6

STRAIT OF JUAN DE FUCA, PACIFIC OCEAN
18 MILES SOUTHWEST OF PORT RENFREW
VANCOUVER ISLAND, BRITISH COLUMBIA

The northwest coastline of British Columbia stretches nearly 17,000 miles, incorporating countless islands, inlets, and bays. Marine life is abundant in these nutrient-rich waters, which serve as feeding grounds for local and migrating populations of Humpbacks, Orca, Greys, and Minke whales. For saltwater fishermen, the deep waters off the Queen Charlotte Islands (*Haida Gwaii*, to the Haida Aboriginals) and Vancouver Island are home to chinook and coho salmon, rockfish, lingcod, and the giant halibut, the major carnivore fish of the Pacific northwest. Found in the more open waters off Vancouver Island, halibut can weigh upwards of two to three hundred pounds, with pregnant females pushing the scale over four hundred.

The fishing charter *Bite Me-2* trolls north at three knots just off Sombrio Beach, a cobble-covered coastline rising to mountainous terrain, covered in heavy vegetation. A dense fog drifts over the cedar-hemlock forest, becoming denser as it moves out to sea.

Heath Shelby tugs on the bill of his San Francisco 49ers

baseball cap and buttons his waterproof parka as the morning mist turns to a steady drizzle. An avid fisherman, the former Associate Vice President of Operations at Enron Corporation has chartered the *Bite Me-2* for the week, hoping to land a prize halibut to adorn the office of his new summer getaway in Prince Rupert Sound. The first two days of fishing have yielded seven forty-pound chinook and a sixty-three-pound halibut, but the "big catch" had gotten away—a 330-pound beast that snapped his line after an exhausting hour-long struggle.

The rain gets heavier, convincing Shelby to seek shelter inside.

His wife's nephew, Mark Allen, greets him with a fresh cup of coffee. "Nasty weather, huh?"

"Brilliant observation."

"Captain says it'll probably get worse before it gets better. Maybe we should head in? Rachael's getting a little seasick."

Shelby glances inside an adjoining cabin where a slim, green-eyed English beauty is lying on a sofa, nursing a headache. Mark's fiancée had joined Shelby's excursion earlier that morning, hoping to get in some scuba diving, but after six hours at sea, the schoolteacher from Wolverhampton looks ready to fly back to the United Kingdom.

"Tell her to pop a few more Dramamine."

"Uncle Heath—"

"This is my charter, Mark, and I'm not heading in 'til we haul in my fish." Shelby ascends the ladder, climbing up to the flying bridge to speak with the skipper.

Matt Winegar has been fishing in these coastal waters for eight years, ever since retiring from a brief stint in the United States Navy. Even-tempered and easygoing, it takes a lot to bother the fishing boat captain, but the arrogant Texas millionaire is clearly getting on his nerves.

"So? Where's my fish? With all this fancy equipment, I figured you'd have found him by now."

"Her, and I'm doing my best, Mr. Shelby. A big female like the one you hooked prefers hanging out near piles of rock along the bottom. We'll keep trolling the Swiftsure Bank between Port Renfrew and Sombrio Beach until we relocate her, but there are no guarantees."

"Damn fishing line . . . I need something heavier this time 'round."

"I told Michael to switch to the heaviest test we have on board. Hate to exceed seventy-pound, if we snag we'll never get it off the bottom."

"So we'll cut away and start again. I don't care what it costs, Captain, I want my fish."

Winegar grits his teeth and grins. "Yes, sir, we'll do our best."

The rain lightens. Shelby heads back out on deck, where first mate Michael Rybel is securing a halibut rig to a braided Dacron line.

"Heavy line . . . good. What bait are you using?"

"Squid lure. Dogfish tend to stay away from them. Saves time."

"Is that what you used before?"

"Yes, sir."

Shelby stares at the first mate's left pant leg, now riding up past his calf. "What is that? A prosthetic? You get attacked by a shark or something?"

"Nothing so glamorous." The electrical engineering major taps his plastic leg. "I have neurofibromatosis—elephant man's disease. It's congenital."

"Tough break for you."

"It's not as bad as it sounds, although the dialysis is a pain in the ass. I have another brace on my—"

"Okay, I don't need the full medical, let's just get that line back in the water before we lose my fish."

Rybel's retort is interrupted by Winegar, who is calling out from the flying bridge. "You ready, Mike? I think she's below."

"About time." Shelby wipes excess water from the deck-mounted steel fishing chair.

Rybel finishes baiting the hook, then hobbles over to the transom.

The captain shifts the boat into neutral. The twin engines putter, spewing clouds of blue-gray carbon monoxide.

Shelby covers his mouth, choking on the fumes. "Come on, before she gets away."

"Big halibut are territorial, bullying the rest away. She's probably the biggest fish in the area, so she won't be so quick to run." The first mate releases the tackle over the side, the rig's two-pound lead ball dragging the heavy line below. "I scented the squid jig, the females tend to like that." He turns back to the captain. "Hey skipper, how deep?"

"About one-ninety."

Rybel feels the sinker hit bottom, then reels in five quick turns before anchoring the pole. "We're set here."

Winegar puts the boat in reverse, trolling backward to keep the line directly beneath the boat, a maneuver necessary to compensate against the fast-moving waters of the Swiftsure Bank. "Okay, Mr. Shelby, saddle up. Let's see if we can't rehook your monster."

The currents along the Pacific northwest coastline move like powerful rivers as they channel south past the Welker and Bowie Seamounts, driving the deep waters of British Columbia toward the Juan de Fuca Ridge.

The male *Carcharodon megalodon* zigzags in and out of the Swiftsure Bank current, tasting its new surroundings. For weeks the adolescent giant has followed the Alaskan Stream, its senses guided by the lingering chemical traces of the female's estrus. Then, upon entering the nutrient-rich waters of the Gulf of Alaska, the male's testosterone-driven lust had turned to hunger.

Whales, sea elephants, seals, dolphin . . . the Gulf was a

thriving ecosystem of marine mammals—a veritable banquet for a hungry Megalodon. But the young adult had never hunted in surface waters before, and never against such large prey.

The male's first hunting lesson came during a night attack. Stalking a pod of Grey whales, the Megalodon had attempted to pluck a defenseless calf from the adults. Instead of feasting, the Meg was forced to flee after being buffeted by the flukes of two 60,000-pound bulls.

Several more frenzied attempts yielded more failures, forcing the big male to devise a new strategy.

Moving along the western coast of Banks Island, the predator had detected the presence of an elephant seal swimming along the surface. Instead of a direct assault, the male remained deep, circling its prey from below . . . before launching a stealthy, vertical attack.

Like the Great Whites that stalk the waters off the coast of South Africa, the Megalodon drove straight out of the sea, propelling its entire girth out of the water as it snatched the half-ton elephant seal in one explosive shake-and-toss bite. Swallowing the mammal's upper torso, the overly cautious male continued to circle the gushing lower torso before finally moving in to finish off its meal.

Lesson learned: blind attacks were more effective than bull-rushing prey along the surface.

With its newfound knowledge, the male continued its southerly trek along the Pacific northwest coast—a lone wolf picking its way among nervous flocks of sheep.

The squid dances against the current—a marionette enticing its 330-pound suitor.

The six-foot halibut, a pregnant female, carries over four million fertilized eggs within its bloated ovum. Hungry, she inhales the bait's scent and eyeballs the lure, growing more and more agitated.

She circles the bait again, watching . . . waiting—

Heath Shelby's heart leaps as the heavy Dacron line sings on the spinning reel. "Got her—ha! And this time, she won't get away."

Michael Rybel secures Shelby's harness to the deck-mounted chair. "Okay, nice and easy. Just let her run a bit along the bottom, probably doesn't even know she's hooked."

The tension on the rod eases.

Shelby clips the end of the rod to the steel chair, giving his arms a moment's reprieve.

"Okay, Mr. Shelby, let's take her in a bit, slow and steady. We gotta knock some of the fight out of her."

"We? You mean me, this is my fish." Shelby takes up the slack, then leans back with all his weight, pulling against the immovable object. Leaning forward again, he rewinds several feet of line, then repeats the maneuver, his entire body shaking from the effort.

"God, what a monster!"

"Stay with her, wear her down a bit, then reel her in again."

"Wear her down? She's wearing me down! We need to cleat the line."

"Can't, she's too big. She'll rip the cleats right out of the boat."

Shelby grimaces, beads of perspiration pouring down his face "I can barely hold her."

The skipper shifts out of reverse, moving the boat forward at two knots.

Mark Allen joins them. "You caught her again, excellent. Hey, Uncle Heath, you okay? Your face is purple. Want me to take—"

"Stay . . . back!" Shelby tightens his grip on the rod, the veins in his neck popping out like rope.

Rybel moves to the transom, carrying a harpoon with a

rope attached to a fluorescent-orange float. "Get her close to the surface and I'll gaff her."

Shelby pulls and reels, pulls and reels, the weight of the unseen fish actually turning the boat, dragging it backward. "She's coming up a bit . . . I can feel her weakening!"

The halibut swims in great looping arcs, twisting and rolling against the invisible force stabbing into its gill, its frenzied fight for survival broadcast across the deep, fast-moving waters of the Swiftsure Bank.

Two miles to the north, the big male changes course, its sensory system drawn to the low-frequency random reverberations like a magnet to steel.

A cloudburst of rain pelts deck and sea, the splatter of a trillion droplets rising to cloak all other sound.

Water pours off the soaked bill of the 49ers baseball cap. Shelby shakes his head, trying to see. His arms burn from lactic acid, his back and legs tremble from muscular exhaustion. Still he refuses to give an inch.

The line plays out, the slick pole slipping within his aching grip.

Exhausted but too stubborn to quit, Shelby locks down the tackle and holds on, relying on the strength of the deck-mounted chair to tire his catch.

The line goes taut, the fish unable to run.

Shelby grits his teeth. *Okay, time to haul this bitch in.* Wrapping his elbows around the rod, threading the slack of heavy line around his forearms, Shelby allows the tackle to tighten around the insulated waterproof material of his parka as he leans back, drawing in line with his entire body.

"Got you now, you're not getting away this—"

CRACKKKK!

The line is snagged by a runaway freight train, a titanic force that causes the deck boards to splinter and rupture, spitting free the base of the mounted fishing chair, catapulting the entire assembly, harness, fishing rod, *and* Heath Shelby, over the transom and into the sea.

The halibut bursts inside the Megalodon's mouth like a ripe strawberry.

The fishing line threads out a gap between two teeth in the Meg's upper jaw.

The big male swims off, dragging an annoying weight behind it.

Mark Allen stares dumbfounded at the hole in the deck that, an eye-blink ago, had been his Uncle Heath.

Captain Winegar kills the engines, then half-stumbles, half-jumps down to the splintered deck and leans out over the transom. For a split-second he sees a wake racing away from the boat before it disappears behind the endless sheets of rain. Then he remembers his first mate.

"Michael! Mi-chael!"

Michael Rybel surfaces, blood gushing from a head wound. "What happened?"

"You were knocked overboard." Winegar grabs a reach-pole and hooks his first mate around the waist, dragging him back to the boat. With his skipper's help, Rybel pulls himself on board, his body shivering from the cold, then his eyes turn to saucers as he sees the massive hole in the splintered deck. "Jesus, what could have done that?"

His reality shattered, Heath Shelby twists and turns within the heavy steel chair as he torpedoes purple-face-first into the bone-numbing blue depths, his bursting lungs screaming at him to release the harness.

Prying his fingers free from the fishing pole, he struggles in vain to loosen the vice-like grip of the line, still entangled around his forearms and clipped to the chair.

Seventy feet . . . eighty. . . . the pressure squeezes his ears, his heart pounds in his brain as he continues the rapid 30-degree descent to his grave.

And then he stops moving forward, the pressure on his arms suddenly easing as the fishing line snaps—

—and the weight of the chair takes over, plunging him straight for the bottom.

Shelby gurgles out his last bits of air as he tears at the seat belt, freeing himself from the anchor.

He kicks away the chair, which drops below, disappearing out of sight.

Shelby ascends, the flotation device secured beneath his rain gear guiding him toward an unseen surface. The former power industry executive pinches his nose, willing himself to hang on. *You're alive . . . it's okay.*

He focuses upon the undulating surface, counting the seconds before he can breathe.

Damn charter . . . by the time my lawyers are through with them . . .

The heavenly light rising from below startles him.

A whale . . . you hooked a goddamn Belukha whale . . . sonuvabitch—

The male Megalodon closes to within ten feet of the strange fish, staring at it with its right eye.

Oh, sweet Jesus . . . A burst of adrenaline ignites Heath Shelby's arms and legs, sending him stroking and kicking to the surface like a madman.

The message of distress is universal, the predator's response primordial.

Closed jaws animate open as the great head lurches for-

ward, engulfing a swimming pool of sea, along with the
body of Heath Shelby.

Dragged backward into an insanity of blackness, Shelby's
tortured mind is too shattered to recognize his own an-
guished screams as his mangled body is compressed by a
puncturing, existence-crushing embrace.

CHAPTER

7

BIG SUR VALLEY, CALIFORNIA

Big Sur, christened by landscape painter Francis McCormas as "the greatest meeting of land and water in the world," lies between San Simeon and Carmel—seventy-two miles of rocky coastline where the violent Pacific waves crash against the foot of the Santa Lucia mountains. Weaving precariously along this panoramic eye candy is Highway 1, a mountainous roadway with harsh grades, twin bridges, and blind turns, made all the more dangerous by the drivers' overwhelming desire to gaze down upon its awe-inspiring coastline.

"The Lord is my shepherd, I shall not want. Fresh and green are the pastures where He gives me repose—"

From her father's backyard, Terry Taylor gazes numbly at the Pacific—a majestic blue carpet stretching as far as the eye can see.

"Near restful waters He leads me, to revive my drooping spirit. He guides me along the right path—"

Scenes of her childhood play across her mind's eye: the nature hikes with her father and brother on the Mount Manuel trail, the picnic lunches on the cliff-tops above

Soberanes Cove. Shopping in Carmel, the visits to the Redwood forest . . .

"Yea, if I should walk in the valley of darkness I shall fear
no evil—"

How many winter storms had she watched while sitting
on her father's lap? How many morning fogs? How many
sunsets?

"Surely goodness and kindness shall follow me all the
days of my life. In the Lord's own house shall I dwell, for
ever and ever."

The urn with her father's remains is lowered into the shallow hole.

Terry's dark almond eyes burst into tears, her husband's
grip the only force preventing her from collapsing.

Jonas moves like a zombie through the house, pausing occasionally to listen politely as guests offer their heartfelt
condolences.

"I'm so sorry—"

"How's Terry holding up?"

"He was so full of life."

"Your children have gotten so tall."

"What will you do now?"

"Sell the home?"

"Move back to California?"

"Why isn't Mac here?"

"So I hear you're writing a book?"

"Will you excuse me?" Jonas slips between several
guests, avoids the line at the buffet table, grabs a beer from a
cooler, then heads outside.

The director of the mortuary and his workers have finished their work, the granite marker set in place, the backyard's Zen restored.

Jonas parks himself on the wooden bench, staring at the
tombstone, feeling Masao's presence everywhere. A cool

ocean breeze whips strands of graying brown hair away
from his forehead, soothing his frayed nerves.

"I hear you, old man. I miss you already."

"What?"

He turns, recognizing Mac's girlfriend. "Oh, hey, uh, Patricia. Sorry, just . . . just talking to myself."

"May I?" The blue-eyed blond takes a seat next to him. "I
just wanted to tell you how sorry I am."

"Thanks." He drains half his beer.

"My boss wanted me to make sure I passed along his condolences as well. Would have been here himself, but he had
a closing in Carmel."

"Rodney still representing the Dietsch Brothers?"

"And half of Big Sur."

"That deal still on the table?"

"Whenever you and Terry are ready."

"Give her a few days."

"Tell her to take as much time as she needs."

"So, how're things going with you and Mac?"

"They're not. Mac and I are through."

Jonas turns to face her. "I'm sorry to hear that. I think
you're good for him."

"I tried to be, but I wasn't strong enough to deal with his
problems, and neither was he. But you were. Mac needed
you, Jonas."

"I was there. Did all I could do. In the end, he didn't want
my help."

"It's not the end, not yet, and since when do you give a
drunk the choice? Mac has psychological problems that
need addressing. You should have forced him to enter rehab."

"You think it's that simple? You weren't there, Trish. You
have no idea what I was dealing with. Pulling him out of
bars at four A.M., bailing him out of jail, visiting him in hos-
pitals. Ever baby-sit an adult? It's not easy."

"Still, he was always there for you. You should have done
something. You could have set up an intervention."

"I did what I could. You want to do an intervention, go for it. I have plenty of my own problems right now." He heads back to the house.

"Turn your back on Mac now, Jonas Taylor, and the next time you see him will be in a casket."

It's dark by the time Jonas arrives at the marina.

Mac's boat is berthed between the fourth and fifth pilings from the end of the dock. Plastic garbage bags litter the pier behind the *Angel-II*'s stern.

Jonas kicks at one of the containers. Hears the sound of empty bottles.

"Who's there?!" Mac charges out of the galley, a bottle of tequila in one hand, a baseball bat in the other. His face looks pasty, his eyes bloodshot and glassy, framed in dark brown circles. "Oh, it's you. Come to scold me for missing the funeral?"

"I came to talk."

"Sounds like I'm in for another lecture."

"You look like hell. When's the last time you ate a meal that wasn't out of a bottle?"

"Does la-lum . . . alum-inum cans count?" Mac laughs, then wheezes into a fit of heavy coughing.

Grabbing a stern line, Jonas pulls the boat closer and boards.

"Hey, I didn't give you permission to board. I'm the captain, see, and it's up to me to give you permission to board."

"I'm not here to fight."

"Nah, you're here to judge. Jonas the judge, that's you. What say you, Your Honor?"

"Mac—"

"Hey, I have the perfect nickname for you—Judge Jonas."

"I came to talk."

"Say, Judge Jonas, remember about two or three years

ago . . . remember how you turned against me when I got that li'l strawberry-blond number pregnant? Oh, what was her name . . . wait, don't tell me, Judge, I'll get it . . . Lyla something-or-other."

"Lisa."

"Yeah, Lisa. Man, you were pissed. Caught both barrels from you that time. Didn't talk to your old pal for three months, did you? Hey, I said, did you?!"

"Her name was Lisa Frankel. I know because she used to baby-sit Dani. She was seventeen and fresh out of high school when you picked her up at Giuseppe's."

Mac's mouth drops open. "Seventeen. Shit . . ." He paces in circles, struggling for words. "Well, she looked twenty-three. What am I supposed to do, card her in bed? Anyway, I paid for the abortion. Stayed with her through the whole damn thing."

"I guess that exonerates you."

"I screwed up, okay? Think I was the first? Do you ever screw up, Your Honor, or are you perfect?"

"Far from it."

"That's right. So go away. Go fly away, Mr. Daredevil, fly off to your little adventure in the South Pacific. Oh, didn't think I knew about that?"

Jonas remains silent.

"Yeah, they offered me the same deal weeks ago. Told 'em to shove it. Shove it where the sun don't shine. I may be a no-good drunk, but I know when someone's sticking their tongue up my sphincter. Settin' me up for the big fall, that's what they were doing. But you . . . you'll go. You'll go waggin' your tail."

"I need the money."

"Ha. With Masao gone, you can sell that stinkin' facility and retire. So don't stand there and bullshit your old pal. We both know why you're really going."

"And why's that?".

"Because you miss it. You miss feeling important. Most of all, you miss the action. There's still Daredevil blood in you, Judge Taylor, even if it is mixed with Geritol."

Jonas checks his watch, getting impatient. "I'm only guest-hosting, Mac. I'm doing color commentary."

"Ha!" Mac drains the remains of the bottle, then tosses it overboard. "The call to action will come, Mr. Perfect. It'll blow right up your ass and you'll jump, just to prove to the rest of the world you're still alive and kicking."

Jonas is about to reply when he sees the squad car park at the edge of the dock.

Two police officers step out of the vehicle and walk deliberately toward them.

Mac's eyes widen. "You sonuvabitch. Stab your old pal in the back, will ya?" He reaches for the baseball bat.

Jonas tackles him from behind. He subdues him in a tight headlock, gagging at his friend's rancid breath. "Masao's gone, Mac. Now I've lost two fathers, hell if I'm losing a brother."

Danielle Taylor presses her ear closer to the wall, listening to her parents fight.

". . . and I can't believe you're still going!"

Jonas avoids his wife's will-breaking gaze. "I signed a contract, Terry. I gave Erik my word."

"Erik? Who the hell's Erik? Some stranger you met days ago." She takes several deep breaths. "This is some sort of mid-life crisis thing, isn't it?"

"I don't know . . . maybe."

"Do you still love me, Jonas? Are you still attracted to me?"

"Of course."

"Then why do you feel the desire to leave me, to leave the kids for two months?"

"It's six weeks, seven tops, and it's not that I want to leave you, it's just something I feel I have to do."

"Then take Dani."

"Dani? Terry, you know I can't do that."

"Why not? It'll be good for the two of you to spend some quality time together. You need to bond with your daughter, Jonas, before it's too late."

"I think she'd rather cut her throat."

"For your information, Dani came to me about this."

"About spending more time with me?"

"About going on *Daredevils*. Seems she met a boy while we were in Venice Beach, one of the contestants—"

"Forget it."

Dani curses her father's presence.

"Terry, this is business."

"Oh, please. You'll be sitting around on deck sunning yourself, while scantily-clad women half your age wait on you hand and foot. You want to go and make a jackass of yourself, fine, but you're taking Dani as chaperone, otherwise forget it."

"Terry—"

"I said, otherwise forget it!"

Dani closes her eyes, listening to the heavy silence . . . praying.

"Fine, Dani can go, but I swear, if she starts giving me lip while those cameras are running—"

His daughter's catcalls from the other side of the wall cut him off mid-threat.

LATE PLEISTOCENE

Hungry and exhausted, the pregnant female has arrived at a tropical atoll, a barrier of coral reef whose vast lagoon encompasses a maze of verdant, mushroom-shaped islands. Born by the process of the Pacific Plate thrusting beneath the Philippine Plate, these heavily vegetated archipelagos span hundreds of miles, paralleling the deepwater trenches and subduction zones that gave them life.

Plunging sea levels from the Ice Age have expanded the island chain's borders, creating a labyrinth of azure waterways that snake between these tropical land masses like rivers.

To the pregnant Megalodon, the atoll is an oasis. Nutrient-rich water converges upon the lagoon from the Philippine Deep and the Palau Trench, supplying food to a diversity of sharks, rays, whales, and several thousand species of fish.

Weakened by hunger, the predator glides over the coral reef barrier through the teal and jade sea, her broad, lead-gray back appearing as an ominous shadow against the buttermilk-yellow sandy bottom. She follows a warm easterly current, then enters the mouth of a vast river way. The upper third of her dorsal fin crests above the glass-like surface, her coal-black eyes searching the sun-drenched surroundings for food.

Immediately, her senses are inundated by the scents and sounds of the shallows.

A dozen different species of parrot fish and dogtooth tuna cruise by, drifting lazily in the swift current. Schools of manta ray fly along the bottom. Two sharpfin barracuda swim parallel with their new queen, then disperse into the shadows. A giant mottled eel pokes its head out from an enclosure of coral, then retreats.

The female moves deeper into the maze of coral islands, her senses locked onto something more enticing.

Ignoring the danger, the 233-pound golden grouper hovers close to a cluster of coral, its thick-lipped mouth opening and closing as it gulps the sea.

A dozen powerful strokes of her caudal fin and the female is upon it, her widening jaws inhaling the fish in one devastating bite, her back teeth skewering the grouper before it can escape.

The Meg's thick tongue pushes the refuse down her garage-size gullet, the sudden wave of nourishment rousing the lethargic giant, quickening her pulse, even as waves of new information saturate her primordial senses.

Nostrils the size of gopher holes inhale a current of chemical odors, creating a neural photograph of her new environment.

Stench of earth.
Pungence of urine and feces.
Turbulence.
Muscle movement.
Food.

The Megalodon moves deeper through the saltwater river, stalking her next meal.

Overhead and on either bank, dozens of white-cheeked gibbons leap from branch to branch, chasing after the "Grim Reaper's" lead-gray dorsal fin.

Deeper in the jungle, a group of Micronesian natives follow the hoots and squawks of the simians as they stealthily converge upon their prey from below.

A mile downstream, the twenty-six-foot-long, 7,200-pound prehistoric sea cow, *Hydrodamalis gigas*, continues to churn up silt as it feeds on floating seaweed, oblivious to the jungle chatter and her place on the quickly-assembling food chain. Bulky and bulbous in appearance, the pinniped has adapted well to the Ice Age, its multiple layers of blubber, surrounded by bark-like skin, insulating her against the cold. Lacking teeth, she is a true aquatic herbivore, making her unique among the marine mammals of the Pleistocene.

Size alone has always protected her, discouraging her enemies.

But not this time.

Sensing the approaching wake, the sea cow submerges to take a look, staring curiously into the shaded jade underworld.

Patches of ivory-white skin push forward from the blue-green haze, followed by a conical snout and head so large it occupies the pinniped's entire field of vision.

An electrical twinge of panic courses through the mammal's body. Adrenaline sends its flattened tail churning, its flipper-like forelimbs pulling toward shore.

The Megalodon senses these disturbances in concentric layers: the rapid rise in the sea cow's pulse, the electrical disturbances of its prey's swimming muscles, the scent of its flight or fright amino acid secretions, the cacophony of vibrations echoing through the shallow channel, the sight of the fleeing mammal—

—its acidic taste of fear.

Restricted by the forty-foot depths, the female rolls gracefully onto her side, the blade of her right pectoral fin churning silt as she moves dangerously close to shore.

The waterway erupts as the Megalodon's massive sickle-shaped tail slaps at the surface in a flurry of quick strokes that propel her open mouth upon her quarry.

Seized from behind, the sea cow wheezes a final spasm of pain as dozens of six- to seven-inch daggers puncture its blubbery epidermis seconds before its existence is stifled behind an ungodly 200,000 pounds per square inch of pulverizing pressure. The pinniped's lungs explode, its compressed innards bursting out gaping teeth wounds within its splattering skin.

The Meg shakes its head, allowing the serrated edges of

its incisors to saw the carcass in two. The engulfed lower torso is ground into succulent hundred-pound clumps of hot fat and swallowed, the remains of the head and upper torso squirting free, floating toward shore.

Monkeys squeal overhead as the azure waters are stained a deep scarlet.

The Meg's caudal fin breaches sixty feet behind its groping mouth, walloping the surface with thunderous slaps that soak and scatter the suddenly not-so-curious monkeys. Pushing through a trail of blubber and blood, the upper jaw snaps blindly through the refuse, searching for the sea cow's sumptuous remains.

And then the monster stops.

The Megalodon cannot breathe, her flank beached, her mouth and gills half-clear of the water. In a state of panic she thrashes about, slapping her great tail as she attempts to roll off the limestone shelf, the contortions only serving to dig her swollen belly deeper into the soft sand.

Desperate minutes pass. The female gulps silty sea and air, her tail slaps becoming less and less frequent.

The cackling monkeys return, dropping from the jungle canopy, moving closer, ever curious.

The sun begins to set, beckoning a high tide, and something else—

—the male Megalodon.

The hungry predator glides silently through the darkening waters of the atoll, closing on the stranded female.

CHAPTER

8

LOLOATA ISLAND
PAPUA NEW GUINEA

Papua New Guinea, located in the southwest Pacific, comprises the eastern part of New Guinea, the Bismarck Archipelago, and most of the Solomon Islands. Situated within eighty nautical miles of the northernmost tip of Australia, the territory is a tropical paradise surrounded by an aquatic wonderland of reefs.

Archaeological evidence indicates the main island was inhabited by Asian natives as far back as 50,000 years ago. Eons later, the Portuguese would lay claim to the island in 1526, the Spaniard Inigo Ortiz de Retes naming it New Guinea because he thought the natives resembled those of Guinea, Africa. By the late 1800s, the land fell under Dutch rule before eventually being claimed by the Germans, English, and finally the Australians. A hard-fought independence would arrive in 1975, disrupted by years of internal strife with the locals of Bougainville Island. After many years of civil war, a cease-fire was finally negotiated in 1998, only to be followed by a catastrophic drought that affected more than 650,000 people. As if this were not enough, the main island's northwest coast was struck by three monstrous tsunamis, the waves killing three thousand people, flattening every village in the area.

Despite these harsh beginnings and natural disasters, despite crime waves that forced the local government to barbwire extensive areas in Port Moresby and the Central Provinces, the tourism industry continued to reach out to Papua New Guinea and its private neighboring islands, the beaches of which redefine the word "paradise."

Loloata Island is one such place. Located across Bootless Bay, just south of the capital city of Port Moresby, the island that means "one hill" in the native Motu language offers travelers a private getaway difficult to find in the Western world.

Loloata Island's lone resort dates back to the 1960s when it was constructed as the main house to a chicken farm. Refurbished twice, the hotel offers twenty-two beachfront units, a restaurant, two dive boats, and a few board games, "for those in need of more cerebral pursuits."

The heavyset American bulging beneath a Boston Red Sox jersey and khaki pants adjusts his dark glasses against the burst of morning sun as he makes his way from the hotel lobby across the grassy esplanade to the breakfast buffet spread out along the dockside veranda. Only forty-six, the man walks with a senior's gait that resembles the late Charlie Chaplin, his flat feet almost shuffling, his weight balancing with the aid of a cane. Once a former amateur marathon runner, the scientist—an ichthyologist—was forced to retire from sports due to a severe bout of frostbite that cost him all his toes as well as sections of fleshy padding beneath the balls of his feet. No longer able to jog, the bitter professor from Woods Hole Institute has gained eighty-five pounds over the years and has all but given up on having a social life, though for entirely different reasons.

Michael Maren heads for his usual table, unloading his

sizable bulk onto one of the wicker chairs facing the bay. Using the menu as a fan, he gazes at puffy white cumulus clouds that drift over the distant mainland, the only blotch on an otherwise infinite blue sky.

Maren signals the waitress over, handing her his plate. "The usual, Francine. And don't skimp on the bacon."

Francine flashes her standard Melanesian smile, then heads off to the buffet table as instructed.

The water taxi arrives two helpings later.

James Gelet, former soap opera star and current co-producer of *Daredevils,* climbs out of the small motorboat and onto the pier, his gelled dark hair defiant against the tropical breeze.

Maren holds up his left hand, finishing off a forkful of powdered eggs with the right.

"Mr. Maren. Glad to see you're enjoying yourself on our diminishing production budget."

"It's *Doctor* Maren. Stop whining and sit down, Gelet. Want some breakfast?"

"This isn't a social call. The network has questions that need answering and so do I. We've invested an awful lot of money into this venture, most of it based on nothing more than a handful of promises."

"Which is nothing compared to what I've invested, fourteen long years of field work, not to mention most of my mother's inheritance."

"Still, you understand our concerns. How can you guarantee—"

"There are no guarantees, Gelet. No one controls Mother Nature. Best I can do is tease it to the surface. Whatever happens after that happens on its own accord. Now you tell. Is Taylor on board?"

"He'll arrive in Sydney later today."

"I knew his ego couldn't resist. What about Mackreides?"

"Sorry. He wouldn't commit."

Maren pounds his fist against the table, causing the china

to jump. "I was very specific with my requirements, Gelet. You and Hollander knew that from the get-go."

"As you said, we can tease but we can't control. Mackreides is a drunk who could care less about money and fame. Why all the fuss about these two anyway? Every poll we've taken shows the viewers have no interest."

"I have an interest . . . sharks are my interest. I've dedicated my life to studying their behavior, specifically that of big ocean dwellers like Great Whites and their so-called extinct prehistoric cousins. I published textbooks, gave seminars, and, for a while, I was considered the final word on the subject. Then this ex-Navy sub pilot trips over the biggest discovery in the history of paleontology and suddenly he's the Megalodon expert."

"Got it, it's the whole ego thing. You're still mad because Jonas Taylor stole your thunder."

"It's not about ego, Gelet, it's about setting the record straight. While Taylor's been writing his memoirs and posing in front of cameras, I've been doing real research, designing and testing new field equipment, breaking through new barriers in animal behavioral sciences. Taylor's not a scientist, he's a con man wrapped around a diploma, and your show is the forum I've chosen to expose him to the rest of the world."

"Hey, whatever, as long as we get our ratings."

"You'll get your ratings. What about my money?"

"You'll get your first installment, if and when you deliver the goods. The *Neptune* sets sail in two days. When do you plan on returning to the *Coelacanth*?"

"Chopper arrives in four hours. We'll rendezvous in the Banda Sea at the agreed-upon coordinates."

"And everything's still . . . functioning?"

"I get reports every hour on the hour. Relax, Gelet, it's all under control. Just remember, when the time comes, you'll need to move your shooting schedule to twilight."

"Understood."

Maren pushes up from the table and stands, ending the meeting. "Now be a good boy and settle my hotel tab, I'm late for my date with one of the locals."

"I suppose we're paying for that too?"

"And my breakfast." The fat man with the brown ponytail hobbles off, sticking James Gelet with the bill.

CHAPTER

9

WHALES BEACHING IN RECORD NUMBERS

By NOAH LEWIS
Scripps-Howard News Service

Vancouver Island, B.C.—More than eighty whale strandings have been documented over the last week on Vancouver Island's western (Pacific) coastline, with most beachings occurring between Sombrio Beach south to Rocky Point. Among the stranded mammals were dozens of Grey whales and at least fifteen Orca. Vacationers and other volunteers have been working around the clock to save the dying beasts, draping them with wet towels and pouring buckets of water over their skin to keep them moist. Despite these efforts at least half the whales have perished, with more being euthanized every few hours.

Corey LaBranche, a local marine biologist and assistant director of the Juan de Fuca Stranding Network, was baffled by the scope of the event. "Mass whale strandings are not that unusual among sociable animals, and our coastlines contain a variety of coves, bays, channels, and inlets that can sometimes disorient these creatures. Still, this particular phenomenon seems entirely different as we're looking at not just one pod but dozens of pods covering a variety of species. In the last seventy-two hours we've had to rescue Orca, Humpbacks, Greys, and Pacific White-Sided dolphin. Last night, seven Humpbacks trapped themselves in the shallows along Anderson Cove in East Sooke. That's all rocky shoreline, something these larger baleen whales almost never venture near. We managed to tow a few of the bigger adults into deeper water, but they were back in the cove less than an hour later. It's frustrating."

Rising tides have helped volunteers push many of the Orca and dolphin into deeper water, but it remains to be seen whether any will survive.

STRAIT OF JUAN DE FUCA
PACIFIC OCEAN
16 MILES SOUTHEAST OF EAST SOOKE, BRITISH COLUMBIA
22 MILES NORTHWEST OF PORT ANGELES, WASHINGTON

Named for the man mistakenly credited with discovering the passage in 1592, the Strait of Juan de Fuca is the body of saltwater, fifteen miles wide and more than sixty miles long, that separates the southern coastline of Vancouver Island from the northern shores of the state of Washington. Teeming with marine life, the ocean-access tributary divides at its eastern end into the Georgia Strait before moving north along Vancouver Island into Puget Sound.

Darkness grips the waterway, the new moon remaining partially cloaked behind passing cumulus clouds. Waves lap against rocky shoals. A bell tolls on a distant ferry.

The black waters come to life, glowing a lime-green luminescence in the lunar light as the creature streaks just below the surface. An ivory dorsal fin cuts the waves, the rest of the monster's body visible beneath its illuminating wake.

Night. Time again for the big male to abandon the depths of its new-found honey hole and feed.

PORT DARWIN, NORTHERN TERRITORY
NORTHERN AUSTRALIA

Darwin, the capital city of Australia's northern territory, is the major gateway between Southeast Asia and the land down under. Named in honor of the English scientist and naturalist, Charles Darwin, who landed there in 1839, the port city maintains a harbor twice the size of Sydney's, and is one of the fastest growing capitals in the world.

At ten minutes after noon, the white Mercedes-Benz limousine arrives at the entrance to Pier 139 at Stokes Hill Wharf, releasing its two exhausted American VIPs.

"Dani, wake up. We're here." Jonas Taylor nudges his daughter awake, then climbs out of the vehicle, his brain still fried from jet lag.

Jonas squints against the brilliant sunshine. To his left is the Darwin Wharf Precinct, a dining and entertainment area overlooking the Timor Sea. On his right, across a small channel, are berthed three luxury cruise liners.

Directly ahead, docked along the pier before him, past a gated entrance and two security guards lies the Spanish galleon, *Neptune*.

The reconstructed seventeenth-century warship is a sight to behold. The wooden tall ship displaces over 1,000 tons, measures 203 feet from prow to stern, has a 54-foot-wide beam, and carries over 50,000 square feet of sail. With the canvas down, the ship's two bare main masts stretch high into the cloudless blue sky like giant crucifixes.

Jonas's heart races. *This should actually be fun.*

Dani stumbles out of the car, hung over from traveling. "I feel sick."

"You'll feel better after we eat and walk around a bit. Come over here and check out this ship."

A golf cart motors down the pier toward them, Erik Hollander driving with one hand, waving with the other. He screeches to a halt, nearly colliding with one of the security guards.

"There you are. Welcome to Australia. Long trip, huh? Ah, but it'll be worth it. Wait 'til you see the *Neptune*, she's really something. Polanski didn't spare a dime when it came to the attention to details. Took something like two thousand men two full years and more than eight million dollars to build her. Costing us a bundle to lease her, but she's worth every penny. Makes for great filler between stunts."

Dani squints at the ship. "Are the Daredevils on board?"

"Not yet. They're preparing for their grand entrance at sea. We set sail in four hours, if my lousy soundman ever arrives."

"I was hoping you might be able to use Dani behind the scenes, you know, assisting the film crew . . . something to keep her busy."

"Behind the scenes?" Erik laughs. "Your daughter's eye-candy, Professor, and we can never have too much of that. Dani, as soon as you get settled, come find me and I'll hook you up with wardrobe. They'll pick out some nice bikinis, maybe a few after-hour numbers. We'll pay you to be one of our Candy Girls, my pet name for our Daredevil groupies."

"Excellent." Danielle's gloating smile tweaks her father's blood pressure.

"The crew will get your luggage. Come with me, I'll give you a tour of the ship."

Jonas and Dani climb in the backseat of the golf cart.

Executing a U-turn that nearly tosses Jonas over the side of the pier, Erik accelerates the vehicle back toward the ship, pointing out the two galleries and their open-air balconies that occupy the above-water portion of the ship's stern.

The golf cart skids to a halt. Jonas and his daughter follow the producer up the steep gangway, their eyes widening as they see the rest of the sailing ship.

The *Neptune*'s main deck is a beehive of activity, set among two contrasting periods of time. Local workers load crates of supplies onto old-fashioned cargo nets attached to a modern-day crane. Coils of rope for the sails lie side-by-side with spools of electrical cable. Camera equipment leans against the mounts of fixed muskets. Cargo nets of provisions are being lowered into the holds, directed by men speaking into cellular phones.

Erik raises both arms proudly. "Incredible, isn't she?"

Dani looks disappointed. "I was expecting a real yacht. This is more like a pirate ship."

"Trust me, the *Neptune*'s more fun. These galleons were military vessels, designed almost five centuries ago to replace Spain's oar-propelled galleys." He points to the masts. "Each of the masts are attached to the keel and rise up through the lower decks. The central mast is the main, the other big one is called the foremast, and the smaller ones behind us are the—"

"—the lateen and mizzen masts." Jonas points to a fifth mast, which rises at a 30-degree angle out of the bow. "Don't forget the bowsprit."

Erik smiles. "Forgot you were a Navy man."

"She looks like she's being refitted for your show. Why take away so much of her character?"

"Had to. We've got a big crew to feed, and most Hollywood types don't like roughing it. God forbid they eat powdered eggs and instant coffee. Most of it's behind-the-scenes stuff, backup generators, satellite hook-ups, although we did add underwater lights along the keel so we could film stunts at night."

Dani points to the cabin located at the end of the walkway above them. "Who gets to sleep there?"

"Actually, I do. That's the Captain's gallery. You gotta see it, it looks like a real pirate captain's quarters. Right below my stateroom is the Admiral's gallery, that's for Captain Robertson. You'll meet him later. Good guy. American, like most of our crew."

"Where do we sleep?" Dani asks.

"Below. There are four levels beneath us, just follow the companion ways. The level just below the main deck houses your cabin, Professor, as well as the crew's quarters and the galley. If you get lost, just look for the *Neptune*'s smaller cannon, the *Pedrero*. On the next deck down are the bigger guns, the *Culebruina*. Polanski commissioned working replicas; we're going to fire a few of them on the last day of shooting. Should be wild. Anyway, the Daredevils and Candy Girls occupy that second level. Sickbay's down there too. Fresh water, provisions, sails, and the ship's stores are located on the third deck down. The last deck is more of a narrow crawl space located just above the keel. It was designed to hold the warship's powder kegs, but we'll use it for storage."

"I want to see my room," Dani says.

"Sure. Jonas?"

"You two go on ahead, I'll catch up." Jonas leaves them, heading forward to where a stainless-steel shark cage is being assembled. Seated on the capstan, working on an underwater camera, is a dark-haired, tan man, his hulking frame pressed beneath a sweat-soaked tee-shirt.

Jonas smiles at the familiar face.

Andrew Fox is in his early forties, athletic and introverted, an Australian native with a boyish charm. The founder of the Fox Shark Research Foundation, he is also the son of filmmaker and legendary shark expert Rodney Fox, survivor of one of the most vicious Great White attacks on record.

"Andrew Fox, I should have known. No ocean voyage would be complete without a Fox on board."

"Professor Jonas, as I live and breathe. God, you're looking old. Hey, I know some good hair dye that'll take that gray out in one washing."

"Some people say it makes me look smarter."

"Nah, they're just yanking your chain." The two men embrace.

"How's your dad?"

"Same as always, still doing the tourist bit. You ought to pop down to the museum when all this is over, the folks'd love to see you."

"Sure thing. So, what's with the cages? Didn't think these Daredevils would use them."

"Cages are for me and my crew. I'm in charge of under-water photography. Say, maybe you'll join me inside for a few action sequences."

"Maybe."

"I'll come!" Dani approaches, suddenly invigorated. "Erik said I could use a jet-ski once we leave port."

"Andrew, you remember my daughter."

"Sure. Hey, Dani. Didn't expect to see you on board."

"Dad and I needed some bonding time."

Jonas smirks. "She has a crush on one of the Daredevils."

"Oh, yeah? Which one? Not that Evan Stewart I hope. That boy's just plain crazy."

"His name's Wayne Ferguson. He's Australian, too."

"Fergie?" Andrew shoots Jonas a look.

Dani changes the subject. "So Andrew, what do I have to do to join you in one of these shark cages?"

"You certified to dive?"

"Sure."

"Then it's up to your old man here. As long as you're both comfortable—"

"Great. Dad, Erik said to tell you your stateroom's one deck down, number eleven, next to the TV crew. I'm bunking on the Daredevils' deck."

"The hell you are."

"Chill out. I'll be with the models, the women have their own quarters. It's like living in a big college dorm room."

"How would you know?"

"Don't start, we just got here. Anyway, I gotta unpack. Bye, Andrew."

Danielle waves, then hurries down the closest companion-way.

Jonas shakes his head. "I think I'm gonna need two bottles of that dye before this voyage is over."

MONTEREY, CALIFORNIA

The law office of Kelsey Lynn Cretcher is located on Van Buren Street, a short walk from Fisherman's Wharf.

The blue-eyed attorney with the wire-framed glasses pokes her head out of a conference room and into the adjacent waiting area. "Sorry to keep you, Terry. The two of you can come in now."

Terry motions to David, who is lost in a Sony Walkman. They follow the attorney into the conference room, a rectangular, walnut-paneled chamber adorned in framed certificates and degrees.

Seated behind an oval Formica conference table is an elderly African-American woman, her silver-gray hair pulled up in a tight bun.

"Charlene Holman, this is Masao's daughter, Terry Taylor, and her son, David. Terry, Charlene is Athena's grandmother."

"Athena?"

"Atti. She worked for your father."

"Oh, the, uh—"

"Yes, the girl with the cerebral palsy," the older woman says. "Atti's the light of my life, Mrs. Taylor, and she was dedicated to your father and his work. We're all very sorry to hear what happened."

"Thank you. And yes, I know my father was very fond of Atti."

"More so than you think." The attorney motions for Terry to take a seat. "Terry, as part of your father's will, he bequeathed Athena a two-percent share of the equity in the sale of the Tanaka Lagoon."

Terry attempts to hide her surprise. "Two percent? I didn't know."

"The will was changed several months ago. Anyway, from speaking with Patricia Pedrazzoli I know you want to close a deal rather quickly with the Dietsch Brothers, so I didn't want you to be caught off-guard."

"Okay, fine, two percent." She turns to the elderly woman. "And how is Atti?"

"Not good. She's in the hospital, been in shock since your father died. Must've seen the whole thing. Her doctors say she's suffering post-traumatic symptoms. We're all praying she snaps out of it soon."

"I'm sorry, I didn't know."

"She's always been such a strong child, so we're all a bit worried."

"Terry and I need to speak now, Charlene, but you have my number. Call me the moment anything changes." Kelsey Cretcher helps the elderly woman out of her chair.

"Nice to have met you, Mrs. Taylor."

"Yeah, you too. Hope Atti feels better."

The attorney's smile fades the moment the door clicks shut. "Sorry about that."

"Two percent, Jesus. What the hell was he thinking?"

"He also left twenty percent to David."

"That I knew."

David grins. "Twenty percent. Cool."

"David will have to sign off on any sale of the property. Meanwhile, I've been on the phone with the bank and insurance companies and frankly, the news isn't good. Your father was deep in debt, he owed a lot of people a lot of money."

Terry feels her insides tightening. "How much?"

"After the insurance money kicks in, we're still looking at fifty thousand in personal loans from the Dietsch Brothers, plus the balance of two mortgages on the facility. You'll need to clear at least eighteen million from the sale of the property and any salvage just to break even, which is about a half-million less than what the Dietsch Brothers are offering."

Terry shakes her head in disbelief. "Do you know how much money Jonas and I sank into that money pit? My father kept saying he was close to a deal, then nothing would materialize. I should have never listened to him." She sits back, her frustration mounting. "Okay, Kelsey, now you know our financial situation, what do you suggest?"

The attorney takes a seat across from her. "The way I see it, you have two choices. Either we negotiate a better deal with the Dietsch Brothers, or file for bankruptcy, which will probably lead to the Dietsch Brothers eventually purchasing the property for pennies on the dollar anyway."

"Not much of a solution."

"At least it buys you some time."

"Time for what? My father spent years trying to find another buyer. He was desperate to sell."

"No he wasn't," David removes his headphones. "Grandpa never wanted to sell. He loved the lagoon."

"Yes, David, I know that, but he also needed the money. That's why he borrowed so much against it."

"He said it would all be worth it when Angel returned."

Terry smiles nervously. "Honey, Angel's gone for good."

"You don't know that. Dad says big deepwater sharks like Angel can migrate tens of thousands of miles in one year. He said the fact that Angel was raised in these waters makes it more likely that—"

"David, enough. Angel's gone, and your father and I can't afford the upkeep on this facility anymore than your grandfather could."

"But Mom—"

"We're deep in debt and need to sell, David, end of story."

"All right already." David returns the headphones to his ears, tuning her out.

Terry turns her attention back to the attorney. "Contact Rodney Cotner. Tell him we need to renegotiate the Dietsch Brothers' last offer. Tell him my family needs to leave the table with something to show, or we'll tie the property up in the courts for years."

CHAPTER

10

The Spanish galleon, *Neptune*, sails north through the Arafura Sea, a shallow body of water that lies between the Timor and Coral seas, separating Australia from the western territory of New Guinea.

Jonas Taylor is on the upper walkway, leaning against the rail, absorbed by the leaping antics of a pod of Dusky dolphins frolicking in the ship's bow wake. Breathing deeply, he inhales lungfuls of refreshing salt air. Closing his eyes, he listens to the soothing sound of heavy canvas flapping all around him.

A gust of wind whips his graying bangs away from his forehead. He opens his eyes again, gazing out to sea at the shrinking orange fireball that bleeds the western horizon a tapestry of reds and violets. He feels the wood as it creaks beneath his feet, he hears the ropes as they strain to hold the sails. He registers the power of the wind as it pushes against the sheets, luxuriating in the quiet roar of the ocean as it seeps into his restless soul.

God, I've missed this. All the stress, all the worries, all the bills and arguments and crap that consume my daily life . . . all so insignificant when compared to the sea.

"God, I hate this!"

His moment of Zen shattered, Jonas turns to find his daughter staggering toward him, her face as pale as a ghost. "I'm sick. I wanna go home."

"You just haven't gotten your sea legs yet. Did you take the Dramamine like I told you to?"

"No."

"Why not?"

"Because I didn't feel like it, okay? Stop asking me questions, I'm going to puke."

"Try focusing on the horizon."

"I can't." She sits by his feet, her head in her hands.

"Dani—"

"Dad, can you just leave me alone?"

Jonas bites his tongue, then closes his eyes. He inhales the mist. Listens to the sounds of the heavy canvas and the groan of the planks. Feels the salty kiss of the ocean in his face—

—and the nauseating hot burst of bile as his daughter vomits all over his feet.

EAST SOOKE REGIONAL PARK
VANCOUVER ISLAND, BRITISH COLUMBIA

East Sooke Regional Park, located twenty-one miles west of Victoria, encompasses more than 3,500 acres of preserved coastal landscape and wilderness. Once home to the *T'Soukees* Indians, the land itself is composed of Metchosin volcanic basalt rock dating back some 50 million years.

Manuel Quimper, a Spaniard, would become the first European to sail into Sooke Inlet, but by 1795 all the islands and lands north of the Strait of Juan de Fuca had fallen under British rule, with Vancouver Island being granted to the Hudson Bay Company.

————

Though he has spent most of his life in the States, Joshua Bunkofske knows all about East Sooke's history. His great-grandfather, William Bunkofske, was one of the first Europeans to seek work on the island's docks in Fort Victoria, back when the tall sailing ships ran supplies up and down the Strait. The sea is in the twenty-nine-year-old scientist's blood, at least that's the story he tells the female interns back at the Bamfield Marine Station.

The marine biologist slows his Jeep Cherokee at the checkpoint and flashes his identification to a Park Ranger. Waved on, he continues west, following the access road to the Pike Road parking lot adjacent to Sooke Inlet.

Three more weeks until my contract expires, and still no offers. Knew I should have never left the States to take the Bamfield gig. Too remote. Once they label you a Canuck, that's it, you'll always be the wilderness guy. Sorry, Bunkofske, we were looking for someone with more hands-on animal experience, not a lab tech . . .

The normally occupied Pike Road lot is vacant, save for a dozen vehicles belonging to the Royal Canadian Mounted Police and a Channel 7 news van. Joshua parks, then sees two police officers physically escort a female reporter and her cameraman back to their truck.

"Wait . . . Officer, at least tell us why the whale rescues have stopped."

"Again, no comment, now move along."

The woman turns, spotting Joshua as he exits the Jeep. "You . . . who are you? Some kind of cetacean expert?"

She's cute, get her number. "Well, miss, actually my—"

The police officer steps between them. "All right, lady, that's enough. Now you either follow our escort out of the park or we'll arrest you."

"Just tell me why he's allowed in the park but we're not? Okay, okay, I'm going!"

Joshua shows his identification to another officer, watching as the woman is herded back to her vehicle. *God, I miss California. If I date one more woman with hairy legs, I think I'll—*

"The lab guy, huh?"

"Marine biologist."

"Whatever. Follow the foot trail south, it'll lead you to the beach at Pike Point. You're looking for Commander Steve Sutera. He's with the West Coast Marine Detachment."

' "The Marine Detachment? Exactly what's going on here?"

The Staff Sergeant shoots him an aggravated look. "Sir, I'm a non-commissioned officer, which means they don't pay me enough to know. Now do you need an escort too?"

"I'll manage." Joshua double-times it down the trail, wondering what he has gotten himself into.

The footpath is actually an old logging road. Twenty minutes of level ground leads to a short downhill stretch, the blue waters of Iron Mine Bay peeking between the upper branches of trees. Stepping out of the woods, Joshua finds himself on a beach more pebble than sand, the Juan de Fuca Strait glistening before him.

Stretched out like logs along the shoreline are dozens of dead whales, their stench overwhelming.

Two men in orange bodysuits and masks are takings samples from what appears to be an open wound along one of the whale's flanks. Others cover carcasses using sheets of heavy gray tarpaulin. The rest of the men, all members of the elite Marine Detachment, huddle in small groups.

Joshua targets Commander Sutera, a tall man with brown curly hair who is giving orders over a walkie-talkie. "I don't care if it's the goddamn prime minister, no one enters this park unless it's cleared with me. And have Justin Lahey secure the airspace over Delta site; Unit Six reports seeing another news chopper heading their way. Sutera out."

The commander looks up. "Who the hell are you?"

"Bunkofske. Bamfield sent me."

"Don't need a lab tech, I need someone who knows something about marine life."

"Just tell me what the problem is."

Sutera heads toward the beach. "You're familiar with these recent whale strandings?"

"Sure. We had a few in Barclay Sound. It happens."

"Not like this."

"Guess it must be bad if you had to shut down the entire park."

"Not just the park. We've shut down all diving, water sports, and boat traffic in this section of the strait. Announced two hours ago that we've got a bad algae bloom. You familiar with domoic acid?"

"It's a by-product of a phytoplankton bloom. Originates from the interaction with the eddy at the mouth of the Strait and the Juan de Fuca Submarine Canyon. Nasty stuff. It's destroyed clam and crab revenues, I never imagined it could kill something as large as a whale."

"Pay attention. I never said it was killing the whales, I said that's what we're telling the public. The whales aren't beaching because of a phytoplankton bloom, the damn things are doing it because they're scared out of their skulls . . . at least that's my opinion."

"Scared?" Josh smirks. *What is this guy, a cetacean psychiatrist?*

"You think I'm joking? What would you call it when you tow an Orca into deep water and the damn thing beats your boat back to the shallows? Know what I call it? A waste of taxpayers' money. Now we just euthanize 'em. Quicker and cleaner. I've got a crane and two dump trucks working 'round the clock removing carcasses."

"How many animals are we talking about?"

"Thirty a day, give or take a few."

"Jesus. I had no idea it was this bad."

"And that's the way we want to keep it. All these strand-ings are bad for tourism."

"The carcasses, where have you been transporting them to?"

"You don't want to know. Let's just say nothing's going to waste."

"Commander, if you destroy the evidence, how can I pos-sibly find the cause?"

"The cause?" Sutera grimaces. "Oh, we know the cause."

They approach a Humpback whale carcass, its upper torso covered by a tarp, the lower body and fluke stretching out into the bay.

Sutera signals. Two of his men drag away a section of damp canvas.

Joshua shudders.

It is a massive, gushing wound, eight and a half feet high, six feet wide, four to five feet deep. A bloody ring of teeth marks encircle the mortal bite.

"How did this, I mean what on God's Earth could have . . . I mean, yeah, I know what could have done it, but—"

"But nothing. She's back. That damn monster's back, and she's panicking the resident whale populations."

"Incredible." Joshua fights back the nausea, unable to take his eyes from the bleeding wound. "Has anyone actually seen the Megalodon?"

"Not yet. We're keeping a tight lid on everything. If the public learns the monster's returned to these waters, we'd lose half our tourism industry."

Joshua turns away, the smell finally getting to him. Look-ing past the dead beast's lower torso, he notices the shallows are tinged reddish-brown with whale blood, the surface crisscrossed by a dozen dark dorsal fins.

Finally, a project that might actually get me out of this wilderness. "Okay, Commander, exactly why am I here?"

"You're the closest thing to a Meg expert we could drum

up on short notice. We need you to track and kill this monster before she drives all the whales from our coast."

"Kill a magnificent creature like Angel? Not a chance."

"Then just chase her off. I don't give a damn what you do, as long as you get her out of these waters."

"Assuming I'm even interested, how am I supposed to do that?"

"We're dealing with a fish, sonny, albeit a big one. We know where she likes to hunt, we know she feeds at night . . . figure the rest out for yourself."

ARAFURA SEA
52 NAUTICAL MILES SOUTHWEST OF PAPUA NEW GUINEA

The *Neptune*'s galley, located aft of the crew's quarters, takes up most of the forward gundeck. Rows of long wooden tables and their accompanying benches are bolted to the floorboards behind the anchor cable which runs up to the capstan. Electrical replicas of old-fashioned oil lamps hang from posts. Aluminum buffet tables line the far wall next to a serving window connected to the kitchen. Gun port hatches have been propped open, allowing a cool ocean breeze to enter the otherwise claustrophobic environment.

Jonas and his daughter are seated with Erik Hollander and his production staff at one row of tables, the rest of the film crew at another, the *Neptune*'s hands at a third.

Jonas watches Danielle pick at her plate of chicken and rice. "You still feeling sick?"

"I'm fine."

"Then what's wrong?"

"It's just not what I expected. When you said sailing yacht, I was hoping for something with a Jacuzzi."

"What? You don't like my ship?"

Dani and Jonas turn, surprised to find the ship's captain standing behind them. "Robert Robertson, captain of the

Neptune." The short, rugged looking man with the blond crew cut extends his free hand to Jonas, balancing his dinner tray in the other. "Pleasure to finally meet you, Taylor."

"You too. This is my daughter, Danielle."

"Dani. I hate Danielle."

"I gather the *Neptune*'s rocking has soured your trip."

"It's giving me a headache."

"It'll get better."

"What if it doesn't?"

"Well, I suppose we can always let you ride out the rest of the voyage on board the *Coelacanth*."

"What's the *Coelacanth*?"

"She's the super yacht we'll be rendezvousing with tomorrow, a vessel more to your liking, I'm sure. Whirlpool, sauna, luxury staterooms, king-size beds, even a helo-pad. Best of all, smooth sailing."

"No—" Erik half-gags on a mouthful of food, chasing it quickly with several gulps of juice. "Sorry Dani, the yacht is strictly off-limits. We, uh, use it to film establishing shots of the *Neptune*, coordinate stunts, that sort of thing. Chopper's reserved for VIPs and emergencies only, you understand. Besides, hey, all the Daredevils'll be on board the *Neptune* by tomorrow evening, and that is why you came, right?"

Dani looks disappointed. "I guess."

"She'll be fine," Jonas says.

"Course she will." Captain Robertson takes his place at his reserved seat at the head of the table. "Anyway, luxury yachts get boring quick, but how many people get to say they've sailed on a Spanish galleon?"

"I thought this was a replica?"

"From the masts down to her keel, she's identical to the warships that sailed these same waters hundreds of years ago. What you don't realize, what you need to appreciate is the Spanish galleon's unique role in our history of ocean travel."

Danielle wipes her mouth, barely concealing a yawn.

"For two hundred and fifty years, ships like the *Neptune* sailed the Pacific on year-long voyages, hauling Chinese ivory, gold, and precious jewels back and forth between Acapulco and Manila. Salvage operators are still finding treasure troves from sunken galleons all along the Mariana island chain."

"The Marianas?" Jonas perks up. "Why the Marianas?"

"The islands became a necessary stopover to replenish the ship's fresh water and food supplies, but the area earned a reputation as the graveyard of the galleons. More than forty ships were lost in the Marianas over the centuries, and they only sailed one ship a year, so you can imagine how costly these disasters became. I remember reading about the worst accident, a sinking that took place off Saipan in September 1638. Ship was called the *Nuestra Señora de la Concepcion*."

"How'd she sink?"

"According to the accident report, there was a mutiny on board. Amid the confusion, the ship foundered in bad weather and was hurled onto a reef. Four hundred people died when she went down, no survivors. Lost cargo must have been valued in the millions."

"If there were no survivors, then how do they know what really caused the accident?"

"Don't know, that's all that was ever filed. We'll actually be retracing the *Concepcion*'s voyage once we pass Halmahera Island."

Dani grimaces. "Like that's supposed to make me feel better?"

Robertson grins between mouthfuls of food. "No worries. Weather should hold, we've got an experienced crew on board, and I don't anticipate any mutinies."

TANAKA OCEANOGRAPHIC INSTITUTE
MONTEREY, CALIFORNIA

The executive suites of the Tanaka Oceanographic Institute are located on the second floor of the three-story office building, situated along the western end of the lagoon's 10,000-seat arena.

The venetian blinds in Masao Tanaka's office have been raised, revealing the sun-drenched waters of the three-quarter-mile-long man-made lagoon. Terry Taylor is seated behind her father's cherrywood desk, staring at the once Mediterranean-blue waters, now more the color of pond scum.

She presses the phone tighter against her ear as the man's voice comes back on the line.

"Okay, Mrs. Taylor, I've got that estimate for you."

"I'm listening." Terry reaches for a pen.

"To purge the filtration system, replace the leaking generator, and scrub the bottom of the main tank will run you just under twenty-two thousand dollars."

"Twenty-two thousand?" The pen slips from Terry's hand.

"Yes, ma'am. Now that price does not include replacing rusted pipes, gaskets, or other replacement parts. Shall I go ahead and book the lagoon for service?"

"I'll get back to you." She hangs up, on the verge of tears. *Can't field any serious offers from aquariums unless the tank's clean, but I can't afford to clean the tank. No wonder Dad was forced to deal with the Dietsch Brothers.*

She reaches for the two-way radio. "David, can you hear me?"

David Taylor is one floor up in the control room, testing the circuit board of the master control panel that operates the canal's giant automated steel doors. He raises the radio to his face. "What?"

"Any luck?"

"Yeah, and it's all bad. The control panel's getting juice,

but the canal doors still aren't closing. The problem has to be in the underwater relay. I'll grab some scuba gear and check it out."

"No you won't."

"Mother—"

"No diving, David, it's too dangerous."

"It's only eighty feet. Dad and I explored wrecks way deeper than that."

"I said no."

"You're being overprotective again."

"Find another solution."

She clicks off the radio and sits back in her father's chair, curling her knees to her chest.

A dozen photos, framed in white pine, adorn the paneled wall to her right. A grainy black-and-white photo of her mother. A candid shot of Terry, age ten, with her brother, D.J., brother and sister hamming it up on the deck of a research vessel. A photo of Terry in the cockpit of a Cessna. A shot of her scuba diving with a Grey whale.

Terry stares at the last picture, confronted by her own reflection in the glass.

Who was that person? What happened to her?

If one's life is a series of moments, then it is the random ones, the events we never see coming, that often forge the most lasting impressions. A winning lottery ticket, the loss of a child, a huge career break, being caught in the wrong place at the wrong time . . .

The wrong place . . .

Eighteen years have passed since Jonas had rescued Terry from the *Benthos,* a mobile deep-sea laboratory owned and operated by Geo-Tech founder Benedict Singer. Benedict had designed the massive abyssal habitat in his quest to locate manganese nodules that contained Helium-3, a rare element he believed would allow him to break through the fusion barrier. Tricked into boarding the *Benthos,* Terry found herself at the bottom of the Mariana Trench, trapped like a rat in a maze, 16,000 pounds of water pressure pressing against the ship's hull, seven miles of ocean above her head. Within this stress-filled environment she had become Benedict's plaything, her psyche his to abuse, her body left to the disposal of a murderous Russian thug named Sergei.

Against all odds she had managed to keep herself alive long enough to be rescued, but the experience had left an enduring impression. Night terrors haunted her sleep as her tortured mind dreamed claustrophobic images bathed in inescapable violence. Therapy and medication were prescribed, but things eventually grew worse, forcing Jonas to allow her doctors to commit her to a sanitarium.

Sixty days in the facility were needed to vanquish the nightmares, but the person who emerged was not the same spirit Jonas had fallen in love with years earlier. The lasting paranoia inflicted by Benedict Singer required severe lifestyle changes in order to cope. No more scuba diving, no more plane trips, no more risks. All activities would become vanilla. Vanilla was safe. Vanilla avoided potential conflicts.

In some ways, Danielle's birth made things worse. Terry transferred her overprotectiveness to her child, attempting to shield her from the seemingly increasing random acts of violence that infected society. School shootings. Kidnappings. Acts of terrorism. Snipers.

How was one expected to have faith when there was so much senseless violence? The world had become a dangerous place, too dangerous to venture out into and enjoy.

Terry knew her phobias affected Jonas's career choices, but she didn't care. It was only money, after all, they would find a way to get by. She home-schooled Dani, then insisted Jonas sell their heavily-mortgaged estate so they could afford to send their daughter to a private academy.

To make it up to her husband, she agreed to have a second child.

It only takes one random moment to change a life, but it often takes a lifetime to accept the lie. After nearly two decades, Terry had finally grown accustomed to "wearing her new skin." Deep down she knew it was a shaky foundation at best, like building a home on a geological fault line. At some point, the house always collapses.

Staring at her reflection, she feels the tremors of her father's death wearing on her fragile psyche.

Masao's phone rings, causing her to jump. "Terry Taylor."

"Mrs. Taylor, wow, this is a real honor, I can't believe I actually found you."

"Who is this?"

"Sorry. My name's Joshua Bunkofske. I'm an ichthyologist and I—"

"We're not hiring." She hangs up, returning her attention to the next item on her daily "To-Do" list.

The phone rings again. "Yes?"

"Mrs. Taylor, it's Joshua Bunkofske again, please don't hang up."

"Josh, the Institute's not hiring. If you want, you can send us a—"

"Angel's back, Mrs. Taylor. We need your husband's help."

No tremors. She has heard this line dozens of times over the last twenty years.

"Ma'am?"

"Okay, Joshua, I'll play along. Where are you calling from?"

"Vancouver Island. I work at the Marine Station in Bamfield. You know, maybe I should speak with your husband."

"Jonas is out of the country on business. He won't be back for several months."

"Damn."

"Josh, I don't mean to rain on your parade, but the Institute gets hundreds of these so-called Angel sightings. Every one of them turns out to be false."

"This one's real. You've heard about all the whale strandings in the Juan de Fuca Strait?"

"I may have caught a blurb on the news."

"There have been over a hundred just in the last few weeks. What you won't hear is that several of the beached whales had been attacked. We've documented bite marks that could only have been made by an adult Megalodon."

"Joshua, have you ever seen a Megalodon bite mark?"

"Uh, technically no, but—"

"And has anyone actually seen Angel?"

"No, ma'am, but I promise you, it's your shark."

Terry's face flushes with anger. "For the record, Joshua, she's not my shark, and I seriously doubt Angel's returned from the Mariana Trench. The attack could have come from a pod of Orca. They do feed on whales, too, you know."

"But not on each other. We found several Orca among the dead. Look, Mrs. Taylor, I'll admit Megalodon attacks aren't exactly my line of expertise, heck, I was only eleven when Angel escaped. But since you're familiar with a Megalodon's bite print, maybe I could get you to fly up here and give us your opinion on the wounds we've already documented."

"I don't know . . ."

"Mrs. Taylor, if this is Angel, then we have to do something quickly, before she attacks a boater, or worse. The Marine Detachment needs you. Tell us what it'll cost to fly you up for the day and it's yours."

"How about twenty-two thousand dollars."

Nervous laughter. "You're kidding, right?"

"Three thousand a day, plus expenses, that's the Institute's standard fee for a job like this. And that's American dollars, Joshua, cash up-front."

"Hold the line."

Terry waits, her impatience growing. *This is where they always separated the pranksters from the serious inquiries, or, as her father used to say, the buyers from the liars.*

Joshua gets back on the line. "Okay, Mrs. Taylor, you have a deal. There'll be an open ticket in your name waiting for you at the American Airlines counter in San Francisco. Next flight out leaves in three hours. You'll fly into Seattle, then we'll have a private plane waiting to take you on to Victoria."

Terry's pulse quickens. "Who else knows about this?"

"No one, and the CO in charge wants to keep it that way."

She taps her fingers nervously on the desktop.

"Ma'am?"

She stares at the photograph of herself scuba diving. *Time to choose. Which Terry do you want to be?*

"Mrs. Taylor, you still there?"

"Yes, I'm here. I'll be on the next flight up."

CHAPTER

11

BANDA SEA
43 NAUTICAL MILES NORTHEAST OF MOLUCCAS

The bullet-shaped escape pod barrel-rolls inside the monster's churning stomach, globs of molten brownish-gray whale blubber slapping against the fogging Lexan glass.

As Jonas watches in horror, another object passes through the mini-sub's exterior beam of light . . . a human torso.

Jonas screams . . . as his vessel slips backward into oblivion.
"Ahhhh!"

Jonas sits up, his pulse racing, his tee-shirt soaked with sweat. He looks around, desperate and disoriented.

He is alone in his cabin aboard the *Neptune*, the hammock swaying beneath him, its knots creaking in unison with the motions of the ocean.

"Okay . . . you're okay."

Jonas rolls painfully out of the hammock, his aching lower back stiff and swollen, in desperate need of a chiropractor. He checks his watch. *Four-thirty . . . but is it* a.m. *or* p.m.? He glances at the view port, the late afternoon gray on the other side of the window confirming he's slept all day.

He grabs a bottle of water, staggers to the rinse bucket, and brushes his teeth. Slipping on his tennis shoes, he exits his cabin and heads forward, in search of the community bathroom.

The term "head" adopted into the mariner language, originates from a design first incorporated into the Spanish galleon when the crews' toilets were fitted into the forward space at the front of the ship's forecastle, extending underneath the bowsprit.

Ten minutes later, Jonas climbs up on deck, butterflies in his stomach as he tries to psyche himself up for his new career. He waves to Captain Robertson, who ignores him, too absorbed in directing his crew to lower the forward sails.

The sky is heavy with ominous cumulonimbus clouds, which form a line of white, anvil-shaped towers, their flat bottoms dark and gray.

Andrew Fox calls out to Jonas from the upper walkway. "Afternoon, sleeping beauty."

"Hey, I'm still on California time. Why are we heading for the squall line?"

"Show's about to begin. There are two teams of Daredevils preparing to board, one from below, the other from above." He points to a plane, circling at 5,000 feet. "The team in the plane directed us to the squall line two hours ago. God knows what they're waiting for."

"Lovely." Jonas glances astern. Trailing behind the *Neptune* is the *Coelacanth*.

The Abeking & Rasmusen super yacht is 188 feet long, with a 35-foot beam and 11.5-foot draft. Navy blue, with white upper decks and trim, she is a sleek, luxurious fortress of fiberglass and steel, her twin 1400 horsepower engines able to propel her through the choppy seas at an easy twelve knots.

Jonas whistles. "I'm with Dani, I'd rather ride on board that."

"Jonas, where the hell have you been?" Erik Hollander

waves frantically at him from the deck below. "Come on, you should have been in makeup an hour ago."

Andrew winks. "Be sure to have them work on those crow's feet."

"Makeup?" Jonas rolls his eyes. "Andrew, that cage of yours is beginning to look good."

"Jonas, please!"

He hustles down the companionway. "Sorry, got a late start."

Erik signals to a makeup woman, who begins dabbing his face with flesh-tone powder. "Charlotte will do most of the talking, just comment as you see fit. We're live, but still on tape, so we can reshoot or dub in later. Any questions?"

"Yeah. Who's Charlotte?"

"Who's Charlotte? Only the host for this season's show. Haven't you met her yet? She boarded by chopper about three hours ago . . . wait, there she is." Erik points to the bow where a cocoa-brown African-American woman in a white thong bikini is posing before a photographer and two cameramen.

"Not much of an actress, but who cares, she makes—"

"I know, great eye-candy."

"Absolutely. Girl's been on the cover of *Sports Illustrated*'s swimsuit issue twice in the last three years."

"Three minutes!" A woman in her early forties yells over a megaphone, her heavy New York accent crackling across the deck. "Come on, people, let's move, we're losing the light."

She approaches Jonas and Erik, swapping the megaphone for a walkie-talkie as she speaks. ". . . and have the *Coelacanth* stay back another hundred yards, last thing we need is that yacht appearing in the background." She stows the walkie-talkie in her belt, then thrusts her free hand at Jonas. "Susan Ferraris, director. Next time you're late, I'm waking you with a cattle prod up your—"

"Susan, easy, it's his first day."

"Don't fuck with me, Erik, I'm two cameramen short and

I've got menstrual cramps that would drop a grizzly. You, enough with the make-up, he already looks like a goddamn mannequin." She grabs Jonas by the arm, half-dragging him to the chalked red "X" by the starboard rail. "There's your mark, now where's your mike? Goddamn it, can somebody get a remote on him!"

A soundman appears, clipping a microphone onto Jonas's button-down collar. He feeds the wire down his shirt and out the back, where he reconnects the pronged end to a transmitter. "Shove this in your back pocket and say something."

"Hi, my name is Jonas Taylor and I'm—"

"He's set."

"Charlotte, I need you here, dear." Susan's walkie-talkie squawks to life. "What?"

"Susan, it's Brian. The Makos say they're still not ready."

"Not ready? Do these crazies understand we're losing the light?"

"I doubt they care. But we just heard from the *Waller*. The Hammerheads will be in position in ten minutes. Suggest we shoot them first."

"Agreed." She shuts off the two-way radio. "All right people, change of plans. We'll shoot the opening segment, then move right into the Hammerheads' entrance."

"Susan, the TelePrompTer's not working?"

"Wonderful. What else can go wrong?"

A look of panic comes over Charlotte's primped face. "No TelePrompTer? What do you expect me to do? Memorize everything?"

"It's just the intro, dear. You've done it a thousand times in rehearsal."

Camera crews hustle into position, two teams aiming their lenses off the starboard rail, a third setting up to film Jonas and Charlotte. The supermodel's eyes are closed, her lips moving silently as she hastily rehearses her lines.

"Susan, we're ready here."

"Quiet on the set."

"Lights."

Jonas squints against the hot reflection, wishing he'd made another quick stop at the head.

"Sound . . . speed—"

"Five seconds. Four . . . three . . ."

Charlotte's eyes flash open, igniting a false smile.

Jonas grinds his teeth into a grin.

The director signals silently. *Two . . . one—*

"Welcome to *Daredevils II: South Pacific Challenge*. I'm Charlotte Lockhart, your host for this season's show, and with me is legendary Daredevil and former deep-sea submersible pilot, James Taylor."

Jonas's face cracks into a half-smile. "Actually, it's Jonas. James is the singer."

"Cut!" Susan Ferraris charges him like a mad bull. "Never . . . ever correct the host while we're rolling . . . Jesus." She turns to her crew. "Reset. And Charlotte, sugarplum, for God's sake, it's Jonas, you know, like Jonas and the whale."

"Actually, that was Jonah. My name is—"

"Rolling!"

"Speed."

Susan signals.

The supermodel reanimates. "Welcome to *Daredevils II: South Pacific Challenge*. I'm Charlotte Lockhart, your host for this season's show, and with me is legendary Daredevil and former deep-sea submersible pilot, Jonah Taylor."

"Uh, thank you, Charlotte, it's great to be here."

"Great having you, Jonah. Now let's review the rules. As you know, *Daredevils* airs twice each week, allowing our viewing audience a few days to cast their vote on our official Web site to determine our winning stunt. Our Daredevils have been randomly divided into two teams of five. During each taped segment of our show, the two teams will compete head to head by coordinating a live death-defying stunt, placing at least one member of their party in jeopardy. You, our viewing audience, will then have two days to vote for the

winning stunt. At the start of each new show, the losing team
from the last show will have to vote one member off their
squad. During our third week, we'll combine the remaining
members of both squads into one team and continue the
elimination process, one by one, until we have our winner.
How's that sound, Jonah?"

"Sounds exciting, Sharon."

The supermodel's false smile momentarily flickers.
"Right. And now, let's meet this season's Daredevils!"

"And cut." Blue eyes blazing, Susan is about to engage
Jonas when the first drops of cold rain splatter on deck.
Cursing aloud, she grabs her walkie-talkie as dozens of
golf umbrellas simultaneously open to shelter the equip-
ment. "Brian, it's raining. What's happening with the
Makos?"

"Still circling and waiting."

"Waiting for what? A rainbow?"

"I don't know, boss."

"Radio the Hammerheads. Tell them to get their team in
the water." She calls out to the captain. "We're changing the
sequence of shots. Shift this ship of yours into neutral."

"It's not a car, ma'am," Robertson mumbles, turning the
Neptune's prow into the wind. The massive mainsail flaps
above his head, the ship slowing.

"Susan, we're set here."

"Roll film." She yells into her walkie-talkie, "Brian, signal the Hammerheads."

Jonas and the rest of the crew watch in amazement as a
moving wake appears off the starboard bow, followed by the
steel sail of a Collins-class submarine. The Australian boat
continues rising, its hull plowing the sea—

—along with five surfacing water-skiers, three men and
two women, each being towed by ropes attached to the
ship's bow planes.

Michael Coffey, team captain of the Hammerheads, releases his pony-bottle of air as his head breaks the surface

thirty feet behind the submarine's propeller. Gripping the guide rope tightly in both hands, he glances to his right.

Evan Stewart and Jason Massett, skiing along the starboard side of the sub's wake, offer thumbs-up.

Coffey turns to his left. Dee Hatcher and Mia Durante are on the opposite side of the submarine, facing the *Neptune*. Both women are scantily clad in yellow thong bikinis.

The *HMAS Waller* cruises around the drifting Spanish galleon in a wide circle. As the submarine passes the *Neptune*'s stern, it begins to dive—

—hauling the five Daredevils with it.

Jonas stares at the sea, his heart pounding, his ego wondering if he could have pulled off the maneuver. Thirty seconds pass, then a minute. The cameras continue to roll, focusing on the foamy surface.

Holding his own breath, Jonas watches and waits.

Ninety seconds . . . and then a head appears, then another. Five hands raise out of the water in unison to rousing applause.

Charlotte Lockhart smiles at the camera, her open right hand pointing at the sea. "Ladies and gentlemen, introducing the Hammerheads. Say hello to Dee Hatcher—"

A thirty-ish brunette with slate blue eyes scales the cargo net and climbs on board. She flings her hair back with the attitude of a goddess, then poses, fists on shapely hips, waiting for the rest of her team to join her.

"Evan Stewart."

The marine biologist from Miami is next up the makeshift rope ladder, the rugged man sporting a fourteen-inch half-moon-shaped scar over his midsection.

"Mia Durante."

The dark-haired, olive-skinned Italian-Filipino swings a well-muscled leg over the side, offers her own sultry pose, then gives a martial arts bow to the camera.

"From Massapequa, Jason Massett."

The brown-haired, well-built former lacrosse player with

the piercing hazel eyes flashes a crooked smile, then takes his place beside his teammates.

"And back for another season, last year's overall winner and the captain of the Hammerheads . . . Michael Coffey!"

The senior member of the group somersaults over the rail and onto the main deck, then slaps high-fives with the rest of his team.

Susan Ferraris allows the cameras to roll several more minutes before yelling cut. "One down, one to go." She yells into her walkie-talkie. "Brian, what the hell's going on with team two?"

Five thousand feet above the Spanish galleon, the cargo plane continues to circle beneath the ceiling of dark cumulonimbus clouds.

Wayne John Ferguson peers out the open cargo hatch at the lead-gray sea.

"Fergie, give it up already," argues Barry Struhl, a linebacker-size man with short, wavy dark hair and goatee. "It's been an hour since we saw the last spout and we're running out of fuel."

"Barry's right," says Lexy Piatek. "You can't control the weather. Let's just do the jump as planned and make the best of it."

"It's boring." Fergie spits out the open hatch. "What do you think, Doc?"

John Shinto, a thirty-three-year-old dentist from Virginia, scratches his short-cropped dark blond hair. "Lexy's right, we can't control the weather. Jennie's up front, if she can't find a spout, then no one can. I think we've got about as much chance of pulling this one off as pushing shit uphill."

The plane shakes beneath them, nearly tossing Fergie head-first out the open hatch. That's when he sees it.

"Thar she blows, I told you! Two-o'clock, Jennie—hey Jennie!"

Jennie calls back from the copilot's seat. "We see it. Gear up, we're radioing the *Neptune*."

The plane changes course, banking to the west.

Captain Robertson turns the ship hard to port, refilling the main sheets. The *Neptune* comes to life, bounding over the six foot seas, tacking parallel to the edge of the squall line.

Jonas hangs onto the starboard rail with one hand, wiping a fine mist of seawater from his face with the other. The late afternoon sky has taken on a new appearance, the strong tropical convection currents forming an ominous, triangular white object that seems to be growing from beneath a darkening cumulonimbus cloud.

Dani sidles up to her father. "Dad . . . what is that?"

As they watch, a white funnel cloud reaches down from the heavens and kisses the ocean, uplifting a massive churning vortex of sea spray less than two miles off the *Neptune*'s starboard bow.

"Jesus, that's a waterspout." Jonas glances down at her. "Why aren't you wearing a life preserver?"

"Duh, because no one else is."

"Get one on."

"Come on, Dad—"

"Now!"

Michael Coffey wipes mist from his face, his gaze focused on the base of the ocean-born twister, now a tightly spinning mass of spray. "Okay, Fergie, you crazy bastard, you got what you were waiting for, now let's see what you do with it."

The cargo plane circles just beneath the cloud bank, offering the five members of the Mako team a bird's-eye view of the fully formed waterspout.

"Looks like fun," Fergie says. "What do you think, Jen? Three in the drink and two in the rodeo."

"Who are the two?"

"Not me," Doc Shinto says. "Assuming I survived, my wife and kids would never speak to me again."

"Barry?"

"Hey, I'm a big wave surfer, dude, not a skydiver."

"What about you, Lexy? Care to 'ave a go?"

The petite twenty-two-year-old stares below at the churning column of wind. "I'm with Barry. The sea's more my specialty."

"Which leaves the beautiful Jedi Jennie?"

She bites her lip. "I'm in."

"You sure?"

"Shut up."

"Right. Barry, I want you, Doc, and Lexy off this plane like a bride's nightie before this bird blows itself away. Tail's whipping to the southwest, so stay east before you disperse, then radio us when you're in the drink."

Doc Shinto nods. "How close you planning to be?"

"Don't know, never done this before. Jennie and I will circle once and see how she feels. If you see us flying bare arsed in the wind, then assume we pushed it too close."

The *Neptune* slows, the captain once more changing course, positioning his vessel a half-mile to the east of the churning white tornado.

Susan Ferraris is calling out commands, her camera crews continuing to shoot footage. To the southwest, the super yacht, *Coelacanth*, has moved into position to film the waterspout with the *Neptune* in the background.

One by one, the three Yamaha 701 Wave Raider personal water craft are secured to a mobile winch and lowered over the side. Michael Coffey climbs down a cargo net and straddles one machine, Evan and Jason the other two.

Although Coffey despises Wayne Ferguson, the unwritten

law of adrenaline junkies is that no one is ever alone against the elements. As such, Coffey will risk his own life to save Ferguson, though he secretly harbors hope that the man will be torn apart by the funnel of wind long before his carcass ever hits the sea.

"There!" Evan points to three parachutists who have just emerged from the plane.

"Spotters. We'll each take one, then pick up the pieces from the other two."

Claiming the first parachutist down, Coffey accelerates his Wave Raider away from the ship, the souped-up dual carburetor big bore jet-skis capable of reaching speeds in excess of 58 miles an hour.

Wind and sea spray whip across Doc Shinto's face, blurring his goggles as he floats awkwardly toward a patch of Mediterranean-green surface. Fifteen feet from contact, he releases the chute and drops feet-first into the sea, sinking like a brick.

Inflating his life preserver, he rockets back to the surface, distancing himself from his parachute.

The sea is surprisingly warm, the waves a bit rough. Removing his goggles, Shinto takes a quick look around. He has landed 125 yards southeast of the waterspout's tail. For a long moment he can only stare at the howling white column of wind.

The upper and lower portion of the waterspout are moving at different speeds, causing the funnel to angle slightly to the west. Less powerful than its land-based cousin, the waterspout still generates wind speeds of 80 to 100 miles an hour, making it quite dangerous.

Shinto verifies the tail is moving away from his location, then checks in with the circling cargo plane. "Fergie, it's Doc, I'm in position. Fergie, can you read me? Fergie—"

The plane bucks beneath them, momentarily losing altitude.

"Storm could hit any time," the pilot calls back. "It's now or never."

Jennie presses her hands against her helmet. " I can hear Doc, he's in the drink."

"Pilot's right, if we're going to do this, we need to do it now, before that tail goes snaking all over the place like a madwoman's custard."

Jennie laughs, then stares at him, her eyes wide with adrenaline, her heart pumping faster. "First one down owns bragging rights!" She leaps out of the plane—

—Fergie right behind her.

Wind blasts his face and howls in his ears as he free-falls toward the bolt of white wind that lances down from the heavens as if thrown by Zeus.

Pulling his arms back, Fergie soars past Jennie, flying headfirst at the beast at a 30-degree down angle, the heart of the clockwise-spinning shaft becoming less visible as he nears.

And then the wind blasts into his body as it grabs him, sucking him deep into its powerful vortex, the brackish air howling in his brain as his entire existence is narrowed down to this one single, precious, intense moment of time. His mind screams at him to pull his chute even as his ego commands he continue to body-surf the monster, the sensation too excruciatingly real to abandon, the centrifugal force stretching his vertebrae while it tears at his flesh, his jumpsuit peeling away as he is flung around the shaft of wind like a cowboy tied to a bucking bronco—

—and suddenly he is flung free, the ungodly G-force catapulting him backward into deafening silence.

A fleeting millisecond of self-preservation as he expels his parachute, and then the blackness overcomes him, escorting him back to earth like a warm blanket as the sea reaches up to reclaim her clay.

CHAPTER

12

MONTEREY, CALIFORNIA

David hands his mother her jacket. "If you're just flying up to meet with this potential buyer, then why can't I come too?"

"First, because they only invited me, second, because I need you here to repair the damaged circuit boards in the control room. You're a wizard at these things, David. I really need you on this."

"Fine, but I'll need some help. Where's Uncle Mac?"

Terry zips her carry-on bag. "I told you, Mac's away, visiting friends."

"You mean he's in rehab."

"Who told you that?"

"I overheard you and Dad fighting."

"David, that was a private conversation."

"Next time don't scream so loud."

"Maybe Trish can help you, I asked her to check up on you."

"I don't need a baby-sitter, Mother."

"Humor me, I need the peace of mind." She pauses, hearing the car horn blaring downstairs. "That's my cab. Do you want a lift back to the Institute?"

"No, I'll take one of the bikes."

Terry leans over, kissing him good-bye. "Remember, no scuba diving."

"How about just in the tank?"

"Absolutely not, and I don't have time to argue. Here's eighty dollars for groceries and emergencies, make it last. I'll call you tonight from Canada, and you'd better be home."

Tossing her bag over her shoulder, she heads downstairs and out the front door to the awaiting driver. "San Francisco Airport."

She waves again to David, but he's already shut the front door.

Terry climbs in the backseat. Minutes later, they are heading north along the Pacific Coast Highway.

She gazes out her smudged window at the deep blue horizon. *Three thousand dollars and a round-trip ticket, something's got these guys spooked. Probably turn out to be some kind of parasite in the water.*

Still . . .

"Driver, I need you to make a quick stop at the Institute. It's the gravel road coming up on the left.".

Satisfied, she stares out the window, wondering what she'd do if Angel really had returned from the Mariana Trench.

The mere thought causes her hands to shake.

MONTEREY BAY SANCTUARY
DUSK

Wildlife photographer Brian Hodges pulls his paddle out of the water, allowing his kayak to glide within one hundred feet of the swarm of krill. Stealing a quick glance over his shoulder at the setting sun, he estimates the distance to the phytoplankton patch, then opens his camera bag.

Better switch to the wide angle.

Removing the bright yellow Minolta Vectis Weathermatic Zoom camera from around his neck, Brian quickly swaps out the standard lens for the larger 50-mm. Verifying he has ample shots left on the roll, he pulls the dive mask over his face, positions the snorkel in his mouth, and slips quietly over the side.

A dozen boat lengths away, tens of thousands of tiny shrimp continue feeding along the surface, unaware of the behemoth predator rising from the depths to devour them.

His camera poised at water level, Brian steadies his hand, holds his breath, and waits.

With a breathtaking *whoosh*, the surface erupts in a mountain of foam as the 32-foot juvenile Humpback's jaws engulf a dump-truckload of seawater and krill.

Brian clicks away, catching the 38,000-pound rorqual in mid-body slap, its impact with the surface sending three-foot waves caroming in all directions. As the whale feeds, he recognizes the circular patch of crustaceans located on the animal's right flank. *Evening, Charlie Donuts. Nice to see you again.*

Resting along the surface, its head out of the water, the Humpback benignly eyeballs the wildlife photographer as it compresses the contained volume of sea through its baleen.

A stark-white, twelve-foot pectoral fin slaps playfully along the surface, drenching Brian and his waterproof camera.

"Thanks, Charlie, now what about a—"

Wha-boosh!

A swimming pool of sea buries Brian as the Pacific erupts in an explosion of foam and ocean and blood . . . thick, oily, scarlet blood—driven outward from a mountainous mass of ivory-white flesh.

Angel shakes her head viciously along the surface, her blood-soaked serrated teeth sawing out a gargantuan bite from the shocked Humpback's belly. The wounded whale heaves and twists and flops in agony, forcing the larger predator to release it to the sea.

And then, as suddenly as she appeared, the Megalodon is gone, leaving its prey writhing along the surface in a dissipating pool of its own blood.

Gasping in shock, Brian Hodges treads water, fighting to keep his head clear of the eight-foot swells. Tearing his eyes away from the thrashing whale, he searches desperately for the kayak. *Get outta here, get out of the water . . .*

Heart pounding, his skin tingling in fright, he swims for the kayak. Reaches it. Hoists himself up, his adrenaline-packed effort nearly sending him headfirst over the opposite side. *Settle down and paddle . . . where's the damn oar?*

Brian locates the paddle. Grabs it. Strokes as fast as he can, the shoreline and his girlfriend and his freelance photography shop and the rest of his days a good two miles away.

Stay calm, it's not after you, it's after the whale. You'll be fine, just stay calm and keep paddling . . .

The camera, still looped around his neck, bounces against his chest—

—calling out his name.

Brian stares at temptation, his fear momentarily subsiding. *The whale's dying. Angel's got to be circling below, waiting to feed again. One shot, just a quick one before you lose the light, then get to shore as fast as you can.*

He stops paddling, allowing the kayak to drift as he glances back at Charlie. *Calm and steady and the Meg won't even know you're here. One great shot of her next attack, just one killer shot.*

He checks his camera. Frames the shot.

Looks good, looks real good. I can hear them at the Diamond Club now. Show us your proof, Brian. Okay, boys, feast your eyes on this.

Brian zooms in closer on the dying mammal, which is

swimming in spasms, blood draining from a sickening Jacuzzi-size hole in its abdomen. *Sorry Charlie, but that's life in the food chain. Damn, this looks good. Okay, Angel, one more time for Daddy while we still have the light. Definitely a cover shot on* National Geographic, *maybe even* Time . . .

The Humpback moans as it flails its fluke weakly against the surface, paddling feebly with its oar-shaped pectoral fins.

Come on, Angel. Come and get it . . .

The whale changes directions, propelling itself toward shore—

—and Brian's kayak.

Through his lens, Brian watches the animal glide closer . . . closer . . .

Come on, Angel, time for dessert . . .

"Oh shit, what am I doing?" In a panic, Brian releases the camera and reaches for the oar.

The whale's fluke slaps flat against the surface, the gunshot-like sound startling Brian, who drops the oar overboard, gasping in disbelief as it floats away.

"Jesus H. Christ!" Leaning over, he paddles with both hands, closing in on the escaping oar.

The Humpback expels a gust of air from its blowhole, the mist drenching the back of Brian's neck as he reaches for the paddle.

The kayak spins sideways and away from the oar, nudged from below by the Humpback's barnacle-encrusted head.

"Stupid whale, get the hell away from—"

Orange-red sky flips upside down, deep blue sea downside up, the kayak, the whale, and Brian Hodges's entire existence blasted skyward, launched into the crisp evening air beneath nearly 40 tons of thrusting, angry monster.

So high . . . three stories . . . four stories, and now he is falling . . . his heart in his throat and the air so strangely cold as he plunges headfirst past the still-rising ivory silo of flesh, the world gone mad, utterly mad, as, instinctively, he reaches out and catches hold of an immense pectoral fin . . . the insanity of his act and the tearing flesh in his hands forcing him to let go.

Flipping over again, he crashes feetfirst into the chop, his remaining breath driven from his chest as he sinks—

Water warm . . . just stay here a moment . . . just another moment—

The cursed sea blasts him sideways and out again as the two behemoths re-enter the Pacific like an avalanche, the impossibly powerful impact popping his eardrums . . . *If I could only get a picture, just one prize-winner for my headstone . . .*

Sinking again . . . no, not sinking, dragged . . . *I must have fallen in a river . . .*

Kicking, stroking . . . *which way is up?* Choking on oil and blood and blubber . . . *Why is Nature so violent . . . who knew? Who the hell knew?*

An eternity passes and Brian surfaces, lunging his face above the wave tops for air, his heart pounding in his ears, his battered body overwrought with numbing cold and pain.

All alone now, and he is treading water in a spreading pond of blood, its warmth so soothing, the sensation nauseating.

The kayak is gone. He hears the pounding of surf on rocks and heads for the sound, moaning with each exhausting stroke.

"Ahhh . . . ahhh!" He screams as his throbbing body is lifted out of the sea on a gushing, smelly, oily raft of blubber.

God . . . this isn't happening . . .

His mind momentarily shot, he lies prone on the whale, fingering the dark grooved surface of blubber, palpating Charlie Donuts's crusty barnacles.

The island of lifeless blubber bobs beneath him. The chilled air causes him to shiver.

Snap out of it! Get your ass back into that pool of blood and swim . . . swim for your goddamn life!

Too cold, too scared, Brian refuses to move.

Day slips below the horizon, abandoning him to the night.

Another minute, another lifetime passes and still he refuses to re-enter the water.

The dead whale rolls.

Brian scrambles with it . . . balancing on his knees until the carcass slides out from beneath him and he is tossed back into the sea.

He kicks and screams and climbs . . . climbs right back up onto poor dead Charlie Donuts, gripping those barnacles, *Thank God for barnacles* . . . pulling himself back up by the dorsal fin, blood gushing everywhere . . . *Poor dead Charlie Donuts, such is life in the food chain, please, dead Charlie, keep me out of the sea.*

"Help! Help! Somebody help me!"

Strange how his voice sounds . . . so crisp in the cool dusk air, so desperate.

Brian heaves, vomiting the sea and a small half-dollar hunk of innards, the realization of it causing him to retch some more.

Okay . . . stop . . . just stop before she comes back . . . stop before she comes to take another bite out of your raft.

The whale carcass shudders beneath him, dropping him to his knees.

Too late . . .

He leans over and looks into the water . . . water that was dark a second ago, water that is now glowing a soft lime-green, water that reveals a mouth so hideous that Brian nearly jumps out of his skin when he sees it.

The trailer-size orifice is open, revealing a tunnel filled with teeth, the mouth pushing from below, the jaws opening wider, driving his raft out from under him as the head feeds.

Brian screams as he slides backward down the slippery slope.

"No—"

His head goes under, the sea electricity to his skin, shocking him into action.

And now Brian is Spider-man . . . his lightning-packed muscles pushing him up the slippery slope, his adrenal glands pumping like crazy, refusing to allow his island to escape. Pruned fingers dig into the blubbery flesh and search for barnacles, kicking shoes find toeholds along a lifeless pectoral fin.

The carcass rolls like a log and he slips again—

—stepping into a wound.

Angel removes her snout from the gushing hole and stops feeding, suddenly aware of the presence of a challenger.

Brian claws his way back on top of the lifeless log of blubber and crustaceans and oil and blood, praising God, praying for a miracle.

And then he hears it . . . a high-pitched whine.

A boat . . . oh, thank you! "Here! Over here!"

It's dark now, but he's straddling and waving and shouting and screaming, and damn if that fishing boat isn't turning. "Yes, yes, come on, over here, I'm here!"

He is crying for joy—

—and then he is silent.

The sight of the luminescent-white dorsal fin squeezes his voice box, the circling sail so tall and frightening and ominous as it slices past him at eye level that he must swallow his words and the bile rising in his parched throat.

But the motorboat is still coming . . . any minute now . . . any second.

Go away!

The fin disappears.

Be careful what you wish for, because now Brian has time

to think, and now he is really frightened, so frightened that he can only moan as he urinates in his wetsuit.

"Help! Help me—"

The whale carcass erupts, flipping his legs out from beneath him, the powerful blow from below casting him into the dark, boiling, unforgiving sea.

The motor boat slows.

David Emanuel cuts the engine.

"Hello?" He shines his light upon the floating mound of blubber. "God, what a mess."

His co-worker, Jean Fisher, joins him in the bow. "Eww. What was it?"

"A whale. Must've heard it moaning or something."

"The boss'll be doing a lot more than moaning if we're late for his party. Come on, it smells like sewage around here."

"Right." Emanuel pushes down on the throttle, maneuvering around the bobbing hunk of blubber as he continues his journey north to San Francisco Bay.

Four hundred and seventy feet below the gushing humpback, Angel rolls over on her back—

—swallowing the remains of wildlife photographer Brian Hodges.

CHAPTER

13

The Daredevil "rec room" is located belowdecks, situated forward of the galley in what had once been the Spanish galleon's crew's quarters. At the forward end of this large open chamber is the massive foundation that holds the bowsprit, a tree-size mast that rises out from below decks at a forty-five degree angle. Lanterns hang from the ceiling, creating long shadows in their soft auburn glow. Huge colorful body pillows bearing the *Daredevils* insignia serve as rec room furniture. A pool table has been anchored to the bare wood floor in between two imposing cannons.

The Hammerhead team, dressed in their blue cotton warm-ups, laze about on pillows along one wall, the Makos, in their red outfits, relaxing on the opposite side of the room. Seated between them on canvas folding chairs are Charlotte Lockhart and Jonas Taylor.

Positioned discreetly along the periphery of the room are cameramen and sound people.

Danielle watches from the wings, along with the rest of

the Candy Girls—wannabe models—all dressed in skintight
Daredevils tube tops and mini-pants.

Wayne Ferguson lies back on a throne of pillows, his
teammates reclining by his feet. His head is wrapped heavily
in gauze, his left hip packed in ice. Bandages cover his forehead and cheekbones where the waterspout had torn off
patches of skin.

Groggy on painkillers, he waves in Dani's direction, flashing a crooked smile.

Jennie Arnos flops down next to him, purposely grazing
his bruised hip.

"Oww."

"Serves you right. You were supposed to maneuver
around the funnel, not fly right through it."

"Wasn't trying to go through it, I got caught in the updraft. For a second, I thought God was usin' me to play aer-
ial Ping-Pong."

"And guess who pulled you out of the drink." She motions
to Michael Coffey, who is doing an interview.

"Tryin' to score points off my jump, no doubt."

"I thought it was *our* jump."

"Our jump. Don't be cranky."

Susan Ferraris takes center stage. "A great first day, people, a great first day. Now I know everyone wants to cele-
brate, but first we need to tone it down a bit, you know, keep
it real . . . let our viewers peek inside the mind of the adrenaline junkie. So we're just going to let the cameras roll and
turn this rap session over to Charlotte and Jonas and see
what happens, okay? Remember, the more you contribute,
the more our viewers get to know you, very important when
casting their votes. Charlotte, anytime you're ready."

The supermodel crosses her shapely legs and adjusts the
opening of her blouse, accentuating her dark cleavage for
camera one. "Well, Jonas, it's been an amazing first day.
Over the next forty-eight hours, our viewers at home will be

voting to determine which Daredevil team won the opening stunt. Meanwhile, all of us want to know, what makes a Daredevil tick? Why would someone purposely place themselves in situations of peril? Are they searching for fame and glory? Is it the rush of adrenaline? Tonight we'll ask these questions of the men and women competing in *Daredevils*, beginning with Evan Stewart of Team Hammerhead. Hi, Evan."

Evan waves modestly.

"Evan, I understand you're a marine biologist, originally from Miami, but you recently relocated to Maui."

Evan nods. "If you wanna ride the big waves, you gotta live near the action."

"Tell us about Jaws."

"Jaws, or Pe'ahi, is the mecca of big wave riding. You have these huge swells rolling across the Pacific, converging upon this one tip of West Maui, building into these massive thirty- to forty-footers."

"Can you describe to us what it's like out there?"

"First, the waves are so big and move so fast that you have to be towed out by jet ski just to catch them. You're putting a lot of trust in these guys and they're risking their lives, same as you, so that means a lot. Once you catch a wave, you're totally focused. The power of the water is so intense, it hisses behind your board and thunders in your ears . . . you can't imagine the raw power of Nature. It's terrifying."

"But if it's so terrifying, why do it? Why risk your life?"

"To me, the whole thing's spiritual. The night before, I can't sleep, I'm so psyched up, so full of adrenaline, but when I'm finally towed out, I just lose myself. No more marital strife, no more bill collectors or problems at work . . . everything just disappears. I become one with the surfboard, one with the ocean, one with the wave, and that's when you truly know freedom. There's only you and the wave, and if you screw up at Jaws, you're in the worst possible place in the world, because that wave isn't just going to bounce you around while you hold your breath, it's going to drive you down into the blackest water you ever saw, rolling you in its mouth like a cat in a washing machine before it finally spits you out. But riding these monsters . . . the energy you feel inside, it heals your soul, it makes you whole again. It's a feeling I can't describe."

"I see," Charlotte says, who obviously doesn't. "John Shinto, you're a family man, with a wife and two kids, a respected dentist. You don't seem to fit the Daredevil profile."

"Well, I think respected dentist is sort of an oxymoron. Most people hate going to the dentist. Did you know the suicide rate among dentists is among the highest of any profession? Anyway, an old friend got me into parachuting when I was at dental school and it became my release. See, I hate the daily grind, can't stand it. Living on the edge relieves my stress."

"Doesn't it scare you?"

"I'll tell you what scares me—getting old. Sitting on the couch when I'm ninety, eating a TV dinner."

"And that justifies being a risk taker?"

"We're not risk takers, we're risk technicians. There's a big difference. Everything we do, we plan."

Murmurs of agreement.

"What about you, Fergie? Did you plan to almost die today?"

Fergie smiles sheepishly. "Some things you plan better than others."

"When you hit that waterspout, what were you thinking?"

"No time to think. Your mind . . . it's sort of in a zone and your eyes, they don't see nuthin' except what's right in front of you, sort of like tunnel vision, and everything's moving in slow motion. 'Course, that funnel wasn't moving in slow motion."

"What about fear? You had to have been afraid."

"No time for that. Fear's what happens when you have time to think. Ask Professor Jonas about that one."

All heads turn, all eyes on Jonas—except Dani's. *Like he can relate to any of this . . .*

Jonas shrugs, looking down at his hands. "When I was piloting deep-sea submersibles, long before most of you were born, I always tried to focus on staying in control of my body. That way, I could focus on the task at hand and not the thought of dying."

"Come on, Professor J," calls out Lexy Piatek. "Tell us about being swallowed whole by the Meg."

Catcalls of encouragement.

"That was different. It wasn't a stunt. Rocketing the minisub down the Meg's throat, that wasn't fear, that was rage . . . rage at knowing I was about to be eaten. Knowing I was dead, I tried to inflict as much damage on the Meg as I could."

"But when you realized you were still alive, stuck in the belly of the beast, that must have been the all-time fear," Jennie says. "Knowing where you were, that you're almost out of air, in total darkness—I would have freaked."

"I did freak, but then I forced myself to breathe, to stay calm enough to allow my mind a chance to think."

Dani shakes her head in disbelief. *This is such bullshit. If only they knew him like I do.*

". . . climbing out of the escape pod into the Meg's stomach, God, what balls."

Susan Ferraris winces at Barry Struhl's anatomical reference.

Jonas shrugs. "Hey, it was my only option. You do what you have to do."

"Crawling around in there . . . ripping out the Meg's heart? Aw, man, that is so awesome," gushes Jason Massett. "See, if I had a choice, that's how I'd want to go. A massive, bloody, heroic death."

The others laugh.

"What did it feel like when you realized you were actually going to live?" asks Dee Hatcher.

"I never knew, I just . . . I just tried to accomplish one small task at a time. When I finally came to, staring into Terry's eyes, well, it was euphoric. But I don't think I'm like you guys. Back then—maybe. Not anymore."

"Don't be so modest," Doc Shinto says. "You conquered your fear. You went back into the Mariana Trench four years later to face Angel."

Jonas shakes his head. "That's not why I returned. My wife was in trouble. At that moment, I didn't really care if I lived or died, as long as I could make her safe."

Dani's eyes glisten. She stares at her father as if seeing him for the first time.

"See, I love that," gushes Dee. "That's true chivalry."

Mia nods. "Most people would have frozen in place, praying while being eaten alive. You're a Daredevil, Professor J. You refuse to lose, just like us."

Murmurs of agreement.

"I was much younger, still full of piss and vinegar. When you get older . . . things change. You change. Your body can't do the things it used to do, so you lose that edge, that swagger. I lost it years ago, my mind's just too stupid to realize it."

"And . . . cut!" Susan Ferraris claps one hand against her clipboard. "Very nice, people, and Jonas, a nice human touch there. I'd love to do more, but we need to transfer all this footage to digital and send everything back to our studio for editing. For now, we're calling it a day."

A few cheers.

"Just remember people, there are hidden cameras all over this ship, so don't come to me later and complain that we caught you in a compromising position. After all, all's fair in reality TV."

CITY OF VICTORIA
VANCOUVER ISLAND, BRITISH COLUMBIA

Considered by many as the premier tourist spot in the Pacific
Northwest, the city of Victoria is located on the southern tip
of Vancouver Island, directly north of Port Angeles, Washington, a short boat ride across the Strait of Juan de Fuca. A
thriving seaport city of 300,000, Victoria, while contempo-
rary Pacific Northwest, is still heavily influenced by its 150-
year-old British colonial heritage.

Terry Taylor exits the small Horizon Airline jet and descends the passenger ramp. Waiting on the tarmac below,
holding up a sign with her name on it, is a brown-haired man
in his late twenties.

At five feet five, Joshua Bunkofske is two inches shorter
than Terry, his baby-face features more high-school student
than scientist. The exception is his hazel eyes, focused and
intense, belying his boyish appearance.

"Joshua?"

"Mrs. Taylor, hi. How were your flights?"

"Fine," she lies. "I brought a bag, they made me check it in."

She leads him to the cargo section of the small plane
where passengers are collecting their belongings. "So, when
do I see the whales?"

"Right now. I have a seaplane that'll take us over to East
Sooke."

"A seaplane?" Her heart skips a beat.

One of the baggage handlers holds up an aluminum piece
of luggage the size of a saxophone case. "There, that one's
mine."

Joshua takes it for her. "It's heavy. What's in it?"

"I'll show you after I see the whales."

TANAKA OCEANOGRAPHIC INSTITUTE
MONTEREY, CALIFORNIA

"This is bullshit!" David Taylor crawls out from under the main circuit board in the lagoon's control room. "Damn control panel's shot."

He looks out the bay windows to the lagoon. The olive-green surface of the arena ripples with the remains of an incoming wave.

He watches another swell roll inside the canal. *Only one way to close those doors now.*

The mid-afternoon sun glistens along the surface, tempting him in its tranquillity. He locates a pair of binoculars. Focuses on the canal.

The upper three feet of the parallel concrete slab walls are visible above the wave tops.

Low tide . . . perfect for diving.

He paces back and forth. Stares at the circuit board. "Screw it, what she doesn't know won't hurt her."

SOOKE INLET
VANCOUVER ISLAND

Joshua banks the five-passenger DeHavilland Beaver slowly over East Sooke National Park's Mount Maguire, the tips of the peak's Douglas firs nearly scraping the bottom of the seaplane's big skids.

Terry grips her seat, holding on as they dip to a lower altitude.

"You okay, Mrs. Taylor?"

"Call me Terry, and yes, it's been a while since I was in one of these single-prop jobs."

"You a nervous flier?"

"I never used to be. Believe it or not, I used to fly VIPs to our facility in similar planes all the time. Jonas used to say I flew with 'reckless abandon.'"

"So what happened?"

"I don't know," she lies. "Guess I sort of lost my adventurous spirit. Take my advice. Stay young."

"You're still young." He winks, causing her to flush.

The seaplane touches down in two-foot seas along the coast of Pike Point. Joshua guides the aircraft to a small pier erected along the rocky shoreline.

Commander Sutera is the first to greet them. "Mrs. Taylor, appreciate you coming on such short notice. The Marine Detachment's been moving whale carcasses out fairly steadily over the last week. We left you two animals to inspect, a female Orca and a male Grey whale."

"The strandings have only been occurring in East Sooke?"

"No. We lost a dozen pilot whales about sixteen days ago up in Bamfield, that's a good sixty miles to the north. The larger strandings began once your shark migrated south into the mouth of the Strait, effectively cutting off the pods' escape route into the Pacific."

"Looks like she found a new home," Joshua declares.

"We told the media the whale deaths are being caused by a toxic algae bloom. That gave us an excuse for closing the Strait to diving, but that won't last long."

"Maybe you'd better show me the bite wounds," Terry says.

Commander Sutera escorts them to the largest of the two carcasses. "The Grey's the freshest. Washed up onshore three nights ago. That's been her pattern. At least one kill every third night. The rest of the time she patrols up and down the Strait, driving the pods crazy."

Sutera and Joshua pull the two end stakes out of the ground and roll back the protective tarp.

Terry gasps.

A series of festering bite marks litter the carcass, some as large and as deep as an aboveground wading pool. Thousands of flies buzz the wounds, accompanied by hundreds of crabs.

Terry feels light-headed. "Teeth. Were there any teeth left behind?"

Commander Sutera shrugs. "We weren't told to look for teeth."

Joshua nods. "Sharks often lose a few teeth when attacking larger prey. I took a quick look but didn't find any."

"Maybe you didn't know where to look. I need gloves and a screwdriver or a knife. And a mask would be appreciated."

TANAKA OCEANOGRAPHIC INSTITUTE
MONTEREY, CALIFORNIA

David climbs to the top of the arena's northern bleachers. Locates the hidden gate in the steel perimeter fencing. Keys open the padlock and walks out onto the twelve-inch-wide ledge of the northern canal wall.

The top of the two concrete barriers stretches out into the Pacific for several hundred yards like a narrow sidewalk before ending at warning buoys and a rusted spool of barbed wire that crosses the width of the canal.

David picks up his scuba gear and carefully starts walking.

An incoming swell moves through the canal, racing for him. He stops, maintaining his balance as the wave rolls along the wall, rising to soak his feet. *Tide's coming in, you don't have much time.*

He walks faster.

Halfway there, and now the waves have increased in ferocity and size. Abandoning his original plan to make it to the end of the wall, he pulls on his flippers, hoists the buoyancy control vest and air tank onto his back, tightens the straps of his tool kit, then secures his mask to his face.

David waits for the next wave to pass, then jumps feetfirst into the canal.

The water is murky, the cold Pacific seeping through his wet suit. Adjusting the air in his vest, he control-sinks to thirty feet, then begins kicking toward the canal doors.

The current is stronger than David expected, forcing him to expend twice as much energy. Ten minutes and his muscles already feel exhausted. Desperate, he descends to seventy feet, the pressure increasing in his ears, the current lessening noticeably.

The bottom comes into view. Clusters of coral have formed along the base of the algae-infested wall, providing a habitat for thousands of brightly colored fish. He spots the outline of a stingray partially hidden in the sand. A moray eel sneaks a peek from its burrow.

Then, from out of the misty periphery, he sees it . . . two King Kong– size doors, rising ominously toward the surface like twin towers. Eighty feet high, eight inches thick, the steel doors have been stuck in the open position for nearly a decade, pushed outward toward the Pacific.

David swims out of the canal. His eyes follow the seafloor, which runs another fifty feet, then ends at a dark, ominous precipice that plunges several thousand feet into the Monterey Submarine Canyon.

Pulling himself away, he moves around the open northern door. Swimming behind the hydraulic hinge, he slips through the crawl space between the door and canal wall and searches for the junction box.

The trashcan-size object is concealed beneath ten years of barnacle growth.

Removing a screwdriver from his satchel, David chips away at the crustaceans that have effectively sealed the outer lid. Within the steel box is a self-contained power source secured within a waterproof rubber housing. The junction box powers a pneumatic internal pump that can open and seal the doors, overriding the control room.

After several minutes David again attempts to pry off the lid.

Still stuck.

He checks his air: *twenty-two more minutes.* He continues chipping away at the cement-like debris until his hand aches. Taking another break, he looks out between the crawl space at open ocean and the rocky edge of the canyon's cliff face.

The Submarine Canyon . . . the place Angel's mother inhabited before Dad killed her. Somewhere down there lies about two million dollars' worth of unfossilized Megalodon teeth.

Stifling a shudder, he returns to the junction box and continues hacking away at the steel lid—

—the sounds echoing between the wall and the steel door.

SOOKE INLET
VANCOUVER ISLAND

Terry ties her long ebony hair into a tight bun, then adjusts the heavy hooded gas mask over her head. Gripping the hand ax tightly in a gloved fist, she moves to the largest of the Grey whale's wounds, perspiration already dripping down her face.

Using the ax, she clears away a swarm of crabs and flies, the latter buzzing angrily around her covered head.

Think about the money. Think about what Jonas will say when he sees you're helping to pay our bills.

Taking a deep breath, she pushes her hand inside the circumference of the gushy, pus-laden wound, choking back a gag reflex.

Blubber . . . sinew . . . you need to find bone.

Abandoning the bite, she moves to another wound, this one a deep gouge located above the whale's mangled left pectoral fin.

Terry hacks away at the periphery of the bite until she reaches the whale's rib cage. Dropping the ax, she shines her flashlight into the wound, feeling along the splintered edges of bone with her free hand.

"Ow!"

The glove around her palm has been severed, her hand bleeding.

She hacks at the spot with the ax, pulling away bloody pulp as the flies continue their relentless attack on her senses and the crabs nip at her arms.

And there it is! An ivory-white tooth, chipped yet still a good six inches long, its point solidly buried between two ribs.

Her thoughts racing, she works to free the fang.

After ten minutes of perspiring labor, she returns to Commander Sutera and Joshua, prize in hand.

Joshua pulls off her hooded mask. She sucks in lungfuls of fresh air, holding up the tooth. "It's for real. I can't believe it, after all these years—" The blood rushes from her face and she drops to her knees, the world spinning.

"You okay?" Joshua asks.

"Just dizzy."

"Take it slow." Sutera hands her a can of soda.

"Thanks. Jonas has the stomach for this stuff, not me."

Joshua helps her to her feet. "Come on, you look like you could use a drink. And let's take care of that hand before infection sets in."

TANAKA OCEANOGRAPHIC INSTITUTE
MONTÈREY, CALIFORNIA

His strength and air depleting rapidly, David finally manages to pry open the lid to the junction box. Turning on his flashlight, he peers inside.

An underwater key pad reflects back at him in the light.

Okay, Grandpa told me the combination code a million times. Let's see, the month of his birthday . . . Mom's . . . Dad's . . . Dani's, and mine.

He punches in 10-7-6-4-6.

A green light activates, indicating the generator is on-line. *Okay, now we're making progress.* He locates the OVER-RIDE switch, then presses the rubber insulated button marked CLOSE.

A thunderous groan of metal bombards his eardrums as the pneumatic hoses activate within the hinges, pulling the doors closed at an agonizing two inches per second. The sound continues for half a minute, and then the doors cease moving.

Damn . . . David presses the CLOSE switch again. The motor grinds, but the doors do not move.

WHOMP!

The right steel door shudders as if sideswiped by a bus.

David removes his hand from the junction box, his heart racing. Cautiously, he peers out between the door and canal wall, the space now wider by a good twelve feet.

Disappearing into the murk is a white caudal fin, two stories from upper lobe to lower.

A jolt of electricity jars David's brain. Dropping his tools and weight belt, he kicks like a madman toward the surface, his nostrils gushing blood as he reaches twenty feet.

David grips the top of the concrete wall and pulls himself up. Tugs off his fins and slips out of the BCD vest, allowing the harness and air tank to fall back into the sea. Balancing atop the wall, he runs back to the arena and the safety of the bleachers as fast as he can—

—nitrogen bubbling in his bloodstream.

ABOARD THE *NEPTUNE*
BANDA SEA
75 NAUTICAL MILES NORTHEAST OF MOLUCCAS

The heavy bass pounding from the speakers reverberates up through the floorboards of the cabin, causing the hammock to vibrate.

Jonas stares at the ceiling, his head aching from lack of sleep. "I really am getting too old for this shit."

Climbing out of the hammock, he slips into a pair of sweatpants, exits his room, and heads below, tracking the source of the disturbance.

"Oh, geez—"

Jonas Taylor had attended numerous fraternity parties back in his undergraduate days at Penn State, and he's been to more than a few of the Navy's infamous "tail-hook" conventions, but neither can hold a candle to the spectacle playing out before his eyes.

The darkened chamber, pulsating with gangsta rap, is backlit with neon purple bulbs, the light combining with clouds of marijuana smoke to create a purple haze. The heavy stench of cheap beer and pot inundates his senses, along with the dozens of naked Daredevils and crew members and Candy Girls, many of whom are bonding sexually right on the makeshift dance floor.

From out of the mist appears a dark-haired, olive-skinned woman, wearing nothing more than a silver chain attached to her belly button ring. "Professor J. I'm Mia. Mia Durante. One of the Hammerheads."

"Yeah, sure, I, uh, didn't recognize you out of uniform."

"Don't look so shocked. We work hard, we like to play hard."

"Yes, well somewhere in this orgy of yours is my seventeen-year-old daughter."

"Relax, it's just herb and beer and lust. Nothing heavy,

just a celebration of life." She hands him the end of her chain. "Want to take me for a walk?"

"Thanks, but I don't think my wife would appreciate that." Unsure of what to do next, he moves from room to room, growing angrier, then finally heads back up the companionway, his clothing and hair now reeking of marijuana smoke. Instead of returning to his cabin, he heads up to the main deck to get some fresh air.

He sees Andrew Fox leaning against the capstan. "Evening, Doc."

"Were you down there? Did you see what's going on?"

"I saw. These Daredevils live fast and party hard. You should see 'em when they get together for one of their parachuting weekends, it's like the last days of Caligula."

"And Dani's down there somewhere. Christ . . . I should've known better than to take her on board a ship used in a Roman Polanski film."

Andrew's laugh is drowned out by flapping canvas as the ship sails into the night.

EAST SOOKE
VANCOUVER ISLAND, BRITISH COLUMBIA

The nearest local watering hole is an English tavern, with boars' heads hanging from the walls above dartboards and black-and-white photos of logging camps and iron mine workers.

Terry nurses her third gin and tonic, her belly warm, the knots in her shoulder muscles finally releasing. "I could get stone-cold drunk right here."

Joshua smiles, rubbing her back.

Commander Sutera is not amused. "We're not paying you three grand a day to get shit-faced, Mrs. Taylor. Now that we know your monster's here, what do we do about her?"

"First, as I told your boy wonder here, she's not my monster, at least not anymore. Second, what do you wanna do with her?"

"What are our options?"

"Well . . ." she drains her drink, "you could hunt her down and kill her, I suppose, but you're gonna need a friggin' cannon to stop her, assuming she ever surfaces." She slurs the last words.

"She has to surface sometime," the commander states.

"Not really, sir," Joshua intervenes. "She's a fish. Technically, she could patrol the Strait for the next twenty years and we'd never see her. What we need is something to lure her to the surface. We could chum."

"Chum?" Terry snorts a laugh. "Joshy boy, you've been watching too many *Jaws* reruns. The only thing that's gonna bring Angel up to us is . . . is . . . hey, where's my suitcase?"

"It's in the jeep," Joshua says. "You want me to get it?"

"No, but you can get me another drink," she giggles.

Sutera and Joshua look at one another.

"At ease men, I'm fine."

"What's inside the case, Mrs. Taylor?"

"I told you to call me Terry." She squeezes Josh's hand. "It's called a thumper. It's a portable training device Jonas used when Angel was just a pup. It sends out low-frequency vibrations, sort of like underwater doodoo drums." She giggles. "I mean voodoo drums. Thump away and Angel'll come running."

Commander Sutera nods. "I'll requisition a boat."

"Whoa, Commander Canada. What're you gonna do after you find her?"

"Kill her, of course. We can't have that fish hunting in the same Straits as our tourists."

"No, no, no. You can't kill her, she's protected. Bet ya didn't know that, did you?"

"I don't give a damn about—"

Joshua holds up his palm, cutting him off. "What were you thinking about doing, Terry?"

Terry smiles a drunken grin. "Well, it just so happens there's a vacancy at the inn back where I live that'd be perfect for our little Angel. All we have to do is show her the way in."

CHAPTER

14

The circle of light . . . so precious, as precious as the air he is sucking into his mouth, as precious as the mask shielding his eyes and nose from his toxic environment.

Jonas wiggles like a tadpole, pushing through tightening hot layers of internal organs, moving almost blindly in the suffocating darkness toward the epicenter of the tremors, the circle of light, like a halo, his only friend.

His head pounds with the reverberations, his eardrums and brain and bones buzzing with each double beat.

Stay focused . . . allow your thoughts to stray and you'll allow the insanity of the act to gain a foothold. Keep moving through the chamber of horrors, and stop that god-awful sound.

He is falling and then he is rising, he is slipping, then he is clawing, precious flashlight in one hand, fossilized Megalodon tooth in the other, the latter clenched so tightly that its serrations are drawing blood.

His heart beats in unison with the infernal sound, his ears pound in rhythm with its incessant vibrations. And then the walls that wedge in his existence—the walls of Jericho— slam-dance against his flushed face, announcing the organ's presence, and he slices through the membrane, hacking and sawing with that serrated edge until the walls split apart and reveal the heart of the beast to him.

The precious light fades, but even by its dim halo Jonas can see the basketball-size organ, thumping and squeezing within its protective hive of blood vessels, singing at him like Poe's telltale heart, mocking him in its unholy thunder. Anger swells and Jonas pushes headfirst into the cardiac chamber, nearly tumbling into oblivion as his host descends rapidly like a 747 airbus hitting wind shear.

The first stab spurts a pint of blood that squelches his light. His mind screams in the darkness, the insanity of his plight asphyxiating his brain. Blindly reaching forward, he clutches the pounding organ to his chest and hacks at its blood vessels like Ahab punishing his white whale.

Bracing his legs, pulling with all his might, praying with all his soul, he bellows into the rapidly draining pony bottle of air like a man awakening in a buried coffin.

The dam bursts, exploding hot blood against his face mask.

The god-awful sound ceases, replaced by a suffocating silence and his own muffled screams—

Unable to breathe, Jonas rolls off his face and awakens, his heart pounding like a timpani drum. "Jesus . . . Christ."

He lies on his back, his eyes focusing on the golden slivers of dawn peeking through the cabin's lone porthole.

A knock, and Erik Hollander enters. "Jonas, you awake?"

He rolls out of the hammock, grimacing as his lower back greets him good morning.

"You okay?"

"Lower back's out again. Wish you had a chiropractor on board."

"Want me to get one of the Candy Girls to massage you?"

Jonas responds with a scowl.

"Okay, but I need you one hundred percent. Big day to-day. The results from the first viewer vote are in, which means we'll be setting up to film the losing team's vote. They have to oust one of their members. Before that all happens, we need footage of you supervising the chum slick."

"Chum slick?"

"It's part of the next Daredevil challenge. The *Neptune*'s entering shark-infested waters, at least that's what the previews will say. We'll want to draw a nice crowd of predators before the teams risk life and limb in the next challenge. See you up on deck in ten for makeup."

For the next five minutes, Jonas forces his body to stretch. He struggles through three sets of twenty push-ups, then shaves and dresses. Instead of heading up on deck, he takes the companionway downstairs to the Daredevils' dorms.

Mia Durante exits the coed bathroom, wearing only a towel. "Hello again."

"Uh, yes, hi . . ."

"Mia Durante."

"Right. Sorry, I'm terrible with names."

"So, when do you think you and I can get together for a little one on one session?"

"One on one?"

"I feel a need to share my thoughts with you. We were told you'd be sort of our Daredevil counselor."

"What is it you need counseling about? Your wardrobe?"

"Cute. What I need is advice from a mature man. These idiots have no appreciation for what's important. Not me. I've seen the other side, I have a good idea what's waiting for us out there."

"Excuse me?"

"Death. The great equalizer. I've died before, or didn't you know?"

"No."

"I'll tell you about it sometime soon, but not now, the

vibes are all wrong." She moves closer, then inhales the aroma of his chest. "Mmm. Animals sense fear, but people do too. You hide it well, Professor J, but I can smell your fear, it runs deep."

"Oh . . . Kay. Listen, I'm sorry but—"

"Do you know why I'm a Daredevil? It's because I've lost all my fear of living."

She twirls around, losing her towel in the process. "Bet you won't forget my name so easily next time we meet." Mia laughs, dragging the towel behind her as she walks away.

"Dad!"

Jonas jumps. He turns to face his daughter, who is wearing a thong bikini. "Jesus, Dani, you want to give me a heart attack? And cover up, you're practically naked."

"Hello? I just saw you staring at that nude woman."

"I wasn't staring. Anyway, forget about me, where were you last night? And why are you dressed like that?"

"I've been in a photo shoot all morning. What are you doing down here? We have a rule, no one over thirty admitted."

"Funny. As a matter of fact, I was looking for you. I thought we could talk."

"About what?"

"College, for one thing. You know, it's still not too late to—"

"College is out. I'm going to be traveling. Europe. Australia. Erik said he could get me work as an extra in a movie filming in Sydney next fall. It's time for me to spread my wings and fly."

"Why can't you fly and still go to college?"

"Dad, I know you don't want to hear this, but I'm not interested in taking prep classes for the whole nine-to-five deal. I want to live my life to its fullest, be like you used to be."

"Me?"

"Yeah. You know, before you got tied down with a family."

"Dani—"

"As long as I've known you, you've been miserable, always stressed out, always worried about money. Look at you now, it's like you've been reborn. I was watching you yesterday up on deck, you were actually smiling. That's the first time I've seen you smile in years."

"Untrue."

"Dad, it's cool. Look, college just isn't for me. And think how much money you'll save in tuition."

"Dani—"

"I gotta run. See you at lunch." She hurries down the corridor. "And quit staring at naked women!"

The sea is calm, the sky a deep blue, not a cloud visible. Captain Robertson has lowered the ship's main and foresails, allowing the *Neptune* to drift.

The upper deck adjacent to the captain's galley has been taken over by the Candy Girls, who are using it as a tanning area, their lubricated flesh glistening as they worship the sun. Cameramen bandy about, sweating profusely as they record everything for "stock footage."

Jonas joins Andrew Fox on the main deck. The shark photographer is pulling on a wetsuit as his men lower one of the shark cages overboard.

"Going for a morning dip, Andrew?"

"Just a little appetizer before the main course." Andrew points port side.

The surface of the sea is covered in crimson, the chum slick pooling around the ship. A dozen dorsal fins cut the surface, then scatter as the super yacht, *Coelacanth,* pushes closer through a spreading pool of cow blood and fish innards.

Behind the vessel, being towed by cable, is a large floating object—a freshly killed Humpback whale.

The *Coelacanth*'s twin engines idle in neutral as the vessel's crew, all natives of Borneo, release the 33,000-pound carcass to the sharks.

Within seconds, the predators swarm upon the floating

mass, biting and flailing their streamlined bodies with reckless abandon, tearing off huge chunks of flesh.

Jonas grips the rail, his anger building. "Where's Hollander?"

ABOARD THE SUPER YACHT, *COELACANTH*

The sleek super yacht's interior is a plush palace decorated in polished mahogany and teak. Located in the lowest of the superstructure's three upper decks is a galley, pantry, crews' mess, crews' quarters, laundry room, tool, and supply room. The middle deck contains a sky lounge and VIP suite, as well as the captain's stateroom, located just behind the wheelhouse.

The upper deck remains the private habitat of the yacht's owner. Walls and cabinets are planked in a deep cherry wood, the floors black onyx marble. Large tinted bay windows surround the master suite, which is complete with gymnasium, Jacuzzi, entertainment room, office, and private kitchen.

Built in the Abeking shipyard in West Palm Beach, Florida, for the late Mrs. Evelyn Maren, wife of the deceased real estate mogul, Jonathan B. Maren, the vessel is all that remains of an inheritance left to the departed couple's only child.

Michael Maren is in his master suite dressed in a bathrobe. The wide end of his binoculars poke between the slats of his shiny chrome venetian blinds, his eyes focused on the man standing by the port-side rail of the Spanish galleon. "You've aged, my friend. The years haven't been kind."

"Who are you talking to?"

Maren cringes at the woman's New England accent. "I'm talking to myself, if you must know." He stares at Jonas for another minute, then crosses the plush ivory-colored carpet to his private office.

Maren's assistant, Allison Petrucci, sits before three large computer monitors and a bank of closed-circuit television screens, rubbing baby lotion over her sun-scorched skin. The petite twenty-five-year-old brunette from Boston wears no makeup and bites her nails, more to keep them short than out of habit.

"Any change?"

"No," she mumbles, polishing off the remains of a turkey sandwich. She pauses to wash the mouthful down with a swig of diet soda, then points to the main sonar screen.

A white blip appears.

"He'll ascend every so often as high as fourteen hundred feet, then return to deeper water. The dead whale has his attention, but I doubt he'll rise any higher until the sun begins to set."

"When's the last time he fed?"

She glances at a wall clock. "Eighty-three hours and counting. It'll happen tonight, bet the farm on it." She turns to face him. "Hey, don't you think you ought to radio Hollander?"

"Screw him. He wanted reality television, reality is what he'll get."

ABOARD THE *NEPTUNE*

"For the last time, Professor, it's reality TV. Whales do actually die in reality, right?"

"This was arranged and you know it," Jonas says, stalking the man across the main deck.

"Look, I honestly don't know what you're talking about. The crew of the *Coelacanth* has standing orders to locate bait as needed. Obviously we got lucky, end of story."

"I demand to know how this whale was killed."

"Demand? Jonas, you're not in any position to demand anything. Look, maybe the whale died of old age. Maybe a Greenpeace ship inadvertently clipped it. Who the hell cares, as long as we can use it for our purposes. Now get to your mark or I'll dock you a day's pay."

His blood pressure soaring, Jonas takes his place next to Charlotte. The supermodel adjusts her silver and crimson one-piece Daredevil swimsuit, then nods to Susan Ferraris. "Anytime."

The director shoots Jonas an evil eye. "That's twice you've been late, Taylor. The next I'll be grabbing you by your—"

"And five, four, three . . ."

Charlotte activates her smile. "And welcome back. Earlier today, we finished tallying your votes, which overwhelmingly gave the first round of competition to the Makos and their incredible parachute jump into a waterspout. As you know, by losing the round, the Hammerheads were forced to vote one of their team members off the ship. Jason Massett is our first Daredevil casualty, and we're with him now. Jason, any final words before the chopper takes you back to civilization?"

"Yes, Charlotte." The five-foot-eight former lacrosse player from Manhattanville College flashes a good-natured smile. "Obviously I'm disappointed, not just for myself but for my family and friends back home. However, just to show I'm still a Hammerhead, we've decided that my departure from the ship will count as today's team stunt."

"And what will you be doing?"

The camera pans back to a twelve-inch-wide, eight-foot-long wooden beam that has been hastily mounted over the starboard rail.

"Charlotte, back in the seventeenth century, Spanish galleons like the *Neptune* were often threatened by pirates. Innocent crewmen were made to walk the plank, only to die a hideous death in shark-infested waters. Today, I'll be swimming through these same waters as I make my way to the *Coelacanth* for my journey home."

"Wow, what a stunt. Jonas, any words of advice?"

"Yes, don't do it."

A prerecorded drum roll echoes across the main deck.

The remaining members of Team Hammerhead stand at attention along either side of the plank.

Michael Coffey leads his teammates in a salute. "We honor our brother, Jason Massett, and pray for his safe journey."

Jason hugs his teammates good-bye, then, head held high, he climbs onto the edge of the plank and starts walking. Three feet from the end, he turns and winks at one of the Candy Girls, a Reese Witherspoon lookalike named Natasha, then swan dives into the sea.

Daredevils, Candy Girls, and crewmen rush to the side as the cameras continue to roll.

Safe within his shark cage, ten feet underwater, Andrew Fox aims his camera through an opening in the stainless-steel bars, capturing the scene from below.

The underwater realm swarms with more than two hundred dark projectiles, the sharks darting in and out of clouds of vermillion mist to attack the whale carcass.

Jason breaststrokes calmly along the surface, moving at a controlled speed. He keeps his head above the chum, which pools around his outstretched neck as he swims along the periphery of the slick, the super yacht seventy-five yards away.

Dark fins surface to encircle him, slipping in and out of the turbid waters.

Dusky sharks, a few blues. No real man-eaters. Watch for the brown dorsals, the Gray Reef sharks can get aggressive if they think you want their meal . . .

Below, Andrew Fox zooms in on a school of golden hammerheads, circling well below the melee.

And then the underwater photographer spots the 1,800

pound, sixteen-foot creature rising slowly from the depths. Sees the telltale pattern of stripes . . . the blunt nose . . .

Tiger shark . . . oh Jesus—

Jason increases his pace as he swims beyond the chum pool to cheers. Smiling from ear to ear, he rolls onto his back and kicks up a storm. "Do it, Hammerheads, beat the—

"Ahhh . . ."

A hundred unseen daggers rip into Jason Massett's buttocks and pelvis as he is driven out of the water.

The Tiger shark plows him backward through the sea, shakes loose a hunk of flesh, then releases the Daredevil, whose bloodcurdling scream shatters the calm. "Ahhh . . . help! Help me!"

Jennie Arnos and Doc Shinto are the first to answer the call. Within seconds, the heavy whine of their Zodiac blots out the shouting crewmen.

Jonas stands atop the capstan, focusing on the scene through a pair of binoculars. As he watches, the Tiger shark circles back along the surface to launch a second attack.

My God . . .

Dani pushes through the crowd and clutches her father's arm. "Do something!"

Jonas looks into his daughter's frightened eyes, his expression telling her everything.

Jennie Arnos races the motorized raft to the spot of the attack as the predator charges Jason again.

"Ahh . . . ahh—"

Jason flails at the shark, then is dragged under just as Doc Shinto reaches overboard to grab his hand. "Lost him . . . where'd he go?"

"There!" Jennie points.

Doc falls sideways against the opposite side of the raft and grabs the Daredevil by the roots of his hair just before his head disappears again. Reaching down with his free hand, he secures Jason beneath his armpit and forcibly drags him onto the raft.

Blood gushes everywhere, disguising a ring of puncture wounds that encircle what's left of his waist. Jason's eyes are wild, his mouth gasping at air.

Forcing herself not to look, Jennie whips the Zodiac around and accelerates back to the *Neptune*.

Jason, deathly pale, convulses as he gazes up at Shinto. "Doc, I can't feel my legs. Are my legs still there, Doc?"

Doc Shinto chokes out an affirmative, then presses a blood-soaked towel against the spurting gaps across Jason's stomach, unable to bring himself to look at the ravaged pelvis.

"It's rising, Doc, the numbness is rising. Oh, God, Doc, I'm scared."

"Hang on," Jennie yells.

Michael Coffey and Evan Stewart dangle from the bottom of the cargo net secured to the starboard side of the Spanish galleon. Reaching down, they lift their fallen comrade and place him in a hammock-like sling, where he is quickly hauled up to the main deck. The sheath is soaked in blood within seconds.

Jason's body sprawls out on deck as a team of medics and cameramen swarm him. Like a pit crew at the Indianapolis 500, the EMTs work feverishly on the semiconscious Daredevil, his dark blood pooling beneath them.

"Come on, Jay, stay with us!"

"Get me two more bags of O-positive!"

"It's no good, he's losing it faster than we can pump it in him. Jesus, look at his pelvis. It took his right hip and half his buttocks."

Dani stands on the capstan next to her father, unable to take her eyes off the scene. Blood is everywhere, she has never seen so much of it before, even in the worst horror movies. *How much blood can a human body actually hold?*

The EMTs look at one another, then abruptly stop working. One checks his watch. "That's it. Time of death, fifteen hundred hours, seven minutes."

An eerie silence grips the crowd.

The ship creaks beneath them. A gust of wind flaps harmlessly against the mizzen sail.

Slowly, a chorus of sobs overtakes the wind.

Dani chokes back tears as she buries her face against her father's chest, forcing herself not to look at the inanimate object that, only minutes ago, had been Jason Jon Massett.

COMMUNITY HOSPITAL OF THE MONTEREY PENINSULA
MONTEREY, CALIFORNIA

Patricia Pedrazzoli hurries through the basement corridor of the hospital. She locates the door labeled "DCS" and enters in a huff.

There is no nurse on duty. "Hello?"

"Back here, please."

She follows a man's voice to a small emergency room. Only one of the three beds is occupied.

David Taylor is lying on his back, an oxygen mask strapped to his face.

"Oh my God—"

"He'll be okay." A doctor approaches, dressed in hospital greens. "Trey Harris, I'm the physician on duty."

"Patricia Pedrazzoli. What happened to him?"

"Decompression sickness. Comes from ascending too fast on a dive. The reduction in pressure causes nitrogen to dissolve in the tissues and blood. The bubbles disrupt cellular activity, affecting the organs."

"David was scuba diving?"

"He won't admit to it, but the symptoms are pretty clear. His skin and joints were burning, which is what brought him in. By the time we got him down here, he was doubled over in pain. Fortunately it's just a mild case, the oxygen should clear his symptoms fairly easily. If not, we'll transfer him to a hyperbolic chamber for repressurization."

"Can I talk to him?"

"Yes, but go easy, he's still a bit nauseous."

Patricia moves to his bed and pulls up a chair. "David?"

He moans. Opens an eye. "Don't . . . tell." His voice is muffled by the mask.

"I am going to tell. Diving alone . . . are you crazy? You could've died."

He struggles to sit up. Pulls the mask away. "My mother, she'll give herself a stroke. I won't dive alone again, I promise."

"Put that mask back on your face. This isn't fair, you know. I don't mind helping your mother out, but I don't have time to baby-sit you, either. Where were you diving anyway?"

"The canal. I was trying to shut the canal doors."

"That's no excuse."

"Never happen again."

"I said put that mask back on."

"I need to speak with Uncle Mac."

"Forget it. Mac doesn't even have access to a phone."

"Take me to him?"

"Absolutely not. Now lie back and get some rest. I'll be back tomorrow morning to take you home. But I swear, David, if I catch you anywhere near the ocean, I'll call the police and have them lock you up until your mother returns."

BAMFIELD/BARKLEY SOUND
VANCOUVER ISLAND, BRITISH COLUMBIA

Barkley Sound is a vast marine habitat that cuts through the western coastline of Vancouver Island, running inland more than thirty miles to Port Alberni. Fed by three main channels and the seaward extensions of a group of narrow fjord inlets, the heavily trafficked waterway plays host to rocky coastlines, islands and reefs, as well as caves and tide pools.

On the northwest banks of Barkley Sound lies the city of Ucluelet, a popular destination for tourists seeking to whale watch, fish, dive, and just get back to Mother Nature. Across the waterway on the southwest bank is the tiny village of Bamfield, a sparse community of under three hundred surrounded by Indian Reserves and sections of the Pacific Rim National Park.

In 1972, a consortium of five western Canadian universities established the Bamfield Marine Station, a teaching and research facility that provides year-round assistance to visiting scientists and students studying the marine sciences. In addition to its academia, Bamfield also serves as an outpost for the Canadian Coast Guard Pacific Region.

It is not the hangover that forces Terry Taylor to pry open her eyes, nor is it the cotton mouth. It is the incessant banging on the door, reverberating sounds that echo in her skull and force her to crawl off the strange bed in the strange room, in the—

"—where the hell am I?"

She rolls painfully to her feet. Struggles to walk against the nausea. Looking down against the vertigo, she realizes she is wearing a man's XL gray tee-shirt and her underwear . . . and nothing else.

Jesus . . . what the hell happened last night?

The banging draws her attention away from her gurgling stomach. She unlocks the bolt, then dashes to the bathroom and slams the door shut a second before she vomits.

Joshua Bunkofske enters his efficiency, carrying a plastic container of breakfast and a Styrofoam cup of coffee. "Terry? You okay in there?"

"Go away."

He sits on the edge of the bed and reads the morning newspaper.

Terry emerges ten minutes later, pale and in pain. "Where the hell am I and what is that god-awful smell?"

"You're in my room at the Marine Station in Bamfield and that smell is breakfast."

"Toss it outside. What I need is aspirin and my clothes."

"Of course." He looks under the bed and locates the missing items, then removes a bottle of Advil from a nightstand drawer.

Terry returns to the bathroom. She dresses slowly, mindful of her pounding head. Swallows four Advil, then swishes the remains of a bottle of mouthwash.

Joshua looks up as she steps out of the bathroom. "You okay?"

"Far from it." She nods at the unmade bed. "We didn't . . . you know—"

"No. You passed out in the jeep. No other rooms were available at the station except mine. But, hey, I'm game if you are."

"Stop it. Why are we here?"

"You said you wanted to recapture the Meg. I have access to a boat and supplies. With a little luck, we should make it down to Monterey within the week."

"You're insane. You expect to lead that monster eight hundred miles down the Pacific coast?"

"Yes, but we'll be taking the highway, not the ocean. Remember back a few years when a pregnant Blue whale was struck by a motorboat in Grays Harbor? Sea World transported the mother using a mobile tank they constructed out of two trailers. It's like a giant bathtub, open at the top, containing its own seawater supply and circulating pump."

"I know. Jonas was there, he supervised the crew when they loaded the whale into the unit by crane. He even designed the inflatable padding to support the creature's weight."

"And Angel's not nearly as large as a Blue whale. What we'll do is bait one of the whale carcasses with enough drugs to knock her out, then use that gizmo of yours to bring her to the surface. We'll hook her, haul her to the harbor, then load her into the trailer before she knows what happened. Two days later, she's safe and sound, back in the lagoon."

"And I suppose you already cleared this with Sea World?"

"Spoke to a buddy of mine this morning. The crane belongs to a local cargo service, so it's already at the harbor. Sea World only needs a six-hour notice to move the trailer into position."

"And exactly what do you get out of this?"

"You mean, besides a chance to get to know you better?" He loses the smile. "Okay, what I want is a supervisory position at the Institute working with Angel. I want a six-figure salary and benefits, the rest we'll work out as we go."

"That baby face of yours is deceptive, you're actually a greedy little shit, aren't you?"

"Hey, I'm just like everyone else, trying to keep my head above water. Besides, that creature's going to make your family a fortune. If I can help recapture it, then I deserve a taste of the pie." He winks.

Terry feels herself growing angrier. "Listen, hotshot, what if I said I just wanted to collect my fee and go home?"

"That's your prerogative, of course. But it's an awful lot of money to be walking away from. At least let me show you the boat."

The Canadian Coast Guard Cutter *Cape Calvert* is a multi-task medium endurance vessel relegated for Search and Rescue, as well as fisheries patrol in Barkley Sound and the west coast of Vancouver Island. Forty-eight feet in length, fourteen feet in breadth, she is powered by two caterpillar diesel engines that can achieve a maximum speed of twenty-five knots.

Terry stares pie-eyed at the cutter, its scarlet-painted hull and white wheelhouse glistening in the late morning sun. "This is a joke, right?"

"She's all we need."

"You're not real bright for a scientist, are you? Angel's at least twenty feet bigger than your whole boat, and I know she can outswim it."

"Okay, the truth is she's the only boat I could get my hands on at short notice, but we'll be fine. The cutter can haul up to one hundred and fifty tons, and she's equipped with an excellent sonar and fish detector. None of the attacks have been in daylight, which means Angel's become sensitive to light. We'll just keep close to the coast at night when she's more likely to surface. It'll all work out, I promise."

"And I promise that you have no idea what you're dealing with." She glances at her watch. "Dammit, I forgot to call my son." She removes her cell phone from her belt and dials her father's house.

No answer.

She tries the Institute. "Christ, where the hell is he?"

"I'm sure he's fine. Come aboard, I want to show you our sonar system and fish-finder. If Angel gets anywhere near our boat, we'll know it."

She hesitates.

"Terry, we're not leaving the dock. Come on."

She steps on board, more to test her nerve than appease Josh. "If I decide to go, we need to agree on a few things. First, activating the thumper will get Angel's attention, but I don't want that fish within a hundred yards of this vessel."

"Not a problem, we can tow it from a buoy. What else?"

"I assume you have a crew?"

"A local fisherman and an ex-Navy guy. They do odds and ends for me. I'll cover them, but I expect to be reimbursed."

She points to the Zodiac mounted in the stern. "I want that motorized raft gassed and ready to launch at a moment's notice, and I want a weapon on board."

"A weapon? Like what? A howitzer?"

"I'm serious. I want an insurance policy, just in case things go bad. Something that can stop a tank."

"You just got done telling Commander Sutera that Angel's a protected species."

"So let them put me in jail. I'm not taking this journey without it."

COMMUNITY HOSPITAL OF THE MONTEREY PENINSULA
MONTEREY, CALIFORNIA

David opens his eyes. He is in a different hospital room, the morning sun peeking behind a window shade. A wall clock reads 6:45.

He sits up in bed. The pain is gone, replaced by pangs of hunger.

He finds his clothes laid out on a chair. He uses the bathroom, dresses, then leaves the room in search of breakfast.

He strolls by open rooms, stopping occasionally to listen in. After a half dozen rooms he realizes he is on a children's floor.

An idea hits him. He locates the nurses' station. "Hi, I'm looking for Athena Holman."

"Room three-seventeen."

David follows the signs. Locates the room and enters.

The girl is in bed, her eyes half-open and glazed over. An untouched breakfast tray is by her side. The television is playing softly.

David approaches. "Hi, Atti."

No response.

He sits on the edge of her bed. "Don't you remember me? I'm Masao's grandson."

Her eyes open wider. "Masao?"

"That's right. You and I met before, a few summers ago I think. Do you remember me now?"

She stares at his face. Nods.

"Are you doin' okay?"

She nods.

"Good. I heard you had a tough time of it, seeing my grandfather drown and all. I'm sorry you had to—"

She turns away, her attention refocused on the television. She turns up the volume.

"... *the Phillies lost to the Reds last night, six to three, but Ryan Howard hit career home run number seven hundred and fifty-six, bringing him within three of tying Barry Bonds's all-time record. The Phils are off today, but travel to Pac Bell Park for a four-game series with our Giants beginning Friday night. In other games, the Dodgers rallied in the bottom of the eighth to—*"

Atti turns off the television. "Grandma says I get to go home soon. She says she'll take me to see Ryan Howard break the record."

"Cool." He points to a piece of toast. "You eating that?"

"No."

He spreads grape jam on the slice of burned bread and takes a bite. "Can we talk about my grandfather?"

Her expression darkens and she turns away. He notices her hands are quivering.

"Angel was in the lagoon when he died, wasn't she, Atti? That's what gave my grandfather a heart attack. It was Angel."

She nods into the pillow.

I knew it! "Atti, don't tell anyone else about this, okay?"

"What're you gonna do?"

He leans over and whispers into her ear. "I'm going to recapture her."

CHAPTER

15

ABOARD THE *NEPTUNE*
PHILIPPINE SEA
473 MILES SOUTHWEST OF THE MARIANA TRENCH

Jonas Taylor leans against the starboard rail, watching the western horizon fade in a final spark of crimson.

The arrival of dusk brings a chill, but it is not just in the air.

Jason Massett's death has left a heavy pall over the ship. The Daredevil's girlfriend, Natasha, is under heavy sedation. Groups have segregated themselves throughout the vessel, the series producers holed-up in the captain's gallery, the Daredevils in their rec room, the Candy Girls in their dorm.

Only Jonas remains outside on the bloodstained deck, a lone sentinel standing guard over the contents of a makeshift body bag.

Another case of youth corrupted by the mind-set of immortality.

Many years ago Jonas had felt the same way, risking his life on deep-sea dives, believing he'd live forever. He had cheated death several times, the "hero" who had battled the world's most fearsome predator and lived to tell the tale.

The problem with being a hero was that all heroes eventually die, either devoured in the jaws of their enemy or succumbing to the ravages of age. To Jonas Taylor, a man in his early sixties and the father of two, death is no longer an abstract concept, it is the harsh reality that there is more sand in the lower bulb of the hourglass than the upper, that death will win the final contest. It is knowing that a life-threatening illness could reveal itself tomorrow, or an accident could leave him crippled for the rest of his days.

Jonas is consumed by thoughts of death. He dreams of dying, of lying in the casket as it is lowered into the ground. The thought of leaving this world terrifies him, and, not being a religious man, he is far from comforted by the possibilities of an afterlife.

Where did the years go? What have I accomplished?

Jonas looks at the sea, his eye catching movement.

The bloated carcass of the Humpback whale heaves as it rolls, revealing its ravaged underbelly. Dorsal fins continue to slice the surface, the sea's tranquillity interrupted every so often by a violent thrash.

What happened to all my goals, my dreams? Is it too late to find meaning, or have I become as obsolete as that whale?

A cold wind whips across the deck, causing him to shiver. He tucks his knees into his chest, the annoying arthritis in his left knee stifling the movement. He recalls a poem he had been composing for his memoirs.

The immortality of my youth lacked all direction, avoided truth,
Hustling through my middle age, I burnt through years lost in a haze,
The bells now toll from Father Time,
Fortunes fade, and so do mine . . .

Jonas stares at the darkening horizon, his thoughts lost in its symbolism.

He fails to notice the sudden disappearance of the sharks.

There is no lack of testosterone in the Daredevils' lounge.

"The rules of the contest are clear," Michael Coffey states. "The Makos either complete their stunt or forfeit the contest."

"Who died and made you king?" Jennie demands. "We're here to honor Jason's memory, not to discuss the show."

"I don't know," Doc Shinto says. "What happened out there today . . . I can't stop thinking about it. It was sick."

"It was exactly what we signed on for," retorts Evan Stewart. "Personally, I think it was typical Jason. I've seen him body-surfing at Jaws. I think part of him wanted to die that way."

Dee Hatcher drains her beer. "It's true. Jason knew how to represent. To Jason."

"To Jason." The Daredevils raise their beers.

"This is bullshit," Coffey says, pacing the room. "Jason screwed up out there and everyone here knows it. We've all swum with sharks before, and I specifically reminded him to wade through the chum, not to thrash. It was his goofing around that attracted the Tiger shark. I should have done the damn stunt myself."

"Wish you had," Fergie mumbles.

Coffey glances down at the Aussie. "You, of all people, should be on my side. Nobody felt this way last season after Diane died. We all agreed we'd honor her death by going on. Does Jason deserve anything less?"

"I'm just not ready to dive right back into the killing field," Lexy answers. "I'm into these stunts as much as the rest of you, but I'm not ready to be eaten alive. Someone should have spotted that Tiger shark."

"That's a lame excuse, Lexy, and you know it." Evan Stewart removes his shirt, revealing a series of nasty scars crisscrossing his mid-section. "You see this? That's from a three-thousand-pound Great White. Bastard got me while I was surfing in Australia. First thing I did after leaving the hospital was to grab my board and get back out on the waves. If you guys stop competing now, you'll lose that edge forever. Lexy's already losing it."

"Fuck you, Evan."

"Knock it off," Jennie Arnos yells, quieting the group. "Come morning, we're all getting back in the water, *all of us*, but tonight . . . tonight is for Jason, and nothing competes with his death."

"Nothing can compete with this," Susan Ferraris whispers. "Andrew, play it back again."

Andrew Fox rewinds the underwater footage he took of the attack on Jason Massett. "You sure you want to show this? I mean, it's pretty gruesome, even for reality TV."

"Are you kidding? It's a ratings bonanza."

Erik Hollander looks worried.

"What's wrong?" Susan asks. "You're not going soft on me, are you?"

"I was just wondering, you know, what if things got even bloodier?"

"Bloodier than this? Don't tease me."

"Our next location's supposed to be a Sperm whale nursery. Who knows what could happen."

"We're not going anywhere until the Makos respond to the Hammerheads' challenge," Susan reminds him. "They are going to go through with it, aren't they?"

"Latest word is the stunt's set for seven A.M."

A three-quarter moon slips behind towering cumulus clouds, casting an incandescent glow in the eastern sky.

Danielle Taylor creeps barefoot up the companionway, her hormones overpowering her earlier queasiness. Reaching the main deck, she heads forward, the night air combining with the thought of Jason Massett's ravaged corpse more than a bit unnerving.

She locates the Zodiac beneath the bowsprit mast. Fergie is lying in the inflatable raft, his body covered by a wool blanket.

"Lovely evening, isn't it?"

"It's freezing, and that body bag gives me the creeps. Why couldn't we do this below?"

"Too many eyes, too many cameras. Besides, I'll keep you warm." He pulls back the blanket, revealing his naked body and a six-pack of beer. "Thought you might want to sink a few."

"Yeah, but where's yours?" She strips off her sweatsuit and climbs into his arms.

Jonas stares at the wooden beams above his head, unable to sleep. The angle of the hammock is creating undue stress on his arthritic left knee, and an old rotator cuff injury in his right shoulder aches too much for him to lie on that side.

But it is the pain in his heart that is keeping him awake.

God, I miss Tee. Wish we were lying together in our bed, snuggling beneath the quilt. Life's so short, and here I am, wasting our time together. How am I ever going to get through another four-and-a-half weeks without her?

The stateroom is stuffy, the scent of dried wood heavy in his sinuses. Trickles of sweat run down the small of his back. Rolling out of the hammock, he crosses the room to the portal, unseals the window, and pushes it open.

A cool breeze whistles through the cabin.

Then he sees the glow.

The sea beneath the whale carcass illuminates turquoise with it. *Must be the* Neptune's *underwater lights.* He pushes his face through the portal, craning his neck to get a better look.

Then another possibility seeps through the cobwebs of his brain.

"No, it can't be her . . . could it?"

Jonas bolts out of his cabin and sprints up the flight of steps, nearly knocking over Captain Robertson.

"Easy, Taylor, what's the hurry?"

"The *Neptune*'s underwater lights . . . are they on?"

"Not that I know of. Why?"

"I think something's happening beneath the whale carcass."

Jonas dashes up the remaining steps to the main deck.

Captain Robertson pulls out his two-way radio. "Mr. Lavac, power up the underwater lights."

"Yes, sir."

Jonas hustles over to the starboard rail just as the underwater lights illuminate the sea, creating a luminescent azure pond around the *Neptune*. The whale carcass glows from below, dollar-size fragments of meat twirling in the crossing beams of light.

Captain Robertson joins him on deck. "So? Find what you were looking for?"

"I thought . . . it looked like something was glowing beneath the carcass. Maybe I imagined it, I don't know. Whatever it was, it's gone."

Robertson grins. "Pyrotechnics of the deep. Probably a school of siphonophore coming up from the abyss to feed. I hear some exceed eighty feet. Their bioluminescence is amazing."

"Yeah, maybe. But there's another creature whose hide appears ghostly as well, and it's not a gelatinous eel."

The captain slaps him across the shoulder blade. "Relax, man, you're living in the past. Come on, join me for a nightcap, it'll help you sleep. Been a rough day for all of us."

"Think I'll pass."

"Suit yourself." Jonas watches him head aft toward his stateroom.

The underwater lights power off, leaving only the waxing moon to light Jonas's way.

The former deep-sea submersible pilot stares at the dark shadow that is the dead whale. *Nothing there. Keep it together, Jonas, don't go senile on me just yet.*

Still too hyped to sleep, he decides to walk the main deck, hoping to clear his mind.

He hears the whispers as he approaches the bow.

Jonas follows the sounds to the Zodiac. Two people are hiding beneath a blanket, obviously making out.

Jonas smiles, recalling a few memories from his college days. *God, what happened to all the years . . .*

The blanket slips. Jonas recognizes the woman on top.

"Danielle Taylor!"

"Oh, shit!" Dani folds like an accordion, then whips the blanket around her naked torso before making a mad dash for the nearest companionway.

Still in shock, Jonas looks down at the exposed figure sprawled across the raft.

"Uh . . . evening, Professor Jonas. Just out for a stroll, are you?"

"We've already had one death today, Mr. Ferguson. Would you like to be number two?"

"Easy, big fella. Your daughter's all grown up, if you haven't noticed. At some point you've got to let her make her own decisions."

Fists balled, Jonas fights the urge to pummel the cocky young Australian. "Now listen carefully, hotshot. The law says she's a minor, at least for another week, but no matter how old she is, she'll always be my little girl. As for you, I know what you're after, and I know how this'll come out in the end, so let's just end it with this: I catch you with her again, and you'll wish I had fed you to the sharks."

MOUNT MADONNA
WATSONVILLE, CALIFORNIA

The midday sky is a brilliant royal blue, not a cloud in sight.

David Taylor wipes his wet palms against his sweat-soaked shorts, adjusts the bill of his Philadelphia Phillies baseball cap, then continues pushing his bike up the gravel-covered shoulder of the single-lane highway.

The boy has been riding for nearly five hours and he is exhausted. Having slipped out of the hospital unnoticed, he had hitchhiked back to his grandfather's home, filled a backpack with supplies, then called his mother on her cell phone to check in.

"David, are you sure you'll be all right? I may be another day or two up here."

"Mother, I'm fine. The fridge is stocked, and I have plenty to do. By the way, where's Uncle Mac staying? I wanted to send him a get-well card."

He had found the treatment center in the Yellow Pages, then called for directions.

The ride down the Pacific Coast Highway had been a little harrowing, the highway east through Watsonville a breeze. After a quick bathroom and breakfast break at a Food Mart, he had started the long hike up Highway 152.

The incline had taken his legs after ten minutes.

Once home to the Ohlone Indian tribe, Mount Madonna is part of the Santa Cruz Mountain range. Topped with grasslands and a vast expanse of redwood forest, the majority of the mountain is now a protected state park, offering the public views of Monterey Bay to the west, the Santa Clara Valley to the east.

It is 1:30 before David reaches the access road leading to Narconon.

The Northern California Drug and Alcohol Treatment facility is located on thirty-two acres atop Mount Madonna. More mountain lodge than medical building, the retreat offers its residents a chance to commune with Nature during their recovery, with natural trails and views that overlook the Pajaro Valley.

Causes of alcohol and drug addiction can be traced to hereditary disease, mental health issues, or the addict's environment. The philosophy at Narconon is to help the patient through the difficult withdrawal stage through a strict vitamin regiment, then address the causes of addiction by combining individualized courses with peer therapy, all leading to putting the individual back in charge of their lives. While recovery remains a lifetime commitment and there are never any guarantees, seven in ten patients graduating from Narconon remain drug-free after five years, far higher than most conventional programs.

David parks his bike against a tree, then follows a path to the lobby entrance.

Slipping past the main desk, he hurries down a corridor, finding his way to the closed doors of a classroom. He peeks inside the window.

A dozen people are seated in a circle. Mac is not among them.

"Hey, kid, you shouldn't be in here."

David's heart jumps. He turns, half expecting to be arrested and beaten.

The man is in his early thirties, brown hair and green eyes, dressed in jeans and an old kelly-green Eagles football jersey. "Relax, kid, I'm not a counselor. What're you doing here?"

"I'm looking for a friend. James Mackreides?"

"Yeah? And how is it you know Mac?"

"He's my godfather. I need to see him about something. Family business."

"Didn't know Mac had any family. What's your name?"

"David. David Taylor."

"Now that name I've heard. I'm Rob Parker. Mac's sponsor."

"What's a sponsor?"

"A sponsor's the guy Mac needs to call when he stumbles in his sobriety."

"How's he doing?"

"He's angry and in denial, all par for the course. Come on, I'll take you to him."

Parker leads David down a narrow corridor and outside to a pool. They cross the deck, stopping at the wood door of a sauna. "Mac's inside. Spends a lot of time in there. Be nice to him, he's had a rough go of it."

David tugs open the door and enters.

A wave of dry heats greets him, baking his face.

"Shut the fucking door!"

A lone figure is lying on a wood bench, his head and waist wrapped in towels.

"Uncle Mac?"

Mac removes the cloth from his face. "David? Jesus, kid, what're you doing here?"

"I came to see you."

"Your dad and mom here?"

"No, just me."

Mac sits up. "How the hell did you get here? Ah, who cares, it's nice to see a friendly face. So what's up?"

"Angel's back."

"Angel?" Mac chuckles. "Come on, kid—"

"I saw her. I was diving in the canal, checking out the junction box and I—"

"You went diving by yourself?"

"Forget that, the point is—"

"Where's your mother?"

"She had to fly up to Vancouver on business. Anyway, I saw her, I saw Angel, at least I saw her tail. She was moving into deep water, descending into the Monterey Canyon."

"Let me get this straight. You came all the way up here to see me because you thought you saw Angel's tail."

"Not thought, I did see her, and Atti saw her too. Angel was in the lagoon the day my grandfather died."

Mac's eyes become intense. "Atti told you that?"

"That's what I just said. Now come on and get dressed, I need your help. We have to capture her before—"

"Capture her? Whoa, hold on there, Bucko." Mac reaches for a plastic container of water, then pours the contents over the rocks piled atop the sauna heater's grill, unleashing a cloud of steam. "Just for argument's sake let's say you're right. Let's say that freak of Nature did make it back to California waters. What makes you think I'd want to recapture her?"

"Are you kidding? This is our big chance. Do you know how long my grandfather waited for this?"

"Your grandfather? Listen, kid, your grandfather hated that monster. Her scent, or her ghost, or whatever the hell it was kept his beloved whales from inhabiting his lagoon. He blamed that monster for every bad break he had in the last twenty years."

"You're wrong. Maybe that's what he wanted you and my parents to think, but that's not the way it was. My grandfather told me he had lots of offers to sell the facility, but he wouldn't do it. Said it was karma. He knew one day Angel would come back and he wanted to be ready for her."

"He told you this?"

"Only all the time. He used to tell me how Angel drew these huge crowds, how he met all these presidents and actors and other dignitaries. He said Angel attracted and united visitors from every nation and from every walk of life."

"And frightened the hell out of all of them. If your grandfather really felt this way, why'd he agree to sell to the Dietsch Brothers?"

"He was stringing them along. He said he owed them money, my parents, too, so he had to make it look like he was doing something to repay them."

Mac rolls his eyes and grins. "Gotta hand it to him, he played us like a fiddle."

"He never realized Angel had returned. He must have hit her thumper by accident before he went into the lagoon."

"He died in the lagoon?"

"That's where he had the heart attack. He was cleaning out the main drain. I thought you knew?"

"No." Mac holds his head in his hands, sweat pooling beneath his chin.

"Uncle Mac, can we get out of here, I'm boiling over."

"Then it was my fault he died. Maintaining the tank was my job, not his."

"It was an accident."

"No, I should have been there. I hadn't shown up for a week. The drains needed cleaning but I kept putting it off, I was too busy getting wasted. The night before he died, I was partying my brains out at some local watering hole."

"Uncle Mac—"

"I ended up picking up some college kid . . . really stupid of me. Trish caught me on board with her. An hour later, they fished your grandfather out of the lagoon."

David wipes sweat from his brow. "He had a weak heart, Uncle Mac. He could've died crossing the street."

"But he didn't. He died because of me . . . because I wasn't there for him." He punches the wooden bench. Punches it again.

David feels scared. "Okay, so you can make amends, you can help me capture Angel."

"There's something else you should know. That celebrity gig your father accepted? He's being set up."

"What? What're you talking about?"

"Some big-shot producer, James Gelet, he was hounding me about it for weeks. Said I had to join the cruise, made it sound like it was life or death, like the whole thing would fail if my ass wasn't on board. Basically, I told him to shove it, I know when I'm being had. Your father, well, he sees what he wants to see."

"How's he being set up? By who?"

"I don't know. God knows the two of us have pissed off enough people over the years. Somebody's out there pulling strings, and it's not those studio dorks. Guest hosts my ass. Hell, your old man and me fell out of the public eye so long ago we can't even see the page. Half these so-called Hollywood execs weren't even born during our fifteen minutes of fame, you think they give a rat's ass about us now? Shows like *Daredevils* don't need old farts like us, they want sexy broads with big tits. Anyway, I should have warned your old man but I didn't. I was angry at him . . . hell, I've been angry at the whole freakin' world."

"My dad, is he going to be okay?"

"Yeah, sure. Your old man's like a cat, nine lives and always landing on his feet. Don't worry about him, he'll be fine."

David searches his godfather's eyes. "What about you?"

"Me? Like they say, I just have to take things one day at a time. Come on, let's get out of this oven."

David follows him out of the sauna into the brisk mountain air.

"So all these years, Masao was just biding his time, waiting for his monster to come home to roost."

"Will you help me?"

"Well, I sure as shit can't let you do it alone. Come on, we'll grab my clothes and sneak out of here."

"They won't mind?"

"Who's asking? The real challenge comes when we have to sweet-talk Trish into paying our cab fare."

LATE PLEISTOCENE

NORTHWESTERN PACIFIC OCEAN
18,000 YEARS AGO

Dusk bleeds through the palm fronds of the tropical jungle, lacing the beach with its scarlet hue.

The pregnant female is dying with the day, her massive girth hopelessly stranded on a sandbar. She has been thrashing for twenty exhausting minutes, and now she is spent. Settling in the bog, crushed by her own enormous weight, she twists her head from side to side, allowing the lapping waves to move into her beckoning mouth as she ram ventilates.

Swallowing a trough-size mouthful of sea and sand, the Megalodon shark seizes, the debris choking her gill filaments. In a state of panic she arches her back, raising her truck-size head out of the murky shoal, her mud-laced jaws gasping at the night.

Air races down her gullet and is trapped, adding a sudden buoyancy to her massive frame, allowing her to free one of her trapped pectoral fins.

Energized by the motion, the female whips her head and tail to and fro, the violent movements causing the surface of the river to dance. The barge of sand beneath her gives, releasing its suction grip upon her upper torso.

The Megalodon squirms, slaps at the surface, rolls, and is free.

For a long moment the exhausted female simply lies in the water, her jaws opening and closing in spasms. Then, mustering a lead-like muscular contraction, the Meg propels herself through the soothing sea, the incoming current washing through her mouth, expunging grit from her gills.

As fresh seawater moves through the female, it seeps into her swollen uterus, cooling her unborn pups, further acclimating them to their future environment.

Almost two years have passed since the act of copulation that yielded the Megalodon's brood. As embryos, the unborn pups had been sheathed in protective, transparent capsules, nourished by an external placenta-like yolk sac attached to their gut. Over time these capsules had ruptured, exposing the developing Megs to a womb whose liquified world was far different from the chemistry of the ocean. Now, as the day of their birth rapidly approaches, their mother's uterus has been steadily regulating its ion-water balance, preparing the unborn young for their emergence into the sea.

Undernourished, the eight surviving Megalodon pups have had to endure a longer gestation period than normal, their mother's internal anatomy delaying contractions until the pups can achieve greater size. This evolutionary feature, designed to increase the pups' rate of survival in the wild, is taking a toll on their mother, forcing the female to expend greater amounts of energy during these final weeks of pregnancy.

The big carnivore registers the familiar gnawing in her gut. She must feed again and soon, before she loses any more young.

Primordial senses scan the darkening waterway that snakes between the tropical land masses. The female detects the faint electrical impulses of a beating heart and powerful swimming muscles. Something large is approaching, something familiar—

The male.

Too weak to defend herself from her more aggressive challenger, the female alters her course, retreating deeper into the island maze—

—unaware that downstream, another hunter awaits.

CHAPTER

16

The crew is up before dawn, positioning cameras, filming establishing shots.

Jonas Taylor is seated in a canvas chair, half asleep, while a makeup man applies a layer of skin tone, concealing the dark circles under his eyes.

Andrew Fox approaches. Hands him a cup of hot coffee. "It's a miracle, you look ten years younger. Not a day over eighty."

"Which is just how I feel. Have you seen my daughter?"

"No, why? You two fighting again?"

"I caught her last night in her birthday suit with one of the Dare-devils."

"Uh-oh. What did you do?"

"Nothing yet. But I was thinking maybe you and me could hogtie him later, you know, dangle his ass from the crow's nest."

"Knowing these Daredevils, he'd probably enjoy that."

Erik Hollander joins them. "Andrew, we need you in the

cage, we're about ten minutes from sunrise. Jonas, how're you holding up?"

"I'm not a geriatric patient, Hollander."

"No, of course you're not. In fact, I just spoke with the Makos. What would you think about joining them for one of their stunts?"

"Sorry, pal, my days of swimming with sharks is long past."

"Okay, sure, but next up is a jaunt to a Sperm whale nursery. How about a few shots of you scuba diving with the whales?"

"Show me some zeroes on a bonus check and we'll talk."

"And five . . . four . . . three—"

A crimson ball of fire pokes its head above the eastern horizon and over the bare left shoulder of Charlotte Lockhart. "It's morning here in the South Pacific, the end of a long night, as the cast and crew of *Daredevils* hugged and cried and mourned the tragic loss of our friend, Jason Massett. The body boarder and former lacrosse player was one of our more popular contestants, and team captain Michael Coffey spoke last night to Jason's family back in Long Island."

"And cut." Susan Ferraris checks her notes. "Okay, we've got a minute and twenty seconds of footage with the parents, then we go live to a shot of Jason's body bag being lowered into the drink. Is our underwater crew in position?"

"They're all set."

"Good. Jonas, anything you want to add when we come back live to Charlotte?"

"No, I think you've exploited the moment from every available angle."

Susan's face locks into a false smile, her eyes flashing fury. "Right. Thanks so much for your invaluable input."

Doc Shinto, Barry Struhl, Jennie Arnos, and Lexy Piatek follow Makos captain Wayne John Ferguson onto the main deck. All are dressed in wetsuits. Fergie is carrying a mask and snorkel, Jennie a boom box.

They stand ready at the starboard rail, watching the two-foot swells wash over the barely buoyant remains of the dead whale. The Pacific is lead-gray in the morning light. The sharks have returned in force, their dorsal fins crisscrossing the surface.

"Psst!"

Fergie turns. Sees Dani hiding behind the main mast.

The girl launches into his arms, slipping her tongue into his mouth. "I'm sorry about last night. When can I see you again?"

"Don't know. Your father's as mad as a cut snake. Anyway, I can't talk now, I'll find you after the stunt."

"Fergie . . . I love you."

The Aussie winces.

"What? Does that bother you? I just wanted you to know before you . . . you know."

"Before I what? Before I feed myself to the sharks? Look, this is no time to have a blue—"

Jennie Arnos grabs him by the arm. "Come on, lover boy, they're getting ready to lower Jason's body. As for you, Taylor, this area's off-limits to Candy Girls. Why don't you go find your daddy."

Dani grinds her teeth.

Fergie shrugs, allowing Jennie to lead him away.

Andrew Fox passes the underwater camera to his sound engineer, John Lowry, then secures the top of the stainless-steel shark cage. The *Neptune*'s crew activates the winch, raising the cage off the deck, swinging it over the starboard rail before releasing it to the sea.

The heavy cage strikes the surface and immediately sinks, plunging the two scuba divers into the deep blue milieu of the wolves.

The buoyancy tubes atop the cage catch the sea, suspending Andrew and his assistant ten feet below the surface, twenty yards away from the whale carcass.

Cable is released from above, allowing them to drift closer to the action.

The sea is alive. Sharks dart in and out of view like miniature jet fighters, attacking the bobbing island of whale blubber from below. A few predators circle the cage, evaluating it with soulless onyx eyes. A six-foot Blue shark, agitated by the steel cage's electrical field, launches an attack, managing to ram its snout through the two-foot-wide camera port that encircles the enclosure.

Andrew never blinks, continuing to film as Lowry carefully pushes the muscular fish away.

A heavy splash from above. Andrew maneuvers his camera as the body bag containing the remains of Jason Massett impacts the surface. The dark object floats for a fleeting moment, then slowly sinks beneath the waves.

A Grey Reef shark rises to greet the bag. It circles twice, then attacks, ripping apart the seal before darting out of the frame.

A second Grey replaces the first, its tail whipping furiously behind it as it forces its snout into the bag. Seconds later it escapes with its prize—the severed arm protruding from its horrible mouth.

The fresh blood summons a horde of carnivores, the sea transformed into a swirling maze of brown and gray torpedo-shaped torsos.

Andrew swallows the bile rising from his throat. *This is barbaric. I should have never signed on for this nonsense.*

A portable crane is locked into position next to the starboard winch, the flat six-by-eight-foot aluminum platform suspended beneath the hoist's pulley by four cables.

Team Mako steps onto the grate as it is lifted away from the main deck and swung over the side.

Charlotte takes her cue, reading from the now-functioning TelePrompTer. "Shark. The very word conjures our deepest fear . . . to be eaten alive. Masters of all the Earth's domain but one, when we enter the sea, we enter a liquid universe alien to our own, one in which we are no longer highest on the food chain, one in which death can savagely take us without warning from below."

The platform descends to the sea.

Jennie hangs the boom box on the pulley by its strap.

"Having already witnessed the death of Jason Massett, Team Mako enters the feeding frenzy, where hundreds of predators swarm through the bloodstained sea, their jaws snapping upon anything that moves. Five humans, five hundred sharks . . . stay tuned."

"And cut!"

Cameramen and crew move en masse, taking up positions along the starboard rail.

Jonas leaves the makeshift set and wanders along the main deck, searching for his daughter.

Verifying her teams are in position, Susan Ferraris calls down to the Makos using her megaphone. "Okay, anytime you're ready."

Fergie looks into the eyes of his teammates. "No worries. Just keep it slow and steady, and absolutely no splashing. Okay, Jennie."

Jennie presses the PLAY button on the boom box.

The five members of the Mako team slip into the water, accompanied by the opening licks of "Jumpin' Jack Flash."

Michael Coffey watches from his perch on the lateen mast. "Damn showboats . . ."

Treading water, their backs to one another, Jennie, Lexy, Doc Shinto and Barry Struhl hold hands, forming a tight circle. Fergie is inside the ring, floating facedown, watching the activity from below as he breathes through his snorkel and mask.

Working underwater, out of view of the cameras, Fergie unzips his wetsuit, removing three sections of a steel pool cue, spray painted aqua-blue. He screws the links together, the distal end of which has been shaven to a stiletto-sharp point.

He signals a thumbs-up to the Makos.

With Jennie taking the lead, the team wades toward the pungent island of blubber.

Unable to locate his daughter, Jonas gives up and joins Erik and Susan, who are watching the scene below from a monitor linked to Andrew's underwater camera.

Four pairs of churning legs come into view, dancing at the top of the screen, Fergie barely visible in the center of the cluster.

The camera angle changes, zooming in on a seven-foot Grey Reef shark, rising from the depths. Pectoral fins down, the fish bows its back as it circles the team, its lower torso writhing rapidly, like a rattlesnake warning its prey.

Jonas sucks in a breath. "It's attacking."

Expelling a breath through his snorkel, Fergie descends to intercept, stabbing at the incoming predator with his lance.

The pool cue punctures the shark near its left gill slits, drawing blood.

The shark jerks, then loops away, nearly ripping the makeshift spear from Fergie's grip.

The *Neptune*'s crew gasps in relief.

Fergie surfaces, catches a quick lungful of air through his snorkel, then descends again as the activity intensifies.

Dusky sharks dart in and out of view. Andrew shifts his camera angle, aiming below, catching the ominous silhouettes of several dozen hammerheads, circling the arena like buzzards.

A nosey Blue closes on Doc Shinto. Fergie stabs at the

sleek fish between his teammate's legs, warding it off.

"I'm Jumpin' Jack Flash, it's a gas, gas, gas . . ." Jennie Arnos sings out loud, her body quivering with adrenaline and fear as she leads her teammates toward the dead Humpback.

Fifteen feet . . . ten feet . . .

She hums along with the guitar solo, her eyes scanning the oily slick of dorsal fins and thrashing tails.

Five feet . . . three feet . . . "I was drowned, I was washed up and left for dead. I fell down to my feet and I saw they bled . . . yeah, yea—"

Suddenly she stops, as the hideous face of a Shortfin Mako appears from below, its curved lower dentures tearing a football-size chunk from the dead whale's waterlogged carcass.

The Mako's tail slaps hard against her left knee.

Shouting, Jennie kicks out with both feet, chasing the shark away, then releases her teammate's grip and leaps onto the carcass, scrambling up the mound of blubber, using bite marks as toeholds. "Come on, come on, come on!" She reaches back and pulls Lexy Piatek up.

Thirty feet and fifteen tons of Humpback whale bob like a waterlogged mattress beneath their added weight. The carcass is pockmarked by thousands of pinkish-gray bites, most the size of a small child's head.

Barry and Doc Shinto climb up, smiles of relief breaking out on their pale faces.

"Fergie, come on!"

Barry and Shinto lean over and grab Fergie's wrists, hauling him out of the water.

"Whoa! Whoa!" The team dances atop their sanctuary, high-fiving one another. Fergie stabs the pool cue into the island of blubber. "I declare this Mako island—"

—as the bloated carcass rolls beneath them.

Lexy screams as she tumbles into the sea, followed by Jennie and Barry. Fergie and Doc Shinto grapple for handholds, but the carcass continues to rotate as it seeks a new equilibrium, plunging the two men beneath the surf.

Shouts and screams from the *Neptune* are drowned out by the heavy bass of the Rolling Stones' chorus.

Below, Andrew Fox and John Lowry watch in horror as the fallen Daredevils attempt to close ranks amid dozens of agitated sharks.

"Stay together!" Fergie chokes on the command. "Don't splash!"

Jennie grabs Barry's arm, then kicks at unseen objects darting past her feet.

Lexy thrashes along the surface. She, reaches for Doc Shinto's hand—

—then suddenly disappears amid a spreading pool of blood.

Fergie repositions his mask and surface dives. Amid a flurry of bubbles and blood he witnesses two sharks fighting over the girl's left leg.

He stabs at them with his pool cue, losing the weapon in the process. Grabbing Lexy around her chest, he kicks to the surface.

The Zodiac is there to greet them, Jennie, Shinto, and Barry already in the craft. Evan Stewart reaches for Fergie.

"No, take Lexy!"

Evan and Dee haul Lexy onto the motorized raft. Doc Shinto and Barry lean over, dragging their captain onto the inflatable.

Lexy's lower leg is seeping blood, the torn quadriceps muscle held intact only by the remains of her wetsuit.

Jennie hits the throttle, accelerating the Zodiac back to the *Neptune*.

"I don't want to die. Fergie, don't let me die."

"You're not going to die, it's not so bad, really. Now stay calm."

The medical team stands ready on the platform.

Erik is pacing the main deck, speaking on his two-way radio, trying hard not to look at the cameras. "Contact the *Coelacanth*. Tell them we have a medical emergency. Tell them we need the chopper."

Lexy is brought on deck, all eyes, all cameras focused on the blood trail oozing from her mangled leg as a tourniquet is tightened just below the hip.

All eyes . . . except those belonging to Jonas Taylor.

The paleobiologist remains at the starboard rail, his heart racing as his binoculars focus on the carcass of the dead whale and the sand trap–size bite mark gushing along its exposed belly.

MONTEREY, CALIFORNIA

A late afternoon rain pelts the windows of the Old Monterey Café on Alvarado Street. Patricia Pedrazzoli, seated in a corner booth, stares at the weather and picks at her omelette, her mind swirling with emotion.

She is furious at the obstinate fourteen-year-old seated across from her who thinks he is smarter than her and probably is. She is equally pissed off at the kid's mother, who is still in British Columbia doing God-knows-what.

Most of all, she is angry at Mac.

Look at him, wolfing down that hamburger like he was just released from a prison camp. No calls, no letters, just pops back into my life, then sweet-talks me into paying his cab fare and taking him out to eat. And I fall for it every time.

"How's your burger, kid?"

"Good," David says, spraying a nugget of sirloin into Patricia's hash browns.

She pushes her plate away, disgusted.

"What's wrong, sweetie?"

"What am I to you, Mackreides? A meal ticket you think you can punch whenever you feel like it?"

"David, go take your food over to that counter. Your Aunt Trish and I need to talk."

David gathers his plate and drink and heads for an open bar stool.

"Sure, he listens to you. He hasn't respected a damn thing I've said in three days."

"Ah, he's a good kid."

"Are you joking? Kids like him are the reason I'll never have children. And who do you think you're snow-jobbing with that Aunt Trish crap?"

"I know you're angry, but you don't need to take it out on my godson. I need to make amends to you, and I will."

"How? By leaving me your dry cleaning?"

"Trish, do you realize you're the only decent thing in my life."

"Wish I could say the same about you."

"I need you."

"And I need someone who's going to be there for me, someone I can count on, not some overaged frat boy with an out-of-control libido. When are you going to grow up?"

Mac stares at his hands. "I don't know. I have issues . . . things that date back to my father's suicide. Guess I haven't been dealing with my problems any better than he did."

"I've heard that line before, Mac. You become all contrite, then a week later, you're hitting the booze again."

"Maybe I just need a reason to stay sober?"

"Well it can't be me. Do it for yourself. Until things change, you and I have no future together; in fact, we have no future together period."

Mac nods. "You're right. All I ever gave you was disappointment. But whether you take me back or not, I'm going to change. I did a lot of thinking over the last few weeks, and—"

"Save it. The only reason I'm still sitting here is because you said the lagoon deal was in jeopardy."

"David won't agree to sign."

"What?" Her jaw falls open. "We're closing with the Dietsch Brothers in less than a week. Do you know how much time I've put into this deal, how much money's at stake?"

"David owns twenty percent, and he won't sign off, at least not now."

"Oh, he'll sign or . . . or so help me, I'll strangle him."

"Easy, girl." Mac leans in closer, lowering his voice. "David's convinced Angel's returned to California waters."

"What?"

"When he was diving, his imagination got the best of him. Now he wants to capture her."

"This is ridiculous. Where does he come up with these things?"

"He's fourteen. His grandfather's been filling his head with stories about that monster since he was in diapers."

"And how do we convince him otherwise?"

"We humor him. Give him a few days to make his case. Terry's away anyway, so it's not like the delay's costing you anything. By the time she returns, he'll realize it was just his imagination running overtime, then I'll get him to sign off on the deal."

Mac winks. "Still love me, don't you?"

"God, you're such a jackass."

STRAIT OF JUAN DE FUCA, PACIFIC OCEAN
17 MILES NORTHWEST OF PORT RENFREW
VANCOUVER ISLAND, BRITISH COLUMBIA

The late afternoon sun bursts through a gap in the clouds, its brilliant orange eye casting a golden beam across the surface of the Pacific.

The beacon seems to follow Terry Taylor as she watches it from the bow rail of the *Cape Calvert*. The Canadian Coast Guard Cutter is cruising south along Vancouver Island at ten knots, trailing two three-quarter-inch steel braided cables.

One is attached to an underwater sled containing the Tanaka Institute's portable "thumper." The other tows the remains of an adult Grey whale, one of the more recent beachings.

The mammal is being dragged backward by its tail. Its flanks have been split open, allowing it to bleed.

"Hey—"

Terry jumps. Joshua Bunkofske laughs. "A little nervous, are we?"

"You'd be nervous too if you had any brains."

"Relax, everything's going exactly as planned. Come inside the wheelhouse with me, I want to introduce you to my crew. These guys are good, they'll help relieve your nerves."

She follows him inside.

Piloting the vessel is a man who looks more like a guitarist for a heavy-metal band than a boat captain. His dark hair is wild and bushy, his Fu Manchu mustache and lambchop sideburns straight out of the sixties.

"Fellas, meet the lady who'll be signing our checks. Terry, this is our captain, Ron Marino, Jr.—"

Marino nods.

"—and his first mate, Brian Olmstead."

Olmstead, clean-cut and built like a wrestler, sports a jagged scar beneath his right eye. "Nice to meet you, ma'am."

"You, too. Joshua says you were in the Navy?"

"Yes, ma'am. Last three years as a SEAL."

Feeling relieved, she turns to the third man, a rough-looking Italian with dark hair and eyes. "And you are?"

"A guy who hates fish. Michael Villaire. New York transit cop, retired. I'm here to protect you against the worst-case scenario." He pulls out a heavy waterproof case from beneath the chart table and opens it.

Inside is a stubby rifle with an extra wide barrel.

"This is an M-79 grenade launcher. Single-shot, breech-loading, easy to use, and it fires 40-mm explosive rounds with a maximum range exceeding thirteen hundred feet.

That monster of yours either cooperates or she dies, case closed."

Joshua smiles confidently. "Drugs are set in the bait, the bait's being towed, your thumper's thumping, our fish-finder will tell us the moment she's near, and we've got Dirty Harry here, armed to the teeth. I'd say we've covered all the bases. Now try to relax."

Terry forces a smile. "Okay, I'm relieved."

"I'm not," says Fu Manchu mustache, his voice a heavy rasp. "The fish man says we're getting paid for the job, not by the day. Strait's a big waterway, assuming your fish's even in these waters. Far as I'm concerned, you bought my services for three days, after that we renegotiate."

"If she's in the Strait, the thumper will bring her right to us. Angel was practically weaned on the device, which emits an electronic and acoustical signal that we know sharks are very attracted to."

"That was in your zoo. We're in open ocean."

"Which is where the technology originated from. Many years ago, A.T.&T. consulted my husband about a fiber-optic cable system they had just installed on the ocean floor, stretching from the eastern seaboard to the Canary Islands. The cable was laid in six thousand feet of water and was armored with stainless steel mesh, yet the sharks still attacked it, tearing it up, costing A.T.&T. millions of dollars in repairs. Jonas discovered the sharks' ampullae of Lorenzini were attracted to the electronic booster signals originating in the fiber-optic bundles."

"Ampullae of who?"

"Lorenzini," Joshua answers. "It's a cluster of sensory cells located along the underside of the shark's snout."

Terry nods. "Angel's thumper emits a similar electrical signal, combined with a heavy baritone thumping sound which mimics the cardiac vibrations of a whale in distress. The vibrations are important because they travel much farther than electrical signals, which break up fairly rapidly in

seawater. Naturally, the bigger the predator, the greater its
sensory range."

She picks up the M-79 grenade launcher, testing its
weight. "Of course, they don't come any bigger than our little Angel."

17

ABOARD THE *NEPTUNE*
PHILIPPINE SEA
411 NAUTICAL MILES SOUTHWEST OF THE MARIANA
TRENCH

Erik Hollander hurries across the main deck to the captain's gallery. He keys into his stateroom, looking over his shoulder, then enters, deadbolting the cabin door behind him.

Crawling under his bed, he retrieves the shortwave radio.

ABOARD THE SUPER YACHT, *COELACANTH*

Michael Maren is on the sundeck, drinking his morning espresso in the comfort of his whirlpool. The yacht is cruising north by northeast at ten knots, remaining half-a-mile behind the *Neptune*, now at full sail.

A shortwave radio beeps within its charger.

Without getting up from her lounge chair, a topless Allison Petrucci reaches for the device. "Yes? Hold on, I'll get him. Guess who?" Leaning over, she hands the receiver to Maren.

"Hollander. I was wondering when you'd call."

"What is it with you, Maren?" The static-laced voice of Erik Hollander shrieks at him across the radio. "You were supposed to warn me before your creature surfaced. I didn't have one camera in position!"

Maren winks at Allison, who is biting into a fresh pastry. "Easy, amigo. Like I told your partner, I can't control Nature, I can only tempt it. Our friend decided to come up for a late-night snack. The *Neptune*'s lights were too bright for its eyes so it fled."

"Yeah, well Taylor saw the bite mark this morning and he's furious. He'll be banging down my cabin door any second."

"Did he examine the carcass? Take any measurements?"

"No, he never left the ship."

"See what I told you?" Maren climbs out of the whirlpool, dripping hot water across the non-skid surface. "Taylor's not a scientist, he's nothing but a goddamn phony."

"Now he's an agitated phony. What am I supposed to do about him?"

"Do nothing. Play dumb. Tell him he's mistaken. You've already left the area, it's not like he's going back to check on things."

"What about . . . our friend?"

"Been following you since you set sail, in fact, he's right below you in twenty-two hundred feet of water, and still quite hungry."

"Then the tracking device—"

"Still functioning like a charm."

"Oh, crap—"

Maren hears the sound of someone yelling in the background.

"Taylor's here, I have to go. Will tonight be the night? I need to know."

"Maybe. Maybe not. Welcome to reality TV, Hollander. Maren out."

Allison sits up, pausing from applying a fresh coat of suntan oil to her breasts. "Okay, Michael, what gives? We both know the Barracuda's not enticing that monster of yours, it's following the *Neptune* all on its own."

"As I suspected he would."

"Then you lied to Hollander?"

"Not at all. I simply told him all he needs to know." He returns the radio to its charger, then grabs an orange juice and climbs back into the whirlpool.

"Open up, Hollander, I know you're in there!"

Erik wraps the radio in a towel and stuffs it beneath the bed. "Hang on, Jonas, I'm coming." He strips off his shirt, then pulls back the deadbolt. "Sorry, I was just getting—"

Jonas bursts into the room. "I've been searching this boat for an hour. Where the hell've you been?"

"Calm down. I've been coordinating things between the *Coelacanth*'s chopper pilot and the hospital in Manila."

"Bullshit. I looked for you in the control room three times."

"Then you must have just missed me. I had to go below decks to the storage area."

"To avoid me?"

"Now why would I be avoiding you?"

"Don't give me that. You were out there on deck when that whale carcass flipped. You saw that Megalodon bite as clear as day."

"Meg bite? Easy Tiger, what I saw looked like an Orca bite, nothing nearly as large as a Megalodon imprint."

"You're lying. Where did you really get that white Megalodon tooth?"

"I told you, from an old college buddy."

"What's his name?"

"His name? Krawitz. Artie Krawitz. What difference does it make?"

Jonas gets up in his face. "Don't screw with me, Erik. I want to know what's going on."

"What's going on?" Erik pushes him aside, feigning anger. "I'll tell you what's going on. Jason Massett's dead, Lexy may lose her leg, my crew's losing it emotionally, Andrew's ready to quit, and the Daredevils have locked themselves in their rec room, getting drunk on tequila. And now here you are, barging into my room, ranting like some maniac about a Megalodon bite, of all things."

"I may be old, but I'm not senile. When it comes to these monsters, I know what I know."

"Nobody said you were senile, but everyone's on edge. Look, Jonas, I know all you think I care about is ratings, but that's not true. Remember, I'm the one who recruited most of these Daredevils, I consider them family. Everyone's upset about what's happened over the last few days, especially me. So please, take some advice. Go find your daughter. Spend some quality time with her. It's during times like these that we really need our loved ones."

Jonas feels his blood pressure normalize. "Okay. Maybe I overreacted. But there's been way too much blood shed on this voyage, and the whole idea of following a route that will take us close to the Mariana Trench is making me more than a little jumpy."

"I understand. Believe me, producing a television show is no picnic either, especially one as dangerous as *Daredevils*. Wait, I have something for you." Erik searches a suitcase, then shoves a prescription bottle into Jonas's hand. "Valium. In our business, we consider it an essential daily vitamin.",

PACIFIC RIM NATIONAL PARK
VANCOUVER ISLAND

The last trace of day melts behind a mouse-gray horizon like a fading bulb. Velvet waves roll toward the jagged shoreline, sizzling as they die along the rocks and crevices.

The presence of night takes the western shores of Vancouver Island.

A series of high-pitched whistles shatter the serenity of evening.

Trapped in a tide pool bordered by an outcropping of rock is the Pacific white-sided dolphin. Caught by the low tide, unable to reach the receding sea, the mammal flops on its side, inhaling desperate breaths through its blowhole as it awaits the next wave to assault its prison walls and refill the depression.

From above the coastal cliff face, a low growl advances through the rain forest.

Lumbering beyond the line of Douglas fir and spruce is the grizzly. The big male pauses at the edge of the rocky embankment, its snot-laced nostrils snorting the salty air. Within seconds the animal pinpoints the wounded dolphin's location in the breach of rock, twelve feet below its perch.

The sea rushes in, filling the void with foam, momentarily submerging the stranded dolphin. As the water recedes, the entrapped mammal expels a gust of bloody air from its blowhole.

The scent excites the grizzly. Scanning the rock face below, it maps out a route, then steps gingerly onto a lower shelf, digging its claws into the moss-covered boulders as it shifts its seven-hundred-and-twenty-pound girth. Halfway down, it pauses to peer through a crevice of rock at its helpless prey, then it hops down another level—

—as a ten-foot swell rolls against the escarpment.

The wave sweeps in against the rocks and lifts the grizzly away from its foothold. Floating free, the bear thrashes at the slippery slope, then is swept backward into the receding sea.

The grizzly surfaces fifteen feet from the shore. An excellent swimmer, it shakes water from its mighty head, then, churning its powerful legs, swims back toward the draining rock face against the suddenly strong pull of the Pacific.

The current increases, pulling the bear backward. Struggling to keep its head above water, the bear unleashes a gurgling yelp, then disappears underwater.

For a long moment, silence retakes the night . . . until a bone-chilling roar shatters the calm. The grizzly reappears, launching its bloodied upper torso out of the water, its front legs pawing at the sea as the panicked animal propels itself toward the safety of the rocks.

The Pacific bubbles, and then the hyperextended mouth of the male Megalodon rises around the bear like an elephantine steel trap. Serrated teeth slam shut on the grizzly, the upper row of fangs catching the bear along the nape of its neck, punching through fur, muscle, and bone, effortlessly lopping off the animal's head.

The Megalodon's upper torso continues rising, swaying back and forth across the surface while its hideous jaws clamp down on the tough bear hide. Blood and fur swirl in the wind, and then the big male slips back into the depths.

Safe within the tide pool, the white-sided dolphin whistles into the night.

ABOARD THE COAST GUARD CUTTER CAPE CALVERT
STRAIT OF JUAN DE FUCA, PACIFIC OCEAN
2 MILES SOUTHWEST OF PORT RENFREW

Darkness blankets the Strait of Juan de Fuca, the night interrupted by the heavy thrum of the Cape Calvert's twin diesel engines.

Terry Taylor stands on the upper deck of the cutter, a cold misty rain causing her to wipe her face every few minutes as she gazes at the ebony sea.

The confidence of day has been shattered by the arrival of night and the unnerving emptiness of the Strait, the shoreline of which is still under a small craft and diver dusk-to-dawn quarantine.

Looking to the east, her eyes struggle to locate the dark outline of land. *You're only a half-mile from shore, at most a two-minute ride by Zodiac. Stop worrying. Besides Angel's not interested in eating people, she's stalking the whales.*

Joshua joins her on deck. "You doing okay?"

"Fine," she lies.

"It's cold out here. Why don't you come inside?"

"I'm better outside. I get a little claustrophobic."

He moves closer. Hands her a metal flask. "Here. This'll take the edge off."

"No thanks, I've poisoned my liver enough for one trip."

"W.W.J.D.?"

"Excuse me?"

He smiles. "What would Jonas do? Sorry, bad joke. It's just, I know he went after Angel once, I was just wondering how he'd go about it a second time."

"He wouldn't. You can only look death in the face so many times. Besides, Jonas's attitude toward Angel changed over the years. He no longer believes in keeping big predators captive."

"Obviously you disagree."

"If we don't recapture Angel, then the Canadian authorities will eventually have to hunt her down. The outer doors of the canal have been replaced, so the chances of her escaping again are greatly reduced. Plus, her capture should be good for the local economy."

"Especially yours."

"Listen, my family invested all we had into the lagoon. So far, we've had nothing to show for it but my brother's death and overwhelming debt, so yes, I think we deserve a windfall. These last twenty years . . . they've been very hard on all of us."

"May I ask you a personal question?"

"Ask. I may not answer it."

Joshua leans against the rail. "Do you ever feel like life is passing you by, like your entire existence for as long as you can remember has been predicated on that one big break that never seems to come?"

She looks away. "I don't know. Sometimes."

"I feel that way every day. That's why I decided I needed a change, the more drastic, the better. New career. New city. New romance. New life. When things are bad, change it, that's my new philosophy."

"I'm not real good with change."

"Then you'll be stuck in your rut 'til your last dying day, praying for good things to come but never doing anything to make them happen. Someone once told me the definition of insanity is doing the same thing day after day, year after year, while always expecting different results."

"Probably true, but some things . . . well, let's just say I'm too old to change."

"Old? Terry, when I look at you, I see a beautiful, vibrant woman weary from what I can only imagine is a tired marriage."

She laughs. "That's got to be the worst pickup line I've ever heard."

"Yeah, you're right, but be honest. Have there ever been times when you've regretted marrying a man who's twenty years older than you?"

"First, the age spread is twelve years, not twenty, and the answer is no. Like most couples, Jonas and I have had our challenges, but we still have something special."

"Yes, but is the romance still there? Do you miss him right now, or have you two just grown accustomed to sharing space?"

"Where's this going?"

"I know you were nervous about coming on board, but you pushed yourself, you faced your fears. I dig that. Truth is, I find myself very attracted to you."

"Josh—"

"Just hear me out. Sometimes people just need to take a vacation from themselves, you know, to recharge the old bat-

teries and feel new again. No pressure, no complications."
He leans in closer. "When you're ready for some physical
companionship, the door to my bedroom's always open."

Joshua winks at her, then heads back inside.

Terry stares out to sea, wishing she'd taken his flask.

The male Megalodon prowls the rocky southwestern Pacific
coastline of Vancouver Island, its ghostly dorsal fin rising
and dipping beneath the fog-laced surface. It glides north toward Port Renfrew, then retreats to the south, its swimming
pattern becoming more erratic.

The male is agitated, its last meal creating turmoil within
its intestinal tract.

The digestive system of predatory sharks is relatively
short. After food enters the stomach, it travels through the
duodenum, the beginning of the small intestine. Located inside the duodenum is a series of folds, called the spiral
valve. Similar in shape to a corkscrew, the spiral valve ro-
tates within the small intestine like a Slinky, providing additional absorption area for a shark to maximize the nutrients
of its meal. But the shape of the organ serves another pur-
pose, providing the creature with a means of regurgitating
items that cannot be properly digested.

Perhaps it is the grizzly's thick furry hide, perhaps it is the
animal's heavy musculature, but the Megalodon's last meal
is causing severe duress within its digestive system.

The big male thrusts its huge head out of the water. Jaws
snap open in a sudden spasm, and then the Meg regurgitates,
vomiting out the undigested remains of the grizzly bear. So
violent and powerful is the act that the creature's stomach
actually turns inside out, protruding from its cavernous
mouth like a pinkish balloon.

Just as quickly as it happens, the stomach is inhaled back
down the Megalodon's gullet, its intestines returning to their
normal state.

Exhausted from the effort, the Megalodon rolls onto its side and cruises along the surface with its mouth open, the cool sea soothing its inflamed insides.

PORT RENFREW, VANCOUVER ISLAND
4:22 A.M.

Sixteen-year-old Ryan Muskett wipes dew from the seats of his father's 17-foot Boston Whaler while his pal, Justin Tomasini, unties the boat. Boyhood friends, the two have been fishing the waters off Vancouver Island since they were old enough to hold a rod and reel, and no dusk-to-dawn Coast Guard quarantine is going to alter their routine.

Ryan takes control of the outboard, guiding them away from the dock and out into deeper water. Justin tucks his long blond hair beneath a John Deere baseball cap, then secures a 10-ounce cannonball weight to each of their fishing lines.

"Hey, Musk, did you hear the game last night? Howard hit another homer. Two more to tie Bonds."

"Bet he'll do it against the Giants on Sunday. Wish we could get tickets." Clearing the shallows, Ryan guns the engine, causing the whaler's bow to rise out of the water.

"Shh!" Justin motions for Ryan to ease up on the throttle. "Can't afford another fine, eh."

"Screw the Coast Guard, J.T. How come they're not hassling the big fishing charters?"

"My dad says they don't care about the deepwater boats, just the recreational stuff that stays close to shore."

"This toxic algae story . . . it's a load of crap."

"I don't know. I remember back a few years when the last bloom wiped out the clam industry. My brother was laid off for three months."

"Yeah, well I spoke with Shaun MacVicar last night and he told me they stopped enforcing the curfew north of Bamfield. Shaun MacVicar says the crabbing's fine, and the salmon are running real good too. Says that's where we should be."

"Screw Shaun MacVicar and screw the Coast Guard. I'm not paying for all that extra petrol just to fish off freakin' Bamfield."

Ryan passes a marker buoy, then checks his bearings using a distant lighthouse. They are two miles offshore, in water deeper than four hundred feet. He cuts the engine, allowing the boat to drift. "Okay, J.T. Set the rules."

Justin's line is already in the water. "Ten dollars for the first catch, twenty for the most fish caught, and a six-pack for the biggest fish."

"Done. Hope you brought plenty of money, 'cause you're goin' down." Ryan switches to the open swivel bow chair, then baits his hook with a live herring.

Several minutes pass in silence, the boys' attention focused on the tip of their rods.

"And Bingo was his name-oh!" Ryan rewinds his line as fast as he can, then, with a hard jerk, sets the hook.

"Chinook?"

"Yeah, and a nice one. Putting up a big fight."

"Better let him run."

"No shit." Ryan loosens his grip on the single-action reel, allowing the line to peel out. "I'm giving him a hundred meters to tire, then I'm—"

"Got one!" Justin reels in slack, then strikes up the line with authority. "You know the rules, first fish in the boat."

"Yeah, yeah." Ryan tugs at his feeding line. "Let's double the first bet based on weight."

Justin glances at his friend's rod. "Pass."

"Pussy. You probably hooked a minnow."

"Fine, double the bet. I'll still be in the boat ten minutes before you."

ABOARD THE COAST GUARD CUTTER *CAPE CALVERT*

The pilothouse is dark, save for the luminescent amber glow of instrument panels.

Terry Taylor drains the lukewarm remains of her coffee, her third cup in the last three hours. She is running on caffeine, her adrenaline having petered out hours ago. Through sleep-deprived eyes she looks up at the crew, wondering how much she should trust them.

Captain "Heavy Metal Band" is at the controls, engrossed in a "Stygian-Star" e-zine newsletter. Brian Olmstead is seated before a luminescent green fish-finder display, scanning a SEAL manual. In the last eight hours the former Navy man has located two Orca pods, seven baleen whales, a few dolphin, and no less than a dozen halibut.

Michael Villaire hasn't been seen for hours. The former transit cop is somewhere below, no doubt sleeping.

Joshua Bunkofske is posted outside in the bow. Terry watches him discreetly through the pilothouse windshield. She is playing mind games, imagining herself in bed with the younger man.

Would you really do it? Would Jonas ever cheat on me? Does he think about making one last male conquest? What goes through a married man's mind when he reaches that certain age where he knows his best days are behind him?

She imagines Jonas at sea with a bunch of scantily-clad Daredevil groupies.

Stop it! Jonas isn't like Mac, and he certainly wouldn't take a chance on getting caught with his daughter on board. Then again, if you trust him so much, why'd you insist on him bringing Dani?

She looks up again at Joshua.

Not exactly the rugged type. Still . . . if you knew you could get away with it, would you do it?

"Hey!" Brian Olmstead sits up suddenly, staring at the

fish-finder. "Something just passed 320 feet below us, something big."

"Probably just another whale," Captain Marino mutters.

"No, I don't think so. Change your heading to three-three-zero."

Ron Marino eyeballs his new first mate, then turns hard on the wheel while pushing down on the starboard throttle.

Terry is on her feet, her bladder tingling. "Where is she? How deep? Can you still see her on the fish-finder?"

"Stand by." Brian adjusts the Depth Control Gain. "Got her. She's seventy feet ahead of us and staying deep. The signal's getting stronger. She's rising."

Justin Tomasini sees the flash of silver dancing by the side of the boat. Securing the rod and reel in his left hand, he grabs the net in his right and deftly scoops up the seventeen-pound Chinook.

"Got mine, that's ten you owe me."

Ryan Muskett ignores him, his attention focused on his own fishing rod. His arms burn with lactic acid as he continues his battle with the salmon. "She's thirty pounds easy. Not like that wimpy fish."

"Doesn't count unless you bring her in the boat."

Ryan regrips the rod and leans back, dragging the fish with all his might.

Fifty yards out, a silver dart leaps from the water.

"Hello!"

"Whoa, keep at her, Musk. Make her dance again!"

Ryan takes a few breaths, garnering his strength. "Watch this." Recoiling the slack, he leans back and pulls with all his might.

The thirty-three-pound fish leaps out of the sea, followed by a six-and-a-half-foot ivory-white dorsal fin that cuts the dark surface like a sail.

The boys stare pie-eyed at the ghostly object as it races toward their boat.

"Musk, start the engine."

The teenager remains frozen to his seat.

"Musk, start the goddamn engine!"

The lime-green glow rolls closer, and then the submerged ivory girth collides sideways into the whaler with the force of a bus hitting a bicycle.

Ryan Muskett sees stars, and then he's underwater, submerged in darkness and biting cold. Flailing against the weight of his binding clothes, he kicks to the surface, grabbing hold of the capsized boat.

"J.T.?"

"Over here!"

The two teens swim toward one another.

"What the fuck was that?"

Justin's eyes grow wide, his lower lip quivering. "Look."

The pale dorsal fin breaks the surface, circling them.

The Canadian Coast Guard cutter slows to three knots as it enters a dense fog bank.

Joshua Bunkofske stands at the bow rail, his handheld searchlight barely able to cut through the heavy gray mist. "Where is she, Brian?"

"Gotta be up ahead somewhere," the former Navy SEAL calls out.

Terry joins Joshua out on deck, her legs trembling. "The fog's getting worse. Maybe we should head in?"

"Shh."

Josh's light pauses on an object floating just ahead of the cutter. "I see something."

Terry moves closer. "Looks like a capsized boat."

"I think you're right. Captain, all stop."

Ron Marino shifts into neutral. The vessel's heavy hull rises and falls above its trailing wake.

Joshua scans the surface with his light. "Ahoy! Anybody out here?"

No response.

Terry's heart races.

"Ahoy? Can anyone hear me?"

. The light moves from right to left, the beam striking the fog-enshrouded darkness like a brilliant lance, pausing as it illuminates what appears to be the tip of an iceberg sitting out of the water.

"Oh, Jesus . . ."

The Megalodon's entire head is above water, its chomping jaws oozing blood.

Joshua stares at the creature, awestruck. "My God. She's magnificent."

"Josh, something's dangling from the corner of her mouth . . . oh, God, it's an arm!" Terry chokes back a gag reflex.

Josh's pulse pounds in his throat as he focuses on the lifeless limb, flicking back and forth with the powerful chewing action of the Meg's jowls.

The severed human arm drops into the sea.

The searchlight's beam strikes the beast's cataract-gray left eye.

The Megalodon reels sideways and disappears.

Terry grips the rail, feeling dizzy. "I changed my mind, get us to shore."

Josh grabs her around the waist and leads her back inside the pilothouse. "She went deep."

"I have her on sonar," Brian reports. "Three hundred feet . . . four hundred, moving south on two-one-zero. We must've spooked her, she's really flying, pulling twenty-five knots."

Josh mans the fish-finder. "Stay with her, Marino."

Terry heads below. Enters one of the cabins. Finds Michael Villaire asleep on one of the lower berths. She shakes him until he stirs. "Wake up and get your gun!"

Brian listens at sonar. "This is no good, I can't hear her with all that racket coming from the thumper." He shifts back to the fish-finder as Terry rejoins them.

Marino glances at his charts. "Hey, Bunkofske, that fish of yours is leaving the Strait, heading into open ocean. Gonna be tough staying with her now."

Terry's almond eyes twitch in fear. "Josh, I'm not kidding. Take us in. I don't feel good about this."

"Go lie down."

"Don't patronize me."

"Terry, you hired us to do a job, let us do it."

"I changed my mind. I don't even think that was Angel." The men turn in unison, staring at her.

Joshua smiles nervously. "Terry, of course it's Angel."

"No, I don't think so. It didn't look like Angel. Angel's much bulkier, much bigger."

"And when did you last see her? Eighteen years ago?"

"Take me back to shore, Joshua. Now!"

The marine biologist ignores her. "Steady as she goes, Captain. Do not lose that monster."

CHAPTER

18

ABOARD THE *NEPTUNE*
PHILIPPINE SEA
347 MILES SOUTHWEST OF THE MARIANA TRENCH

Gale force winds whip the midnight sky into a frenzy, driving sheets of rain at the rolling, white-capped sea. Towering cumulus clouds growl at one another, firing off rogue gunshots of thunder and brilliant bolts of lightning that ignite across the charged atmosphere like spiderwebs.

Twenty- to thirty-foot swells punish the Spanish galleon's keel, the undulating mountains of water raising the tall ship heavenward, only to send it plunging down steep valleys with a vengeance.

Captain Robertson and his first mate remain steady at the wheel, both men in heavy rain gear, their body harnesses secured to the main mast. The *Neptune*'s topsails have all been lowered, its hatches battened down to weather the storm.

Below decks is a topsy-turvy world of darkened corridors violatedby screams of Daredevil laughter and pounding heavy metal music. Wooden beams creak with every roll, echoing the groans of the sickened crew.

Susan Ferraris tosses in bed, semiconscious after downing three sleeping pills in the last hour. Erik Hollander is on all fours in a bathroom stall, as are most of his assistants. Andrew Fox and his crew are riding out the storm in the galley, watching a DVD of *The Perfect Storm* while sipping hot tea from plastic containers. Jonas fakes his sea legs with them as long as he can, then heads for his cabin, too sick to focus any longer on the television screen.

As he makes his way through the pitch black corridor, the *Neptune* suddenly rolls hard to port. Jonas is thrown blindly against a wall as the ship continues rotating like a funhouse . . . forty degrees . . . fifty degrees . . .

Fear shoots through him as he holds on in the darkness, his mind awaiting the final deluge of sea.

A deck below, the crash of a boom box ends the music, rending the air with yelling and screams and drunken laughter as the two Daredevil teams, engaged in a nude shaving cream Twister tournament, are flung head-over-heels against the far wall. Half naked Candy Girls tumble into the flesh pile, several of the scantily-clad women vomiting blindly in the darkness as the *Neptune* threatens to sink beneath them.

Danielle Taylor retches into a towel, wishing the end would come faster.

Finally the great ship levels off, the bow fighting the sea as it begins its next ascent.

Alone in the corridor, Jonas drags himself to his feet, not sure if he's walking on the floor or the wall. He hears bizarre noises coming from below and debates whether to find his daughter.

What's the point? She's either puking her guts up or stoned like the rest of them. Either way, I'm the last person she wants to see.

Ignoring his paternal impulse to crash the party, Jonas locates his cabin door and half tumbles through the entry, groaning as he twists his surgically-repaired left knee.

"Are you okay?"

A woman's voice, coming from inside his cabin. "Dani?"

"Guess again."

Jonas feels for his duffel bag. Locating his flashlight, he turns it on, aiming for the voice.

She is lying in his hammock, naked beneath an ebony *Daredevils* bathrobe, which remains untied and parted in the middle.

"Mia?"

"See, I knew you'd remember."

"Mia, have you seen Dani?"

"She's down below in the zoo, losing her cookies with the rest of the animals. Let her be, she's enjoying her misery."

The bow of the ship rises beneath them.

Mia lies back in the hammock, enjoying the roller-coaster sensation.

Jonas feels the blood rush from his head to his stomach as the *Neptune* crashes back into the sea. On hands and knees he searches for his water bucket.

The dark-haired, olive-skinned Italian-Filipino leaps off the hammock and lifts Jonas beneath his arm, leading him over to the viewport. She unseals the hatch, the window immediately swinging open.

Wind howls angrily into the stateroom. Flashes of lightning reveal the Pacific's treacherous hills and valleys.

"Breathe." She pushes his face out the hole, the rain and sea soaking him as he inhales. "Focus on the clouds, not the ocean."

"Okay . . . enough." He pulls his head back inside, reseals the viewport, and wipes his face. Vertigo reaches out for him again and he slumps down to the floor, leaning back against the wall. "What is it you want?"

She kneels by his side, allowing her robe to fall from her shoulders. "We could die out here tonight."

"We're not going to die."

"If you really believe that, why are you so scared?"

"I'm not Superman."

"Neither am I, but I'm not scared."

Jonas lifts his aching head to look at her. "Okay, so what's your secret?"

"Scoot over." She flops down next to him, leaning against his shoulder. "About four years ago, I was driving with two friends at night. It was raining, nothing like this, but the roads were icing up pretty bad. Anyway, I was arguing with my friend, Beth, yelling at her to put out her cigarette, I can't stand secondhand smoke, when the car suddenly skidded sideways. Next thing I know—*bam*—we hit something head-on. My body slammed into the steering wheel so hard it bent the rim back against the dashboard, and my head went through the windshield. I remember seeing cracks in the glass, then I blacked out."

A flash of lightning briefly illuminates the tilting room.

Mia grips Jonas's arm. "The next sensation . . . it was bizarre. I woke up, feeling no pain, and then I screamed, because somehow I was sitting up, looking at the back of my head, looking at my arms sprawled across the wheel."

"I don't understand."

"I was dead, Jonas. My spirit was sitting up, halfway out of my dead, lifeless body."

"Jesus."

"I looked around. Beth was crumbled against the passenger door, bleeding pretty badly, my other friend was in the backseat, still in her seat belt. She woke up, looked at me, then started screaming, 'She's dead, she's dead.' When I reached out to touch her, my hand passed right through her, causing her to shiver."

The *Neptune*'s bow rises again.

Jonas closes his eyes, bracing for the drop. "What happened then?"

"I was scared, but not for me, for my friends. I kept screaming at Ellie to get out of the car, that it was going to blow up. Somehow she must have heard me because she managed to get her door open and pull Beth out through the front passenger window. I was running behind them, at least my spirit was, and then I was hovering above the car. I saw Ellie go back to try to get me out, and then everything went black again.

"When I woke up, I was back in my body, and the paramedics were cutting through the back door, trying to get me out. The pain was terrible, my head pounded like it was going to explode, and I kept fading in and out. Next thing I remember is lying on a gurney as I'm being wheeled down a hall, with doctors and nurses and bright chaotic lights. I saw all this just for a second before I passed out again. This time the blackness enveloped me like a warm blanket and it took away all my fear."

Mia whispers into his ear. "I died again on the operating table. The doctors won't admit it, but I know I did. The next time I awoke, my spirit was looking down at my body from the ceiling of a private room. I looked so small and fragile. My skin was very pale and my lips were blue. And then I saw it, a bright circle of light, hovering above me, above the ceiling, and inside the circle was the purest white light I had ever seen. Well, I wasn't sure what to do, you know, you hear all the stories, but no one had come out to greet me, no dead relatives. So I decided to enter the light on my own, just to see what it was all about. Next thing I know, I'm in this rectangular room made of clouds, at least that's what it seemed like, and then I saw this figure. It was a man, but I couldn't see his face. My mind's racing, and I can't believe what I'm seeing, but I know it has to be Jesus, right, or maybe an angel, 'cause he's so beautiful, but not in a handsome way, more in a loving way, all warmth and sunshine.

"But now I'm scared, because I realize I must be dead, and I don't want to leave my mother all alone, so I pleaded for him to let me go back. He wasn't angry, but I could tell he wasn't happy with that either, but he nodded, and then I was back . . . back in that hospital room, back in my body, except the pain was so great that I couldn't stay in, it just hurt so much. I realized that's why my angel was upset, because he knew the pain I would have to endure, but then I felt him touch my soul and the pain became tolerable, and I woke up, staring into my mother's eyes."

She kneels in front of him, the storm lighting her desperate expression. "You do believe me, don't you?"

"Yes."

She reaches out and touches his cheeks, wiping away tears he didn't know were there as he realizes that he wants to believe her, that her story gives him comfort. And then the *Neptune*'s bow rises once more and the ship begins to roll.

"Don't let the thought of death keep you from living." She takes his hands, pulling him to his feet. "Share the storm with me."

Mia leads him across the swaying floor to the hammock—
—as the cabin door bursts open.

Between flickers of lightning Jonas sees the Daredevils, each one wearing a wetsuit and a Navy-designed body harness.

"Well . . . well," Jennie laughs, "I knew someone was rocking the boat."

Evan leans inside the cabin. "Coffey came up with a great idea. We're going waterskiing."

"I'm in!" Mia announces, stripping off her robe to climb into an offered wetsuit.

Jonas grabs onto the hammock for support. "You people are crazy. Don't your lives have any value?"

"Forget him," says Barry Struhl. "I knew he wasn't one of us."

"Yes he is," Mia answers. "Come on, Jonas, you need this. Fergie, where's his wetsuit?"

Fergie tosses a wetsuit and harness at him. "Yes, come on, Professor. Show the rest of us losers what you've got hangin' between those legs."

Jonas and the Daredevils crouch in the companionway, waiting for the boat to level off.

"Now!" Fergie and Coffey release the latch on the hold, then leap out into the weather, slamming the hatch shut behind them.

Doc Shinto shines his flashlight on Jonas, guiding him into the body harness. "Relax. Nobody here wants to die. We're actually quite good at taking precautions, and you'll probably be less seasick out there than you will down below."

The ship rolls beneath them, nearly tossing Jonas back down the stairwell.

"As we speak, Fergie and Coffey are rigging long coils of rope that will run from the mizzen mast to your harness, so there's no way for us to lose you. Put the life preserver on before you attach the harness, it'll keep you afloat."

Jonas puts on the neon-orange vest and clips it tightly around his waist. "I'm still not doing this."

"No one says you have to. Just come up on deck and make an appearance, then back down you go."

Mia helps him adjust the Navy harness over the flotation device.

Someone stamps twice above their heads. Barry and Evan open the hatch, allowing the clip-on ends of three long tow ropes to fall into the stairwell.

Jennie, Evan, and Dee secure the rope clips to their body harnesses, and then the three leap out of the hole and into the maelstrom, whooping it up like kids.

Barry pulls the hatch closed, shutting out the storm.

Jonas covers his eyes, his heart pounding madly in his chest. *This is insane. I'm sixty-three years old. I'll probably have a heart attack before I even make it out there.*

Mia leans in to the light. "We're all outside on the next shift. Is he ready, Doc?"

"No," Jonas moans.

"He's ready," Doc says, checking his harness. "Remember

Jonas, there's nowhere you can go, you're not going to
drown, so just let Mother Nature do all the work and enjoy
the ride."

"Wouldn't you rather drill one of my cavities instead?"

A double knock signals them from above. Barry and Doc
release the hatch.

Four ropes drop into the hole.

Mia secures one to her own harness, then clips one to
Jonas's gear.

"Mia, I'm not doing this."

"Shh." She steals a kiss, pressing her tongue into his
mouth. "See you on the other side."

She follows Doc and Barry into the storm, leaving Jonas
looking up into a lightning-laced ebony sky. *The Hell with
this.* He reaches up to re-seal the hatch when suddenly he is
yanked out of the hole by his tow rope.

The main deck is a blinding windstorm of rain and sea
that drenches him within seconds. As he opens his eyes
against the fury, he sees the *Neptune*'s bow rise out of the sea
like a great beast, tossing him flat on his back.

Jonas flops like a fish out of water, rolling backward down
the sloping wet deck. He drags himself to his feet, just in
time to see a wall of water—thirty feet higher than the upper
deck—roll toward the port side of the ship.

The swell lifts, then rolls the *Neptune* sideways, sending
Jonas sliding blindly backward, his momentum launching
him toward the starboard rail—

And then he is airborne, screaming into the night.

Then he is underwater.

The high-pitched wind shear is muted by a low baritone
roar and bone-chilling cold as Jonas plummets beneath the
suffocating inky environment, his horrified mind not sure
which direction is up.

He flounders—is driven back to the surface by the flotation device, then forcibly yanked facefirst across a deep de-

pression of water by the tow rope attached to his harness.

He manages to lift his head above water as lightning illuminates the silhouette of the *Neptune*, the ship listing on the other side of a mountain of sea.

Jonas gags and hyperventilates, his fear herding him toward a state of uncontrolled panic as he is again jerked through the water.

Grabbing the rope in both hands, he manages to roll onto his back, then he hears—"Jooo-nasss!"

He turns and sees Mia, racing in from behind him on a pair of waterskis. She flops down on her butt next to him, wraps her left arm around his waist, then shoves an ankle collar and tow rope into his hand.

"For you, lover!"

She is back on her skis and gone before he can stammer a reply. .

The valley suddenly lifts him higher and he finds himself on top of the mountain, looking down at the main deck of the *Neptune* as his stomach goes out from under him.

The ship yanks him forward again, but now he is on his back, collar around his ankle, reeling in Mia's rope and the big-wave surfboard. He slips his feet quickly into the two rubber housings, pulls the board forward between his legs—

—then he is up, balancing out of the water, gripping the rope attached to his harness in both hands as he bends his knees, his surfboard slicing down an endless mountain of water. Jonas yells at the top of his lungs until his voice gives out and the valley becomes a mountain again.

He drops his butt onto the board for the tow back up, his fear ever-so-slightly nudged aside by a bizarre feeling of pride.

He reaches the crest of the swell and stands, this time surfing the wave, no longer needing to hold onto the rope secured to his harness.

And there, beneath the lightning-laced heavens and the

four-story swells, in a storm so harsh the driving rain is leaving welts on his exposed flesh . . . Jonas Taylor smiles.

Dawn's gray sliver appears forty minutes later, chasing the storm to the south. The rain eases, the wind dying down to mere gusts, the waves losing their fury.

An exhausted, invigorated Jonas Taylor is hauled out of the sea to a smattering of applause.

Mia greets him as he slips out of the harness and flotation vest. She drapes a towel around his neck and hugs him. "Welcome back, Papa Daredevil. How does it feel to be alive again?"

Shivering, his legs still a bit unsteady, he returns her hug. "That was the second stupidest thing I ever did, and I loved it. Thank you."

He looks up as groups of Daredevils and crewmen rush to the opposite side of the ship.

Jonas and Mia join them.

Coffey and Fergie are standing by the port side rail, arguing.

"You attached the tow ropes!"

"And you attached the clips!"

"Do you even know who it was?"

"I don't know. Who's not here?"

Mia steps in between them. "What happened?"

Coffey holds up the severed end of a rope. "We lost somebody."

Dee Hatcher hurries over. "The captain's turning the ship around to begin a search. We accounted for everyone but Barry and Doc."

"Doc's below," Evan says. "I haven't seen Barry."

"Oh, shit." Fergie shakes his head in disbelief. "I was with him. We were surfing together. He's a big guy, but the rope should've held him. How could this have happened?"

"It couldn't," Coffey states, the anger rising in his voice. "These harnesses are the best the Navy offers, and this rope's strong enough to haul a small truck out of the sea. There has to be another explanation."

Jonas examines the end of the thick, nylon cord. The edges are slightly frayed, as if the rope had been cut by a very sharp saw.

CHAPTER

19

TANAKA LAGOON
MONTEREY, CALIFORNIA

Mac cuts the *Angel-II*'s engines and weighs anchor. The fishing boat bobs in three-foot seas next to the coil of barbed wire and a series of bright orange buoys that mark the submerged entrance of the lagoon's canal.

David Taylor, dressed in his wetsuit, remains seated by the transom, his dark brown eyes searching the horizon.

Mac slaps him on the back, startling him. "Come on, kid, get your gear on, we're burning daylight."

"I don't feel so good, Uncle Mac. Maybe you oughta go without me?"

"This was your idea. No sense luring Angel into the lagoon if we can't shut the doors behind her."

David starts to reply, instead, he rushes below to the head.

Mac grins. "Relax, kid! Ghosts can't harm you." He slips his arms inside the upper half of the wetsuit dangling around his waist, then hoists the buoyancy control vest and its air tank onto his shoulders. Balancing on the edge of the transom, he tightens his fins, then secures his weight belt.

David peeks out from the companionway, his complexion pale. "Sorry."

"Stay on the boat, I won't be long." Mac spits into his mask, rubs saliva around the glass, then jumps into the Pacific.

The cold water snaps him awake.

Bobbing along the surface, he repositions his mask, then waving to David, releases air from the BCD hose. Mac sinks feetfirst into the ocean, plunging within arm's reach of the barnacle-covered steel facing of the open northern door.

It has been seven years since Mac last dived the canal. Still, the former naval engineer has a pretty good idea why the hydraulic doors will not close.

He checks his depth gauge. *Fifty feet . . . sixty feet . . .* He pinches his nose and equalizes. *Seventy feet . . . eighty feet . . . there's the bottom.*

Mac stops his descent, then swims around the front of the door.

His first stop is the junction box. In David's haste to surface, the boy has left the lid off the barrel-size device. Reaching into the mechanism, Mac punches in the code to activate the override control panel.

The red light flickers green, then red again.

Mac shakes the junction box with both hands.

The light turns green.

Damn generator must be going. Add another five grand to this money pit . . .

Mac reaches into the box, feeling for the OVERRIDE switch, and presses the rubber insulated button marked CLOSE.

A crescendo of groaning steel thunders all around him as the two canal doors inch along their track, then grind to a halt.

Mac shuts down the system, then swims out from behind the door to confirm his suspicions.

Piled high against the inside of each door, preventing them from closing, are small mountains of silt.

———

Mac surfaces behind his boat ten minutes later. He removes his fins and hands them to David, then climbs up the dive ladder.

"Well?"

"Generator's going, but the real problem's sand. Tide brings it in by the ton. I'm not surprised, it's been seven years since your grandfather last dredged the canal opening."

"So what do we do?"

"Do? I don't know. Do you have an extra ten grand lying around in some bank account?"

"Ten grand?"

"Ten grand minimum. Have to get a barge out here, the entire expanse of seafloor between the doors needs to be dredged. We're talking a two- to three-day job. And you can add another five grand to replace the generator that powers the junction box."

"Fifteen thousand dollars. Geez . . ." David flops down onto a seat cushion.

"Welcome to 'Life Sucks 101.' Want my godfatherly advice? Sign off on the Dietsch Brothers deal and walk away from this whole mess while you can."

"No."

"No?" Mac slips off his BCD vest. "Okay, so what're you gonna do? Grab a bucket and shovel and clear the mess yourself?"

"Maybe there's another option."

The main office of Jericho Mortgage is located in downtown Monterey in an old brick-face building that once belonged to a bank. The original lobby still contains the old stainless-steel vault door leading to the walk-in safe, only now it's being used to store company files.

Rodney Kenneth Cotner, CEO and President of Jericho Mortgage, is a self-made businessman originally from the central Ohio valley. After years of selling cars, the fast-talking workaholic opened a mortgage company specializing in refinancing. From one location in Lancaster, Ohio, he opened a dozen more, then decided to sell the business and "settle down" on the West Coast.

But wheeling and dealing was in Cotner's blood, and after three months of fishing and sunshine he jumped back into the game, this time courting only the high-end business. Six years of hard work, coupled with a flair for "schmoozing like John Gotti," established Rod among the Northern California elite.

Rodney leans back in his leather chair, his neatly cropped brown hair a contrast to the rough-looking whiskers of his mustache and goatee. Puffing on his cigar like a wannabe gangster, he blows a lungful of smoke at the fourteen-year-old boy. "You're yanking my chain, aren't you, kid?"

David shakes his head. "No sir. Angel's in California waters. It's only a matter of time before someone else spots her."

"You're killing me, you know that. I've invested years into pulling this sale together."

"The lagoon was designed to be an aquarium, not some stupid wharfside condominium. My grandfather said Angel's shows were sold out two years in advance."

"No offense, kid, but your grandfather was a kook. If business was so good, then why'd he have to sell controlling interest to Benedict Singer?"

"There were lawsuits. Grandpa said the Feds were behind most of it. In the end, they returned the title and—"

"Yeah, yeah, I know the story." Rodney stands, circling his desk. "Look kid, I'm a businessman, not a bank. You need money, I got it, but I want a piece of the action, not the kind of return I could get from a CD. How much did your grandfather leave you?"

"Twenty percent."

"I want fifteen."

David's eyes widen. "No way."

"Okay, you're the boss. Listen, best of luck to you and your parents. Don't let the door hit you on the ass on your way out."

"Five."

David and Rodney turn. Patricia Pedrazzoli is standing in the doorway, a smug look on her face.

Rodney's eyes glare daggers. "Something I can help you with, Ms. Pedrazzoli?"

"How much money do you need, David?"

"Mac says fifteen thousand, plus another ten for bait and supplies."

"Okay, I'll do it for five percent, plus a position on your staff, once you catch the Meg. Something in public relations."

David looks at Rodney, grinning from ear to ear. "Done deal."

Rod is livid. "David, wait outside, I need to speak with my ex-employee a moment."

"Go on, David, I'll be right out." Patricia shuts the door behind him.

"What the hell do you think you're doing?"

"Preventing you from taking advantage of a kid."

"Bullshit. You're buying in on the Dietsch Brothers deal at pennies on the dollar."

"Consider it insurance. Face it, Rod, the kid's got both of us by the short and curlies. If I go along with him now, become his 'partner,' I stand a better chance of persuading him to sign once his mother gets back from Canada. Besides, I deserve it. I'm the one who's been working that deal, not you."

"It'll never hold in court. Kid's a minor."

"I checked the will. Masao gave Mac power of attorney. He'll sign off on the deal, and once money actually exchanges hands, it'll be impossible for David or Terry to back out of the Dietsch Brothers contract."

Rodney sits back in his chair. "I like it, but five percent? Jesus, Trish, we could've at least gotten ten."

NORTH PACIFIC OCEAN
34 NAUTICAL MILES NORTHEAST OF PALAU
268 NAUTICAL MILES SOUTHWEST OF THE MARIANA
TRENCH

The Republic of Palau is an archipelago, more than 400 miles long, consisting of several hundred islands that dot a lagoon-like azure sea. Only eight islands within this maze of mushroom-shaped land masses are inhabited, with most of the population living in the capital city of Koror. In this lost tropical oasis one can find five-star hotels, museums, Japanese shrines, and rusting military relics left over from World War II.

What really attracts tourists to this jewel of the Pacific are the islands' unusual dive spots, named "Number One" Underwater Wonder of the World. The Kayangel atoll and its tropical lagoon are a favorite among snorkelers. The island of Peleliu, located along the southern boundary of the Palau Lagoon, once a center for the Japanese defense forces, offers an abundance of downed World War II aircraft and boats for those who enjoy wreck diving. Ngemelis Wall, also known as "Big Drop-off," is a reef covered with coral, sea fans, sponges, and fish, its vertical drop plunging more than 1,000 feet. For the more experienced diver, Palau's coastline contains vast underwater catacombs and ominous blue holes, fast currents and one of the planet's greatest concentrations of marine life.

Over 1,500 species of fish and seven hundred types of coral inhabit seas that average a balmy eighty-two degrees Fahrenheit. Palau's predators include Grey Reef sharks, barracudas, snappers, manta rays, and Orca. It is not unusual for divers to run into an occasional Whale shark.

What attracts such a diversity of animal life to Palau's islands are a series of nutrient-rich currents that originate from several neighboring deepwater trenches which frame the eastern boundary of the Philippine Sea Plate. The Izu-

Bonin Trench, Palau Trench, Yap Trench, and Mariana Trench, together with the Ayu Trough, are all part of a complex region of tectonic convergence points that feed the island's underwater food chain.

The Spanish galleon, *Neptune*, moves through calm seas at two knots, eighty-five hundred feet above the slice of underwater geology known as the Yap Trench. The tall ship is slowly circling thirty to forty Sperm whales, the mammals resting along the surface in their standard mating ritual "logging" formation. Females and their calves congregate in the largest groups, while young bulls form "bachelor" clusters along the periphery. Competing for attention, these adolescent males use echolocation to blast loud clicks through the sea, hoping to entice a female.

Jonas Taylor watches the scene below from his perch atop the main masthead. One hundred feet above the deck, he spots a powerful vaporous plume of whale breath, signifying the arrival of a mature bull Sperm. The dominant leviathan moves toward the cows like a conquering king, its silvery-grayish head nearly twice the girth of his juvenile counterparts.

Through binoculars, Jonas sees "Gray-head" duck underwater, his enormous thirteen-foot-wide fluke remaining above the surface. With a resounding *slap*, the bull's tail strikes the surface over and over, the sounds carrying across the sea like gunshots.

Jonas looks below as a high-pitched whine buzzes the air.

A Zodiac has launched from the *Neptune*. Jonas focuses his binoculars on the small craft and its lone passenger.

Erik Hollander aims his Zodiac for the super yacht, which has come to rest a half-mile east of the *Neptune*. Cutting the engine, he guides the motorized raft along the port side of the sleek ship. Two Micronesian crewmen greet him, one ties off his raft, the other helps him on board.

"Where's Maren?"

The crewman points to the upper deck.

Hollander ascends the spiral staircase, his fair complexion burning beneath the noonday sun.

Michael Maren lounges in a padded chair beneath an umbrella, working at a laptop.

"Maren, we need to talk."

The marine biologist never looks up. "Mr. Hollander. To what do I owe this unscheduled visit?"

Hollander slams Maren's laptop shut. "Don't screw with me. I know what you did, and I'm angry as hell."

Maren looks up, glaring at him behind dark sunglasses. "Be careful, Hollywood. You're on my ship now."

"Barry Struhl was one of my most popular Daredevils. He was water-skiing the storm last night when his rope mysteriously snapped."

"And this is my fault?"

"You and I both know what really happened. You're out of control."

"I was never in control. As I keep telling you, I can only coax the animal to the surface, I can't force it to behave. It's not a trained seal."

"You're lying. You knew Jonas Taylor was in the water with our Daredevils. You used that device of yours to lure it up last night."

"I wonder if you'd be so upset if your camera crew had managed to catch your Daredevil's death on film."

"You pompous ass, I didn't hire you to kill off members of my team."

"No, they seem to be doing quite a good job of it themselves."

"Now you listen here. My company's financing this venture, and so far, we've got nothing to show for it."

Maren re-opens his laptop, punches a few keys, then spins the monitor around for Hollander to see.

The image displays a topographical map of their location in the North Pacific. Maren strikes another key, the image animating into a real-time depth chart. A blue dot indicates the position of the *Neptune*. Three dozen green dots congregating along the surface designate the Sperm whales.

A lone red dot hovers at the bottom of the screen.

"See this red dot? That's our friend. As you can see, he's circling the *Neptune* at 3,500 feet. That's what you're paying me for. Now get back to your ship."

"I need him to surface tonight."

"I don't control Nature—"

"I know, I know, just use that device you stole from Woods Hole to lure him up."

"Stole?" Maren's face flushes purple. "Satoshi!"

A mountain of a Japanese man emerges from the hot tub, the water line receding to half its previous depth. The half-naked, 375-pound former Sumo wrestler causes the deck to shake as he lumbers toward Hollander.

"Satoshi, show this Hollywood leech back to his boat."

Hollander backs up against the rail. "Okay, Maren, I'm sorry. I know you didn't steal the drone, the plans were yours to begin with. Maren, did you hear me? Call him off."

Satoshi grabs Erik Hollander by the neck with one paw, the producer's groin with the other, pressing him effortlessly above his head.

Hollander thrashes within the big man's grasp "Let . . . go or no . . . payment."

Maren scoffs. "You'll get what you desire soon enough, and then you'll pay me double. Until then, stay on your own ship and do your job."

Maren nods.

With a grunt, Satoshi launches Erik Hollander over the rail.

The flailing man screams as he plummets two stories into the sea.

Hollander surfaces. He swims to the Zodiac, then hauls himself painfully over the side of the inflatable. "You're through, Maren. By the time I'm done with you, you'll . . . you'll never work in Hollywood—or anywhere else again!"

Two decks up, a grinning Satoshi blows him a kiss.

OLYMPIC COAST NATIONAL MARINE SANCTUARY
NORTHWEST COASTLINE OF WASHINGTON
PACIFIC OCEAN

The Olympic Coast National Marine Sanctuary spans 135 miles along Washington State's rocky Olympic coastline, extending thirty-five miles offshore, covering more than 2,500 nautical miles of Pacific Ocean. The boundary between land and sea encompasses rugged cliffs, hundreds of offshore islands, and sandy, desolate beaches bordered by dense forests.

The northernmost end of the sanctuary begins in the Strait of Juan de Fuca. Follow the Pacific seafloor to the southwest and the geology makes a sudden drop into the Juan de Fuca Submarine Canyon, a deepwater gorge that spreads across the Juan de Fuca Plate.

The tectonic plate is part of the Cascadia Subduction Zone. As the Juan de Fuca Plate slides beneath the continental plate, its action pushes the Olympic Mountains higher at a daily rate approximating that of the average fingernail growth. Driven back into the Earth's core, molten materials form along the western edge of the plate, creating a new seafloor, along with a string of underwater volcanoes.

The big male descends into the depths of the Juan de Fuca Submarine Canyon, its slack jaw opening and closing, its ampullae of Lorenzini registering the presence of several whale pods feeding in the shallows. While its last meal was far too small to satiate its hunger, the Megalodon refuses to

venture into the painful sun to attack, its left eye still stinging from the searchlight.

And so the creature remains within the dark recess of the
canyon, rising every so often to test the upper shadows of
gray as it follows the abyss south, waiting impatiently for the
arrival of night.

ABOARD THE COAST GUARD CUTTER *CAPE CALVERT*
GIANTS GRAVEYARD
NORTHWEST COASTLINE OF WASHINGTON

The early morning sun sparkles brilliantly against the kelp-
strewn surface of the Pacific. A cold wind drives the ocean,
lashing it against the rocky shores and towering cliff faces of
Giants Graveyard—monolithic pillars, carved by Nature,
that dot the coastal landscape for miles.

Terry Taylor leans against the port side rail, her mind
wandering as she gazes at the scenic coastline.

She had argued all night with Joshua, who steadfastly refused to drop her off on land, fearing they'd lose the Megalodon. Remaining deep, the creature had led them on a wild
chase as it continued its journey to the southwest through the
Juan de Fuca Submarine Canyon.

Exhausted, her nerves frayed, Terry stares at the coastline,
contemplating a decision. *Either stay on board and continue
tracking the monster or take the Zodiac to shore while it's
still light out. Whatever you're going to do, do it now. Take
charge. Don't allow yourself to be manipulated into a dangerous situation by another controlling man.*

Joshua joins her on deck, offering her a cup of steaming
hot cocoa. "Thought you might accept this as a formal peace
offering."

"This isn't a game, Josh. We either resolve this now, or
I'm taking the Zodiac."

"Okay, let's resolve it. This is your expedition, you're

calling the shots, but I'm still the one fronting the expenses, which means I should have some say as well. Last night you became overly emotional. You panicked. If I had listened to you and dropped you off, we'd have lost the Meg for sure."

"It doesn't matter. Next time I order you to take me in, then you'd better damn well do it."

"Be reasonable, Terry. We were never in any danger. In fact, Angel seemed more scared of us than we were of her. She won't venture near our underwater lights, and the engines probably freaked her out, too."

"It's not your decision. This is my life, Josh, and I won't allow you or anyone else to control me." She takes the cocoa from him, then sits down on a wooden bench outside the pilothouse. "You think you know me, but you don't. I used to be able to handle this stuff, but that was a long time ago, way back before Angel first escaped."

"I think you're still pretty tough."

She ignores the compliment. "There was this man... Benedict Singer. When things got bad for us financially, he became majority shareholder of the Tanaka Lagoon. We had no choice at the time, the courts were really putting the screws to us. Anyway, right before Angel escaped, Singer manipulated me into descending with him into the Mariana Trench aboard his abyssal habitat, the Benthos. We were seven miles down, exploring the Challenger Deep. I was supposed to be investigating the disappearance of a submersible. While we were down there, the ship was attacked by creatures that dated back to the Jurassic Age."

"Kronosaurs. I read about that. Pretty frightening."

"As bad as they were, the monsters aboard the Benthos were even worse. One of the crewmen, a Russian, tried to molest me. I went to Benedict, fearing for my life, but he was just playing head games with me, always promising we'd surface soon, though he never had any intention of letting me go. Turns out he was only down there to locate a specific type of manganese nodule, one he thought would

unlock the secrets of fusion energy. I became expendable after I learned what he was after. There was nowhere to hide,
no way to escape. I tried, but was caught by his mistress, Celeste, a woman who had it out for my husband. When all
seemed lost, Jonas rescued me, but the experience—" she
pauses, "—let's just say Benedict really did a number on me.
That was almost twenty years ago, and I still suffer from
nightmares. Believe it or not, I used to be pretty daring in my
day, piloting airplanes and submersibles; I was even into
mountain climbing. Not anymore. Now I avoid risks I suffer
from claustrophobia, even commercial airliners make me
queasy, and God help you if you ever corner me."

"But look how far you've come just over the last few days.
You flew up to British Columbia, then let me take you up in
my puddle jumper. You were able to get on board this boat,
you hung in there last night when we saw the Meg."

"It's only because I'm desperate. My family's in a real fix,
we need this to work. Don't be fooled by what you see. I'm
just as frightened as I've always been. The only reason I'm
still here is because I was too scared to pilot that Zodiac last
night."

"Don't be scared. Angel will take the bait and then we
have her. Let's stick to the plan, it'll all work out in the end."

"And if I insist on you putting me to shore?"

"Then I'll order the boat to the nearest port."

She studies his face. "Okay, Josh, I'm giving you one last
chance, but—"

"You have my word."

"Fine." She heads for the companionway.

"Where are you going?"

"I need sleep. Wake me before the sun sets."

"Hey, one question. Whatever happened to that Russian
guy?"

"Sergei?" She turns, looking the young scientist straight
in the eye. "I killed him."

ABOARD THE *NEPTUNE*
34 NAUTICAL MILES NORTHEAST OF PALAU
268 NAUTICAL MILES SOUTHWEST OF THE MARIANA
TRENCH

Susan Ferraris and the seven remaining members of the Daredevils file into the captain's gallery. Mia, Dee, Mike Coffey, and Evan Stewart flop onto the mattress of the antique four-post bed. Fergie, Doc Shinto, and Jennie squeeze together on the love seat.

Erik exits his bathroom, smoothing out the patches of hair still wet from his shower. "Afternoon. Susan and I called you here, away from the cameras, to discuss what happened last night."

"There's nothing to discuss," Coffey says. "It was an accident."

"I spoke to Barry's family this morning," Jennie says. "They're taking it pretty hard, but they're not pointing fingers."

"Wait until the lawyers get involved," Doc Shinto mutters.

"You people are missing the point," Susan interjects. "Last night's escapade was an unscheduled, foolish stunt that had nothing to do with our show."

Dee Hatcher smirks. "Foolish, compared to swimming with sharks?"

Fergie looks at Erik. "You buggers are just peeved because it wasn't captured on film."

"And if it had been part of the show, maybe Barry'd still be alive," Erik snaps back. "Like it or not, all of us are being paid to entertain. If you wanted to do an impromptu stunt, you should have come to us first."

"We're not a dog and pony show," Mia snaps. "We do these things to feel alive, not to satisfy the Nielsen ratings."

"This is still a business," Susan retorts. "All of you knew that going in. All of you signed contracts. We could have filmed last night's stunt, or, at the very least, we could have rigged one of you with a Minicam."

"Should have rigged Barry," Fergie states. "Maybe then we'd know what happened to him."

Erik glances at Susan. "Yes, well that brings up our next little item. Our official statement regarding Barry Struhl is that he's been lost at sea. Two Coast Guard choppers out of Manila have joined the search. Since Barry was wearing a life preserver, there's still a good chance he may be found."

None of the Daredevils seem convinced.

"Meanwhile, the show must go on." Susan looks around the room. "Barry's disappearance gives the Hammerheads an unfair advantage. Since the accident occurred outside the parameters of competition, we feel the Makos should be allowed to add another member to their team."

The Daredevils look at one another.

"Who're you going to add?" Coffey asks.

Erik paces the cabin. "Keep an open mind here. We were thinking about Jonas Taylor."

Susan mumbles, "We sure won't miss him as a color analyst."

Jennie shakes her head. "He's too old."

"He handled the storm just fine," Mia retorts.

Erik looks to Fergie. "You're the Mako captain, it's your call."

"Ask him, but he won't do it. Years ago, yes, but he's lost his balls." The Australian grins. "But I think I know someone who will."

A late afternoon sun seeps through the galley's open viewports, brightening the chamber with its orange hue. The meeting area is packed, the cameras rolling.

A cake is wheeled out on a cart for the guest of honor.

"Happy birthday, dear Dani, happy birthday to you."

"Go on, Dani," Fergie winks, "make a wish and give us a blow."

Dani laughs, then blows out the candles.

Overexuberant Candy Girls bounce in their revealing bikini tops as they clap, parading before the camera lenses.

Fergie scoops up some icing with his index finger, then offers it to the eighteen-year-old. The crowd whoops it up as Dani suggestively sucks the icing from the Daredevil's finger.

Jonas watches from behind the cameras, seething.

Charlotte maneuvers toward center stage. "Quiet please, quiet. Before the Makos offer us their next challenge, we have an announcement. As you know, one of the Makos, Daredevil Barry Struhl, was swept overboard in last night's storm. The Manila Coast Guard has joined the Palau Island authorities in the search, and we still believe Barry will be found. Meanwhile, the show must go on, a new Daredevil selected to take Barry's place. I'm happy to announce that joining the Makos on their next stunt is our own birthday girl, Danielle Taylor!"

"What?!" Jonas's throat constricts as the throng cheers and the Makos raise his daughter onto their shoulders, taking her for a victory lap around the galley.

Jonas pushes through the crowd. Spotting Erik Hollander, he lunges at the man, grabbing him by the collar.

"Jonas, easy—"

"You sonuvabitch, what the hell do you think you're doing? My daughter's not a Daredevil. I never agreed to any of this!"

"You declined our offer, she accepted. She's eighteen now, take it up with her."

Jonas throws him to the ground, chasing after his daughter.

TANAKA LAGOON
MONTEREY BAY, CALIFORNIA

David Taylor is frustrated.

He has searched every storage room in his grandfather's facility and every office. Unpacked dozens of sealed cartons and gone through every shelf. Moved forklifts-full of equipment and even checked the trash bins, and still he cannot find Angel's portable thumper.

He removes the two-way radio from his belt. "Uncle Mac?"

"Yeah, kid?"

Mac is on the *Angel-II*, unloading equipment, his boat tied off in the southern end of the tank.

"The thumper's gone."

"Did you look in the mechanical room?"

"Ten times. And I searched the whole building. It's gone."

"Well, if it's gone, it's gone. Wouldn't be the first time we've been vandalized. Of course, now there's no way to prove Angel's really out there." Mac looks up as Patricia climbs over the concrete seawall and boards his boat, briefcase in hand. "David, I'll call you back."

Mac tosses the radio against a seat cushion. "You've got some nerve, lady. Is this your idea of striking back at me?"

"What are you talking about?"

"Your little deal with David. Did you really think I'd sign off on that?"

"Wake up, Mac. This facility's deep in debt. Terry and Jonas have one chance of walking away with a few dollars in their pockets, and David's about to blow all that because of some delusion."

"It still doesn't give you the right to—"

Patricia falls against Mac's chest as the entire lagoon reverberates as if struck by a gigantic tuning fork.

"What the hell is that?"

"It's the underwater speakers. David's activated Angel's signal. He's trying to prove the Meg's really out there."

"Persistent little shit, isn't he?" She opens her briefcase, removing a stack of contracts.

"Forget it, Trish, I'm not signing. Let his mother deal with it."

"Yes, well I received a message from his mother yesterday. Now she says she'll be gone until the end of the week. Meanwhile Rodney met with the Dietsch Brothers. They're rescinding their offer as of midnight tonight. David's signature saves the deal, but only if you endorse it."

"Forget it." He heads below.

Patricia chases after him. "You drunken bastard, you owe me. Who do you think made the last three payments on this boat? Who's been taking care of you for the past six months while you've been partying your brains out?"

"That's between us. You're ripping my godson off." Mac ducks as she tosses a plastic dish at him.

"Nobody's ripping anybody off! Grab a calculator and look at the damn figures."

David is in the subterranean observation room, staring at the olive-green waters of the main tank. The seven-inch-thick Lexan glass reverberates every fifteen seconds from the underwater speakers, but David is not listening to the signal, he is more focused on his two-way radio and the static-laced conversation bleeding through.

As he eavesdrops on Mac and Patricia, his eyes remain focused on the *Angel-II*'s keel, which occupies the upper right-hand corner of the viewing glass.

Mac finishes his calculations. "According to my figures, David's ten percent adds an extra forty gees to your commission."

"Minus the twenty-five thousand I'm advancing him for expenses."

"Fifteen of which is being used to dredge the canal. Seems to me the Dietsch Brothers ought to be paying for that themselves."

Whomp!

The *Angel-II* rocks as if pummeled by another vessel, the sudden lurch sending a stack of dirty dishes crashing to the floor.

Mac helps Patricia to her feet, then races up the short companionway to the outer deck.

"Oh, Jesus . . ."

Angel's gargantuan head is protruding out of the water next to the boat. The creature's gray-blue eyes gaze longingly at the rusted main frame towering overhead, her hideous lower jaw quivering as if she is talking to herself.

Mac stares at the frightening beast, his body trembling. *She's waiting to be fed . . .*

Patricia climbs topside. Mac grabs her mouth in midscream, whispering, "Don't move, don't make a sound."

David is on his feet, his pounding heart threatening to punch its way out of his chest. He stares at Angel's flapping gill slits, mesmerized by the sheer size of the creature's snowy-white forty-ton girth.

Tired of waiting for food, the Megalodon slips beneath the surface, revealing her face to the boy.

David's mouth drops as he sees the massive head for the first time. He stares, incredulous, at the cantaloupe-size nostrils that inhale streams of seawater. His eyes dart to the powerful jaws, large enough to drive his father's car through, and those hideous pink gums that mark a boundary of bone that can unhinge and jut forward as it delivers the most devastating bite in the history of evolution.

Inches of glass separate him from rows of triangular

white teeth, as large as his face, as sharp as the most deadly
scalpel. He gazes into the dark gullet that leads to hell. He
looks into the pupil-less eye, gray-blue and sinister—

—that now stares back at him!

David's skin tingles, his constricted chest laboring a
breath. His eyes dart to his far right and the cinder-block
wall with the red button beneath the sign that reads: EMER-
GENCY ONLY.

Angel nudges her snout against the Lexan barrier, her
enormous weight bending the glass within its frame. A distant memory tugs at the Meg's brain . . .

A distant memory of food.

The Megalodon moves away from the viewing window
and circles the southern end of the tank.

"Oh, geez!"

David leaps for the wall, the boy's right palm slamming
against the red button as Angel charges the glass.

A veil of bubbles explodes along the outside of the glass
as the two ends of the titanium barrier slam shut over the
Lexan glass seconds before the colossus barrels snout-first
into the obstruction.

Mac grabs Patricia and holds on as the seven-foot dorsal fin
circles back toward the boat, Angel's left flank skimming
the bow.

A sonic *BOOM* shakes the tank. Ten-foot swells crash
over the side of the boat, the *Angel-II* rocking in the sudden
chop, its hull banging against the interior concrete wall of
the tank.

"You okay?"

Patricia nods, then screams.

Angel's head has surfaced next to the boat, the Meg eyeballing the two humans.

"Move!" Mac half-carries, half-pushes Patricia toward
the starboard rail as the Megalodon's jaws gnaw at the port

side of the transom, her upper teeth puncturing the fiberglass surface, splitting it into kindling.

Mac grabs Patricia around her waist and practically throws her over the concrete seawall as the boat tilts beneath him. He sees her tumble safely over the barrier as his boat is bashed again from below, the inertia causing the bowline to snap.

Horrified, Mac can only hold on as his boat drifts free of the seawall toward the middle of the lagoon.

Whomp!

The angry Meg pummels the hull again, driving the bow clear out of the water.

Mac falls against the aluminum ladder leading up to the flying bridge. He pulls himself up a rung at a time—

Whomp!

Angel wallops the hull again, tipping the boat sideways.

Patricia screams, "Mac, start the engine!"

Mac stumbles up the ladder to the flying bridge. He falls against the control panel and presses the POWER switch.

The twin engines jump to life, the propellers catching water. He shifts out of neutral and the boat leaps forward—

—until the mangled driveshaft clanks and screeches, sputters, and dies.

Whomp!

The boat is bashed again, only this time Mac hears the sickening report of splintering fiberglass and wood as the hull buckles and the lagoon's waters rush inside his ruptured vessel.

The *Angel-II* rolls slowly to port, the flooding boat already listing.

Angel circles, waiting for her prey to die.

Patricia looks around. Spots Masao's old rowboat. Grabbing an oar, she races to the northern end of the tank.

Mac stands on the spinning deck, already knee-deep in water. His heart races as the pale dorsal fin glides by. He is thirty yards from the nearest concrete seawall, thirty seconds from sinking, thirty seconds from death.

Whack.

Patricia leans over the seawall and slaps the surface hard with the paddle.

Whack. Whack . . . whack . . . whack . . .

The *Angel-II*'s bow rises vertically as the boat's half-chewed transom begins slipping beneath the surface.

Mac grabs one of the aluminum ladder's rungs for balance and does something he has not done in twenty years: Pray.

Whack . . . whack . . . whack . . . whack . . .

Waist-deep in water, Mac feels Angel's powerful tug as the 76-foot albino beast glides by, heading for the northern end of the tank.

Not yet . . .

Mac treads water, slipping away from the *Angel-II*'s deck as the gurgling boat continues sinking beneath the surface.

Wait . . .

He watches the Meg continue toward the sound of the disturbance.

The transom strikes the bottom of the tank with a resounding *thump.*

Halfway across the lagoon, the dorsal fin turns.

Oh, hell . . .

Mac ducks his head into the olive-green water and swims, his arms digging, his legs kicking like mad, his hands straining to reach the eastern seawall of the tank, his mind screaming at him to move faster even as he stresses over how he's ever going to pull himself up the five-foot-high incline of concrete.

Angel homes in on the new disturbance, cruising along the surface at twenty knots.

As Mac reaches the wall, he sees his godson straddling the barrier, offering him his hand.

Three body lengths away, Angel raises her head above water, her mouth opening to engulf her prey.

Mac snatches David's arm in his right hand, step-kicks up

against the seam of the tank, snags the top edge of the wall in his left hand, and, in one adrenaline-enhanced motion, heaves himself over the barrier, dragging the boy with him.

The two roll into the first row of seats as Angel pulverizes the seawall, the vertical concrete slab bursting on impact, sections of the decimated wall tumbling into the tank. The dorsal fin glides by, followed seconds later by the towering caudal fin, which slaps at the remains of the crumbling barrier.

Mac drags David to his feet, the two shell-shocked survivors hurrying up the arena stairs, not stopping until they reach the tenth row.

Angel circles the sunken boat, her inertia causing the *Angel-II*'s transom to dance along the bottom of the tank. The agitated female drives her snout into the pilothouse and pushes the sunken vessel toward the pulverized eastern seawall.

Whomp!

The boat buckles against the side of the tank, its momentum sending eight-foot waves washing into the arena.

The monster circles four more times before gliding out of the lagoon. Moving through the ocean-access canal, she slips past the open steel doors and disappears into the depths of the submarine canyon.

Patricia hurries over to Mac and hugs him, seawater dripping from his soaked clothing.

"Hey!" David taps his godfather on the shoulder, breaking up the embrace. "So? Do you believe me now?"

CHAPTER

20

"Dad, you can give me all the advice you want, just don't be upset if I ignore it." Danielle Taylor defiantly zips up her wetsuit. "I'm eighteen now. I'm old enough to vote, old enough to make my own decisions, old enough to finally live my life and make my own mistakes."

Jonas follows her as she collects her scuba gear. "You may be eighteen, but you're still my daughter, and I forbid you to do this."

She turns on him. "What're you going to do? Ground me? Lock me in your cabin for the rest of the voyage? I'm not a kid anymore."

"Then stop acting like one. Use some common sense. What you're about to do is dangerous. Wild animals are unpredictable. What're you trying to prove?"

"Nothing. Can't you just accept the fact that I'm my own person? It's my life. I've earned the right to make my own decisions and take my own risks."

"Dani, I'm not the enemy. I'm a lot older than you, more experienced at these sort of things. Trust me, you're not ready for this."

"How old was Andrew Fox when his father first took him diving in a shark cage? How old were you when you decided to become a deep-sea submersible pilot?"

"That was different. I didn't just jump into a sub and descend. The Navy trained me."

"And the Daredevils are training me."

Fergie signals her from the lifeboat. "Dani, come on."

"I know it's hard, Dad, but you can't control the world. Learn to let go." She hugs him. "Hey, I'm about to be a star. Be happy for me."

Jonas watches her go, wondering what happened to the little fair-haired girl who he used to bounce on his knee.

The juvenile male Sperm whales have been frolicking among the females for hours, swimming in tight clusters as they rub their bodies against one another.

Now, as the setting sun ignites the western horizon in a blaze of oranges and reds, the mammals' activity slows and the sexes segregate themselves once more, the females huddling around the calves, the bachelors moving off into groups of four or five.

Approaching quietly from the east are two vessels, a wooden rowboat containing the four members of the Mako team, and a Zodiac, carrying Andrew Fox and two of his film crew.

Fergie brings the lead boat to within twenty feet of a half-dozen brownish-gray females. "Okay, here's the drill. We'll spend a half hour just moving in and about the females, lettin' them get used to us. Don't fret about the ju-vee males, they won't bother us this late in the day."

"What about the old bull?" Doc Shinto asks.

"Him we have to watch for. Can't miss him, his head's as big as a building, full of scars and silvery-gray. Our lookouts say he went deep to feed about ten minutes ago, which buys us maybe forty minutes. Since he's already had his way with the ladies, he'll probably just doze off after surfacing. Let's do twenty minutes in the water, then meet back at the boat. We'll wait until after dark before we do the deed."

The Makos nod.

"Doc, hand me that bag."

Shinto passes Fergie a plastic trash bag stuffed with nylon rope.

"I rigged this while we were back in Port Darwin. Fit it to the museum's whale they have on display. The noose should fit nicely around the whale's peduncle."

Jennie shakes her head. "No offense, Fergie, but we're not exactly dealing with plastic models here. You honestly expect us to lasso one of these animals? Look at them, they're rolling like logs."

"Lasso? Of course not. Once it gets dark, these animals will be off to sleep. Sperm whales sleep vertically underwater with their heads up. As soon as they're in la-la land, we'll target one of the females, set the noose around her tail, then tie the free end to the bow of the boat. Should make for one helluva Nantucket sleigh ride."

Dani slips nervously over the side and into the sea, her mouth so dry she cannot spit. Giving up, she dunks the mask into the ocean, then fixes it over her face.

Fergie floats beside her, waiting patiently. Strapped to the top of his head is an underwater camera. "Doc and Jennie went left, we'll go right. You ready to pop your cherry?"

"I'm a little scared."

"You'll be fine. Here, turn me on." He ducks, allowing

her to flip the toggle switch on the camera assembly.

From the second boat, Andrew Fox gives them a thumbs-up.

Fergie positions his regulator in his mouth and releases air from his buoyancy control vest. Dani follows his lead, then, hand in hand, the two Daredevils sink into the darkening blue void.

Three-foot-long tissue-thin pieces of whale skin float like algae in the water—chafing from a day's worth of body rubbing. Stringy white clusters of goo—ejaculation from the excited juvenile males—swirl in the sea like bizarre spiderwebs.

Fergie leads Dani down to a forty-foot depth. They head west, approaching a cluster of females rolling ten feet beneath the surface. Each whale is no less than thirty feet, weighing in at fifteen tons. Dani squeezes Fergie's hand as they move closer, then she points.

Playing among the adults is a ten-foot calf, the newborn's flank still ringed with vertical creases from having been curled within its mother's womb.

The curious two-thousand-pound infant sees the two humans and squirms free of the adults to investigate.

Dani's eyes widen as the animal accelerates straight for them. Fergie slides in front of her, absorbing the brunt of the blow as the newborn playfully nudges them with its head, pile-driving them backward through the water.

The calf's mother quickly intervenes, prodding the infant back to the group.

A single downward stroke of the adult's powerful fluke sends Dani and Fergie rushing to the surface on a cushion of water.

Fergie spits out his regulator, pulling Dani by his side. "You okay?"

Dani clears water from her mask. "Oh my God, that was so cool. Let's do it again!"

"Easy, girl, once is once, twice gets the momma whale peeved." He points west, the last violet rays of daylight disappearing quickly. "C'mon, let's head back to the boat and get ready for some real fun."

A full moon rises, igniting the depths in its pale yellow lunar light. Twinkling stars ascend from the abyss to greet it—luminescent creatures whose nightly pilgrimage represents the largest migration of life on the planet.

Andrew Fox hovers in eighty feet of silky gray water, his underwater camera aimed below at a thin trail of rising air bubbles. Somewhere in these depths, ascending from its three-thousand-foot feast, is the king of the sea, the enormous adult bull Sperm whale.

Andrew's eyes widen as the colossal gray head appears majestically from out of the murk, followed by its impossibly large undulating girth.

The bull rises surreally, and then it is upon him, filling his entire screen—a sixty-foot, eighty-five-thousand-pound predator, expelling its last few seconds of air as it drives itself toward the surface to breathe.

An awestruck Andrew Fox is towed upward within its powerful wake, and then the filmmaker's skin crawls beneath his wetsuit as he sees blood gushing from a jagged bite wound where the bull's right pectoral fin used to be. Before he can react, the male's powerful fluke swishes by, its turbulence flipping him upside down.

Once more, the photographer finds himself staring into the abyss, the intense pressure squeezing his ears. Before he can right himself, he sees something else rising from below—a glint of metal, coming from a narrow, silvery object. Aiming his camera, he follows the dart-like life form as it moves past him after the whale.

What is that thing? A barracuda?

Andrew zooms in on the object as it soars past him toward the surface. He looks below one last time—
—and then he sees the glow . . .

The sleeping pods of Sperm whales hover motionlessly in sixty feet of water, their bodies vertical, their heads pointed upward at the surface.

Fergie floats within an arm's reach of the selected cow's motionless fluke. He waits until the cameraman, Stuart Starr, signals, then motions to his three teammates.

Doc, Jennie, and Dani widen the nylon noose, then ascend slowly, threading the whale's tail carefully through the rope.

Fergie hovers by the base of the peduncle, drawing the noose tighter so that it cannot slip off. Feeding out line, Fergie swims back toward the rowboat, followed by his three teammates and the cameraman.

Stuart Starr climbs aboard first. The Daredevils wait for him to get settled in the stern, then they climb in, one by one, trying hard to pretend the camera is not there. Doc and Jennie find seats in the middle of the lifeboat, Dani and Fergie riding shotgun. The Australian secures the free end of the rope through the brass bow ring, he and his mates giggling like schoolchildren.

"The noose'll tighten the moment the female wakes up and swims. I left us fifty meters of slack. Should be an amazing ride."

Having stopped filming, Stuart Starr communicates with the second boat using his two-way radio. "Understood. Fergie, don't stampede them yet, we're still waiting for Andrew to return."

A motionless Andrew Fox watches breathlessly as the glow gradually illuminates brighter in the lunar light. The son of legendary shark expert Rodney Fox has spent a lifetime filming Great Whites. He has photographed them at night and in murky waters, while in shark cages and in open ocean. He is always wary, but has never been scared.

Now, as the sixty-foot albino ancestor of the Great White ascends beneath him and sheer terror paralyzes his muscles, he wonders if this is how his father felt moments before nearly being ripped in two by his own worst nightmare.

Despite his fear, Andrew continues filming, knowing all too well that the electronic impulses discharged by the device in his hands will most likely lead to his own hideous death.

Back on board the *Neptune*, Jonas Taylor feigns interest for the camera as Charlotte Lockhart continues reading from the TelePrompTer.

"... the largest predator in the sea, the Sperm whale is equipped with eighteen to twenty-five comical teeth in each side of its lower jaw—"

"Cut!" Susan Ferraris bites her lower lip until it bleeds. "Charlotte, darling, that's conical, not comical. Con-ick-cal. Okay dear? Let's try it again."

"Roll tape."

"Speed."

Charlotte licks her lips. Resets. "The largest—"

"Shit!"

Susan slams her clipboard to the deck. "Somebody is just begging me to commit murder."

Her assistant signals from behind one of the side monitors. "Susan, Erik, you have to see this, come quick!"

A crowd gathers. The director and producer push their way through to oohs and aahs. "My God, is that thing real?"

Jonas cuts through the crew. Sees the image. Feels the blood drain from his cheeks.

The devil's face appears first, its right eye and nostril ringed by a series of gruesome scars that extend down to the upper jaw line and an exposed section of gum. The deformed mouth twitches as it opens, revealing rows of six inch teeth.

The creature's pigmentless hide glows luminescent-white in the moonlight as it ascends past the camera, the undertow of its wake spinning the cameraman around as if he is caught in a washing machine. A wing-like pectoral fin momentarily blots out the view, and then the image refocuses, zooming in on a mutilated alabaster dorsal fin, the back end of which has clearly been bitten off.

The final image—a twin set of claspers and a thrashing caudal fin.

A dozen thoughts scream into Jonas's mind at once, entwined by a dozen commands. *Help Andrew ... it's a male ... Terry was right ... the Venice shark tooth festival ... the male Meg tooth ... Erik set you up ... find a weapon ... how did it get here ... locate a boat—*

"—save my daughter!"

Jonas races across the main deck to where Team Hammerhead waits. The cargo net is in place over the side, a Zodiac already in the water, tied off below.

Mia Durante looks up. Sees the expression on his face. Says nothing as she follows him over the rail and down the cargo net to the motorized raft.

Buzzing clicks of echolocation from the surfacing bull fill the sea, alerting the sleeping whales. Shaking off their slumber, they race for the surface, the cows surrounding the calves, the juvenile males circling the females, as the mammals organize a mass exodus.

The adult female harnessed to the Daredevils' boat awakens with a start. As she thrashes toward the surface, the noose tightens around the base of her peduncle and pulls tight.

Registering the sudden tug, the cow panics.

"Say again?" Stuart Starr presses the radio tighter to his ears, unable to hear over the din of helicopter blades pounding above their heads. "A meg-ala what?"

Dani turns, staring at the cameraman—

—as the nylon line suddenly jerks taut, sending the rowboat shooting through the sea at twenty knots.

"Whoa-ho!" Fergie grabs Dani around the waist and holds on as the wooden vessel bounds across the wave tops like a bucking bronco.

Dani ducks her head, showered by heavy spray. She turns and yells back to Stuart Starr, "Did you say Megalodon," but the cameraman cannot hear her over her shouting teammates, the *Coelacanth*'s helicopter, and the wind in his ears.

Looking back, she sees the dorsal fin.

The male Megalodon, surviving "runt" of Angel's first litter, avoids the cluster of whales, its senses targeting the lone female, which has separated from the group and is racing away from the pods, remaining close to the surface.

The Meg goes after her, its mangled scythe-shaped dorsal fin whistling as it cuts the night.

Within seconds, the hunter detects another creature, trailing in the whale's wake.

Smaller. More vulnerable.

The Megalodon alters its course, mistaking the lifeboat for a calf.

Dani screams. "It's gaining on us, do something!"

Fergie holds on as the boat bashes bow-first into a six-foot swell. "It's after the lifeboat. Maybe we're better off in the water? It'll pass us. The chopper could pick us up."

"Bullshit," says Jennie, staring at the fin. "That chopper's here for one reason, to film our deaths. I'll take my chances in the boat."

The panicked cow has towed the lifeboat a good two miles. Exhausted, sensing the larger Meg closing along the surface, the whale goes deep.

The rowboat skims over another swell, then suddenly plunges bow-first, straight into the dark Pacific.

Dani sees an explosion of lights, and then somehow she is underwater, being dragged into the suffocating depths. The boat groans in her ears as her shattered mind screams at her to let go.

Releasing her grip, she tumbles free, then kicks to the surface for what seems like an eternity. Her head pops free and she gasps several breaths.

And then she freezes.

The white wake rolls toward her, moving just below the surface like a submarine, and before she can scream, before she can command her frozen muscles to move, the monster is upon her, gliding beneath her. Her bare feet touch its ivory back and she jerks them away, tucking her knees to her chest as a mangled dorsal fin slices by, nearly colliding with her face. Caught in the creature's current, she is dragged several yards, spinning around and around until she rolls away from the submerging white beast and sinks.

Dani resurfaces, panting, and then she hears a scream, the worst scream she has ever heard, a man's scream, and it is so horrible, so inhuman, that it actually curdles her blood, but what is worse, what is so much worse, is that the scream suddenly stops.

So scared is Danielle Taylor that she cannot find her voice to answer the scream, and that is a good thing, because a

thrashing ivory tail suddenly appears, whipping past her face
as it slaps at the sea before disappearing beneath a wave,
leaving her in deafening silence that becomes a roar of rotor
blades.

Looking up, she sees a light and the outline of the *Coelacanth*'s two-man chopper, its thundering blades causing the
water to reverberate beneath her.

"Help me! Help—"

The airship remains thirty feet directly overhead. She sees
someone hanging out the side of the craft . . . a large man
holding a camera.

"You bastard! Help me!"

A swell rolls over her head and Dani screams into the
night, screams at the cursed helicopter, screams even louder
as a pair of hands lifts her out of the water and drags her
backward into the Zodiac, and she keeps on screaming until
she smells her father's aftershave and feels his arms tightening around her.

"Daddy?"

"It's okay." Jonas wraps a blanket around her shoulders as
Mia slows the Zodiac, allowing Stuart Starr to grab hold.
Jonas hauls the frightened cameraman up by his wetsuit as
Jennie Arnos climbs aboard from the opposite side of the
raft.

The helicopter pilot redirects the beacon of light, blinding
them.

Jonas shouts to Mia above the din of noise. "Get us away
from these assholes before they get us killed."

"Wait!" Dani is frantic. "Where's Fergie?"

"Where's Doc?"

Mia pushes down on the throttle, accelerating in a widening circle as five pairs of eyes desperately search the sea.

"Shh! Listen!"

A man's voice calls out from the darkness, barely audible
over the booming helicopter rotors.

Jonas points. "There! Two o'clock."

Beyond a rolling swell they see someone waving frantically, as a tall sliver of dorsal fin bears down upon him thirty yards away.

"Hold on!" Mia slams down on the throttle, the rubber raft leaping ahead, bounding over wave tops.

Jonas straddles the starboard side of the boat, bracing himself in a prone position, his legs straddling the raft, his right arm reaching out into the blinding spray.

Faster, Mia, much faster—

The man is swimming now, kicking like a demon, the Megalodon's snout rising clear out of the water right behind him.

Jonas sees the upper jaw jut forward. *We're too late . . . oh, Jesus, Mia, don't try it, don't—*

Jonas snags the offered forearm in his right hand, his fingers tightening like steel clamps against the man's cold rubber skin, his own elbow straining beneath an unbearable weight that threatens to yank him over the side—

—as a cavern filled with teeth reach out for him and Jonas bellows a cry into the creature's mouth, the Megalodon's rancid breath gagging him as he shuts his eyes to die.

Mia veers the Zodiac hard to port, so hard that Jonas and the man he is somehow still holding onto are nearly tossed inside that cavernous gullet.

But Dani is gripping her father's left leg and Stuart and Jennie are holding Dani, and now the Zodiac is racing across the ocean, leaving the monster in its wake.

Jonas rolls Wayne Ferguson into the boat, the two men hyperventilating.

Unable to find his voice, the Australian simply nods at Jonas before Dani embraces him.

The survivors remain silent. The Zodiac's high-pitched whine rattles their ears, the wind buffets their faces. Fear tightens their guts, acid reflux rising in their throats.

Mia searches the horizon. "Where the hell's the *Neptune*?"

Jonas is more focused on the expanse of sea behind them. *It missed its last surface attack, it won't be fooled again.* "This isn't over, Mia. It'll come up beneath us. You need to keep zigzagging."

"What?"

"Zigzag!" Jonas grabs the wheel, sending the Zodiac veering hard to port.

"Yo, what are you—"

The sea erupts to their right as the gargantuan beast explodes into the night, three-quarters of its twisting upper torso clearing the surface, its ferocious jaws snapping at air.

Dani and Jennie scream. Fergie falls backward against Stuart Starr, both men trembling.

Mia stares wide-eyed at Jonas, clearly out of her element. "Okay, you drive."

Jonas takes the controls as the creature disappears in the Zodiac's wake. *Think, Taylor. You can't outrun it and you won't be able to outmaneuver it much longer.* He scans the dark horizon, all sense of direction gone. *The* Neptune *was south of the lifeboat, but which direction's south?* He glances skyward at the stars, then snaps out of it. *Dammit, pay attention, you should be counting the seconds between surface attacks.*

"Hold on!" Jonas veers hard to starboard, altering their course.

The Meg's scarred dorsal fin surfaces ahead to their left, then disappears.

Mia looks at him, amazed. "How did you—"

"I've played this cat and mouse game before."

"How does it turn out?"

"You don't want to know."

The pounding of rotors reappear as the helicopter soars past them.

Allison Petrucci drops the chopper to twenty feet and hovers, waiting for the Zodiac to reach them.

Michael Maren taps her on the shoulder. "Perfect. Hold it here." Looking into his viewfinder, he pans down on the approaching craft. *Smile for the camera, Taylor. Smile before you die.*

Maren completes the shot, then slides back into the co-pilot's seat, placing the laptop on his thighs.

Mia grinds her teeth. "Look at these assholes."

"That thumping sound'll lead the Meg right to us." Jonas veers away from the hovering chopper, cursing to himself as the airship stays with him. Watching the waves, he counts to himself, estimating the big male's rate of descent and closing speed, when he notices a glint of metal, coming from a dart-shaped object that is trailing just beneath the surface along the starboard side of the boat.

Before he can get a better view, the object disappears.

The three jet skis converge upon the Zodiac, Michael Coffey taking the lead, Evan Stewart and Dee Hatcher on his flank. The Daredevil trio races directly for the Zodiac, then closing to within one hundred yards, they veer to the south, signaling for Jonas to follow.

Mia points to the three jet skiers. "Jonas, follow the Daredevils, they'll lead us back to the *Neptune!*"

Jonas changes course, keeping his bow in the jet skier's wake.

Dani and Mia cheer as the *Neptune* appears on the horizon.

Jonas looks back. The dorsal fin has abandoned them to circle the dying Sperm whale.

The gray-headed bull swims on its side, languishing in a pool of its own blood.

Michael Maren stares at his display monitor, cursing the dying beast's existence as he works the laptop's joystick.

"Michael, should I follow the Zodiac or stay with the Meg? Michael?"

Maren slams his laptop shut. "Just take us back to the *Coelacanth*."

The three jet skiers are already on board by the time Jonas docks the Zodiac alongside the Spanish galleon. He ties the raft's bowline to the bottom rung of the cargo net while the others ascend to rousing applause.

Fergie motions for quiet. "Knock it off, you bloody mongrels. I said stop!" He stares at the smiling crewmen, shaking his head. "Doc's dead. Hope you got your bloody shot."

Expressions drop, replaced by a heavy silence.

Jonas climbs on board. "Where's Hollander?"

Captain Robertson steps forward. "He's locked in his stateroom with Susan and a team of editors. They're already uploading footage."

"And Andrew?"

"He's in sick bay. He'll be all right, just some nasty abrasions."

"Take us to the nearest port, Captain. This voyage is officially over."

"Can't do that, Taylor. I've been ordered to stay within two clicks of the dead whale."

LATE PLEISTOCENE

A westerly breeze accompanies a violet twilight as night takes the island atoll. The pregnant female, exhausted from her stranding and near-suffocation, follows the tropical waterway, determined to avoid a confrontation with the stalking male.

Gliding just above the silty seafloor, the Meg rounds another bend, its primal senses immediately inundated by heavy surface vibrations and the telltale scent of blood.

The hungry Megalodon beats her tail rapidly from side to side, accelerating toward the disturbance.

The young Micronesian boy is perched midway up a slender coconut tree. Spotting the dorsal fin, he takes the conch shell from around his neck and blows, the shrill sound sending a group of howler monkeys scattering to the safety of the canopy.

A second boy appears from out of the jungle, blowing his own conch shell warning as two runners race along the beach, keeping pace with the moving current of water.

A mile upstream, the waterway dead ends at a shallow lagoon. As the sound of the conch shell relay grows louder, brown-skinned women line the tiki torch–lit bank, slapping the lagoon's dark waters with flat wooden sticks and coconut rattles. A tribal elder, his painted face protruding from a head-piece made from a Tiger shark jaw, tosses the carcass of an eviscerated monkey in and out of the water, dragging the bloody remains by a long vine.

Tribal hunters are posted along the three banks of the lagoon, their heavily calloused hands gripping the ends of a crude fishing net, the bulk of which is concealed along the waterway's bottom. Their job: to entangle their quarry in the net and drag it onto the beach where priests will bless the beast before slaughtering it.

To the natives of these Micronesia islands, the shark is not merely a source of food, it is an ancestral species, reborn as a sea creature to offer itself as sustenance from the depths. According to legend, the ocean realm is ruled by a fearsome Shark God. The tribesmen have no doubt about this deity's existence, for they often find the creature's massive triangular teeth buried in the shallows.

Each day, natives pray to the Shark God for food and health and good tidings. A mature Tiger shark can feed the village for two days, a coveted Whale shark for two weeks.

For as long as anyone can remember, fishermen have been worshiping this ancient lord and master of the sea.

The sound of the conch shell grows nearer.

The villagers grow excited as reports of their quarry's size reaches the lagoon. On this blessed day, the Shark God has been extraordinarily giving.

The natives are about to meet their Maker.

The female glides slowly into the shallows; the upper lobe of its caudal and dorsal fin towering above the dark waters.

Children chase after the creature, gesturing at its enormous size.

Warriors regrip the net, anticipating a fierce battle with what they are convinced is a 15-ton Whale shark.

The submerged 32-ton Megalodon enters the mouth of the

lagoon, its tail slapping the surface as it nears the bleeding morsel of food.

Teams of fishermen push their canoes away from the lagoon's banks. Paddling quietly, they position their boats at the center of the waterway, cutting off their quarry's retreat.

The Megalodon's snout rises to hoots and hollers as it devours the dead monkey.

The elder wearing the Tiger shark jaw signals.

Natives along both banks wade into the lagoon as they gather in netting, their muscles straining to drag the immovable submerged weight. More villagers enter the fray to help, their excitement peaking as the size of the catch is realized.

The dark waters boil. A massive tail rises, bludgeoning the surface. The natives in the canoes toss their spears, drawing blood, causing the enraged Megalodon to rear its mammoth head out of the water.

Villagers scream. Net bearers howl in agony as the monster lurches, its raw power jerking the net, tearing clenched fingers from their hands.

Whipping its head around, the Megalodon snatches the two closest net bearers within its chomping jaws, spewing blood and body parts in all directions.

More villagers rush to help the hunters, who continue to strain at the net.

Caught within the shallows, the Meg rolls like a crocodile, entangling itself in the tightening webbing.

Millions of razor-sharp, teeth-like denticles, laid out along the Megalodon's skin in a ridge-and-groove fashion, make quick work of the rope, slicing it to ribbons.

Churning up sand, the panicked beast whips its upper torso around, attempting to escape the beachhead. Snapping jaws lash out, snatching another stunned native as he wades to shore.

Maneuvering free, the Meg confronts the canoes of warriors.

The fishermen panic. A brave few toss spears, while others leap into the lagoon, paddling for their lives.

The provoked female seizes a canoe and three shrieking

elders within her outstretched jaws, crushing the mass into a mangle of kindling and bloodied flesh.

Screams rend the night air. Natives along either bank fall to their knees, babbling in worship.

With a final slap of its tail, the "Shark God" glides out of the lagoon—

—directly into the path of the oncoming male.

CHAPTER

21

". . . the Megalodon's skin is covered with these razor-sharp, teeth-like scales called denticles. As you can see, it raked me pretty good. Thank God I was wearing a wetsuit, or there'd probably be nothing left of my skin."

Andrew Fox raises his left arm, exposing his chest wounds to the cameraman, his bleeding skin appearing as if it had been scraped by a cheese grater.

Jonas enters sick bay. Seeing the film crew, he ushers them out. "Damn vultures. Andrew, you okay?"

"Two broken ribs and some scratches that should make the wife jealous. Other than that, I'd say I'm lucky to be alive. Is Dani okay?"

"Yes, but we lost Shinto."

"Damn." Andrew shakes his head, still in shock. "Jonas, how do you suppose Angel—"

"It wasn't Angel. The Meg's a male."

"A male?" Andrew grimaces as the physician swabs his wounds with antibacterial ointment.

"Judging by its girth and teeth, I'd say it was a young adult. Right now, it's feeding on the bull Sperm whale, but he'll go deep in about an hour, as soon as the sun starts to rise."

Andrew lies back as the physician finishes. "Pretty amazing coincidence, huh, this Meg just showing up like this while we're filming. I mean, I know we're close to the Mariana Trench, but—"

"I don't believe in coincidences."

"I didn't think you did."

Jonas waits for the physician to leave, then pulls up a chair. "This whole thing reeks of one big setup. My recruitment on this voyage, the selection of the *Neptune*, the course our ship's been following—"

"Whoa, you lost me. What about the *Neptune*?"

"Remember that story Robertson was telling us our first night out, about the history of these Spanish galleons and how so many of them sank off the waters of the Mariana Islands?"

"You think they were attacked by Megalodons?"

"I do. Back when Angel first escaped the lagoon, we had her trapped along the Washington coast, in Grays Harbor. There was a tourist attraction there, a reproduction of an eighteenth-century tall ship—the *Lady Washington*. Same basic design, same wooden hull and keel. Angel went berserk, she attacked that vessel like she hadn't fed in a month. Took me a while to figure it out. Seems these big wooden ships strain and creak as they move along the surface. To an adult Megalodon, the reverberations must sound similar to those a dying whale would make."

"You think the *Neptune* lured this male up from the deep?"

"Actually, I think it's been following us. I'm sure it fed on that Humpback carcass, and I'm pretty sure it took Barry Struhl."

"That means it's been with us since we entered the Philippine Sea. I thought these Megs of yours preferred to stay deep?"

"They do. Where's that footage you filmed tonight?"

"Susan's team's already editing it. I hear the network's doing cartwheels. They're preempting all prime-time programming tomorrow to run the episode."

"I want to take a closer look at your footage. When we were in the Zodiac, I thought I saw something metallic shadowing us."

Andrew sits up. "Like a barracuda? I saw it too. It followed the Sperm whale up from the depths. You think it's some kind of lure?"

"It's possible. These Megs have large brains, bigger in relation to their body weight than most whales. Back in the lagoon, we were able to train Angel to respond to certain electronic stimuli. She learned how to press a target that sounded a bell, signaling her to swim to another section of the tank for food. She could even distinguish colors. Using shock therapy, I taught her to avoid the color yellow. I had all my trainers in yellow wetsuits, just in case they accidentally fell in."

"You think Hollander's behind all this?"

"He definitely knows something, but I think the brain behind this affair is hiding out on that yacht. Hollander got a pretty nasty reception the other day when he boarded her. If you remember, the yacht's crew were also the ones who supplied the show with that first whale carcass."

"What are you going to do?"

Jonas stands. "I think it's time I paid a little visit to the *Coelacanth*."

TANAKA LAGOON
MONTEREY BAY, CALIFORNIA

Mac watches from the eastern bleachers of the arena as the tugboat winch recoils, dragging the remains of his boat off the bottom of the lagoon.

Gregory Stechman, co-owner of Stechman Salvage, flops

down in the seat next to him. "Okay, Mac, let me get this straight. You were coming home late last night in some rough weather when your keel struck the edge of the canal wall."

"Yep. Barely managed to make it back into the main tank before she sank."

"Uh-huh. And that's what you expect me to write on the insurance claim?"

"That's what happened."

Water pours from the *Angel-II* as the vessel is hauled transom-first onto the tugboat's barge.

Stechman stares hard at his boyhood friend. "Nothing else you want to tell me? Like how a concrete wall managed to chew through half your pilothouse?"

"Must've happened when she went down. Speaking of going down, remember the time you picked up that biker chick in that bar? Geez, was she horny. But hey, how were you to know her old man was in the bathroom? I still remember the look on your face when he caught you in your Buick with her, doing the nasty."

"Okay, okay, we'll call it even for the tow, but there better not be any of those rocks attacking my barge, if you catch my drift."

Mac gazes out to the canal entrance, now blocked by a rusted steel barge supporting a loud-clanking generator. Water and silt are being pumped up from the bottom, the latter piling into small sand dunes. "I notice you're not using the jet-flow dredger."

"The back-hoover'll do you just fine. Lucky for you, we don't need a cutterhead to stir up the sediment. Then again, for what you're paying me, you're lucky I didn't give you a straw and tell you to suck it up yourself."

"How long until the entrance is clear?"

"I don't know, another day or two . . . and no, my guys aren't working overtime."

David Taylor is in the control room, on the phone with a slaughterhouse. "Yes, sir, we'll need two sides of beef a day, but they have to be freshly killed. We'll take the first delivery tomorrow afternoon, along with as much blood and innards as you can possibly spare. Yes, sir, cash on delivery."

He hangs up as Patricia enters in a huff. "Was that your mother?"

"No, and I've been trying her all morning. Her cell phone's dead."

"There are two reporters downstairs, wanting to interview her."

"What for?"

"They want her reaction about this." She turns on the television.

The scroll along the bottom of the screen reads:

MEGALODON SHARK ATTACKS DAREDEVIL TEAM. WHO WILL LIVE AND WHO WILL DIE? DON'T MISS TONIGHT'S MUST-SEE *DAREDEVILS II* SPECIAL, 9 P.M. EST.

ABOARD THE COAST GUARD CUTTER *CAPE CALVERT*
HALF-MILE NORTH OF DESTRUCTION ISLAND
NORTHWEST COASTLINE OF WASHINGTON

Destruction Island is a remote stretch of rock, 300 feet wide and half a mile long, located off the Washington coastline about a mile south of Ruby Beach. Once used as an anchorage for Spanish ships back in 1775, the tiny land mass eventually became the home of the Destruction Island Lighthouse, the beacon of which can be seen up and down the coast for twenty miles. Now a U.S. Fish and Wildlife sanctuary, the island is the protected habitat of seabirds, bald eagles, and rabbits, the latter descendants of the lighthouse keeper's pets.

The island has also become an enclave to seals and sea lions, which laze about the rocky beach by the thousands.

The Canadian Coast Guard cutter slows to a drift, its captain weighing anchor a hundred yards off the western coast of the island.

Below decks, Joshua Bunkofske slips into the cabin, the late afternoon sun's reflection on the water causing the far wall to dance. Terry is lying on the cot, sleeping on her stomach, one shapely leg remaining free of the blanket.

The scientist sits gently on the edge of the bed, whispering into her ear. "Terry, it's almost time."

She stirs. "I could sleep all day."

"You practically have." He massages her shoulders.

"Mmm, that feels good."

"Your traps are really tight." He kneads her neck and shoulder muscles, working his way slowly down her spine to her lower back and that tantalizing leg. "Hey, I'm sorry if I came on a little too strong the other day. It's just, well, I find you very attractive and I'd really like to get to know you better."

She rolls over. "Joshua, you do understand I'm married?"

"Happily married, or just married? I know, it's none of my business, but—"

"Josh—"

"Okay, okay." He stands. "Get dressed and meet me in the pilothouse, there's something you need to see."

Terry enters the pilothouse, surprised they have weighed anchor. "What's wrong? Why have we stopped?"

Brian Olmstead looks up from the fish-finder. "It's your fish. It left the canyon about two hours ago and headed closer to shore."

"It's hungry," Joshua says, pointing out the window to Destruction Island. "It can taste the sea lions."

"Sea lions?" Terry heads out on deck.

The Destruction Island Lighthouse looms over the tiny anchorage like a concrete sentry. Seals are everywhere, frolicking in the water and along the rocky shoals, while six-hundred-and-fifty-pound male sea lions belch and bay at one another on the beachhead.

Joshua joins her. "She's out there somewhere, waiting until the sun goes down. She can sense the sea lions. I'll bet my right arm it'll happen tonight, in these waters."

Captain Marino exits the pilothouse, spitting a hunk of chewing tobacco into the sea. "Nothing gonna happen tonight with that crappy bait we're dragging. All soggy and washed out, even the sharks don't want it. I told that cop of yours to find us some fresh meat."

Terry looks aft, sees the Zodiac is gone. "The sea lions? You can't kill them, they're protected under Federal law."

"Easy, Terry," Joshua says. "No one's killing a sea lion, isn't that right, Captain?"

Marino reads the scientist's expression. "Yeah, sure. You always find a few dead ones among the living."

"Exactly. We'll haul the freshest two or three carcasses on board and bait them with the drug pouches. Then we'll circle the island and catch our fish, simple as that."

"Nothing's as simple as that."

"Be positive," Joshua says, "Grays Harbor's less than fifty miles south. With any luck, we'll have Angel secured within Sea World's transportation vehicle by tomorrow evening."

The thought of Angel back in her pen causes Terry to smile.

Then she remembers. "The lagoon . . . David was supposed to repair the canal doors. My phone's dead, I need to call my son."

Joshua hands her his cell phone. "Don't say anything to him about the Meg. The last thing we need is the press catching wind of this before Angel's captured."

TANAKA LAGOON
MONTEREY BAY, CALIFORNIA

David Taylor listens to his mother's voice on the other end of the phone, wondering if he should say anything about his father and sister.

"I'm sorry, David. Business took longer than expected. I'm in Washington now, traveling down the coast. I should be home in a few days. I'll have a big surprise for you."

"Ma, you didn't sell the facility, did you? You can't do that you know, not without my signature."

"No, I didn't sell. I'll explain everything when I see you. David, were you able to fix the canal doors?"

David glances out the bay windows of the control room, focusing on the barge and its growing dunes of sand. "Not yet, but it should be ready by the time you get back."

"Good. I'm counting on you, don't let me down. I love you."

"Yeah, okay. Bye." David hangs up.

Patricia shakes her head. "Why didn't you tell her about Angel or your father?"

"Are you kidding? She'd freak. Besides, that network lady called and told Uncle Mac that Dad and Dani are fine. We'll watch the show tonight, bet the whole thing's just a big hoax."

"Those reporters were sure taking it serious."

"Ah, that stupid network probably sent 'em over just to get publicity. Just wait 'til we fix those doors and call Angel. Man, it'll be sweet. We'll have every TV station in the world lining up to see her."

The sleek thirty-eight-foot F-2 Top Gun Racing Series Cigarette boat skims across the five foot seas like a flying fish, soaring past Monterey doing 72 miles an hour. Devin Dietsch is at the helm, his hands gripping the padded Latham steering wheel, his older brother, Drew, in the middle bolster, working the throttles. They continue south until they spot the familiar outcropping of rocks and the orange warning buoys.

Drew slows the boat, allowing its long bow to settle back into the water. The twin Mercury 500-horsepower engines rumble at their backs, spewing blue exhaust.

Devin points to the barge, now occupying the entryway of the Tanaka Lagoon's access canal. "There it is, just like I told you."

"You're right, they are dredging. The question is why."

"No, bro, the question is who's paying for it. Tanaka's daughter's as broke as her old man. Somebody's spotting her money."

"Rodney claims Terry's been out of town all week."

"You think she cut another deal?"

"Don't know, but I'm gonna find out. Let's get back to the office." Drew pushes down on the throttle as Devin executes a sharp turn, guiding the craft back up the coast.

Angel moves through the inky depths of the Monterey Submarine Canyon, her thick caudal fin snaking back and forth like a slowly waving scythe-shaped fan. Ampullae of Lorenzini, attuned to the canyon's distinct magnetic field, guides the Meg through the twisting abyssal chasm. Grayish-blue irises are rolled back, revealing the bloodshot white sclera of her eyeballs. The female's pulse has slowed, her great conical-shaped head, as large and wide as a school bus, swinging from side to side in long, easy movements.

The albino predator glides through the gorge on autopilot, as close to being asleep as Nature allows. And yet, even in this semiconscious state, Angel hears every sound, registers every movement, tastes every trail, and sees every sight, for *Carcharodon megalodon* does not just move through the sea, the sea moves through the Megalodon.

Water passes in and out of her nostril passages, feeding information to her brain. It flows through her mouth, causing her gill slits to flutter as she breathes. It moves along the underside of her snout, plugging her in to the faint electrical fields generated by the swimming muscles and beating hearts of her quarry. It runs along her lateral line and stimulates her neuromast cells, allowing her to "feel" ocean currents and the presence of solid objects within her environment.

Thu-whomp. Thu-whomp . . . whomp . . . Thu-thu-whomp . . .

The surface disturbance reverberates through the Submarine Canyon, the anomaly disrupting the sea's bioelectrical field.

Thu-whomp. Thu-whomp . . . whomp . . .

Fluctuating currents are processed by the sensory cells embedded along the creature's flank. Pressure-wave detectors alert Angel's ampullar system to the turbulence, exciting the Meg's respiratory functions.

Thu-whomp. Thu-whomp . . . Thu-whomp.

Vibrations of sound reach the creature's inner ears, sounding an internal alarm.

The Megalodon's mouth opens wider, the increased flow of water causing her gills to flutter faster, her pulse to jump. The creature's muscular keel, as wide as a sewage pipe, pumps Angel's powerful vertical tail briskly through the water.

Cataract-gray eyes roll forward.

Angel awakens.

Fourteen hundred feet above her head, the racing boat whizzes by, its fiberglass hull blistering the waves.

The Queen of the deep rises away from the bottom, accepting the challenge.

ABOARD THE *NEPTUNE*
34 NAUTICAL MILES NORTHEAST OF PALAU
268 NAUTICAL MILES SOUTHWEST OF THE MARIANA
TRENCH

Jonas is up with the sun. Dressing quickly, he heads out on deck, greeted by a glorious warm breeze and the possibilities of a new day.

The sight and stench of the dead bull Sperm whale slams him back into reality.

He scans the horizon until he finds the *Coelacanth*, the super yacht drifting a mile to the south.

Jonas makes his way aft, stepping over passed out crewmen and their dozing, half-naked Candy Girls until he reaches the cargo net, mounted along the starboard side. The Zodiac is below, rigged for launch.

"You're up early."

Jonas turns, startled.

Mia smiles at him and stretches, her well-defined physique pressing against the insides of a see-through black kimono. "Where you going?"

"Business trip. Thought I'd pay my respects to the captain of that yacht."

"Sounds like fun. Mind if I tag along?"

"Not this time."

She moves closer, brushing back a comma of his graying brown hair, allowing her right knee to press between his legs. "You missed a great party. I was waiting for you all night."

Ten feet away, hidden behind the mizzen mast, Danielle Taylor stirs in Fergie's arms.

"Mia—"

"I like you, Jonas. I want to share myself with you."

Jonas backs away, feeling himself getting aroused. "Mia, I'm married."

"Jonas, it's just sex. Two lonely people, attracted to one another, sharing an innocent moment. We're only in this physical world a short time, let's enjoy it."

Dani's eyes flash open. Slipping out from under Fergie's arm, she crawls on all fours until she's close enough to eavesdrop.

"Mia—"

"Aren't you attracted to me?"

"That's not the point."

"Actually, that's the entire point. I'm not looking for a commitment, I only want to enjoy the moment." She moves closer. "Let yourself go, it's completely harmless."

"Mia, you're a wonderful girl, and believe me, I'm flattered. But at the end of the day, I need something more. See, it's never just harmless sex, it carries a price, and that price, at least for me, is my own sense of morality, something both our generations have been a little too quick to shortchange of late."

"Funny, I never pegged you for a conservative Republican."

"Last I checked, morality had no political affiliation."

"There's nothing immoral about being happy."

"There is if it means forsaking your family."

"Jonas, no one has to know."

"I'll know, and that's enough. See, I've come to realize a few things of late. Like it or not, I'm getting older. Physically, I'm half the man I used to be. My body's falling apart, my mind wanders at times . . . and God knows I'm not the poster child for success. The years and the poverty and the public humiliation have all taken their toll on my dignity, but at the end of the day, whether I'm lying in some coffin or dying in some hospital bed, or serving as fodder for some overgrown Great White shark, the only thing that matters, the only thing I might have to show for my years in this world, *is* my morality and the example I set for my children. And maybe, in the end, that's the only thing that counts."

Mia smiles. "You don't know what you're missing."

"Believe me, I do. But you know what else I miss? I miss cuddling with my wife. I miss her waking me in the middle of the night, complaining about my snoring. I miss tossing a baseball with my son. And I miss my little girl's love. I miss her trust. I want all those things back, which means I can't be with you, because I refuse to compromise myself for a fleeting moment of senseless passion."

"Okay, I respect that. So who's waiting for you in the yacht?"

"I don't know, but whoever it is has succeeded in pushing me into this frying pan. I need to confront them before we all get shoved into the fire."

Jonas climbs over the side and down the cargo net to the Zodiac. He verifies half a tank of gasoline, then unties the bow rope and starts the engine.

Dani lies back, wiping tears from her eyes as the whine of the single motor echoes across the sea.

DESTRUCTION ISLAND
NORTHWEST COASTLINE OF WASHINGTON

The night is dying now, reeling beneath a vaporous pre-dawn fog that ignites into a silvery-gray beacon with each pass of the lighthouse's beam. An ominous ocean, enveloped in darkness, rises and falls against the faces of rock.

The cutter continues to circle Destruction Island, dragging the thumper, its buoy, and the three dead sea lion bulls in its wake.

Terry is wrapped in a wool blanket, dozing in the Zodiac. Joshua is stretched out next to her, watching the sea between whiffs of fog. The heavy baritone pulse of the thumper reverberates across the surface, mixing with the rumble of the *Cape Calvert*'s twin engines.

Joshua drains his mug of coffee, then casually snuggles

closer to Terry, entwining one of his legs between hers.

She stirs. "What are you doing?"

"Just trying to stay warm."

"Here, take my blanket." Terry pushes him aside and stands, stomping her boots, forcing circulation back into her cold feet. "What time is it?"

"Just after four."

"In the morning? Ugh, this is ridiculous." She heads forward, climbing an aluminum ladder to the pilothouse.

Ron Marino is snoring in a folding chair, his head lying in the crook of his arm atop a chart table. Brian Olmstead has taken his place at the controls.

Terry enters, visibly upset. "Why's he sleeping? Who's watching the damn fish-finder?"

"It's handled." Brian motions to the console. "Your Meg's been playing cat and mouse with us all night. Every time we circle by, she disappears off the screen, returning to deeper water."

"Then stop the boat."

"Can't. If we drop below three knots, the bait'll sink."

"I don't care. If the cutter's engines are scaring her off—"

"Weren't you the one that told us Angel wasn't scared of boats?"

"Don't tell me what I said, just do what I say. Shut off the engines."

Brian shrugs. "You're the boss." Pulling back on the throttles, he reduces speed, powering down.

The *Cape Calvert* slows to a drift, its trailing wake rolling the vessel.

The sea grows silent, save for the heavy *thumpa . . . thumpa . . . thumpa . . .* coming from the buoy.

The hungry male is frustrated.

For the last nine hours, the agitated hunter has been moving back and forth along a two-hundred-foot cliff face located at the edge of the Cascadia basin. It can taste the sea lions, it can feel them as they swim along the surface, but every time the Meg ascends to feed, its senses become overloaded by a wave of sonic vibrations that reverberate within its skull like a tuning fork.

Hunger drives the predator once more. Ascending beyond the continental rise, the big male begins another assault, its overwrought senses guiding it through the shallows toward its meal.

"Here she comes again," Brian announces. "Watch, she'll race over the plateau, then retreat about three hundred yards to the west."

Terry focuses on the luminescent-green fish-finder display and the approaching red dot. Her heart rate increases, her palms sweaty as the object closes in on their location.

The blip slows, wavers, then abruptly reverses.

"Why's she doing that? The engines are off and she's still spooked."

Brian motions to the captain. "Maybe Marino's snoring chases her away?"

Or maybe it's really not Angel? Terry heads back out on deck.

Joshua has gone below.

For a long moment she stares at the sea and the insulated electrical cable which runs from the thumper buoy back to the cutter's storage trunk.

Reaching inside the box, Terry disconnects the cable from the truck battery powering the sonic device.

The big male slows. Shakes its head.

The annoying electrical disturbance has ceased.

The Meg turns east again, zigzagging warily toward its prey.

———————

Terry returns to the pilothouse in time to see the red blip moving across the screen, closing on the *Cape Calvert.*

"That did it, here she comes," Brian says. "Hey, Marino, wake up and take the helm, we've got company."

The captain stirs, scratching his Elvis-like sideburns as he staggers toward the controls. "Okay, where is she?"

"Two clicks east, staying deep. What do we do, boss? Troll or drift?"

Terry's thoughts are more focused on fear than strategy. *It's not Angel, at least I don't think it is, I mean, who knows? Whatever it is, it's still a Meg, which means we're in real danger. Do we risk our lives trying to capture it? Will the public pay to see it? Of course they will, but—*

"Terry?"

"Yes, yes, start the boat. Keep us moving, keep us close to that island."

Marino shoves a wad of chewing tobacco into his mouth and restarts the engines, driving the cutter forward.

"Marino, mind those rocks," Brian warns.

"Just watch your damn screen."

Brian shakes his head at Terry, adding to her worries. "She's still circling along the bottom . . . wait . . . yes, she's coming up to take a peek. Two-fifty . . . two hundred . . . still coming . . . one-seventy—"

Terry feels her insides tighten on her bladder.

"One-twenty . . . hold on, she's leveled off at seventy feet . . . she's circling the bait. She's not sure. Marino, slow down a bit."

Marino spits defiantly into a paper cup, but pulls back on the throttles.

"Still circling . . . she's still not sure . . . okay, she's rising again. Sixty feet . . . forty—"

Terry hurries out on deck, her body trembling from fear and excitement.

Joshua is leaning out over the transom, gesturing at the sea.

A lime-green radiance of movement, as large as a bus, is circling the buoy and its sea lion bait. "Can you see her? Angel's homing in on the bait, just like I said she would."

A triangular ivory fin breaks the surface, rising six feet out of the water.

"My God, look at her," whispers Josh. "She's amazing."

The fin circles back behind the trailing sea lion rigging and disappears.

"She'll come up from below," Terry whispers. "She'll—"

The sea explodes in a geyser of foam as the Megalodon leaps halfway out of the ocean, the sea lion snatched firmly within the beast's clenching jaws.

"Wow!"

The Meg plunges back into the sea and disappears as the eight-foot spool of cable jumps to life, whirling into the night as it feeds out line.

"We did it, we hooked her," Josh yells. "Hold on, she's going deep."

Terry watches, terrified, yet giddy, as Joshua dashes up to the pilothouse. "Full reverse! Give her plenty of line, we need to allow the drugs to take effect."

The big male races into the depths, its mouth radiating in pain from the five-foot titanium hook embedded in its lower jaw. The Meg shakes its head, writhing in agony, its pulse and blood pressure soaring from the massive dose of pentobarbital now being absorbed by its digestive system.

Then, as the monster soars past three hundred and twenty feet, it registers a sharp tug of resistance that tortures its bleeding jaw.

The Meg writhes and twists on the steel cable but cannot pull free. Its nostrils flare as it tastes the warm sweetness of its own blood, its mouth quivering in spasms against the throbbing ache. Excited by the drugs, its primal brain is unable to fathom cause and effect.

Whipping its caudal fin against the sea, the brute forcefully drags the thirty-three-ton cutter after it.

The *Cape Calvert* is towed backward through the Pacific, its stern sending six-foot waves crashing over its dipping transom.

Terry grabs Joshua, shouting over the sea and wind. "How much pentobarbital was in each pouch?"

"Don't know. Maybe fifteen pounds a pouch. Who knows how much she swallowed?"

"What if it wasn't enough?"

"Give it a chance."

The boat dips beneath them, the sea momentarily rushing over the transom.

"Release the cable before it drags us under!"

"A couple'a more minutes."

"Hey, fish boy!" Marino calls out from the pilothouse. "Hope you're a better swimmer than you are a fisherman."

The *Cape Calvert* rolls to starboard and keeps going, the now empty hydraulic spool groaning as it strains to maintain a grip on the length of steel cable dragging them sideways.

Terry falls against the starboard rail and holds on, her eyes wide in fright as the cutter continues bending toward the sea. *I told you not to come. I told you it was too risky. Get to the Zodiac, get to land while there's still a chance . . .*

The steel cable suddenly goes slack, the boat rolling back to port, righting itself.

Joshua grins from ear to ear. "See? The drugs took effect, just like I knew they would. Who's the man now?" He thumps his chest, doing his best Denzel Washington impression. "King Kong ain't got nuthin' on me!"

Terry laughs, pinching tears of relief from her eyes. "Okay, hotshot, what do we do now?"

"Hey—" Brian calls out from the pilothouse. "I think you'd better get up here."

Terry's heart pounds as she hurries up the ladder, Joshua right behind her.

The red blip is still moving, only now it is rising.

Brian looks at them, his perspiring face ghostly-green in the luminous light. "She's coming up fast. I'd say she's pissed. What do you think an angry Megalodon'll do?"

"We're not waitin' around to find out." Marino slams both throttles down. The cutter's twin diesel engines jump to life, the two fixed-pitch, four-blade propellers churning the sea, driving the boat forward.

Terry stares at the fish-finder, her mind too exhausted to grasp what is happening. "You can't outrun it, Captain. Our only chance is to beach us. Did you hear me? You have to beach the cutter on Destruction Island, that's an order."

"No," Joshua interjects. "The rocks'll tear the hull apart."

"So will the Meg."

"Head for the mainland, Captain. Give the drugs a chance to kick in."

"Again with the drugs? Forget the drugs and forget the mainland, it's too far," Terry protests. "We'll be lucky just to make it back to the island."

Brian's eyes widen. "Hold on!"

Wha—boom!

The sudden impact rocks the vessel like a sports car striking a speed bump doing ninety miles an hour, sending Terry crashing sideways against the chart table.

· Marino picks himself up off the deck. "When the lady's right, she's right. Destruction Island it is."

Blood gushes from the big male's wounded left nostril, its head aching from its collision with the cutter. The Meg's senses are jumbled and on fire, its nervous system sizzling in convulsions from the heavy dose of drugs. In blind rage, the Megalodon rises again to bull rush its challenger—

—as a strange lead-like numbness creeps into its tail.

The lighthouse beacon cuts across the *Cape Calvert*'s windshield as Ron Marino closes on the western shoals of Destruction Island. Searching for a soft place to beach the cutter, he targets a stretch of flat coastline, oblivious to the jagged outcropping of rocks that lie in wait just below the wave tops.

"Captain, don't!" Spotting the rocks, Joshua pushes Marino aside and yanks hard on the wheel, veering the boat away from the island.

Terry tumbles to the deck, only this time she remains there, her limbs paralyzed in fear. She grips a leg of the chart table as terrifying images from her past play across her mind's eye.

The blade of Sergei's hunting knife pressed against her neck.

The isolation of the abyss as her submersible is attacked by unseen creatures.

"Terry?"

The taste of vodka on the Russian assassin's breath.

The maniacal gaze of Benedict Singer's emerald-green contact lenses as he pronounces her death sentence.

"Hey, Terry!"

She opens her eyes, gazing up at Joshua.

The cutter has slowed. Marino, Brian, and the former cop, Villaire, are crowding around the fish-finder.

Joshua offers her his hand. "You okay? You blacked out there for a few minutes."

She allows Josh to help her up. "I'm . . . okay. What about the Meg?"

"Drugs finally knocked her out. Come on." Joshua heads back outside and down the aluminum ladder, Terry right behind him. "We need to pull her in fast, keep water flowing through her mouth or she'll drown."

Terry delights in the graying eastern horizon, the new day vanquishing the terrors of a long, exhausting night. She watches as Joshua reverses the steel spool of cable, rewinding the taut line.

Fifteen long minutes pass before they finally see the glow of the unconscious Meg, its upper torso trailing fifty yards behind the thumper buoy.

Joshua calls up to the pilothouse. "Marino, follow the coastline south, our destination is Grays Harbor. Keep her steady at three knots. I'm going out in the Zodiac to make sure she's breathing." He turns to Terry. "Join me."

Like a dutiful zombie, she follows him to the Zodiac, fatigue and relief quelling her resistance. They climb over the port side rail and into the inflatable.

Josh releases the bowline, then loops it around the steel cable, allowing the free-floating Zodiac to drift backward along the line. He maneuvers them beyond the thumper buoy until they reach the glowing ivory monstrosity that is being towed four feet beneath the waves.

"My God, will you look at her. She's bigger than a tractor trailer." Josh fixes the line so the raft is directly over the Megalodon's head.

The sixty-one-foot ancestor of the Great White has rolled belly-up, its lower jaw open and raw, the razor-sharp hook embedded deep within its mouth. "Look, she's breathing, I can see her gills fluttering." He turns to Terry. "You see the old footage taken twenty years ago, but it just doesn't do her justice. I can't believe how big she is."

"It's not Angel."

"Of course it is."

"Loosen the line. Drift us back toward the tail."

Joshua obeys. The current takes the Zodiac back another fifty feet toward the Meg's inert caudal fin.

Terry points.

Just visible between the creature's two pelvic fins are a pair of five-foot-long male claspers.

"Well, I'll be a sonuvabitch, it's a . . . a son of a bitch. Or maybe it's Angel's mate? Or her sibling? Or even her pup?"

Terry's teeth chatter against the cold. "I don't even want to think about where this male came from."

"Right. Anyway, it doesn't matter. Just think about where she . . . I mean he's going."

Joshua unties the line, allowing them to free float beyond the tail, then he starts the Zodiac's engine, accelerating back to the cutter.

Michael Villaire ties off the boat and helps them on board.

"I need to radio Sea World," Josh announces. "It'll take us most of the day to get to Grays Harbor. Terry, you should get some sleep. Come on, I'll walk you to your cabin."

She nods, following him down the companionway as if in a dream.

They pause outside her cabin door.

Josh brushes strands of black silky hair away from her cheekbone. "See," he whispers, "now that wasn't so bad, was it?"

"I suppose not."

"What have I been telling you? You just have to give in and take a few risks. It's what makes life worth living."

"I guess so," she whispers, staring into his chestnut brown irises as he leans closer.

And then she closes her eyes, inviting him in, her heart racing, her face flushing as their lips meet, his tongue pressing into her mouth.

The sudden release of emotions overwhelms her, and suddenly she is panting in his arms, their hands groping beneath one another's clothing, her insides electric to his touch.

"Wait!" She holds his hand to her breast, forcing him to pause. "Go. Go call Sea World. Business first."

"Okay . . . business first, but I'll be back." Grinning, he hurries up the companionway like a kid on Christmas Day.

Terry leans against the cabin door, her groin tingling, her limbs shaking.

CHAPTER

22

Jonas cuts back on the throttle, slowing the Zodiac as he moves to within one hundred yards of the sleek 860-ton Abeking & Rasmusen luxury super yacht. *Looks like no one's out on deck. Still, better to be safe than sorry.* Shutting off the engine, he grabs an oar and paddles the rest of the way in.

The rising sun glints off the yacht's tinted bay windows and navy blue steel hull. An imposing eleven feet of draft separates the ocean from the rail of the main deck. Jonas looks from stem to stern for an access point, then paddles for the portside bow and the three-foot rectangular opening that houses the anchor.

Jonas stands, balancing carefully in the raft as he ties off his bowline to a palm-size link in the anchor's heavy iron chain. Supporting himself against the side of the boat, he reaches inside the anchor housing and pulls himself up, using the opening to gain a foothold. Reaching higher, he feels for one of the drainage slits, shoves his hand inside, then, after a bit of a struggle, manages to drag himself up and over the bow rail.

Jonas steps quietly onto the white fiberglass decking, his sneakers squeaking against the nonskid surface. Slipping off his shoes, he makes his way aft, staying low as he approaches the yacht's infrastructure.

Rising on his toes, Jonas peeks inside the corner bay window of the wheelhouse. Through the tinted glass he sees a heavily tattooed Micronesian man snoozing in the captain's chair.

Jonas continues past the wheelhouse, pausing at a circular steel staircase. Creeping up the steps, he finds himself standing on a balcony and the open double doors of a sky lounge.

A wave of chilled air rushes past him as he enters a beige-carpeted stateroom. At the far end of the chamber is a wall-mounted projection screen surrounded by three large crushed-velvet charcoal-gray couches. A circular coffee table is set between the sofas, a recessed oval ceiling complementing the table. Dark drapes match the furniture, venetian blinds covering the large vertical windows. A polished mahogany bar is set off against the wall opposite the movie screen.

Standing behind the bar is a heavyset man with a bulldog face, dressed in a monogrammed white bathrobe. Dark brown hair peppered with gray is pulled back into a tight ponytail. A beer belly hangs over a pair of blue and purple Bermuda shorts.

The man looks up nonchalantly. "Good morning. Orange juice?"

Jonas scrutinizes the man's features. "I know you, don't I?"

"Could be. Think real hard."

A petite brunette wearing a matching robe enters from an interior corridor. "Sorry to interrupt. The chef wants to know how your guest wants his eggs."

"Taylor?"

Jonas stares at the double "M" monogram. "Michael Maren?"

"See, Allison, I told you he'd figure it out."

"Jesus, Maren, what happened to you? You look like you swallowed a manatee."

Maren's eyes flash menacingly in the overhead lights. "Allison, inform the chef that our guest will be skipping breakfast."

The overweight marine biologist hobbles out from behind the bar, exposing his toeless bare feet. "I see the years have taken their toll on you as well."

"Maren, what are you . . . Jesus, what happened to your feet?"

"An unscheduled trip to the Alaskan wilderness eighteen years ago, courtesy of your friend, Mackreides. My only wish was that he was here to share this moment as well."

"Don't tell me you planned this whole thing for revenge? That's pretty pathetic, Maren, even for you."

"Don't flatter yourself. You're just a minor distraction."

"From what? Eating?"

Maren grins. "Go on, keep pushing my buttons. It'll make things more enjoyable later when you're begging me to spare your life." He calls out through the connecting corridor. "Satoshi, join us, please."

The floorboards groan beneath Jonas's bare feet as the largest human being he has ever seen waddles into the lounge.

"Satoshi, this is the man I told you about. Show him to a chair."

Jonas backs away, but the former sumo wrestler is too quick. In one motion he lifts Jonas off the ground as if he were a small child and tosses him onto a couch.

Jonas bounces off the cushions and onto the marble floor, his lower back twisting in agony. "Not too bright, are you, Satoshi? He said show, not throw."

Satoshi grins.

Maren sips his drink. "Let's play catch-up, shall we? Since our last encounter, you've become a pathetic old man, scraping the bottom of the barrel for money while seeking to relive those lost fifteen minutes of fame. On the other hand, I, being a real scientist, have continued the work you tripped over twenty-two years ago."

Jonas crawls onto the sofa, remaining under the watchful eyes of Satoshi. "I take it you've been exploring the Mariana Trench."

"The Mariana Trench is nothing. The real ancient marine sanctuary is located along the Philippine Sea Plate. The area is a paleobiologist's gold mine. At least four major submarine canyons feed nutrients into this valley, creating a habitat that has sustained primitive life since the very first marine reptiles returned to the sea over a hundred million years ago. I've discovered species long believed extinct, and evidence of creatures we never knew existed, all endowed by Nature to adapt to the pressures of the deep. Prehistoric sponges with immune systems that could potentially cure cancer. Jawless fishes with bony armor plating. Undiscovered ray-finned life forms. Ichthyosaurs and Pliosaurs possessing gills, giant sea turtles with teeth that could tear open a small truck. This labyrinth of the deep is a lost world just waiting to be explored, and the ruler of these primal waters is *Carcharodon megalodon.*"

"Congratulations, you've made an incredible discovery. But why lure a Meg to the surface?"

"Megalodon have been surfacing long before you or I happened upon them." Maren drains the rest of his drink, then pours himself another. "Back in 1918, for instance, one of the creatures migrated across the Western Pacific into Canadian waters. Local fishermen reported seeing it after it had become entangled in their craypots. Another sighting was documented in the late 1950s when one of the creatures attacked the *Rachel Cohen,* an Australian fishing boat. The crew on board never knew what hit them—until the cracked hull was repaired in Port Lincoln and a five-and-a-half-inch white tooth was discovered, embedded in the ship's keel."

"And this male?"

"I came across him about five years ago. He was in pretty bad shape, in fact he was close to death, having recently lost a territorial dispute with another Megalodon. We weighted down sea lion carcasses loaded with medicines and fed him in 19,000 feet of water. Took us seven months of gradually raising the lures to get Scarface to finally surface."

"Scarface?"

"My assistant named him. It seems to fit. Over the years we've managed to tag him with several homing devices. As you can see, he's doing quite well now. I estimate he's gained at least ten tons since our first encounter."

So have you. "How did you do it, Maren? How did you manage to explore the extreme depths? Benedict Singer tried and failed."

"Singer was a businessman, not a scientist. Manned trips into the abyss are far too expensive and dangerous, as you already know. Come with me, I want to show you something."

Jonas follows him through a wide connecting interior corridor and down a plush companionway. Satoshi remains close behind them.

The winding stairwell descends two flights to the crew's level. The three men move aft past staff quarters, then through a tight corridor lined with pipes and bulkheads. Passing through the engine room, they arrive at a pair of sealed metal doors.

Maren keys an entry pad and the doors click open.

Satoshi shoves Jonas ahead with one thick paw, propelling him over the threshold.

It is a mechanical room, converted into a workshop. At the center of the chamber, situated within the steel-plated decking, is a rise holding a recessed hatch, six feet across, three feet in depth.

Jonas hears the sea lapping against the other side of the door.

Next to the elevated hatch, strapped to a padded work-table, is a five-foot-long sausage-shaped underwater drone, its contours mimicking that of a large barracuda.

Maren pats the device proudly. "My abyssal hound dog. Micro-subs like this drone do my exploring for me. The Navy's been developing the technology for years, using them for long-term mine reconnaissance. My drone's a bit more complex, its multiple shell design enabling me to go far deeper. The Barracuda contains a sophisticated fish-finder, thermal imager, sonar, and an infrared beacon at-tached to a video camera. I've programmed the drone to emit a variety of bioelectronic signals, similar to the acoustics you trained Angel to respond to. When I want Scarface to surface, I simply locate him, circle a few times while emitting the feed stimulus, and up he comes, like a 30-ton Pavlov dog."

"Then it *was* your Meg that attacked us during the storm?"

"Yes, but Scarface surfaced on his own. It seems *Carcharodon megalodon* is attracted by the surface vibrations of Spanish galleons."

"Which is why you insisted on Hollander leasing the *Neptune*."

Maren smiles. "He thought it was an inspired idea, though he still has no concept why."

"And me? Why am I here?"

"Because I despise you." Maren circles the Barracuda, staring at him. "You're not a scientist, Taylor, you never were. Yet for years, you pretended to be one, giving ridicu-lous lectures about these magnificent predators, how they avoided extinction, how they might be alive in the Mariana Trench. Tell me, *Professor* Taylor, when you became an overnight sensation, did your newfound celebrity serve any-one but that ego of yours? And those sold-out shows at the

Tanaka Lagoon, did any percentage of the gate ever find its way back to the science you so flaunted all those years? It takes money to explore the abyss, and the abyss needs exploring, for there are life forms down there that might harbor cures for disease . . . discoveries just waiting to happen. You had the means, you had the world's attention, you could have spearheaded the movement, instead you destroyed it. Angel's escape and eventual return to the abyss chased away dozens of potential investors . . . major universities, pharmaceutical companies, scientists like myself, who could have opened the realm to real exploration."

Maren shakes his head sadly. "Times have changed, the window of opportunity has closed. Education and science have taken a backseat to war. Federal grants under this current political regime have become almost nonexistent, unless one's researching a new vaccine for anthrax, or involved in the space weapons program. Since I can't afford to hire lobbyists like the fossil-fuel industry or the NRA, I've had to resort to another means of gaining the public's attention."

"The *Daredevils* show."

"Exactly. Scarface's appearance on the last show will be watched by more than sixty million people, with the final episode leading to my own series on the exploration of the Philippine Sea. Within six months, I should have the funding necessary to spearhead a full investigation of the abyss."

"So you dared the devil up from his purgatory just to raise money?"

"Scarface is far from the devil; in fact, it turns out that Megalodon isn't even the meanest fish on the block. Many years ago, my first drone crossed paths with a real monster of the deep, a creature one hundred and twenty feet long, weighing in excess of one hundred tons. The beast had jaws that could snatch a fully grown Megalodon. It destroyed my drone, and has been eluding me for eight years. But it's down there, perhaps the last of its kind, and with the proper funding and equipment, I'll find it."

"Maybe some things are best left alone."

"Spoken like the phony paleobiologist I know and love. It really is going to be fun watching you die." Maren nods at Satoshi.

The hulking bodyguard grabs Jonas by the crook of his arm and forcibly drags him across the room to a set of wrist and ankle chains bolted to the base of a bulkhead.

Jonas struggles.

The wrestler punches him hard in the gut, driving the air from his lungs.

Jonas wheezes and folds, gasping for a breath as Satoshi shackles his wrists and ankles.

Maren stands over him. "You wanted to know why I arranged to bring you here, I'll tell you. It's because of Celeste. I know what you did to her in the trench."

Jonas struggles to speak. "She used me . . . she tried to kill Terry."

"And so you murdered her, you led Angel to the *Prometheus*. You watched as the Meg attacked her sub."

"She wanted me dead. Would have killed us—"

"And so you anointed yourself judge and jury, and now, eighteen years later, so do I. Jonas Taylor, this court finds you responsible for Celeste Singer's death, as well as the deaths of the crewmen aboard the *Prometheus*. Found guilty, you are hereby sentenced to die. But don't worry, I'm not going to kill you just yet. First I'm going to tenderize the meat."

The sumo wrestler pulls on Jonas's shackles, pinning his arms painfully behind the bulkhead.

Maren slips out of his designer bathrobe, balling his fists . . .

ABOARD THE COAST GUARD CUTTER *CAPE CALVERT*
NORTHWEST COASTLINE OF WASHINGTON
36 MILES NORTH OF GRAYS HARBOR

Terry lies back against the sheets, her eyes half-closed, the fingers of her right hand entwined in Joshua's brown hair as she guides his face to her aching groin. She grinds her hips against his mouth, panting as she forces him deeper.

She writhes beneath his touch, and then he is on top of her. She wraps her legs around his waist and guides him in, digging her nails into his flesh as she thrusts her hips faster.

"Excuse me, Mother. What exactly are you doing?"

Terry turns her head, shocked to see her daughter seated in a folding chair, watching.

"Dani?"

"How can you do this to Dad? I mean, look at this guy, he's not even that cute."

Joshua pauses. "Who're you talking to?"

"My daughter."

"Oh. Mind if I keep at it, I'm nearly finished."

"You see, Mother? He couldn't care less about you. Is he even that good?"

"No, but it's never that good the first time you do it with someone new."

"Does that mean you're planning on seeing him again?"

"I don't know."

"You haven't really thought this through, have you?"

"No. It was just sort of . . . spontaneous."

"Spontaneous?"

"A part of me needed it, Dani. It was like having an itch that only someone else can scratch."

"I guess if we try hard enough, we can justify anything, is that it?"

"That's not fair."

"So, are you planning on divorcing Dad?"

"Of course not. I love your father."

"You have a funny way of showing it."

"Dani . . . Look, I don't expect you to understand. Maybe when you get older."

"Oh, please."

"Sometimes things just happen. You never intended it that way, but they just do. It's like . . . it's like sticking your hand in a pot of cold water and turning on the burner. If the heat's gradual, you can boil your flesh away without ever noticing."

"Then I guess the lesson here is not to put your hand in the pot in the first place."

"Huh?!"

Terry opens her eyes and sits up in bed.

She is alone, Dani and Joshua gone.

Just a dream . . .

She hears pounding outside her cabin door. "Hey, Terry, it's me. Open up."

"Josh?"

"Sorry I took so long. Can you open the door please?"

"Josh . . . I, uh, I can't. I have a bad headache."

"Let me in and I'll massage your shoulders. Takes all the tension away."

"No. I mean, its menstrual cramps. I . . . I need to sleep."

"Are you serious?"

"Let me rest, Josh. I'll see you later, okay?"

A long pause. "Fine."

She hears him stomp away.

What am I doing, I must be out of my mind. She recalls her dream, replaying Dani's words—her words—spoken to her daughter three years ago. *I'm stewing in boiling water and I don't even know it. Get away from this guy before you ruin everything.*

She dresses quickly. Presses her ear against the cabin door. Hearing nothing, she opens the door, verifies the corridor is empty, then hurries up the companionway to the main deck.

The morning sky is overcast and gray. Brian is lying on a bench, asleep beneath his baseball cap. She creeps past him, then climbs over the rail and into the Zodiac.

"Hey!" Joshua climbs down from the pilothouse. "Where do you think you're going?"

"To buy tampons. See you in Grays Harbor." She waves as the Zodiac slips away, drifting behind the *Cape Calvert*.

Starting the engine, she presses down on the throttle and heads for shore.

Twenty yards away, the big male stirs.

ABOARD THE *NEPTUNE*
34 NAUTICAL MILES NORTHEAST OF PALAU
268 NAUTICAL MILES SOUTHWEST OF THE MARIANA
TRENCH

Susan Ferraris ushers the Daredevils into the captain's gallery.

Erik Hollander pulls Danielle Taylor aside. "Where's your father?"

"He went to see someone aboard that yacht."

The producer's eyes widen. "Who gave him permission to do that?"

"My father doesn't need permission." She pushes his arm away and joins the others inside.

Susan looks around the room. "So, we have some amazing news. The network went bonkers over last night's footage with that Megala-shark. Everything airs tonight. We've spoken to our local, uh, experts, and they feel confident the Meg will surface again tonight to finish off that whale. The network's so excited they've decided to offer a bonus. Are you ready? Any Daredevil who participates in a stunt involving the creature will receive a half-million-dollar bonus."

The Daredevils look at one another.

"Amazing, isn't it? Dee, I know you're in."

"A half million dollars to be eaten? You've got to be kidding."

"Count me out too," Evan says.

"Whoa, hey, slow down guys," Erik says, "maybe Susan didn't explain this right. We're talking about a half million dollars guaranteed, just for doing one stunt. Mia, that's five hundred thousand dollars to experience the ultimate adrenaline rush."

"I know what half a million dollars is, Erik, and I'm passing, too. I'm not afraid to die, but I am afraid of that monster."

Erik turns to Jennie Arnos.

"No way. I was up all night just thinking about that nightmare."

"Same here," Fergie says. "I was nearly eaten last night. Once is enough for me."

"Don't even bother asking me," Dani says.

Erik looks on the verge of tears. "Michael . . . Michael, you'll do it, won't you? One quick stunt and you're set for life."

"On half a million dollars? Who are you kidding?"

"Okay, good, at least we're negotiating. Tell you what, let me call the network and see if we can't just adjust that figure up a bit."

"You still don't get it, do you?" Fergie says. "It's never been about money or fame, we do what we do for the rush."

"Exactly. And what could be a greater rush than surviving a Megalodon attack?"

"This is different. Maybe jumping out of planes and swimming among a school of normal sharks seems haphazard to you, but everything we do falls under 'planned mayhem.' Each stunt has degrees of safety built in. With this monster, there's no degree of safety, no predictability. It eats, it's huge, and we're messing in its backyard, at night no less. That makes any stunt Russian roulette with five bullets, and we don't play those odds, not even for half a million bucks."

Erik slams his clipboard against his desk. "For two seasons, all I've heard out of your mouths is how you people live for the ultimate challenge. Now I've put my butt on the line and get you everything you ever wanted, and you're chickening out?"

"It's not chickening out," Mia says. "Everyone has to know their limits."

"If you're so damn brave, let's see you out there," Jennie retorts.

Erik turns to Susan, exasperated. "Do you believe this? Tonight could be the most watched broadcast in the history of television and the stars of the show are walking out on me. After all I've done for them. Nothing but a bunch of talkers."

"Maybe we ought to replay them that segment taken a few weeks ago, the one where they had their noses so far up Jonas Taylor's ass they couldn't breathe."

"That's it, I'm out of here." Dee stands, the others following suit.

Susan pulls Erik aside. Whispers something quickly into his ear.

Erik nods. "Whoa, hey guys, hold up! Please."

They pause at his door.

"Look, I'm sorry, I was completely out of line. It's been an amazing show up until now, let's not ruin it. Go eat something, enjoy the day, we'll figure things out. Michael, Fergie, if we can just speak with the two of you? Everyone else can go."

Dani looks at Fergie, who shrugs. "Go on, I'll catch up with you later."

The remaining Daredevils file out, leaving behind their two leaders.

Erik closes the door.

Susan makes her pitch.

"You're right. Half a million is just our first offer. But let's forget about the money for just a second. Do the two of you know why you were selected as team captains? It's not because you're the best Daredevils, which, of course, you are, it's because the two of you are leaders. You accept responsibility for your teammates, you lead by example. The two of you are the heart and soul of this show."

"Now the·show needs you," Erik chimes in. "Before you object, at least hear us out. We need five shows to complete the season. Figure three, since the last two episodes are combined into a reunion, slash final vote, slash season in review, which takes place back in the studio. Even if we cancel the team competition now, we still have to determine a winner."

Susan nods. "What if the final competition was changed from a team event to a personal duel between the two of you? Instead of going live, we'll shoot as much stock footage as we can, filming everything in one night. All we need is a simple stunt, something that places you in the same frame as the Meg but never really endangers you. We'll get our shots, then let the editors enhance the risk back at the studio."

"No danger, huh?" Fergie snorts a laugh. "Tell you what. Have the Meg swim by the *Neptune* and we'll wave."

"Yes, well, I'm sure we can do better than that."

"Okay," Coffey says, "you want a little *mano a mano* bull-shit, you've got it, but you'll pay the winner four million, the runner-up two. And we'll want everything in writing, signed, sealed, and sent to our attorneys before we set foot off this boat."

Fergie stares at Coffey, dumbfounded. "Hey, I said it's not about the money."

"Sure it is, especially when it's Erik's high-paid ass in a sling."

Erik shakes his head. "Six million for one episode? Make it two and you have yourself a deal."

"Come on, Fergie, we're out of here." Coffey drags the younger man out by his elbow.

"Hey, hold on now," Erik says. "We're negotiating."

"Sorry, Hollander, this is non-negotiable. So if I were you, I'd get on the radio real fast and start pimping your network pals before the sun sets on this whole bloody affair."

TANAKA OCEANOGRAPHIC INSTITUTE
MONTEREY BAY, CALIFORNIA

The Pacific Ocean has receded, the early afternoon's low tide revealing the upper three feet of the canal's reinforced concrete walls.

Mac guides the 29-foot *Fountain Sportfish* slowly toward the canal entrance, his pulse racing, his hands quivering noticeably. It has been twenty-two days since his last drink, and if ever James Mackreides needed one, it was now. *Is it just the D. T.'s, or are you scared?*

Rather than weighing anchor, he ties the bowline to the steel barge still anchored between the canal walls. Three mountains of sand are piled high across the middle of the steel expanse. The massive suction hose remains in the water, but the generator and pump have been shut down for the weekend.

Okay, if things go bad, where do you retreat? The barge or the boat?

Thinking fast getaway, he decides on the boat.

Mac pulls on his wetsuit and weight belt, searches the horizon nervously, then takes out the two-way radio. "David, you there?"

"Yes."

"I'm in position. Start the thumper."

"Uncle Mac, you sure about this? How do we even know the doors'll close this time?"

"Stechman assured me we have minimal clearance. If we wait until the next high tide, we could lose it."

"And the dive?"

"Don't see how we have any choice. Only way to close the doors now is directly at the junction box. With the bait in place, I should have an extra five minutes or so."

"Uncle Mac—"

"Start the thumper, kid. I'll call you the moment she enters."

David enters the Mechanical Room. He locates the thumper mechanism, then flips the switch, activating the underwater sound system.

The heavy thrumming sound resonates through the wall, giving him goose bumps.

Hurrying topside, he waits by the rusted steel A-frame, now bending beneath the weight of a 320-pound side of raw beef. Blood drips from the freshly killed bovine into the southern end of the man-made lagoon.

Mac paces nervously. *The boat or the barge? Boat'll get you to shore, but the barge is tougher to sink.* Recalling his adventure aboard the *Angel-II*, he grabs his equipment and climbs onto the barge.

Screw the boat, it's just a rental.

Mac sits back against a small dune of silt and sand, his eyes focused on the canal entrance.

ABOARD THE *NEPTUNE*
34 NAUTICAL MILES NORTHEAST OF PALAU
268 NAUTICAL MILES SOUTHWEST OF THE MARIANA
TRENCH

Danielle Taylor finds Fergie in the Daredevils' lounge making plans with Michael Coffey.

"Dani, I can't talk right now."

"Is it true? Are you really going through with it?"

"Two million is a lot of money," Coffey says.

"Hope you make it last," Fergie shoots right back, "since I'm taking the four."

Dani is on the verge of tears. "Fergie, we need to talk. In private."

"Go on," Coffey says, "I could use a beer."

"Grab me a coupla' cold ones, too, would you mate." Fergie nuzzles Dani's neck. "So what's on your mind, love?"

"Stop it." She pushes him away. "I want to talk about this stunt. You promised me you wouldn't participate."

"Whoa, I never promised anything. At first I decided against it—"

"And then Hollander bribed you."

"Actually, it was Coffey's idea, but he's right. This'll be the ultimate rush for the ultimate payday, and this time, Coffey's the one going down, not me."

"Listen to you, all of a sudden it's about competition and money. Everything you told me . . . it was all bullshit, wasn't it?"

"Wasn't bullshit, but I still need to make a living. Parachute jumps and surfing at exotic beaches and the rest of the lot, it all costs money. This is how I earn my keep."

"Is it really worth risking your life? That monster will kill you."

"It might, then again, maybe it won't."

"Ugh!" She turns to leave.

"Dani, wait—"

"You know, I thought we had something special. I thought I meant something to you."

"You do."

"Then why throw it all away? Why risk your life just for one stupid testosterone-filled moment?"

"I thought you understood. It's who I am."

"Well, you know what? It's not who I am." She storms out of the lounge, tears streaming down her cheeks.

CHAPTER

23

Ronald Roehmholdt runs his fingers through his silvery-gray hair as he stares at his reflection in the bathroom mirror. Flexes his muscles. The former Navy man and recent divorcée is still quite fit, thanks to beach volleyball and a half-mile ocean swim three times a week. *Maybe it's time I washed the gray out? Look a lot younger with black hair again. Got to make some serious changes, Ronnie, now that you're officially back in circulation.*

Ronald dresses in a tee-shirt and swim trunks, then searches his half-empty bedroom closet in vain for his warm-up suit. "No . . . no way. That lousy bitch . . . she swiped my brand new warm-up!" He kicks at his laundry bag, cursing his ex-wife's name. *Twelve hundred a month in alimony and still she robs me blind . . .*

Locating an old gray N.U.W.C. sweatshirt, he checks the alarm clock by his bed. *Two-twenty. Just enough time to pick up a lottery ticket, get to the marina, then head out to Pac Bell before the first pitch. Can't be late, not with Howard only one home run from history.*

Ronald double-times it through the kitchen and out the garage door to his car, checking his mental "to-do" list. *Fish-*

ing net . . . extension pole . . . portable television . . . extra bat-
teries . . . sun-block . . . camera . . . boat   keys . . . cooler . . .
sandwiches . . . beer . . . you're all set.

He grabs his newspaper and climbs in his Jeep Cherokee,
then checks his horoscope in the Lifestyle section before
starting his car.

Aquarius: Your financial pressures will soon be relieved.

He starts the car, smiling to himself.

ABOARD THE *NEPTUNE*

The late afternoon sun inches toward a cloudless horizon,
casting a warm golden glow over the Spanish galleon.

Danielle Taylor leans against the starboard bow rail, her
eyes red-rimmed from crying, her heart aching in her chest.
*I don't deserve to be treated this way. How could he do this?
Doesn't he know how much I love him?*

She stares at the dark object floating less than a half mile
from the *Neptune*, a dozen shark fins continuing to circle the
Sperm whale carcass. *Maybe he doesn't know? Maybe I
should have told him before I ran off like I did? I mean, who
am I to change him? Being a Daredevil is who he is. Besides,
it's not like we're married or anything.*

She stands, wiping tears from her eyes. *I have to find him.
I can't let him go out tonight feeling confused. I'll . . . I'll let
him know I support him, that I'm here for him, that I only
said what I said because I love him so much.*

Dani races down the nearest companionway, nearly trip-
ping over Evan Stewart.

"Evan, I . . . I have to find Fergie. Have you seen him?"

Evan looks her over, smiling a sly grin. "Fergie? As a
matter of fact, I just saw him in Captain Robertson's state-

room, that's the big gallery in the stern. Just go on in, he'll be happy to see you."

"Thanks." She heads back up on deck, hurrying aft to the Admiral's Gallery.

The cabin door is closed but unlocked. "Fergie? You in there?"

"Dani? Wait, don't—"

She pushes open the door.

Fergie sits up in bed, his eyes wide, the covers pulled up to his naked chest. "Dani, I . . ."

A woman's hand appears from beneath the blanket.

Jennie Arnos pokes her head free from the sheets, exposing her disheveled hair and naked upper torso. "Fergie's a little busy right now. Why don't you take a number and come back in about an hour."

Dani swallows the bile rising in her throat, unable to speak.

"Dani, I'm sorry, but it's for the best. It just wasn't going to work out."

Dani grunts a guttural scream, grabs a candleholder off a nearby wall shelf and hurls it at the Aussie.

The toss misses his head, shattering a framed painting of *Dante's Inferno* hanging on the wall behind the bed.

"I hope the two of you rot in Hell!"

Dani turns to leave, shocked to find an audience of applauding, snickering Daredevils and Candy Girls waiting outside the door.

"Ugh!" Red-faced, bursting with tears, she pushes past the crowd, wishing she was dead.

TANAKA OCEANOGRAPHIC INSTITUTE
MONTEREY BAY, CALIFORNIA

Mac's eyes follow the whalewatching boat as it continues its journey north, a half mile out to sea. He can just about hear the tour guide over the loudspeaker. He can see the tourists aiming their cameras at the canal.

Been eighteen years since she escaped and the pen still excites a crowd. Mac checks his watch. *Three-fifteen.* He calls David on the two-way. "Hey, kid, you still there?"

"Yes."

"It's been almost five hours. Where's the Meg?"

"She'll come. Trust me."

"Yeah, well that thumper's giving me a goddamn headache. Shut it down, I'm calling it a day."

"But Uncle Mac—"

"A buddy of mine got me tickets for this afternoon's Giants-Phillies game. Thought we could use the break."

"Yes!"

"It'll take me twenty minutes to return the boat. I'll pick you up in the lagoon's northern parking lot at four."

ABOARD THE *COELACANTH*

Jonas Taylor forces his eyes open against the pain.

His lower lip is swollen and bleeding, his nose broken. His ribs are badly bruised, his stomach muscles ache. Still, as hurt as he is from the physical beating, he knows Maren let up.

Crazy bastard wants me alive and kicking when he feeds me to his shark.

He tests the shackles, then notices Satoshi seated on the floor by the opposite wall. The Japanese wrestler grins at him, holding up four stubby fingers.

Jonas closes his eyes, conserving his strength.

Message received: Four more hours until I become live bait.

PIER 39 MARINA
SAN FRANCISCO BAY, CALIFORNIA

The Pier 39 Marina is a virtual city of boat slips, located on
the San Francisco waterfront between the Golden Gate and
Bay bridges, just southwest of Alcatraz.

Ronald Roehmholdt follows Powell Street north to the
Pier 39 garage and parks. Gathering his equipment, he
crosses the street to the Marina and walks along Dock D until he reaches Slip 36.

Ronald's blood pressure soars as he spots the strawberry-
blond sunning herself in the back of the boat . . . *his boat,*
while her scum-sucking attorney boyfriend fills an ice chest
with beer.

"No way, Sue, no goddamn way!"

His ex-wife looks up, almost bored. "Spencer, handle this
please."

Spencer Bullock greets Ronald as the man attempts to
climb on board. "Back off, Ronald, or I'll hit you with a re-
straining order."

"And I'll hit you with a right cross. This is my boat!"

"Better re-read the settlement agreement. It's yours when
you pay Susan her fair share of the equity."

"Fine, use it all next week if you want, but I'm using it
today."

"Sorry," Sue chirps, "we were here first."

"Shut up! Since when do you give a damn about fishing?"

"I don't. We're going to Pac Bell to see the Giants."

"You mean, you're trying to catch Howard's home run ball."

"They say it'll be worth between three and five million."
Spencer says, eyeballing Ronald's equipment. "Apparently
you're after the same prize."

"You're damn right, and when I get that ball, the two of
you get nothing. Now get off my boat!"

Sue holds up a cell phone. "Back off, Ronald, or I'll call
the cops."

"Go ahead. My name's on the title."

"And we were here first."

Spencer holds up his hands between them. "Okay, let's all just calm down. Susan, since Ronald's going to McCovey Cove too, I suggest we let him come along for the ride."

"Absolutely not."

"Well I'm not leaving. How do you like that?"

"I'm calling the cops."

Spencer pulls her aside. "The game starts in an hour. Call the cops now and we'll miss at least one at bat and our only shot at finding a decent spot in the Cove. Do you want to risk all that just for him?"

She glances over at her ex-husband. "Fine, he can come, but he stays on his side of the boat."

PACIFIC BELL PARK
SAN FRANCISCO BAY, CALIFORNIA

Pacific Bell Park, home to the San Francisco Giants baseball team, is arguably the most enjoyable stadium to watch a game in the major leagues, offering breathtaking views and an outfield that backs up to the glistening blue waters of San Francisco Bay. Erected in 2000, the privately financed park features a nine-foot statue of Willie Mays, an 80-foot Coca-Cola bottle with playground slides, and a mass transit system second to none.

Perhaps the most unique feature of Pac Bell is McCovey Cove. Named after the former Giant Hall of Fame outfielder, McCovey Cove is the stretch of public waterway situated beyond the right-field wall, 420 feet from home plate. Prior to each Giants home game, watercraft ranging from rubber rafts and kayaks to luxury yachts and tall-masted sailboats congregate in the cove to party and perhaps even catch a home run ball.

Today's crowd rivals only that of the one that overwhelmed every Giants late-August home game more than a decade ago when Barry Bonds surpassed Hank Aaron's long-held record of 755 career home runs. When Bonds finally did catch Aaron, it was on the road, disappointing the Bay Area crowd.

Now, with Philadelphia Phillies slugger Ryan Howard closing on Bonds's record, the San Franciscans are arriving in droves, some to cheer, most to boo, all wanting to be a part of baseball history.

The boaters in McCovey Cove want something more.

Twenty-seven percent of Howard's home runs at Pac Bell have been hit over the right-field bleachers, thirty-four percent of those being mammoth shots that made it into the bay. With the odds of catching Howard's record-breaking home run several hundred times better than hitting the California lottery, nearly everyone in the Bay Area with a watercraft is converging on McCovey Cove.

The super yachts had begun arriving last night just before midnight, only hours after Howard had tied Bonds's record with a seventh-inning two-run blast over the left-field wall. By dawn the cove was packed with rubber rafts and kayaks, fishing boats, pontoons, and two AM radio stations. By midday, the bay had become a flotilla of fiberglass, a virtual floating parking lot filled with barbecuers and sunbathers, beer brawlers and dreamers, all jostling for position, hoping and praying that one man's athletic achievement will change their lives forever.

Angel glides along the mollusk-laden seafloor of San Francisco Bay. Having followed the Dietsch Brothers speedboat into the waterway, the creature abandoned the chase when its senses had become overwhelmed by a myriad of alien scents and electrical impulses. For more than two hours the Meg had circled the depths of the Golden Gate Bridge, its sensory system buzzing with the reverberations caused by

the bridge traffic. From there the Meg had moved east to
shadow an Alcatraz Island tour boat. Confronted by a nox-
ious mountain of dredged materials, the big female left the
area, moving farther north.

Now, as the sun begins to set and the night teases its appetite, a new set of signals gains the Megalodon's attention,
causing the monster to once again alter her course.

"Oh, hell, I don't believe this." Ronald Roehmholdt slows
his boat, confronted by the sight of hundreds of watercraft
jammed into a square mile expanse of bay located just beyond the low-lying right-field bleachers and public pier.

Undaunted, Ronald nudges the bow of his fishing boat between the stern end of an 85-foot yacht and a 31-foot catamaran, desperate to enter the melee.

The baseball stadium is a beehive of humanity, standing
room only for all but the lucky 41,000 ticket bearers. The
lights towering over the horseshoe-shaped open-air arena
have been turned on, brightening the otherwise overcast,
gray sky. A man's voice crackles over the public address system, announcing the day's starting lineups.

"Batting clean-up and playing first base, number six,
Ryan Howard."

A resounding chorus of cheers mixed with boos echoes
across the bay.

Mac shows his tickets to an usher, then leads David to
their seats, which are located in right field in fair territory,
just inside the foul pole. "Great seats, huh? Would you believe scalpers are getting three times the face value for anything in the outfield, four times for the left-field bleachers."

"I'm just psyched to be here. I think I was seven or eight
the last time my dad took me to a game." David pounds his

fist into the worn leather pocket of his first baseman's mitt, then hands it to Mac. "You'd better take this. If Howard does hit a deep one, you stand a better chance of getting it than me. This crowd'll crush me if I try getting near that ball."

Mac hands David back his glove. "Tell you what, if he hits it out this way, I'll lift you up onto my shoulders."

"Okay. But if I catch it, we split everything fifty-fifty."

"Done deal." Mac smacks him affectionately on the shoulder as he eyeballs a beer vendor heading their way. *Lord, give me strength . . .*

Ronald has managed to maneuver his boat a third of the way into the traffic jam, irritating at least a dozen boat owners by the time the sold-out crowd has risen for the national anthem. "Guess this is about as close as we're gonna get. Burrell better really get hold of one for us to stand a chance. Hello? Am I talking to myself?"

Ronald climbs down from the flying bridge, looking for his ex-wife and her attorney. "Where'd they go?"

He heads below. Sees the closed cabin door. Feels the boat rocking as he hears the sound of two people making love. "Oh great, that's just great. On my own boat, no less." He yells against the door. "Guess what, pal, she's all yours. Now do us both a favor and marry her so I can stop paying her monthly ransom!"

Stomping back up on deck, he grabs his battery-operated television, flops down in a canvas chair, and turns on the game.

The Phillies leadoff man singles to left field to open the game. The second batter sacrifices him to second. With one out, Philadelphia's number three hitter draws a walk on six pitches.

"Now batting for the Phillies, number six, first baseman Ryan Howard."

A chorus of boos rains down on the second leading home run hitter in major league history as he steps to the plate, attempting to become number one.

High up in the right-field bleachers, psychology major James Hollen turns to his fiancée, Jessica Burna. "Ready for some fun? This is a little psyche experiment I call 'teaching Pavlov's dogs to fetch.' Watch and learn."

Howard takes the first pitch for a called strike.

Reaching into his backpack, James Hollen discreetly removes a baseball.

Howard takes the second pitch high for a ball.

James powers on his palm-size video recorder. "See, Jess, greed is an amazing thing. It actually conditions us to do stuff we'd normally never do in a million years."

The runners lead off their bases. The pitcher delivers the one-one pitch—

Howard swings, sending a towering fly ball to deep left-center field.

The crowd roars, rising to their feet.

James turns toward the right-field wall and throws the baseball as far and as high as he can, then aims his camcorder at McCovey Cove.

The boaters are on their feet, screaming and rushing to track the tiny white baseball that is soaring over the right-field wall, falling from the heavens.

The ball lands on the bow of a catamaran, caroms ten feet in the air as it deftly eludes a pack of sunburned, half-drunk boaters, then causes a jump ball/scramble/rugby-like scrum that sends sixty-three people diving overboard and into the water.

As Ryan Howard's deep fly ball is caught at the warning track and the Phillies runners tag up, a horde of inexperienced swimmers find themselves treading water and surface diving, jostling each other while attempting to avoid being crushed to death by the hulls of a dozen anchored boats and at least four kayaks.

"Hey, it was a fake out, a dork ball! Knock it off, it wasn't even a homer!"

It takes another ten minutes of yelling before the last of the wannabe millionaires crawls dripping wet and bruised back onto his vessel.

Ronald Roehmholdt drags himself up the aluminum dive ladder with one hand, his left shoulder aching from his collision with a paddleboat camouflaged as a floating golf green.

Sue laughs hysterically as her ex-husband pulls off his drenched sweatshirt and wrings it out over the side. "Hey, genius, you were watching the game on television. Didn't it ever occur to you that the ball was hit to left field?"

"Shut up."

"You're such an idiot. I bet these fans'll have you jumping in and out of the bay all night."

"When I want your opinion I'll ask for it."

Spencer Bullock hides his grin as he attempts to change the subject. "You know, I hear Major League Baseball has tagged every ball in use today with a specially encoded computer chip, just to make sure no one tries a stunt like this."

"Thanks for the insight, Mister ESPN. Now why don't you go down below and bang my ex for another few innings."

"Come on, Spencer. Obviously Ronald's jealous that I've found someone and he hasn't." She leads him below as the partisan crowd cheers wildly for their Giants, whose pitcher strikes out the number five hitter, ending the Phillies' first inning threat.

"Hey, if you're what's out there, I'd just as soon skip the marriage and divorce and buy a boat for a stranger I hate!"

Angel moves slowly through the shallows, her towering dorsal fin coming within twelve feet of the keel of a super yacht. A cacophony of reflected sound echoes through her brain from the ceiling of watercraft, stirring her curiosity and appetite.

Rising, she pushes her snout gently between a catamaran and a paddleboat, "tasting" the hulls, nearly flipping two inebriated men in the small vessel backward and into the water.

"Whoa! Hey, watch it!"

"Goddamn rich folk . . . think they own the whole damn bay."

Angel descends. The surface vibrations are enticing, but the source is not edible. She moves off—

—then her senses detect a different kind of disturbance.

Dwarfed by sailboats and yachts, floating in the middle of the chaos of McCovey Cove, is Paul Barkmeier. The thirty-eight-year-old accountant and father of two is exhausted from straddling his surfboard for the last three and a half hours. Tucking his radio into his waterproof backpack, he zips up his wetsuit, then swings his right leg overboard, slipping into the cool water.

Laying his arms and head down on the surfboard, he allows his cramped legs to dangle as he urinates into the bay.

Circling thirty feet below the flotilla is the Great White shark. A rogue hunter, the fish moves in and out of the murk, lured by the scent of prey. At 2,800 pounds and eighteen feet, the female is easily the largest creature in the bay . . . save for its prehistoric cousin.

Zigzagging along the bottom, the shark suddenly rises, its nostrils inhaling the scent of urine in the water, its ampullae of Lorenzini homing in on the electrical discharge created by Paul Barkmeier's beating heart.

Paul finishes relieving himself, then registers a bizarre sensation as the hairs on the back of his neck stand on end—

—and a fifteen-foot tsunami-like swell rolls beneath the

boats spread out before him, sending one after another rising and crashing into the next.

"What the hell?"

He pulls himself back onto the surfboard and holds on tight as the wake crests and falls beneath him, sending his board hurtling into a dinghy.

Angel accelerates just beneath the ceiling of boats, her wake causing havoc among the anchored vessels.

Detecting its immense cousin, the Great White breaks off its attack and descends—too late.

Angel snatches the eighteen-foot shark within her jaws, shakes it twice, then crushes its spine.

The chaos below creates a massive domino effect as hundreds of tightly packed watercraft are lifted and bashed against one another as if caught in a powerful eddy. For a moment the baseball game is completely forgotten as irate boaters yell and scream and threaten one another, all unaware of the ominous presence still circling beneath their vessels, feeding on the remains of the Great White.

The sound of the Pac Bell crowd restores order as Ryan Howard comes to bat in the fourth inning.

Ronald readies his fishing net.

Sue and Spencer emerge from below, the couple holding hands as the radio blares: ". . . Jackson takes his lead off first, and here's the two strike pitch to Howard . . ."

Craack!

"And there's a long fly ball to deep right field . . . Perry Meth is way back . . . he's at the warning track . . . and that ball is outta here! A two-run monster shot for Ryan Howard, who has just become baseball's all-time leading home run leader! Wow."

David looks up into a forest of raised arms. For a scant second he glimpses the ball as it loops high overhead, spinning majestically, seam over seam, the roar of the crowd in his brain, the shoving wall of flesh and beer and popcorn becoming a sudden, fading avalanche—

—as the ball continues its fateful journey over the right-field bleachers and beyond the public pier.

And now 41,000 fans turn to Pac Bell's fan-o-vision as a thousand pair of eyes look up from McCovey Cove into the twilight sky, searching the heavens.

Ronald sees the tiny white meteorite of rawhide, and he can't believe it, because that ball is flying right toward him as if magnetized. His eyes widen as he reaches out with his bare hands and yells, "I got it! I got it—"

—his ex-wife and her boyfriend crash into him, the impact sending all three tumbling over the side of the boat and into the bay.

A dozen more people jump into the water before Ronald can surface, another hundred leaping from boat to boat to join them. Within thirty seconds, the bay has become a chaotic screaming, splashing, thrashing mass of human beings, all intent on drowning one another as they search in vain for a small white baseball.

Ronald is underwater, spinning like a bug in a flushing toilet, his right hand clenched firmly around the precious object, his lungs screaming at his brain to surface, but there is no surface to ascend to, just a ceiling of churning limbs.

He kicks as hard as he can, wedging his head between a choking teenage girl and an Asian man in his forties. As he sucks in a mouthful of air and foam, he hears his ex-wife shout above the din, "There he is! Spencer, he has the ball, quick—" as she leaps upon his head and her boyfriend bites Ronald's fist.

And now he is underwater again, his heart pounding in his ears as the life-changing object is forcibly ripped from his hand and a dozen bodies converge upon him, grabbing and tearing at his clothes, pummeling him deeper, and now Ronald must make a decision—the ball or his life—because this time he really is drowning.

A desperate surge of energy courses through his being and he punches and kicks his way free of the mob. With no place to surface, he is forced to swim beneath the melee, his scorching lungs about to burst, the dark sea spinning in his vision as he sees the white object looming overhead.

Ronald reaches up, dragging himself onto the aluminum ladder as he gasps a life-quenching breath of air. His body is lead, his muscles drenched with lactic acid, but still he forces himself up and over the side of his boat, collapsing onto the decking.

For a long moment he just lies there, his chest heaving from the effort. *God, I hate that woman* . . . Ronald Roehmholdt pushes himself onto his knees and leans against the transom, cursing his ex-wife's existence—

—as a halo of lime green appears beneath the mob, the glow gradually brightening into a twelve-foot-wide bear trap, filled with nightmarish white teeth.

Ronald is on his feet, watching breathlessly as the horrible set of jaws rises higher to become the monstrous head of a ghostly albino Great White shark—only the creature is way too big to be a Great White.

And now Ronald is screaming with the others—giggling and screaming—as his ex-wife and her boyfriend fall into the Megalodon's beckoning mouth, and then he is gagging as he witnesses those snapping jowls devour a half dozen flailing, shell-shocked people, and now he is on his knees again, thanking God that he is still alive, and to hell with money, to hell with his boat, just please get him home safely.

David and Mac are looking up at the big screen along with the rest of the mesmerized crowd as Angel torques her mammoth head back and forth along the surface, driving boats sideways, sinking canoes and kayaks and paddleboats as she creates a larger hole in which to feed.

"Sweet Jesus . . . it's like a human smorgasbord out there." Mac grabs David's arm. "Come on!"

They race down the aisle, heading for the parking lot, leaving behind the shrieking crowd and the thundering helicopters and the home run music still blasting from a thousand speakers, and the stunned commissioner of Major League Baseball, who stands in horror in his skybox seat, wondering whether he should call the game an inning before it becomes official.

CHAPTER

24

WESTPORT MARINA
GRAYS HARBOR, WASHINGTON

Grays Harbor is a massive body of water carved out of the northwest coast of Washington, accessed by an estuary guarded in the winter by large waves, harsh wind, and heavy fog. Named after Captain Robert Gray, a Boston sea captain and trader who eventually managed to negotiate the inlet, the harbor was first colonized when it was mistakenly believed to be the entrance to the long-sought Northwest Passage. The area eventually prospered as a trading hub between East and West, and became an important resource for timber, pulp, and paper.

These days, the harbor supports nine incorporated cities and close to 50,000 residents, which swell each summer as more than two million tourists come to visit the area's pristine waterways, beaches, and shopping areas, all set at the foot of the Olympic Mountains.

Grays Harbor is also home to Westport Marina, the largest coastal marina in the Pacific Northwest. Once a shipyard, the marina is now a docking area for deep ocean salmon and tuna trawlers, crabbing boats, and a thriving charter business specializing in deep-sea fishing. A promenade of shops, restaurants, museums, and an aquarium draw visitors year round.

Terry Taylor is in a local eatery, sipping her clam chowder. She gazes out the bay windows at another crab boat unloading its wares at the Crab Fishery dock. She had arrived in Westport four hours ago, her journey beginning earlier that afternoon with a nerve-racking Zodiac ride across two miles of rough Pacific, dodging waves, weather, and a bulwark of beached ships. Landing in Kalaloch, she had ditched the raft, then followed a forest trail through dense spruce until she found her way to a rustic lodge perched on a bluff overlooking the ocean. A warm breakfast and a two-hour cab ride later and she was in Westport, refreshed and satisfied with her decision to leave the *Cape Calvert.*

A short, muscular man with a marine haircut enters the diner, his huge forearms sporting a dozen tattoos. He looks around, then approaches. "You Mrs. Taylor?"

"Yes."

"Sean Justus. Call me Popeye. Sea World hired me to transport your animal."

"You brought the mobile tank?"

"It's parked out back."

"Come on, I'll show you where it needs to go." She pays her bill, then follows him outside.

At the end of the pier is a deepwater dock. A large crane towers overhead.

Sean nods. "So what are we transporting? Orca? Gray whale?"

"Something like that."

The former Coast Guard seaman looks at her with suspicion. "Look, lady, you want to be coy, that's your business, but whatever it is we're hauling had better be heavily sedated. This truck's a bitch to drive even when she's not loaded down with ten thousand gallons of seawater."

"It'll be sedated."

"Did you arrange a police escort?"

"Yes. Can I see the truck now?"

He leads her around back to the parking lot. A massive double-wide tractor trailer sits cater-corner to the road, its twenty-six wheels and reinforced shock absorbers supporting a twenty-foot-high, eighty-foot-long steel tank, connected to a circulation pump mounted on top of the cab.

Four lanky young men in their early twenties lean against the truck, eating the remains of their fast-food lunch.

"Mrs. Taylor, meet my crew. Ashley Davidson, Jeff Gruman, and our Georgia boys, Josh and Cory."

"Ma'am."

"So, Mrs. Taylor, when can we expect this mysterious specimen of yours to arrive?"

"Sometime within the next few hours, I'm guessing."

Sean checks his watch. "Jeff, move the rig down to the end of the pier and start filling her with seawater."

"How big a fish we hauling?"

"Sixty feet, probably weighs thirty tons," Terry answers.

Ashley whistles. "Humpback or Gray?"

"The lady's not saying. Some kind of secret."

"It'll be heavily sedated, trust me," Terry says. "I'll meet you down by the dock in fifteen minutes, I just need to make a phone call."

Leaving them, she locates a payphone and places a collect call to David at her father's home.

No answer.

She tries the Institute, but he's not there either.

Where the hell is he?

PACIFIC COAST HIGHWAY, CALIFORNIA

Mac exits Route 280 and drives south along the Pacific Coast Highway. "Well, at least we know why she wasn't responding to the thumper. The question now is, how do we get her back down the coast to Monterey?"

"We need the portable thumper," David says. "We could drag it from a boat and lead her right into the lagoon."

"Not in this lifetime. Bad enough what happened in the lagoon, I don't want to be in open ocean with that monster bearing down on me." Mac turns up the volume on the radio.

". . . Coast Guard now confirming seven dead, eighteen wounded, with two more boaters suffering heart attacks. A small craft advisory has been issued for San Francisco Bay and the surrounding areas. Meanwhile, Major League Baseball commissioner Garret Peck has announced that tonight's game between the Phillies and Giants will be postponed until Monday, play resuming from the fourth inning on. Once again if you're just joining us, fans at tonight's game between the Phils and Giants witnessed history when Ryan Howard broke Barry Bonds's all-time record for home runs, only to see play stopped when the once-captive Megalodon shark known as Angel brutally attacked boaters in McCovey—"

Mac turns the radio off. "Not a sighting in eighteen years, now we've got Megalodons coming out the ying-yang. What time's your old man's show come on?"

"Nine o'clock."

"We'll watch the show, then search the Institute again for that thumper. Maybe there's another way we can lure that Meg of yours home."

WESTPORT MARINA
GRAYS HARBOR, WASHINGTON

Terry Taylor is seated on a wooden bench, watching the last rays of day melt beneath the darkening Pacific. Somewhere out there is the *Cape Calvert*, towing a creature she selfishly hopes can save her father's legacy.

For the first time since her journey began, she thinks about her family's future. *What will Jonas say when he learns we captured another Meg? Will he even want to work at the In-*

stitute again? Maybe it's better he doesn't. It'll be hard enough having to deal with Josh on a daily basis. Then again, with Jonas around, maybe the cocky little shit will back off. If he doesn't, I can always fire him . . . no, then he'll sue me, or worse, he could threaten my marriage.

She stomps her feet in frustration, wishing she'd never left Monterey.

Terry gazes absentmindedly at a raucous crowd gathering around the entrance of a local sports bar. *Must be some game.*

Then she hears the screaming.

Terry heads for the bar, quickening her pace as she hears more shrieks and a name that sends shivers down her spine. "It's Angel, the monster's returned!"

Terry pushes her way through the mob until she can see one of the ceiling-mounted television screens.

The slow-motion replay of Angel gnashing a mouthful of screaming boaters is too horrifying for her distraught mind to absorb. For a bizarre moment, her brain seems to short-circuit, then blackness takes her as she faints dead away.

ABOARD THE *NEPTUNE*

The night is electric, the production crew tense as they wait behind their cameras and monitors, boom mikes and sound equipment for Mother Nature to begin the show. Captain Robertson has his ship pointed into the wind, her sails up, ready to power a quick getaway.

Susan and Erik huddle behind monitors linked to three underwater cameras mounted beneath buoys. The images appear blurred and bouncy in the heavy seas.

Susan shakes her head. "These cameras are useless. I'm getting seasick just trying to watch the damn picture."

"It's the best we could do," Erik says. "Andrew's crew refuses to enter the ocean."

"What about Andrew?"

"Not for all the tea in China. But I may have another means of getting some great shots."

Susan's eyebrows rise. "I'm listening."

"Part of my arrangement with the captain of the *Coelacanth* was that he provide me with underwater footage of the finale."

"How's he going to do that?"

"Sorry, can't give you details."

"Erik—"

He grins sheepishly. "Okay, okay, I have to tell somebody. The captain owns one of those naval drones, complete with an underwater camera. If the Meg shows up, he said he'll release the drone and shoot all the footage we need."

"Fantastic. So who is this mysterious captain?"

Erik loses his smile as Dani steps out from behind the main mast.

"Answer the question, Erik. Who's the captain, and what does he want with my father?"

"Honestly, Dani, I have no idea. You'll have to ask your father."

"I would, but he still hasn't returned from the *Coelacanth*. Captain Robertson tried contacting the yacht, but they won't answer. What happened to him, Erik?"

"Again, I wouldn't know. I'm a television producer, not a gypsy."

"You're lying." She moves closer. Whispers. "If something happens to my father, I'm going to kill you."

Dani backs away, then heads aft, ignoring the whispers coming from a group of scantily clad Candy Girls. Moving past the mizzen mast, she pauses to watch Charlotte Lockhart's live interview with Fergie and Mike Coffey.

"Fergie, I understand you're up first. Would you tell us a little about your stunt?"

"Charlotte my love, all I can say is it's a helluva lot more dangerous than Michael's here. I'll be stranded alone on that whale carcass, it'll be just me and that monster. God only knows how I'll survive."

"And how will you get out to the dead whale? Swim?"

"Lord, no, I'm not that crazy. One of my brave-hearted teammates'll be taking me out by jet ski." He checks his watch. "Should be ready to go any time now."

Dani continues aft, then slips inside Erik's stateroom.

Jennie Arnos is in her wetsuit, primping before a mirror. "Well, well, if it isn't our little Daredevil wannabe. Tell me, jailbait, when you decided to come on board, were you expecting this to be a cruise on the Love Boat?"

Dani moves past a bookshelf, palming a hardbound copy of Gideon's Bible.

Jennie applies more eye shadow. "Poor little schoolgirl. I bet you thought Fergie would propose. So sorry to disappoint you."

"Actually, I only came on board to share some quality time with my father." Gripping the bible in both hands, Dani slams the heavy book on top of Jennie's head, knocking her out.

The cameras are rolling as Fergie climbs down the cargo net to his awaiting jet ski. Beneath one arm is a Wipika Inferno 144 wakeboard and boots. Strapped to his back is a canvas bag, loaded with equipment. Looking up at the cameras, he calls out, "come on, Jedi Jennie, we can't keep Nature waiting!"

The female Daredevil climbs down the cargo net to the awaiting jet ski, straddling the pilot's seat in front of Fergie.

"Dani? Dani, what're you doing here? Where's Jennie?"

"She has a bad headache, I'm taking her place."

Before he can object, she powers up the jet ski, guns the engine, and races for the dead Sperm whale.

ABOARD THE *COELACANTH*

Satoshi leads Jonas Taylor up to the sun deck where Michael Maren is waiting. The marine biologist and his girlfriend are seated at a dinner table, finishing their shrimp cocktail appetizer.

Jonas's mouth waters. He has not eaten for twenty hours.

"Sorry, Taylor. I'd invite you to join us for dinner, but then you'd have to wait a full hour before going swimming, and we wouldn't want to hold up the show."

"Of course not." Jonas eyes the Nighthawk 2.8 ¥ 53 night-vision binoculars dangling from the fat man's neck. "So, where's your monster now?"

Maren swallows the remains of his shrimp, then turns the laptop's monitor away from Allison Petrucci so it faces Jonas. On-screen, a tiny blue blip is rising from the depths, a large red blip following it up. "He's still deep, but he's coming up fast. Scarface is hungry."

"Then if I were you, I'd stay out of the water. Megalodons love sea elephants."

Maren's eyes narrow as he forces a smile. "So nice seeing you again, Professor Taylor. Give my regards to Celeste when you see her."

"Maybe you'll see her first."

Satoshi grabs Jonas by his wrist and the seat of his pants and tosses him clear over the rail.

Jonas plunges painfully into the black Pacific, the impact and sudden cold driving the wind from his lungs. He kicks to the surface, wheezing at the sharp pain stabbing at his rib cage.

Looking up, he sees Maren and Satoshi waving from the starboard rail.

Forget them. Stick with the plan. Searching the darkening horizon, he locates the *Neptune,* the ship a good mile away across rough, four- to five-foot seas.

Jonas ducks his head and attempts to swim, but the crawl

stroke is too much for his bruised ribs. He switches to side-stroke, his skin tingling, his mind insane with the knowledge that he is only minutes away from being eaten alive.

Wayne Ferguson holds Dani tightly around her waist as the girl drives the jet ski across the windswept sea, her blond hair whipping in his face.

For Danielle Taylor, fear has been replaced by rage. She loathes the man holding her, and feels sickened by his touch. She hates "Jedi" Jennie and the rest of the Daredevils, despises their legion of whores, and wishes the show's producers would die a painful death.

Most of all, Dani hates herself. She hates that she has succumbed to vanity, hates that she allowed others to manipulate her, hates that she attempted to "fit in." She has lost her self-esteem and her direction, and part of her hopes she'll die horribly tonight, just to teach them all a lesson.

She spots the floating hump of blubber, surrounded by a sea of dorsal fins. The presence of the sharks makes her even angrier, and she zigzags back and forth, running over as many of the soulless creatures' fins as she can before driving the jet ski right onto the dead whale's back.

Skidding to a halt, she pries Fergie's arm loose from around her waist, then turns, looks him square in the eye and says, "Get off."

"Dani—"

"Now."

He slides off the seat, stunned and strangely turned on by the girl's sudden maturity. "Dani, I know you're as cross as a cut snake, but don't go yet. You know part of this is your fault too. You were getting way too serious."

Ignoring him, she climbs off the jet ski and pushes its nose back into the water.

"You know, there's a good chance I could die out here tonight. Is this how you want things to end between us?"

"It's your life, Wayne. If you want to throw it away, who am I to stop you?" Mounting the jet ski, she pushes it off the island of blubber, then accelerates away from the carcass, heading for the super yacht.

Jonas stops swimming, then looks back. He has succeeded in distancing himself from the *Coelacanth*, the yacht now a hundred and sixty yards away. He knows Maren is watching him through the night-vision binoculars, marking his progress as he guides the barracuda up from the depths to greet him.

Jonas waits for a five-foot swell, then sucks in a deep breath and ducks beneath the wave, swimming as hard and as long as he can underwater, altering his course from north to west. Timing his ascent, he raises his head just before another swell passes by, using the wave to conceal his presence. Stealing another breath, he ducks underwater and continues swimming, moving parallel to the *Coelacanth*.

Michael Maren lies back in his lounge chair, his binoculars focused on the splashing form moving along the surface. "Allison, where's Scarface now?"

"Twenty-six hundred feet."

"When the barracuda reaches one hundred feet, level it out and circle Taylor. I want to frighten him a little more before he dies."

"You're sick."

"An eye for an eye, Ali. I've waited a long time for this."

"Taylor didn't kill Celeste, Angel did."

"And I'm doing precisely the same thing he did eighteen years ago."

"It's still sick."

Maren refocuses his glasses on the sea. He scans the surface, then sits up suddenly. "Dammit, where'd he go?"

Jonas's legs burn with lactic acid, his chest from a lack of air, yet still he swims underwater, his mind, crazed with fear, counting the breaststrokes between swells.

Twenty-two . . . twenty-three . . . twenty-four . . . now!

He rises, his head clearing the surface seconds before another swell washes over him.

Remaining on the surface, he steals a quick glance at the yacht, verifying that he has moved past the vessel.

Ducking underwater again, he changes course, this time heading south, back toward the *Coelacanth.*

Maren, Satoshi, and two more crewmen stand by the sun deck's starboard rail, all searching the Pacific through their night-vision binoculars.

"Fourteen hundred feet. He's coming up faster now, he must smell the dead whale."

"Adjust the barracuda's ascent, Allison. Keep Scarface away from that whale until we relocate Taylor."

"Maybe he drowned," Satoshi offers in broken English. "You hit him many time."

"He didn't drown. He's up to something. Keep searching."

"Uh-oh, we've got company." One of the crewmen points off the starboard bow.

A jet ski approaches from half a mile away.

Maren refocuses his night glasses on the rider. Recognizes the long blond hair. "That's Taylor's daughter. Satoshi, did you sink Taylor's Zodiac as I instructed?"

"*Hai.*"

"The three of you find Taylor. I'll greet his daughter."

Dani slows the jet ski as she approaches the bow of the sleek super yacht.

A searchlight ignites, blinding her. A man's voice calls

out from behind a megaphone. "The *Coelacanth* is off-limits. What is it you want?"

She squints up at the light, unable to see anyone. "My father's Jonas Taylor. He boarded earlier. I need to speak with him."

"Professor Taylor left hours ago."

"What?" Dani's heart races. "But he never returned to the ship."

"Then you need to contact the Coast Guard. Get back to the *Neptune*, before the Megalodon returns."

He's lying. "It's already dark. I'm frightened. I don't want to run into that creature. Let me board, please."

A long pause. "Very well. Come aft, I'll lower the swim dock."

Fergie kneels on the belly of the dead Sperm whale as he finishes assembling his equipment, the wind-driven swells repeatedly washing over the bloated carcass. The *Neptune* remains sixty yards away, its two powerful spotlights illuminating the island of blubber. He imagines his image displayed to hundreds of millions of viewers around the world, and knows that many are hoping to see him die.

Sorry to have to disappoint you, folks, but tonight is my night.

Fergie finishes attaching the last strut and climbs into the harness of his kite board. He slips his feet into the open-toed boots of the small surfboard, but does not raise the kite.

Okay, God, looks like it's you and me again. Anytime you're ready.

He scans the sea surrounding the dead whale, waiting for the glow to appear.

His body trembles when he realizes the smaller sharks have fled.

———

Jonas surfaces, checking his progress. He has moved to within fifty yards of the *Coelacanth*'s dinghy, tied off at the stern. He is about to duck beneath another wave when he hears the jet ski.

Treading water, he kicks hard to see above the swell.

Dani?

Maren stands in the stern, speaking into his two-way radio as the yacht's hinged swim platform is hydraulically lowered to the sea. "Allison, how close?"

"Circling at two hundred feet."

"Have Satoshi and his men direct their search closer to the ship." Maren waves at Dani as she climbs aboard the retractable ramp.

The light on his radio flashes. "Michael, we've got him. He's fifty yards off the stern."

Maren smiles. "Restart the engines. Move us two clicks to the south, then send in the barracuda."

Dani shuts down the jet ski and climbs aboard the steel platform. Gripping the end of the jet ski's guide rope, she presses the spring snap against the metal rail, locking it in place—

—as the sea percolates beneath her and the yacht's powerful engines jump to life. Before she can react, the boat leaps forward, dragging her jet ski sideways in its frothing wake.

"Dani!"

She turns. Searches the darkness. "Dad?"

Jonas's heart sinks as the *Coelacanth* moves off, its growling engines fading—

—replaced by a strange, high-pitched, pulsating *whine.*

Jonas's eyes catch movement. A small metallic dorsal fin cuts the surface five feet away, the barracuda's red mechanical eye videotaping him as it circles.

Looking down, Jonas sees the glow.

The male Megalodon circles sixty feet below the surface, its senses struggling to disseminate the barracuda's concentrated electrical pulse from the faint heartbeat coming from another life form.

Seconds later, the barracuda's signal abruptly ceases, allowing the predator to "feel" its prey.

The fifty-eight-foot prehistoric killer ascends, its scarred mouth yawning open to feed.

Jonas Taylor's skin tingles as if charged with electricity, his heart and chest gripped by an invisible force that paralyzes his muscles and his voice box as the lime-green patch brightens and he sees the outline of an ivory mouth opening beneath him.

No . . . no . . . no!

Desperate energy surges through every adrenaline-enhanced fiber of his being as Jonas dives to meet the rising upper jaw. Wrapping his arms and legs around the tip of the conical snout, he holds on for dear life, his heart pounding like a racehorse as his hands grope blindly for something to grip.

The Megalodon's head keeps rising, its upper jaw jutting forward and away from the skull, attempting to skewer its prey with its lower row of stiletto-like triangular teeth.

Seconds from falling backward into oblivion, Jonas shoves his fists into the monster's grapefruit-size nostrils, driving his arms deep into the nasal cavities clear up to his elbows while wrapping his legs around the monster's upper gums.

The incensed Megalodon bucks like a bronco, thrashing its mammoth head back and forth along the surface. The creature's jaws snap open and shut, but are unable to dislodge the being from its upper lip.

Jonas steals a quick breath and holds on, his knees squeezing the sandpaper-like hide, his fingers gripping flaps of internal flesh within the Meg's nostrils as he rides 29 tons of fury, refusing to let go.

Dani sees the Megalodon's head break the surface, a dark figure spread-eagled atop its snout.

"Oh my God—"

Her jet ski is being dragged sideways behind the ship. Tugging with all her might, she frees the tow rope's snap from the swim platform's rail and releases the machine to the sea, then dives in after it.

Jonas squeezes his eyes shut, his legs swinging wildly behind him as the gargantuan head torques back and forth across the sea with bone-jarring swipes, the insane creature abusing him with every lashing.

Unable to withstand the punishment any longer, Jonas withdraws his forearms from the Megalodon's nostrils, allowing his body to be flung into the night.

The Pacific reaches up and swallows him, and he falls into her suffocating embrace.

Wind blisters Dani's face, the swells retaliating against her watercraft's shock absorbers as she races the jet ski for the monster.

She watches helplessly as her father is flung through the air.

The creature descends.

*It'll come up from below and swallow him. I've got to beat
it to the spot!*

She aims for the splash, her entire body trembling with
adrenaline. Sees her father floating facedown. "Dad?"

Without waiting for a response, she leans over, grabbing
his wrist—

—as the sea glows green beneath her.

Go!

Dani digs her fingernails into the cold, wet flesh of her father's wrist, then accelerates, the jet ski hauling Jonas's unconscious form through the sea.

The Megalodon punches up and out of the water, its eyes
rolled back, its jaws snapping sea and foam.

Dani screams as her father's limp body twists within her
grip and falls back into the water.

Wheeling about in a tight circle, she relocates him,
reaches down with both hands, grabs him by the shirt, and
with an adrenaline-enhanced surge of energy, physically
pulls him up and out of the sea, laying him awkwardly
across the seat of her jet ski.

"Damn the man!" Maren bashes his walking stick against
the bow rail, shattering it. "Allison, send the barracuda after
the jet ski."

"No." She pushes the laptop away. "You want to commit
murder, do it yourself."

Maren shoves her aside and grabs the keyboard. Working
the miniature joystick, he sends the drone after Dani and her
father.

Dani grips the jet ski throttle in one hand, holding her father
in place by his waistband with the other. The *Neptune* is still
half a mile away, but she is afraid to go full speed, fearing
the waves will jar her father loose from his unsteady perch.

Turning, she sees the mangled ivory dorsal fin slicing through her jet ski's wake.

Forget the Neptune, *head for the whale.*

Fergie stands on the belly of the bobbing sixty-foot log-shaped carcass, his eyes focused on the approaching jet ski.

What the hell is she . . . oh, no—

"Look out! Dani, no . . . don't do it!"

The watercraft bounces over a five-foot swell and becomes airborne, smashing ski-first against the truck-size mound of blubber. The force of the crash crushes the jet ski's engine, collapsing the chassis like an accordion.

Forward inertia tosses Jonas and his daughter over the handlebars. Dani tumbles sideways, splashes down on the submerged blubber, then slides backward and drops over the edge of the slippery carcass, into the sea.

She surfaces seconds later, shakes loose the cobwebs, and crawls onto the dead whale.

"Dad?" Spotting him, she stumbles in calf-deep water across the Sperm whale's huge rectangular head and turns her unconscious father onto his back. Verifies a pulse. Shakes him until he stirs. "Dad, wake up!"

Jonas opens his eyes, grimacing in pain. "I'm still alive?"

"For the moment."

Jonas forces himself to sit up, and then Dani falls into his lap as the Megalodon clamps its jaws over the dead whale's fluke, savagely shaking its garage-size head until its serrated teeth excise an eight-hundred-pound hunk of blubber from the lifeless tail.

Warm, bloody four-foot swells roll over Jonas and Dani as they struggle to hang on. Fergie slogs across the belly of the destabilizing mass and joins them. "Are you two crazy? Get off this whale before it rolls and tosses you off."

"And what are you going to do?"

"Complete my stunt. Maybe I can lead it away." He turns

to Jonas. "Hey, man, no hard feelings. Seeing these things up close . . . you really were a Daredevil."

"Shut up and get us some help!"

"Right." Yanking back on the steel cable, he releases the oval-shaped, canary-yellow kite to the heavens.

A gust of wind drives it high into the night sky, quickly taking up seventy feet of cable attached to his harness.

"Woo-hoo!" Fergie skis across the dead whale on his board, then jerks hard on the control bar and leapfrogs over the feeding Megalodon, the tail-wind lifting him thirty feet into the air.

The twin beams from the *Neptune*'s searchlights cut through the darkness to follow his flight, the crew of the Spanish galleon applauding wildly.

The Megalodon abandons its meal and disappears.

Jonas and Dani hold onto one another as the dead whale suddenly heaves, then rolls like a log beneath them, tossing them into the Pacific.

"Dad?"

"Over here."

She swims over and he pulls her close, the two of them huddling against the Sperm whale's still intact flank.

Fergie eases up on the control bar, allowing his wake board to touch down. He can feel the strength of the wind as the kite pulls him through the water, knows he can launch himself high into the air whenever need be. Zigzagging, he heads for the *Neptune,* surfs a swell, bounds over another, then allows himself to become airborne once more.

Looking down, he spots the monster's telltale white hide as the sea appears bright green beneath him.

The Megalodon surfaces, gliding on its side, its cold, gray-blue eye watching its escaping prey.

"What's the matter, big boy, can't catch Superman?"

The Meg goes deep.

The wind dies.

Bugger . . .

Fergie loops toward the sea, touches down, then yanks back as hard as he can on his control bar, fighting to regain altitude, somehow knowing what the creature is doing.

Come on you bastard, higher!

The wind catches his kite and yanks him into the night, just as the Megalodon raises its upper torso out of the Pacific directly beneath him. *Come on, come on!* Fergie tucks his knees to his chest, registering the tip of the Meg's snout glancing off the bottom of his board.

As gravity takes over and the monster falls beneath him, Fergie stomps down on its nose with his wake board, bringing wild catcalls from the *Neptune.*

Try topping that, Coffey!

Dani and her father huddle in the water, hiding between the dead whale's remaining pectoral fin and its flank. .

Jonas feels his daughter shake uncontrollably in his arms. "Sweetheart, I know you're scared, but try not to kick or thrash. Just hold on to the fin and hang here in the water. Stay as quiet as you can."

"Okay." Her lower lip trembles from cold and fear. "Dad, look . . . the *Neptune*—"

Jonas turns.

The Spanish galleon is sailing right for them.

Ignoring the verbal threats spewing from the television producer, Captain Robertson turns his ship, aiming the prow of his vessel straight for the whale carcass. "Andrew, can you see them?"

Andrew Fox leans out over the starboard rail. "Steady on this course, skipper."

Evan Stewart and Mia Durante have climbed down the

starboard cargo net, the two Daredevils holding onto the
lowest rung as they reach out for Jonas and Dani.

The *Neptune* bounds through the sea, its heaving prow
spouting foam.

"Get ready!" Jonas wraps his right arm around Dani's
waist. "Now!"

Father and daughter kick away from the dead whale's
pectoral fin, lunging for Evan Stewart's offered hand.

Jonas misses, bouncing off the side of the sailing ship.
Sinking, his lower extremities are instantly caught in the
Spanish galleon's powerful vortex. As he is dragged under,
Mia reaches out and grabs Dani's arm, securing both daugh-
ter and father to the cargo net.

Jonas grabs onto a rung and holds on, then climbs out of
the raging current. More hands pull him higher, and then he
is on the main deck, lying next to his daughter, the two of
them exhausted, gasping breaths of air.

"Dani . . . you okay?"

She nods.

Jonas squeezes her hand. "I'm proud of you. You really
saved your old man's butt."

Dani smiles, then turns and retches across the deck, her
overwrought bravery spent.

Fergie circles fifteen feet above the whale carcass and looks
back, shocked to find the *Neptune* distancing itself from
him. Shifting his body weight, he executes a wide ninety-
degree turn and lands, surfing the waves in pursuit.

Captain Robertson alters his course, slowing his ship as
he turns into the wind.

Fergie bounds over another swell and pulls hard on his
control strut—

—as a powerful updraft catches the kite.

For a moment, the Aussie loses control, soaring up and over the *Neptune*'s lateen mast. Fighting the wind, he gazes below at his cheering comrades waving in the stern and the blotch of emerald-green sea keeping pace along the starboard side of the Spanish galleon.

Fergie jerks at his controls, sending his kite crashing into the upper reaches of the main sail. Losing the wind, he plummets—a seabird with clipped wings—

—as the Megalodon breeches, its head rising at him like a missile, its jaws yawing open, offering an impossible target to miss.

And once more time stands still, each adrenaline-enhanced heartbeat pounding in Fergie's skull, his entire existence caught in a vacuum as he falls feetfirst toward the monster's beckoning mouth.

A split-second decision—

Instead of thrashing, the Daredevil pulls his knees to his chest and plunges past the widening jaws, straight down the Megalodon's ten-foot-wide gullet into instant, suffocating darkness.

Fergie claws blindly at the constricting walls, his screams muffled, his eyes useless, his mind barely able to grasp his dilemma as he punches and kicks and wedges his body against the unseen slippery slope, the inhuman stench causing him to choke on his vomit.

A dizzying lurch as the Megalodon crashes back into the Pacific and the ocean invades Fergie's tomb, pummeling him like a swiftly flowing river—

—squeezing him headfirst out a gill slit!

Fergie clutches the blessed flap of skin, then squirms free like a newborn riding a contraction. Righting himself, he kicks to the surface, the Meg's thrashing caudal fin gliding past him.

The Daredevil's head pops free and he inhales the incred-

ible night, bellowing at his utterly shocked and crazed legion
of worshipers, who are screaming wildly from the main
deck of the *Neptune.*

Swimming to the ship, he leaps for a rung and scales the
cargo net like Tarzan, pausing to howl at the cameras, his
mind so engorged with endorphins that he can barely contain his glee.

"Screw you, Mike Coffey, screw you, Jonas Taylor, now
I'm King of the World, do you hear me? I am King of the—"

The Megalodon's ghostly upper torso lifts gracefully out
of the sea along the starboard hull, its nightmarish teeth
plucking Wayne John Ferguson free from the cargo net, its
chomping jaws crushing the feisty Australian's remains into
bloody pulp.

CHAPTER

25

MONTEREY BAY, CALIFORNIA

It is after eight by the time Mac arrives at Masao Tanaka's house. Driving up the cobblestone path, he maneuvers beneath the porte cochere and parks.

David cracks open the passenger door and looks at his godfather's face, chalky and perspiring in the interior light. "Uncle Mac, you okay?"

"Fine. Touch of the flu, that's all. Go on, I'll be back soon."

"Where are you going?" David glances down at Mac's trembling hands. "You're going to a bar, aren't you?"

"Just get out of the car."

"No."

"Listen, kid, I'm the adult here, now do as I say."

David pulls out his cell phone and dials a number.

"What're you doing? Who're you calling?"

"I'm calling that rehab place."

"Give me that!" Mac snatches David's cell phone, which suddenly rings.

Mac eyeballs David, then answers it. "What?"

Terry's voice cries out from the speaker. "Who is this? Where's David?"

"Hold on." Mac tosses the phone out David's open door and onto the grass. "Better get that, it's your mother."

David jumps out of the car.

Mac drives away.

"Uncle Mac! Ahh, crap." David picks up the cell phone. "Hello?"

"David, where've you been? I've been trying to reach you all night."

"Angel's back."

"I know, I just saw the news. Are the canal doors functional?"

"Only the manual override. But I can't get her back into the lagoon without the portable thumper."

"I have the thumper."

"You have it? Why? Are you after Angel, too?"

"No. I should have told you earlier. There's another Meg, a big male."

"You mean the one they've been advertising all day on *Daredevils?*"

"What?"

"It's just some bullshit promo. Hello?"

"David, no, there's . . . there's another Meg. It's been feeding in the waters off Vancouver Island. We captured it. That was the surprise I was telling you about."

David feels the blood rush from his face.

"David?"

"Ma, you can't put two Megalodons in the same lagoon, you know that, don't you? It'd be like sticking two betas in the same fish bowl."

"I know. I didn't know Angel had returned."

"Well, she has, just like Grandpa knew she would. Where'd this male come from anyway? From the trench?"

"Who knows? What difference does it make now? David, I don't want you to—"

"Just keep that male away from here, Mother. And bring home that thumper!" He hangs up, then dials the number for information. "Yes, I need the number of the Northern California Drug and Alcohol treatment facility, the one in Watsonville."

ABOARD THE NEPTUNE

The hysteria of the moment eventually subsides.

Mia Durante holds Jennie Arnos, who is sobbing uncontrollably against her shoulder. Michael Coffey goes below to share a bottle of Jack Daniel's with Evan Stewart, the two of them swearing off stunts for a year. Candy Girls weep in pairs for the cameras, then return solemnly to their dorm room to get high and calm their nerves. The rest of the cast and crew huddle in small groups, still shell-shocked by what they have just witnessed.

Captain Robertson fights nausea as he turns the *Neptune* leeward, distancing his ship from the dead Sperm whale, guiding his vessel away from the scene of the nightmare. The Spanish galleon groans and creaks as it cuts a swath across the wind-swept sea, its billowing sails driving it north.

Danielle Taylor rants and screams, the events of the last two hours having fried her nerves and overloaded her capacity to reason. Jonas and Andrew Fox carry her below to sickbay, the ship's physician injecting her with a heavy sedative.

Erik Hollander and Susan Ferraris have snuck off to their editing room, their bodies quivering with adrenaline.

Erik locks the door behind them. "My God, was that the most amazing . . . the most frightening thing ever filmed or what?"

"Absolutely, without a doubt. Jesus, I'm still shaking."

"I told the crew I want them down here to start editing in twenty minutes. That'll give us about two hours before we have to upload everything to L.A."

"With the extra footage we took earlier of Jonas and his

daughter, we should have more than enough to end tonight's episode just as Fergie passes over the ship. That should make for the cliffhanger to end all cliffhangers."

Erik paces, too wound-up to sit. "The ratings'll be through the roof. Geez, I can't calm down. Want a drink?"

"You have to ask?"

He searches the desk drawers until he locates a bottle of scotch and a stack of paper cups, then pours each of them a double shot. "To Fergie."

"To Fergie." Susan downs her drink. "Damn . . . hit me again."

Wa-boom!

The resounding blow from below shudders the Spanish galleon from its keel through its masts, sending an avalanche of equipment crashing from the editing room's shelves.

Erik drops the bottle, he and Susan staring at one another like passengers on a doomed airliner.

"What the hell was that?"

"You know what it was. Come on." Erik races out of the cabin and up the companionway to the main deck, Susan lagging behind.

A dozen cast and crew members are already topside, nervously watching the choppy black seas.

And then it appears, a luminescent jade-green bolt in the moonlight that streaks just below the surface, heading right for the *Neptune*.

"Oh, shit, here it comes again . . . hold on!"

Screams take the ship as the Megalodon bashes its skull against the starboard hull, rattling the *Neptune* from mast to keel, the collision knocking half the passengers off their feet.

Captain Robertson grabs at the wheel, then looks up as he hears a sickening gunshot-like sound, followed by an agonizing *craaaack*.

"Look out! Clear the deck!"

The main mast splits at its midsection, toppling like a redwood. The gallant and topsail twists slowly as they catch in an entanglement of rope, and then the sheer weight of the mast breaks through the barrier and the pole crashes sideways against the port-side rail.

Panic breaks out among the passengers. Robertson orders them back to their quarters, but they ignore him.

One of the *Neptune*'s crew hurries up from below, the man's clothing soaked from the chest down. "It's bad, skipper. The cordage chamber vented in that last attack. We're trying to seal off the lower deck, but she's taking on too much water."

"How long?"

"If we can seal the chamber, hours. If not, we'll be swimming in fifteen minutes."

The news unleashes another wave of panic.

"Quiet! I want everyone in flotation vests and back up on deck in five minutes. Mister Berkowitz, prepare to launch the lifeboats. No one boards with any personal possessions."

"Aye, sir."

"Mister Lavac, have you sent out a distress call to the Palau Coast Guard?"

"Aye, sir, but there's still no response. That makeshift antenna's not doing the job."

"Where's Hollander?"

"Right here, Captain."

"Contact that yacht. We'll need their assistance."

"I'll, uh . . . try."

"Hold on, here it comes again!"

Passengers gawk as a luminescent emerald streak glides beneath the dark surface, angling toward the starboard beam.

Jonas Taylor pushes through the chaos. "Captain, it doesn't like bright light. Blast your keel lights, maybe you can hold it off."

Robertson speaks into his two-way radio. "Jackson, turn the underwater lights up, fast!"

A yellowish halo appears around the ship's hull.

The Megalodon closes to within a hundred feet of the *Neptune,* then veers away, going deep.

Cries and gasps of relief take the passengers.

"All right Taylor, you bought us a few minutes. Now what?"

"The Meg's senses are confusing the *Neptune*'s reverberations in the heavy surf for an injured whale. It won't let up until it sinks us."

"Which won't be long at this rate."

"Have you sent an SOS to the Coast Guard in Palau?"

"Can't, antenna's down. Our only chance is to stay afloat until dawn, then signal the *Coelacanth* to rescue us."

"I wouldn't count on it." Jonas grabs Erik Hollander by the crook of his arm, dragging him into the conversation. "It's no coincidence that Meg's been following us. The yacht's owned by a guy named Michael Maren. Hollander hired him to lure the Meg up from the depths, his way of jacking up the show's ratings."

"What?"

"Maren's using a sophisticated acoustic device rigged to an underwater drone. The sounds attract the creature."

The crowd closes ranks around Erik and Jonas. Jennie Arnos pushes through the mob. "Throw Hollander overboard. Let him see how it feels to be eaten alive."

Murmurs of agreement.

"No, wait, I didn't know . . . I mean, he said he could lure one of the Megs up from the deep so we could put it on film. I never imagined any of this would happen. I'll . . . I'll order him to use the drone to lead the monster away. I'll demand he bring his ship alongside the *Neptune* and rescue us." Without waiting for a reply, the producer hurries to his stateroom.

Jonas pulls the captain aside. "How far are we from Palau?"

"Palau's too far south. Closest island's thirty-eight miles

to the northwest, in the Ulithi Atoll. We're heading there now."

Jonas feels the ship list to port. *We'll never make it . . .*

ABOARD THE *COELACANTH*

Michael Maren takes the radio from Allison Petrucci. "Go on, Hollander, I'm listening."

"Things have gotten way out of control. You need to call off your beast."

"As I've told you countless times, I can't control him. Scarface wants what it wants, and right now, it wants the *Neptune*. Makes for great drama, don't you agree?"

"Screw you, you bastard. Your little plan backfired. Jonas Taylor's alive, and he just told the entire crew about your drone. And here's another little newsflash for you—if we sink, so does all the footage we shot tonight."

Maren sits up in his lounge chair. "You haven't uploaded tonight's episode?"

"No, we changed the format. Tonight's footage was supposed to be edited on board the *Neptune* into three episodes, then sent on to Los Angeles, one episode at a time. But your monster's changed all that. We're sinking, and if I die, the tapes die with me. So what's it gonna be, Maren? Are you willing to lose all this great publicity?"

Maren grinds his teeth. Checks his watch. *Less than an hour before daylight.*

"All right, Hollander, listen closely. Scarface will head deep within the hour, I'll try to keep him off you until then. At first light, have the captain organize an evacuation. As soon as you see the *Coelacanth* move in, I want you in a Zodiac loaded with all of tonight's footage. Make sure everything's sealed in watertight cases. Once I verify the images, I'll allow the rest of the crew to come aboard."

"What about Taylor?"

"Taylor, too. Far be it from me to hold a grudge."

TANAKA LAGOON
MONTEREY, CALIFORNIA

It is dark by the time Mac arrives at the deserted arena. Parking on the sidewalk, he makes his way through the facility, the three-quarter moon lighting his way.

Stumbling up the concrete steps, he flops down on an aluminum bleacher, an open beer in one hand, the remains of a six-pack in the other. Draining the can, he crushes it in his palm and tosses it into the dark waters of the lagoon.

"That's for you, old man. Choke on it!"

He pops open another can and takes a long swig.

"Evening."

Mac turns around, startled to find his sponsor. "Parker? That you? What're you doing here? Wait, the kid called you, didn't he?"

"He cares about you, James."

"Hey, don't call me James! Nobody calls me James! Only my mother calls me James, and the name died with her."

Rob Parker walks down the bleachers. "You never mentioned her in group. What was she like?"

"My mom? She was a saint, God's apology for my father. She protected me from him. Passed away eight years ago."

"I'm sorry."

"Not a day goes by that I don't miss her."

"The drinking got worse after she died, didn't it?"

"You're a regular Sigmund Freud, aren't you?"

"Just a friend."

"I didn't ask for any of this, you know."

"No one asks to be an alcoholic or addict, just as you never asked to be abused by your father. You've been using alcohol as a painkiller. It won't solve your emotional and physical anguish, it only provides an illusionary escape. Alcoholism is a disease, Mac. The more you use, the more problems it creates. In order to move beyond the addiction, in order to face reality, you have to accept what happened in the past and set boundaries for the future."

"Yeah, well, I tried. It's still too hard, so leave me alone."

"It's hard because you're trying to do it alone. If you want me to be your sponsor, then you have to do exactly what I say. That means calling me whenever you're struggling. And it means you absolutely cannot drink." He takes the beer from Mac and pours it out. "You have to want to stay sober more than you want to drink. You have to get to meetings in order to learn how to live your life without drinking. You need to work your steps. AA is not for people who need it, Mac, it's for people who want it."

Mac pinches tears from his eyes. "I feel useless. Like I'm no longer in control."

"Which is why we teach you to turn your life over to a higher power. If God got you to it, He'll get you through it."

ABOARD THE *NEPTUNE*
NORTHWEST PACIFIC OCEAN
33 NAUTICAL MILES SOUTHEAST OF THE ULITHI ATOLL

A blurred line of gray streaks the cloud-strewn eastern horizon, signaling the dawn. Gusts of wind drive the ocean, sending seven-foot swells rolling against the sinking Spanish galleon, the vessel now listing thirty degrees to port. The ship's lower two decks are already underwater and half her remaining sails have torn, the lateen and lower mizzen sails flapping wildly in the stern.

Huddled on the slanting main deck are ninety-three frightened passengers and crewmen, all dressed in orange flotation devices. It has been thirty minutes since the Megalodon was last sighted, but the drama of the last few hours has not eased, even with the graying of dawn. Candy Girls, production staff, and sailors stay close to their assigned lifeboats, the crashing sea spraying them with mist as they wait and pray, hoping the dying *Neptune* doesn't sink beneath them before the sun comes up.

A lone cameraman, Stuart Starr, continues to document the journey using a handheld underwater camera. The rest of the equipment has already been packed and loaded onto the lifeboats.

Erik Hollander waits by his Zodiac as his production assistant places three heavy watertight cases into the motorized raft.

A horn blasts. The jittery crowd cheers as the super yacht moves into position fifty yards off the starboard beam.

Susan joins Erik, tossing two suitcases stuffed with her personal belongings into the Zodiac. "We're all set. Stuart will film everything from the last lifeboat." She looks out at the yacht. "Why doesn't this Maren fellow move closer?"

"Maybe he's afraid the *Neptune*'s too unstable to risk getting close."

"To hell with that, that damn Meg could still be lurking below. I'm not going anywhere until—"

An eight-foot swell rolls over the port side rail, heaving the *Neptune* hard to starboard. Passengers scramble for their lifeboats as the ship begins to spin counterclockwise.

"Jesus!" Susan jumps into the Zodiac, the raft now free-floating on the submerged deck. "Well, don't just stand there, get in!"

A strong current pulls at Erik's ankles as he slogs across the tilting flooded deck to catch the moving raft. *Why does Maren have to be so darn far away?*

Jonas Taylor stands in the balcony of the admiral's gallery, watching the steadily rising sea.

Captain Robertson enters. "We've set aside a lifeboat for

you and your daughter. Andrew said he'd join you, none of the others want to take a chance."

"No one will be boarding the *Coelacanth*, Captain. Not Hollander, not you, not your crew. Maren's only interested in saving the *Daredevils* footage, not potential witnesses to murder."

Six overloaded lifeboats drift in the rough Pacific sea, the *Neptune* crewmen stationed aboard each vessel rowing quietly, distancing themselves from the sinking Spanish galleon. Nervous passengers watch the ocean, praying the Megalodon has gone deep, cursing the owner of the super yacht, wondering why it is taking so long for him to allow them to board.

The seventh lifeboat remains lashed to the *Neptune*'s starboard bow rail.

Andrew Fox is in the boat with Danielle Taylor, the girl still heavily sedated and wrapped in a flannel blanket.

Come on, Jonas, where the hell are you?

Michael Maren holds the length of celluloid up to the light. "Nice. Very nice. You and your staff did a wonderful job."

Erik Hollander smiles. "You can thank Susan and her team. Now, if you don't mind, we'd like to get the rest of the crew on board. It's been a long night and—"

"You know, I wish I could do that, Hollander, I really do, but I can't. It's Taylor's fault. Had he died, we'd have no issue. But as you rightly pointed out, the rest of your crew now knows about the barracuda. Not good, Hollander, not good at all. See, technically, they could pin those Daredevils' deaths on me."

Erik's heart pounds in his throat. "But you said the Meg chased the *Neptune* on its own. And Taylor's still alive."

"His word against mine, I know, but a jury could be swayed. It would be much cleaner if there were no witnesses."

"You're abandoning my team?"

"And you with them. Satoshi."

"Maren, don't do this."

Satoshi grabs Erik by his arm, dragging him back outside to the sundeck.

"You murdering bastard! No, don't . . . don't—"

The sumo wrestler lifts Erik Hollander off the deck and tosses him overboard.

Jonas Taylor wades through knee-deep water on the starboard gun deck, working on the *Culebrina*, a functioning replica of a seventeenth-century Spanish cannon. Tearing open the waterproof sack of gunpowder given to him by Captain Robertson, he sprinkles a fistful of powder on the touch hole, then pours the rest into the cannon's bore.

Grabbing a mop, he rams the powder down as best he can, as he hears Erik Hollander's scream, followed by a splash.

Some people never learn . . .

Reaching to the flooded deck, he feels for the thirty-two-pound cast-iron shot, dries it off as best he can with his shirt, then positions it in the barrel.

The *Coelacanth* turns to starboard, distancing itself from the *Neptune*'s lifeboats.

Jonas removes the captain's lighter. *You've got one shot at this, make it count.* Aiming for the yacht's stern, he lights the touch hole with the flame, then leaps aside.

A brilliant flash—

Boom!

The cannonball blasts out of the barrel at the speed of sound.

The heavy cannon recoils like a mad bull, tears itself free from the starboard wall, and plunges through the flooded deck.

Looking up through a cloud of smoke, Jonas sees the smoldering impact of the hot iron shot as it pummels the aft section of the yacht, crashing through the main deck, igniting flash fires in its devastating wake.

Michael Maren hobbles out to his sundeck as a second explosion rocks his vessel. "What happened? Allison? Satoshi?"

A ball of flame belches upward from the engine room, followed by another explosion.

"Taylor, you sonuvabitch, I'll kill you, I swear to Christ!" Ducking back inside, Maren grabs the watertight cases, then hurries to the helo pad.

The Spanish galleon has begun its death spin, its bow pushing out of the water as it sinks stern-first into the Pacific.

· · Jonas rubs his head, his ears still ringing, the chamber spinning. A river of sea pours through the gun port. Holding his breath, he dives through the flooding opening.

Surfacing, he swims hard, fighting the *Neptune*'s current.

"Over here!" Andrew rows toward him, helping him on board. "Nice shooting, Blackbeard. Guess you were right, Maren was only interested in the footage."

A chorus of screams fills the air.

The disfigured dorsal fin cuts through the sea between two of the *Neptune*'s lifeboats, circling slowly.

Susan Ferraris pulls Erik out of the water as the Megalodon swims by, its snout casually nudging their Zodiac. The creature's current drags them forty feet before releasing them.

Another explosion rocks the *Coelacanth*, engulfing the super yacht in flames.

Members of the yacht's crew leap into the sea, swimming for the overloaded lifeboats.

Satoshi emerges from the main deck of the burning ship, the former sumo wrestler howling in agony, his gasoline-drenched clothing on fire. Hurdling the port side rail, he plummets into the Pacific like a miniature asteroid.

The wrestler surfaces, gasping for air. His cherub face is purple, his exposed back swollen and blistered. Unable to raise his burned arms, he kicks on his side, sculling toward the nearest lifeboat.

Jonas watches him approach, holding his oar like a baseball bat. "Not in this lifetime, fat boy."

Satoshi's eyes bulge insanely as an abominable head rises from the sea beneath him, collecting him within its gruesome scarred jaws.

"Aeiyyyyyyyyy . . . ahhh haaa!"

Jonas stares in horror as the sumo wrestler thrashes about in the Megalodon's gnashing mouth as if caught in a giant garbage disposal, his head barely visible within a shower of blood.

Poised above the wave tops, Scarface's ghostly belly quivers as it swallows.

Abruptly, the screaming stops, replaced by the beating of helicopter blades. Jonas pries his eyes away from the monster to see the airship climb into the sky above the burning *Coelacanth.*

The sun pokes its glorious crimson head above the eastern horizon.

The Megalodon cataract-gray eyes roll back, the prehistoric predator slipping beneath the pink froth, vanishing with the night.

Allison Petrucci pulls back on the helicopter's joystick, sending the chopper climbing into the gray morning sky.

From the co-pilot's seat, Michael Maren gazes below at the spectacle that is his burning yacht, the burly scientist cursing beneath his rancid breath as he programs his drone.

CHAPTER

26

WESTPORT MARINA
GRAYS HARBOR, WASHINGTON

The *Cape Calvert* arrives just after midnight, pushing slowly through Grays Harbor at three knots.

Terry paces nervously along the pier. She spots Joshua standing in the bow. He sees her, but doesn't wave.

Then she sees something else—the big male's tail fin, lifting lazily in and out of the water behind the boat.

The Canadian cutter glides past the pier, slowing as it reaches the location of the construction crane.

Terry looks down into the calm, dark waters. The Megalodon is lying on its side, its jaws opening and closing in spasms. No longer being towed, the thirty-two-ton fish begins to sink, its tail striking the murky bottom.

Joshua hastily loops the bowline to one of the pilings and jumps down to the pier.

"Josh . . . what took so long?"

"Don't talk to me, lady." He pushes past her, approaching Sean Justus and his crew. "Hey, Popeye, sorry to keep you. Ran into some rough seas."

Sean Justus stares at the blotch of ivory hovering just below the surface. "Dude, is that what I think it is?"

"Yes, and we need to get it into the flatbed as quickly as we can or it'll drown."

"Is this a Megalodon invasion or something?"

"What're you talking about?"

Terry steps into the conversation. "Angel attacked a bunch of boaters in San Francisco Bay about six hours ago."

Sean nods. "There was also some wild rumor about a Meg showing up on that *Daredevils* TV show, but tonight's episode was just a rerun."

Brian Olmstead calls out from the stern. "Hey, Bunkofske, give me a hand!"

Joshua climbs back on board, Terry following him. "Josh, listen to me, I know you're mad—"

"Mad doesn't begin to describe how I feel."

"Well, you're going to be even madder. I don't want the Meg."

Brian looks up from the heavy hydraulic spool, where he has detached the end of the steel cable. "What's she talking about?"

"Ignore her." Joshua takes the end of the thick cable from him and passes it overboard to Sean Justus. "Attach this to the crane's line and start hauling my fish out of the water before it drowns."

"Josh, listen to me, this isn't about me and you, it's business. Angel's back. With that thumper, we can get her back into the lagoon."

"This *is* business, lady. You committed to this voyage. We accomplished what we set out to do, now you're going to keep your end of the bargain. Popeye, where's that flatbed?"

"Hold your bowel, my boys are moving it into position."

Michael Villaire climbs up from below decks, the former transit cop looking ghostly pale. "I hate boats. I never want to see another damn boat again."

Terry pulls him aside. "Mr. Villaire, where's your gun?"

"Locked up below."

"You need to get it. I saw the Meg's tail moving."

"It was just an involuntary spasm," Joshua calls out. "Marino, move the boat!"

The captain looks out from his pilothouse, then drives the *Cape Calvert* forward another thirty feet.

The double-wide flatbed truck beeps as it backs into place along the pier, water sloshing out the top of its steel tank.

With a belch of blue diesel smoke, the crane jumps to life, its towering arm rotating counterclockwise, its winch retracting steel cable from out of the sea.

The line goes taut, then slowly, inch by inch, the monster's snout rises from out of the harbor. Seawater pours from the creature's flaring gill slits as its triangular head continues elevating, the strain on the crane increasing, the pull of the five-foot titanium fishhook creating greater stress on the festering wound along the Meg's punctured lower jaw.

With a mighty spasm, the male Megalodon awakens, its eyes rolling forward as it jerks the line.

"Look out," Brian yells, as the enraged creature dances halfway out of the water, its lashing upper torso blasting waves in all directions.

Planks splinter along the pier. Metal groans in protest as the crane fights to maintain its hold on the behemoth fish.

Cory Akins and Josh Jenkins are bounced around in the crane's cab as if they are on the losing end of a demolition derby. With each powerful jolt, the seamen from Georgia can feel the tracks of the derrick lifting away from the pier.

"Drop it back 'fore we get pulled in!"

"Can't! Line's tangled!"

Terry is still on the boat, crouching behind the transom. She is drenched and too afraid to move, the Megalodon thrashing wildly in the water behind her, the swaying crane towering over her, the support beams of its steel arm screeching and bending beneath the gargantuan weight.

The cutter's engines growl to life. *Get off the boat!*

Leaping to her feet, she dashes through raining buckets of

seawater, colliding with Michael Villaire, who has emerged from below, his hands wrapped around the barrel of his M79 grenade launcher. Breaking open the breech, he inserts an M203 cartridge into the barrel and marches toward the end of the boat. "Time to end this bullshit."

"No!" Joshua heads him off, grabbing the weapon, as a rifle shot cracks overhead and the steel cable snaps.

The thick cord whistles past Villaire's ear and lashes his left kneecap, shattering his patella. The former police officer howls as he crumples to the deck, writhing in agony.

Terry covers her mouth, then looks up as the crane buckles, its arm tumbling surreally toward her before smashing through the pilothouse, blasting it into kindling.

Terry opens her eyes, amazed to be alive and intact. She crawls out from beneath the carnage of twisted steel, her eyes focusing on the slithering cable playing out across the crushed deck.

The line disappears overboard.

The big male is gone.

NORTHWEST PACIFIC OCEAN
16 NAUTICAL MILES SOUTHEAST OF THE ULITHI ATOLL

Sparkles of sunlight dance across the deep blue surface like fireflies.

Seven lifeboats and a Zodiac plod along a half-mile swath of ocean, spent passengers roasting beneath a noonday sun. Captain Robertson commands the lead boat, using a handheld compass to plot their course. Somewhere across this vast plain of sea is the Ulithi Atoll and its haven of tropical islands. Somewhere below, following their boats in depths that run black, is their relentless stalker.

Puttering behind Robertson's boat is the Zodiac. With a final triple belch, the engine inhales the last ounce of gasoline and shuts down, returning the sounds of Nature to its two irate passengers.

Susan Ferraris grabs an oar and tosses it at Erik. "You got us into this mess, now get us out."

Erik dunks the torn sleeve of his sweatshirt in the water, wrings it out, then repositions the rag across the pink skin of his receding hairline. Without saying a word, he begins paddling, cursing the day he left med school to become a television producer.

Danielle Taylor slouches uncomfortably in the bow of her lifeboat, gazing absentmindedly at the sweaty sunburned backs of her father and Andrew Fox. The two men have been rowing at a steady pace for what seems like forever, her inner voice chanting with each downward stroke.

Ninety-one bottles of beer on the wall, ninety-one bottles of beer . . . if we manage to find the Atoll, ninety bottles of beer on the wall.

Dani is hungry and thirsty and tired and scared and sunburned and her butt hurts from having sat on bare wood for seven hours and twenty-three minutes. If not for the constant pain, she'd swear she was dreaming.

Stuck in his own head, Jonas feels blood from his blisters soak the cloth wrapped around his palms. Still, he refuses to stop rowing, the last five-minute break having lasted over an hour when he and Andrew had passed out from exhaustion. With Dani asleep and no one else on board to relieve them, they had quickly fallen behind.

Erik Hollander had finally turned back for them, towing them back to the pack.

Jonas steals a quick glance at the sun, continuing his equations.

. . . fifteen feet with each stroke, figure ten strokes a minute . . . that's one hundred and fifty feet every minute . . . nine thousand feet an hour . . . one point seven miles an hour . . . with only six hours left until the sun sets.

Christ, we're moving too slow, we'll never make it to the atoll before dark . . .

PALAU PACIFIC RESORT
KOROR, PALAU
4:45 P.M.

Michael Maren opens the door of his hotel suite, allowing James Gelet to enter. Twenty minutes later, the *Daredevils* co-producer stares open-mouthed at the raw footage playing on the laptop monitor before him. "Jesus, Maren . . . do you have the *Neptune* going down, too?"

"Allison managed to capture a few minutes on her video camera before the *Coelacanth* sank. It's rough and a bit jumpy, but you can see the cannon shot that cost me my ship and quite possibly the lives of your crew. Uh . . . speaking of which, any word from the Coast Guard?"

"Nothing yet, and I'm worried as hell. Wish you could have given them some decent coordinates."

"Hey, it was chaos out there. I was lucky just to make it back alive."

"Maren, we're dealing with a third world island nation. It could take them weeks just to organize a search party."

"Which is why I'll be heading out again in my chopper. I'll find them."

"And I'll be going with you."

"Sorry, Gelet, there's no room. Allison and I will radio you as soon as we locate them." Maren stares at the producer. "Now what's wrong?"

"There's still something I don't get. Why would Jonas Taylor open fire on your boat?"

"As I've explained, Taylor lost it out there."

"But to interfere with a rescue at sea?"

"Who knows why a man does the things he does? I'll tell you this: Jonas Taylor was desperate. Why else would he accept Hollander's offer to get in the water with that Meg?"

"That's just it. Erik radioed me days ago, telling me Taylor refused the deal."

"Refused the—" Maren wipes sweat from his brow. "Well, he changed his mind, didn't he? Just look at the tape. Taylor's in the water, his daughter rescues him, then he flips out and sinks my boat. Man's a lunatic."

"Maybe. All I know is that I've got over ninety people lost at sea—"

"And I said I'll find them! Just make sure my money gets wired and this footage airs as soon as possible."

WESTPORT MARINA
GRAYS HARBOR, WASHINGTON
7:12 A.M.

The marina is overrun with members of the media, local officials, and insurance men, all of whom seem to be snapping pictures of the 65-foot hunk of mangled metal embedded in the roof of the cutter's collapsed pilothouse.

Terry Taylor finishes giving her statement to the Grays Harbor police, then locates the salvage operator. "Excuse me, there's something of mine I need to claim. It's a sound device attached to that buoy." She points to the bobbing object, still anchored to the *Cape Calvert*'s transom by steel cable.

"Sure, lady. Give me half an hour."

Avoiding two local newsmen, she ducks beneath police tape and loses herself in the crowd, finding her way to a donut shop.

"Large coffee and a cream donut." She pays the woman, then locates an empty booth.

Joshua Bunkofske slips in beside her.

"Josh, go away, I have nothing more to say to you."

"You think you can just walk away from this mess, leaving me holding the bag? You owe my crew money."

"Use the money you owe me."

"And what about the damage to the cutter? And that crane?"

"That's not my problem. I warned you the big male was conscious, but you didn't listen. You lost the Meg, not me."

"Yes, but now Angel's back in California waters. I can help recapture her."

"Angel's not your concern. Our arrangement's over."

"What arrangement?"

Terry turns, caught off-guard by her son, now standing next to her booth. "David!" Terry pushes the table away, slips past Joshua, and hugs her son.

"Mother, who is this guy?"

"He's the marine biologist who captured that big male."

David smirks. "You mean the one that got away?"

"Never mind that. Where's Mac?"

"Waiting by the chopper. Where's the thumper?"

"Someone's getting it for me."

"Thumper's gone," Joshua states. "Removed it from the buoy last night."

"Give it back," David demands.

"Sorry, kid. The thumper covers the loss of my Zodiac, which your mom stole from me yesterday." Joshua winks at Terry. "Like I said, this is far from over."

CHAPTER

27

NORTHWESTERN PACIFIC OCEAN
4 NAUTICAL MILES SOUTHEAST OF THE ULITHI ATOLL
DUSK

The helicopter follows the orange ball of fire as it begins its day-ending descent over the Pacific.

Michael Maren pilots the two-man airship. He is alone, his laptop balanced on his thighs, the monitor displaying a real-time cartography of the Northwestern Pacific.

Maren knows the eight tiny green dots sprinkled along the upper-right portion of the screen are the boats holding the *Neptune*'s shipwrecked crew. For the last fourteen hours, his drone, represented by a blue dot, has been trailing the survivors, remaining within sonar range of the acoustical signatures being created by the lifeboats' surface disturbances.

The red dot trailing the blue is Scarface. Maren knows the Megalodon, trained to follow the drone's sensory lure, will remain in the darkness of the mid-waters until nightfall, when it will surface and attack.

Would have been a perfect plan, but Gelet's too suspicious.

Maren checks his watch. *Less than an hour of daylight left, and then all hell breaks loose.*

He contemplates the impending loss of life. *If you can*

lure Scarface into attacking Taylor and Hollander first, then maybe you don't have to allow the others to die. You can tell the authorities you weren't abandoning the Neptune's crew, that you saw Taylor aim the cannon and got scared. Yes, that's why you veered off, to avoid being hit.

He grits his teeth. *Fool. The crew witnessed Satoshi tossing Hollander overboard. Stupid, stupid, letting your ego get in the way of the bigger picture. Celeste always warned you never to react emotionally when it came to business. Premeditate each move, she said, calculate each worse-case scenario before it happens. Mistakes are made through smokescreens of optimism created by the human ego.*

Glancing down at his laptop, he rechecks the drone's coordinates, then adjusts his course.

If you had only taken the time to think things out, you could have at least made it look like you were rescuing the crew. No, that wouldn't have worked either. Taylor's escape forced the issue, and Hollander knew too much. The only solution would have been to put a bullet in Taylor's brain when you had the chance. But what fun would that have been?

The monitor's display changes, the swath of Pacific now showing the islands of the Ulithi Atoll.

To hell with it. Boats sink all the time, and the shipping industry never loses any sleep over it. It's the price of doing business, the risks associated with technology. The Neptune sank, case closed. What happens now will be based on the reality of perceptions. Create the perception that you're a hero, not a villain.

Better start the cameras.

Maren activates the onboard camera strapped to the helicopter's landing struts.

Stick with your story. The Megalodon sank the Neptune, then Taylor destroyed my yacht, and with it, the crew's chance at being rescued. All I need to do to exonerate myself is show the world that I tried, that I risked my own life to go

back and find the survivors. As long as the effort's there,
that's all that'll be remembered, not the results.

He checks his laptop again.

They should be just up ahead. Wait . . . don't fly right over
them, that'll look too obvious. Fly past them, then circle
back. Yes, that should get them cheering. Great psychologi-
cal effect, too. A miracle I found them in all this ocean, an
absolute miracle. If only the Coast Guard had arrived an
hour earlier.

Hover over them a few minutes, then contact the Palau au-
thorities. Be sure to sound real excited, like you just found a
needle in a haystack. Give them the coordinates, then tell
them you'll lead the survivors to the nearest island in the
atoll. Be sure to use the loudspeaker to inform the survivors,
that way the camera documents everything. Better give Scar-
face a few minutes before sending him in to mop up this
mess. Wait until he takes out the first boat, then start yelling
out warnings.

Ninety-three people . . . what if Scarface doesn't go after
all of them? Humans are too bony to be part of a Mega-
lodon's diet, he'll probably stop feeding after a half dozen or
so. It's a two-mile swim to the atoll, a few of Robertson's
crew could make it.

"Dammit!" He alters his course, delaying the rescue to
think.

Perception . . . got to create the perception of being the
hero. Okay, what if you actually rescued a few of the crew?
Let Scarface take out the lead boat, then lead him away, send
him after Taylor. Descend real fast and instruct a few of the
survivors to grab hold of your struts—oh, this is perfect!
Make a quick run to the nearest island in the atoll, then
hurry off, like you're going back to rescue a few more. I can
hear them now . . . "Undaunted, our hero never let up. If it
wasn't for him, we'd have died too."

As long as Taylor and Hollander die, it's just your word

against the survivors, and they'll be kissing your ass, thanking you for saving them. It's not a perfect plan, but it's damn good, and it'll keep you out of prison.

Maren checks his location once more, then adjusts his course for the fly-by.

Celeste would be proud.

Hours of rowing in the relentless sun and heat without fresh water have left Jonas Taylor a physical wreck. His lower back is out, and his shoulders and arms ache from muscular exhaustion. His skin, exposed to the unrelenting sun, is fried to the point of blistering. His broken nose aches, his ribs are swollen. A thick white spittle has dried around his lips, and his parched throat is so tight that he can barely swallow.

Andrew Fox moans next to him as he manages another stroke. The underwater photographer, twenty years his junior, is nearing physical exhaustion.

Danielle Taylor stirs from her feverish catnap, her hands covered in open blisters from having rowed hours earlier. Turning to face the bow, she sees they have fallen behind the pack once more. A lifeboat and the Zodiac are visible some sixty yards ahead, the rest of the boats out of visual range.

The end of daylight is coming fast, the heat replaced by a cool evening breeze that sends shivers across her sunburned skin.

We're going to die out here . . .

She thinks back to Fergie's death and shudders.

The helicopter roars overhead out of nowhere, its clapping thunder jump-starting her pulse.

"Hey . . . stop," she rasps, her voice so hoarse it is barely audible. "Dad, splash or something."

With great effort, Jonas manages to lift the oar from its socket and slap it twice against the surface.

Andrew reaches for his binoculars. With quivering hands,

he lifts them to his face, focusing on the aircraft, now hovering a quarter mile ahead. "It's Maren," he whispers.

A wave of adrenaline shoots through Jonas's body. He looks at Andrew, their thought patterns synchronizing.

Gripping their oars, they begin stroking, this time with vigor.

Maren hovers his chopper sixty feet above the lead lifeboat. "Palau Coast Guard, this is Michael Maren aboard the *Coelacanth* helicopter, Bravo-niner-two-five-zero. Have spotted the survivors of the *Neptune*. Seven lifeboats and a Zodiac, located approximately two nautical miles southwest of the Ulithi Atoll. I am going to attempt to lead them to the nearest island. Please send a rescue ship immediately, these poor people need assistance."

"Roger, Bravo-niner-two-five-zero. We'll dispatch the first vessel available. Well done."

"Roger, that. Maren out."

Maren flips the radio's toggle switch, changing to the loudspeaker. "Attention. This is Michael Maren. I've just alerted the Palau Coast Guard that I have located you. A rescue ship is on the way."

He pauses to allow the video camera to record the cheers.

"The Ulithi Atoll is approximately two miles to the northeast. It is imperative I lead you to one of the islands before the Meg returns."

He turns his airship and heads north, maintaining a crawl-like speed.

Okay, give it about five minutes, then send in your fish.

Erik Hollander stares at Susan Ferraris, a sickening feeling gurgling in his stomach. "Maren? What's that bastard doing here?"

"What difference does it make, as long as we're safe and I can see my daughter again."

Hollander swallows hard, struggling to find enough moisture to speak. "We're not safe, not as long as he controls that drone. I think . . . I think he means to kill us."

Maren focuses his night-vision binoculars on the sea, jumping from one lifeboat to the next. He pauses at the Zodiac. Sees Hollander and the woman suddenly double-time it with their paddles. *Sorry, Hollander, you can run but you can't hide.*

As he watches, the last lifeboat pulls alongside the raft.

Maren smiles as he focuses on Jonas Taylor.

Patience. First we play the hero, then we have some fun . . .

"Hollander, come aboard." Jonas's voice cracks in the wind as he maneuvers his lifeboat alongside the powerless Zodiac.

Andrew steadies the raft as Susan and Erik climb aboard with their paddles. "Taylor, it's Maren. He means to kill us."

Jonas nods. "The atoll. Our only hope."

Susan and Erik stroke from the bow, Jonas and Andrew rowing from the stern.

Michael Maren's right hand quivers with a sudden rush of adrenaline as he types in a command on the laptop keyboard, deactivating the barracuda's automated sonar tracker. Switching to manual controls, he works the laptop's joystick, sending the drone to the surface.

Jonas Taylor's shoulder muscles ache with each pull, his sun-scorched skin tightening like a vise with every movement. He focuses on the sea to his left and behind him, making sure each stroke of the oar is placed at its optimal point in the sea before he pulls with all his might.

A glitter of metal in the water catches his eye.

The silver drone streaks past his oar, leaving a trail of bubbles in its wake.

Maren selects one of the two lead lifeboats, circling it with the barracuda. *Okay, get the passengers in the water, then send Scarface after Taylor while you play hero for the camera.*

Typing in another command, Maren changes the drone's acoustical signal, overlapping it with a chaotic electrical impulse.

Twelve hundred and seventy feet below the surface, the male Megalodon known as Scarface glides through the pitch black depths, cruising on autopilot, its ampullae of Lorenzini mesmerized by the acoustical stimulus pulsating above its head.

Now, as the last rays of light diminish in the shallows, the signal abruptly changes, jolting the male's sensory array, causing its pulse to quicken. The pattern increases in voracity, agitating the Meg, stimulating a primal response within the predator's physiology.

The Megalodon's back stiffens and arches, its half-moon-shaped tail lashing at the sea.

The signal mimics that of a dying whale.

The 57,000-pound fish rises to feed.

Michael Coffey and Mia Durante work the oars in the second lifeboat, which is overloaded with camera equipment, eight shivering sunburned Candy Girls, two cameramen, a sound man, and three production assistants.

"Mich-ael . . ." Mia chokes out a warning as she spots the tall, mangled ivory dorsal fin break the surface thirty yards behind their boat.

The Megalodon plows through the sea, chasing their wake.

The passengers scream.

Mia and Michael stroke faster.

The monster's broad back rolls under the hull of the over-loaded vessel, spilling its occupants into the water.

Mia Durante plunges facefirst into the water, the rim of the lifeboat cracking against the back of her skull as it escorts her underwater. Echoes of ocean fill her ears as she sinks, followed by a bizarre metallic *buzzing* sound that snaps her awake.

Mia opens her eyes and sees what she believes is a heavenly light.

The Megalodon's snout continues rising, driving the wind from her lungs as it lifts her straight out of the sea, her back colliding painfully against the inside of the overturned lifeboat.

Daredevil and vessel rise fifteen feet above the wave tops, the pinned girl thrashing wildly against the creature's upper jawbone, rows of triangular teeth searching for her flesh.

Hyperventilating, Mia punches at the receding upper gum until she loses her balance and falls into the widening mouth.

"My God, it . . . it just devoured that poor girl. Oh, God, oh my God—"

Michael Maren casually checks the sound levels of his voice as he continues maneuvering his drone. "Mayday, mayday, Coast Guard, this is Maren again. The Megalodon's returned, the *Neptune*'s crew under attack. One boat's already down, I . . . I have to do something!"

Maren flips the toggle switch back to loudspeaker. "Hold on, people, I'm coming! Try to grab onto my landing struts!"

Maneuvering the laptop's joystick, he sends the barracuda back in the direction of Jonas Taylor's lifeboat, then shifts out of autopilot and descends the helicopter toward the pack of thrashing passengers.

Jonas and Andrew pause, staring in horror as, one hundred yards away, the breaching monster drives the lifeboat and one of its passengers clear out of the water. *Damn you, Maren* . . .

Staring at the surface, he notices a line of streaking foam heading in their direction.

The barracuda!

Jonas stands, his arthritic knees popping as he steadies himself in the boat.

"Dad, what are you doing?"

"Jonas, don't—"

Jonas dives overboard, then swims into the path of the on-coming drone.

"Dad!"

Come on . . . come on . . . "Owfff!"

The barracuda's nose cone strikes him in the gut, driving him backward through the sea.

Jonas holds on, draping his upper body around the cylindrical object, his right hand clenching the drone by its dorsal fin-shaped antenna, his knees wrapping around the propeller shaft as the slender torpedo hauls him along the surface at twenty knots.

The barracuda zigzags wildly, slows, then descends at a sixty-degree angle.

Refusing to let go, Jonas kicks at the propeller, then drives his shoulder against the head of the drone, angling it back toward the surface.

Bursting up through a swell, he gasps a quick breath of air—

—as the Megalodon's dorsal fin surfaces less than a hundred feet away.

Candy Girls and crewmen gasp and grope and shove one another as they tread water and fight for position beneath the descending helicopter and its life-saving landing struts.

Michael Maren hovers five feet above the melee, the desperate cries for help blotted out by the chopper's whirling rotors. "Easy now, I can only hold five or six at a time. Did you hear me? Hey—"

Jonas snaps off the fin-like antenna, overriding its remote signals, as he wraps his calves around the back of the torpedo-like object, freeing his feet to manipulate the barracuda's propeller. By pressing the soles of his shoes against either side of the shaft, he can steer the drone, by pushing against the nose cone, he can maintain his surface presence.

Pushing back with his feet, he loops the barracuda into a tight figure eight—

—sending the drone rocketing headfirst toward the opening jaws of the monster!

"Shit!"

Pressing down with his left foot, pulling up with his right toes, he executes a sharp ninety-degree turn.

The creature's right pectoral fin slices the sea beneath him like the wing of a 727 airbus.

Jonas lifts his head above the surf, regaining his bearings.

"Easy now, hey watch out!" Maren pulls back on the joystick as the airship wobbles beneath the additional weight of eleven panicky adults. "Some of you have to let go, do you hear me? I can't save all of you! Idiots, I said let go!"

Maren jerks the controls, pitching and yawing his aircraft, casting the desperate flock of humans back into the sea. *Christ, you try to be a hero and look what happens.* "Now listen to me, I can only take four people at a time, but I'll be back, okay?"

Steadying his airship, he descends again, stealing a quick glance at the laptop monitor.

"What?" The barracuda has changed course and is heading right for the downed boat.

Pausing his descent, Maren engages the autopilot once more, then grabs at the laptop's joystick. *Something's wrong. The damn thing's jammed.*

Jonas aims the barracuda toward the mob of thrashing people, then, rolling beneath the streaking cylinder, props the nose cone high out of the water and drives his legs down, sending the barracuda leaping out of the sea like a marlin.

Flying through the air, the drone's antenna secured in his right hand, Jonas manages to catch the helicopter's strut around the crook of his left arm. Dangling in midair, he curls his legs around the landing strut for support, then looks down at the swarm of passengers treading water six feet below him. Eyeballing Mike Coffey, he yells, "Move! Get them out of here!"

Coffey sees the drone. "Oh, shit. Everyone with me, the Meg's coming!" The Daredevil captain swims away, the others following his lead.

Maren breathes a sigh of relief as the laptop's joystick finally unjams. He checks the drone's position. "No . . . that's impossible."

Opening the cockpit door, he looks below. "Taylor?!"

"Tell Celeste I said hello." Mustering all his strength, Jonas heaves the forty-two-pound cylinder into the open cockpit, then kicks away from the landing struts and drops—

—as the male Megalodon's upper torso rises out of the sea.

Jonas bounces sideways against the Megalodon's right gill, then plummets into blackness, the sounds of the helicopter's beating rotors dulled by the density of the Pacific.

Scarface bites down on the landing strut, its clenching teeth splintering the aluminum.

Maren screams, fighting the joystick with both hands.

For a surreal moment, the chopper's thrust matches the Megalodon's extraordinary girth, and then gravity takes over and the outmatched airship is dragged from the sky, monster, man, and machine hurtling sideways into the sea.

Maren is blasted by a wall of water that fills the cabin within seconds. He fumbles desperately for the seat belt buckle, but the cabin is reeling end over end now, and it is all he can do to hold on. Pressure stabs at his ears, panic rises in his brain as he can no longer tell up from down.

The struggle wanes at eighty feet, his anger venting with the remains of his final breath.

At one hundred twenty feet, he loses consciousness.

At two hundred feet, his limbs cease twitching.

Cockpit glass shatters at seven hundred feet, the aluminum frame groaning as it buckles.

The barracuda, still wedged firmly under Maren's seat, continues transmitting.

The Megalodon escorts its prey into the depths, the prehistoric killer embraced by the primal waters of its birth.

LATE PLEISTOCENE

NORTHWESTERN PACIFIC OCEAN
18,000 YEARS AGO

The adolescent male circles the pregnant female warily, its senses probing the larger adult. It can feel the tantalizing heartbeats and muscle movements of the pregnant female's unborn young. It can taste the alkaline embryonic discharge now seeping from her cloaca.

The female's two-year gestation period is coming to an end.

The male Megalodon is hungry.

·A sudden contraction causes the female's thick back muscles to spasm, arching her spine.

The male moves closer.

With a lightning reflex, the female snaps at her assailant, her jaws finding flesh.

The male darts away, a dozen crimson claw-like teeth marks striping its flank.

The female leaves the lagoon, seeking more open waters to birth her young. Retreating through the widening river way, she races through the atoll, her swiftly stroking tail churning up silt along the bottom.

The wounded male keeps its distance, biding its time.

A second contraction grips the female as she moves be-

yond the last island into open waters. Anxious young dance
in her belly. A cloud of blood spurts free from her widening
ovum.

Shaking her titanic head, she fights through the contraction and continues onward.

As she clears the outer ring of coral, a powerful muscle
spasm sends her caudal fin wriggling in short bursts. Unable
to control her own body, the female swims in ever-tightening
circles, her back arching violently, her ovum widening, until—

—the head of a wide-eyed Megalodon pup pokes its way
through her trembling orifice.

The nine-and-a-half-foot, thousand-pound male squirms
free of its mother's womb, enveloped in blood and embryonic
fluid. Shaking its head, it opens its mouth and inhales the
sea, clearing its gills.

The pup swims off to explore its world.

The adolescent male moves in.

There is little the mother can do. Even as a second pup
emerges, the first is speared within the jowls of the aggressive male. The hunter shakes the newborn until it stops struggling, then swims off with its meal to feed.

The second newborn squirms free, followed by six more
pups, all brownish-gray, their bellies stark white. Of these
seven survivors, five are female, averaging more than twelve
hundred pounds, the two male runts just under eight hundred. Leaving their mother's side, they stalk the coral reef of
the atoll in twos and threes, more miniature adults than newborns.

Carcharodon megalodon: apex predator of all time.
Blessed with primordial instincts 200 million years in the
making, cursed by Nature to remain a rogue hunter.

For these seven heirs to the throne, survival now depends
upon their ability to endure an ocean realm stricken by diminishing temperatures, stalked by Sperm whales, wolf packs of
Orca . . . and their own kind.

Detecting the lurking presence of the adolescent male, the
pups remain close to their birth mother, whose instinct to
feed makes her a threat in her own right.

Exhausted from labor, the adult female moves off, scanning her surroundings for prey.

The pups trail in her wake, the adolescent male closing from the shadows.

CHAPTER

28

NORTHWESTERN PACIFIC OCEAN
THE ULITHI ATOLL, MICRONESIA
DAWN

Scattered across three million square miles of Pacific Ocean are more than two thousand volcanic islands collectively known as Micronesia. Formed millions of years ago, the island chains are divided into three major archipelagos: the Carolines, the Marshalls, and the Marianas.

Many of these lush, tropical islands are merely the tops of massive underwater mountains, others formed from the rims of sunken volcanoes. Atolls surround many of these islets, their protective coral reefs harboring azure-blue lagoons.

Ulithi is a coral atoll located southwest of Guam, its 1.75 miles of land laced across the fourth largest lagoon in the world, occupying some 200 square miles of sea. In September 1944, this tropical waterway was made famous when it was occupied by U.S. forces and converted into a temporary naval base. After the war, the atoll, along with the rest of Micronesia, fell under a United Nations trusteeship known as the Trust Territory of the Pacific Islands. The TTPI was eventually disbanded in 1994, replaced by four distinct, self-governing districts.

Fewer than two thousand people occupy Ulithi's tropical islands, a forgotten paradise that lies just west of the Mariana Trench.

The cool tropical breeze from the overhead fan soothes his fever, the shadows of daylight chasing away his nightmares.

Jonas Taylor opens his eyes.

He is lying in an infirmary, staring into the smiling brown eyes of a Micronesian nurse whose dialect he cannot comprehend. White gauze covers his arms and chest, a petroleum-aloe salve moistening his sunburned skin.

Raising his arm, Jonas points to a metal pitcher, cringing in pain as his aching muscles tighten beneath the bandages.

The nurse pours him a drink.

"Thank you," he rasps. "Where am I?"

"Mokomok." Erik Hollander appears at the foot of his bed, the producer's receding forehead covered in moistened gauze. "Mokomok's the chief village of the Ulithi Atoll, about half a step above Gilligan's Island. You've been fading in and out of consciousness for the last day and a half."

"My daughter?"

"She's fine. Probably snorkeling in the lagoon as we speak."

"Maren?"

"He's history, thank God." Erik moves closer. "Bastard wanted us both dead, the rest of the crew too. You really came through, you old Daredevil you. Saved all our butts. You're a real hero. Network won't forget it. None of us will. I mean that literally. Stuart Starr got the whole thing on tape. Worth half a million extra to you, my friend."

"Go away."

"Yeah, sure. Hey, fella, if it means anything . . . I'm sorry."

Jonas closes his eyes. "Find Dani."

"Dad?"

Jonas opens his eyes. Dani is dressed in a *Daredevils II* tee-shirt and shorts, her wet blond hair pulled back in a pony-tail. "You look . . . so beautiful. When did you grow up?"

Her lower lip quivers. "I think I still have a long way to go."

"I'm proud of you, you know that?"

"I'm proud of you, too." Her metallic-blue eyes tear up. "Dad, can we go home now?"

Jonas smiles. "Yes. I think I've had enough excitement for one lifetime."

29

FARALLON ISLANDS, PACIFIC OCEAN

It is a landmass known to native Americans as the "Islands of the Dead," a craggy landmass first visited by Francis Drake who sought its abundance of sea lion meat for his long voyages.

The Farallon Islands are a series of windswept rocks situated twenty-six miles west of San Francisco's Golden Gate Bridge. Of the four islands that make up the archipelago, three are mountain peaks that jut just above the Pacific, the fourth, Southeast Farallon, being the largest, and only one that is habitable. Marine mammals like the Northern Elephant Seal dominate the jagged landscape, their presence enticing another species to visit the remote island chain.

Carcharodon carcharius: the Great White shark.

The shadow of the Tanaka Oceanographic Institute's helicopter passes over Middle Farallon, an inaccessible slice of rocky terrain covered by bird droppings. Mac hovers the chopper sixty feet above the dark blue Pacific, then signals Terry to lower the portable thumper, now rigged to the chopper's winch by steel cable.

The acoustic device touches down in the heavy surf and sinks, drawing a crowd of curious seals.

Mac turns to Terry, her reflection distorting in his mirrored sunglasses. "Last time I flew over this spot was twenty-two years ago, back when Angel's mama was on the loose. Crazy, huh?"

She nods, adjusting the microphone attached to her headset. "Where do all the years go?"

"I don't know, but I've come to the conclusion that I've wasted most of mine. Tell me something, Terry, is marriage all it's cracked up to be?"

The seriousness of his tone throws her. "James Mackreides, don't tell me you're actually thinking about settling down? Has Hell frozen over already? Are pigs flying?"

"Guess you think I'm too old, huh?"

"Too old? Actually, I think it's the first mature thing that's come out of your mouth in years. You and Trish make a great couple. Uh, we are talking about Patricia Pedrazzoli, right?"

"No, I was thinking of proposing to Bimbo Betty down at Shakey's Bar and Grill. Start your damn fish-finder."

Terry smiles, activating the sonar device, now rigged to the thumper. A swarm of small blips representing the inquisitive seals appears on her laptop monitor.

Mac sends the helicopter to the south, the airship dragging the thumper into deeper waters. "Getting back to the marriage thing, I, uh . . ."

"You're worried about the whole monogamy thing."

"Sort of, yeah. With you and Jonas, is the spark still there after twenty years?"

Terry stares at the horizon. "It's there. It just gets overshadowed sometime by the familiarity. Then you spend time away from each other and realize it never left."

"Miss him, huh?"

She nods. "He and Dani are coming in on the red-eye

from Hawaii. I'd love to have Angel back in her pen before
he arrives."

"I'd love to see the look on his face." Mac glances at her.
"So what's the story with this Joshua character?"

Terry's expression changes. "What do you mean?"

"Come on, Terry, I see the way he looks at you. If ever a
guy wanted to jump your bones—"

"Josh knows I'm married."

"So? Marriage never stopped guys like my old man.
Maybe I need to say something to this Joshua guy before
Jonas gets back."

"Let it be, I can handle it."

"You're the boss."

ABOARD THE DREDGING BARGE
CANAL ENTRANCE, TANAKA LAGOON

The dark blue hills surge toward shore in sets of six, cresting
seven feet as they race through the access canal before crashing against the lagoon's interior eastern seawall.

Joshua Bunkofske closes his eyes as another swell lifts the
dredging platform. The wave tugs at the anchors, then rolls
beneath the orange buoys and through the line of barbed
wire strung across the canal entrance.

The marine biologist zips his wetsuit against the cold
wind as the two-way radio buzzes to life.

"Base to rig, come in."

Joshua reaches for the communications device. "Yeah, go
ahead, Donald."

David's voice squawks over the receiver. "David, not
Donald!"

The biologist smiles. "What is it you want, kid?"

"The bait's been set. I'm starting the lagoon's underwater
acoustics."

"Let her rip."

"You'll call me the moment she enters the canal, right?"

"Yes, Douglas." Joshua sets the radio aside and turns on his CD player.

David shakes his head at Patricia. "Who does this guy think he is?"

"Don't let him get to you." The blond-haired realtor shields her eyes against the sun, gazing up at the 350-pound carcass of beef swaying thirty feet over the southern end of the lagoon. "You sure that A-frame will hold? Looks pretty old and rusted to me."

"I don't know. I'm not even sure we set the bait right. I wish my father were here. He'd know just what to do."

ABOARD NORTHWESTERN FLIGHT 6002

The Boeing 767 jumbo jet cruises 40,000 feet over the Pacific Ocean, continuing its seven-hour trek east.

Jonas Taylor stirs from his catnap as a stewardess sideswipes his shoulder with her drink cart. "Excuse me, miss, when do we land in San Francisco?"

"About an hour."

Jonas turns to the window seat. Verifying Dani is asleep, he removes the *Honolulu Advertiser* from his jacket pocket, turning to the second part of the front page article.

Monster shark attacks Giant Fans:
Susan Tunis, editor of *Discover Diving Magazine*, witnessed the attack from her dive boat, *Genie's Folly*. "This wasn't the first time I've seen that monster. About twenty years ago, my sister and I attended an evening performance at the Tanaka Lagoon. The moment I saw the glow in McCovey Cove, I knew it was Angel. But seeing her up close . . . I can't begin

to describe how frightening she was. When she surfaced, it was like watching the tip of an iceberg jut out of the water. When her mouth opened and all those people were eaten . . . it must have felt like falling into a mine shaft."

Terry Tanaka-Taylor, wife of Professor Jonas Taylor, issued a statement following the attacks. "There's really no way to tell how long Angel's been back in California waters because we know she prefers the depths. Her appearance in San Francisco Bay was most likely a fluke, a result of the tremendous surface disturbances going on during the [baseball] game. As horrible as this event was, I can assure you that humans are not a staple of Angel's, or any other shark's, diet, and while it will be difficult and dangerous, the Tanaka Oceanographic Institute will not rest until we've recaptured the Megalodon. Meanwhile, our prayers go out to all the victims and their families."

Jonas stares at the quote. *Don't do it, Terry. Please don't try to prove anything to me.*

He tucks the article away as his daughter stirs. "I'm hungry."

"Want some peanuts?"

"I hate peanuts. When do we land?"

"Soon."

"Why'd we have to take an earlier flight anyway? The rest of the cast and crew got to stay in Hawaii the whole week, all expenses paid."

"I miss your mother."

"So? Erik offered to fly her out. We could have had a free week in Honolulu and you blew it."

"I'll make it up to you. Go back to sleep."

ABOARD THE DREDGING BARGE
CANAL ENTRANCE, TANAKA LAGOON

The baritone acoustics reverberate across the water and through the steel barge, pounding Joshua's brain like a bad sinus headache. He reaches to turn up the volume on his CD player when the radio buzzes with a burst of static.

"Base to rig, come in."

Josh snatches the annoying device. "Hey, Donald, how about turning down those drums, my head feels like it's in a freakin' vise."

David ignores him. "Listen, I was thinking, while we're waiting for my mother and Mac to locate Angel, maybe we should restart that dredger, you know, just to make sure the canal entrance is still clear."

"By 'we,' I take it you mean me?"

"All you have to do is crank up the generator."

"Mackreides said it was clear, that's good enough for me."

"It was clear three days ago. Now it might need to be dredged."

"You can't just turn on the generator. Somebody has to be down there, guiding the suction hose, and damn if I'm going anywhere until I know for certain where Angel's lurking. Call me back when your mother spots her; meanwhile, turn down those damn underwater speakers."

ABOARD THE TANAKA OCEANOGRAPHIC INSTITUTE'S
HELICOPTER

The lead-gray shadows appear just beneath the surface, six sinister silhouettes moving in unison, following the thumper as it is dragged through the sea.

Terry watches the scene below through binoculars as three more sharks join the pack. "Definitely Great Whites. Never saw so many in one place."

"I have," Mac says. "Eighteen years ago, when Angel was in heat. Must've been a dozen of 'em, all males, circling the canal door like a bunch of horny marines on shore leave."

"Angel was giving off a powerful scent at the time. Why would these sharks be following the thumper now?"

"Maybe they're not. Hang on." Mac pulls back on the joystick, driving the chopper higher.

The thumper lifts out of the water, dancing on the end of its sixty-foot steel towline.

Seconds later, the Great White sharks break formation as Angel's upper torso rises out of the Pacific, its jaws snapping at the dangling acoustic device.

"Sonuvabitch!" Mac climbs higher as the angry monster falls sideways back into the sea.

Terry grabs the radio. "Chopper to base, chopper to base—"

"Base to chopper. Go ahead, Ma."

"We've located Angel, we're on our way."

TANAKA LAGOON

David grabs the two-way radio, his heart beating in time with the baritone drums echoing across the empty arena. "Base to rig! Pick up, Josh, it's Donald, I mean David!"

"Go ahead."

"They found Angel. She's twenty-three nautical miles north, heading our way. Even pulling twenty knots, that should still give you at least forty-five minutes to dredge."

"Tell you what, kid. Instead of dredging, how about I just try the doors and see if they'll close?"

David shrugs. "Yeah, okay. Makes sense."

ABOARD THE DREDGING BARGE
CANAL ENTRANCE, TANAKA LAGOON

Joshua snaps the buckles of his buoyancy control vest and air tank in place, checks his regulator, then spits into his face mask. *Check this, do that . . . who does this Taylor kid think he is?*

Securing his face mask, Joshua steps off the rig, plunging feetfirst into the sea.

The Pacific envelopes him in its deep blue aura, the water crystal clear, dive conditions excellent. Adjusting the pressure in his vest, he slows his descent, then kicks toward the towering gray steel facing that is the open northern canal door.

Joshua inspects the barnacle-encrusted surface, poking three fingers into one of the door's thousand pores. Then, remembering the monster, he continues his dive, his heart beating more rapidly in his chest.

Touching down on the silty bottom, he looks around, then locates the junction box. Peering inside, he finds the key pad David had described.

The generator light glows red.

Joshua presses the sequence 10-7-6-4-6 and waits.

Nothing happens.

He tries it again, then a third time.

Still nothing.

Cursing into his regulator, the marine biologist kicks away from the bottom, expelling air as he surfaces.

TANAKA LAGOON

"Rig to David, pick up!"

David pulls the radio free from his belt. "What's wrong?"

"The damn generator's getting no juice, that's what's wrong. I thought you said you tested this thing?"

David looks at Patricia, dumbfounded. "I, uh . . . shit."

"Yeah, shit. Now get your ass in gear and find us an alternative power source before Angel gets here."

SAN FRANCISCO INTERNATIONAL AIRPORT

Jonas and Dani exit the boarding ramp, entering the terminal to a sea of blinding flashbulbs.

"Professor Taylor, is it true you returned early to recapture Angel?"

"What makes you so sure your facility will hold her this time?"

"Jonas, how many people actually died on *Daredevils?*"

"Did you know the final two-hour episode airs tonight?"

"Professor, is it fair to keep a wild animal like Angel locked up?"

"Enough!" Jonas grabs his daughter by the crook of her arm and bulls his way through the mob of reporters.

James Gelet and a security guard intercept them as they hurry down the escalator. "Jonas, hey, James Gelet, Erik's partner. I have a limo waiting for you and your daughter outside."

"Good, get us the hell out of here."

"Give the guard your baggage claim tickets, he'll take care of your luggage."

Jonas digs into his pocket. Hands the guard the stubs as Gelet leads them outside into daylight.

The limo driver opens the rear door. Dani climbs in first, followed by her father.

Gelet peeks inside. "Be back in two shakes, just want to make a quick statement, then we're off."

The door slams shut as a crowd surrounds the limo.

"Dad, what's going on? They were talking about recapturing Angel."

Jonas reaches into his pocket. Hands her the article.

Dani stares at the AP photo on the front page. "Oh, no . . . oh my God."

"Shh . . . it's all right—"

Outside the limo, the shrill shriek of a woman screaming forces James Gelet to pause from his speech.

TANAKA LAGOON

David emerges from the subterranean stairwell, dressed in his wetsuit and diving gear, carrying his fins, mask, and a coiled length of underwater cable.

Patricia chases after him as he hurries through the arena. "David, wait—what're you doing? David—"

"We need power. I can rig this cable to the generator on board the barge. That should give us plenty of juice to close the canal doors."

"No way, I'm not letting you go down there. David, did you hear me?"

Ignoring her, he hurries to the top of the arena's northern bleachers. Pushes open the hidden gate in the perimeter fencing. Keys open the padlock.

"Hey!" Patricia grabs his arm. "Don't do this."

"I'll be okay, we still have plenty of time." He walks out onto the twelve-inch-wide ledge that is the northern canal wall, swallowing the lump in his throat.

Patricia watches him as he follows the concrete barrier beyond the beachhead and out into the Pacific.

Then she notices the cigarette boat.

ABOARD THE CIGARETTE BOAT

Devin Dietsch powers down the speedboat a hundred yards south of the southern canal wall. "You want me to get us closer?"

Older brother Drew glances up. "Nah, this is good enough. Any closer and we'll draw attention. Get your gear on, I'll be through in a minute."

Balanced on the real estate magnate's lap is a small underwater platter mine.

ABOARD THE DREDGING BARGE
CANAL ENTRANCE, TANAKA LAGOON

Joshua sits on the edge of the swaying rig, watching with amusement as David Taylor stumbles along the edge of the submerged seawall. "Come on, kid. Just swim over already."

David holds his breath and ducks, gripping the concrete wall between his knees as another swell rolls over his head.

"Come on, Dagmar, we don't have all day!"

Shoving his regulator angrily into his mouth, David waits for the next swell to pass, then jumps into the canal, stroking with one arm, holding the roll of underwater cable with the other. Surface diving beneath the four-foot-high roll of barbed wire, he surfaces on the other side, kicking toward the platform.

Joshua reaches down and drags the teenager onto the rig. "Took you long enough. Now what are we supposed to do with this?"

David kicks off his swim fins, then starts unraveling the 600-foot cord. "You wanted power, I'll give you power. We'll hook one end to the rig's generator, the other end to the junction box."

Joshua checks his watch. *Twenty-eight minutes, give or take.* He takes out the two-way radio. "Hey, Tracy, you there?"

Patricia answers. "Funny."

"Contact the helicopter. I want to know exactly how far out they are before we get back into the water."

ABOARD THE TANAKA OCEANOGRAPHIC INSTITUTE'S HELICOPTER

Terry scans the surface with her binoculars. Spots the ivory dorsal fin. "Here she comes again."

Mac yanks back on the joystick, causing the thumper to spring from the sea.

Angel disappears, going deep.

"Guess she's tired of all that leaping," Terry yells over the headset.

"Base to chopper, come in."

Terry flips the radio's toggle switch. "Go ahead, Trish."

"What's your ETA?"

Mac checks his instruments. "We're only averaging ten knots, and we're still a good fourteen miles out. Say an hour at the least, just to play it safe."

ABOARD THE DREDGING BARGE
CANAL ENTRANCE, TANAKA LAGOON

"Mac says you've got another hour if she holds her present course and speed. But we've got another problem. There's a cigarette boat just south of the canal. I'm guessing it belongs to the Dietsch Brothers."

Joshua climbs one of the sand dunes and looks to the south. "Who the hell are the Dietsch Brothers?"

David stares at the distant boat. "Coupla' guys who want to turn the lagoon into a housing development and mall."

"Yeah, well we don't have time to worry about them now. Rig that end of the cable to the generator and I'll escort you below."

David swallows hard. "Can't you handle it yourself?"

"Listen, boy genius, I'm a marine biologist, not an electrician. Go, get moving."

David grabs the free end of the cable and drags it with him over a sand dune. A trail of hoses leads him to the oil-stained, fire-engine-red 7,700-kilowatt diesel generator.

David locates the connection box, attaches the electrical cable, then double-times it back to Joshua. "Okay, we're set here."

"Let's make this fast." Joshua fixes his mask, then jumps back into the ocean, disappearing in a haze of bubbles.

David tries spitting into his mask, but finds he has no saliva. Bending down, he leans over to wash off his mask, as another swell rolls under the platform, flipping him head over heels into the Pacific.

The panicked teenager thrashes to the surface, quickly dragging himself back onto the rig. Panting nervously, he looks around at empty ocean. *Okay, you gotta do this . . . stop being such a pussy.*

Tightening his mask over his eyes, he bites down on his regulator and jumps.

TANAKA LAGOON

Patricia leans against the steel fencing at the top of the western bleachers, her binoculars trained on the two men seated in the cigarette boat.

"Okay, boys, exactly what are you up to?"

She watches as Devin climbs overboard in full scuba gear. Drew leans out and hands him a heavy-looking, disk-shaped object.

Devin submerges.

Patricia's blood runs cold. *A mine? They mean to blow up the canal doors!*

Taking out her cell phone, she dials the number for information. "Monterey Bay. I need the number of the Coast Guard."

TANAKA CANAL

David kicks toward bottom, following Joshua's trail of air bubbles. The haunting echo of voodoo drums meshes with his pounding pulse, the thumper reverberating in his bones. He thinks of his grandfather. *You'll be okay, Angel's still miles away.*

Slowly, the silty seafloor comes into focus, nestled beneath a forest of mustard-tan coral.

Joshua waits impatiently by the trash can–size junction box, the end of the underwater cable in his hand.

David hovers above the seafloor, then turns, looking over his shoulder at the underwater canyon and its ominous dark drop-off.

The sight of the abyss causes him to shudder.

Joshua taps impatiently on the junction box.

Swimming over, David searches the outside of the steel container until he locates a barnacle-encrusted seam. Removing his dive knife, he chips away at the crustaceans with the steel blade.

Josh moves in to help.

The stark, ivory-white creature moves through the valley of perpetual darkness, its lower jaw quivering in spasms, its breathing erratic.

For days, the big male has been moving south along the Pacific coast, its senses detecting traces of the ovulating female. Crossing the currents of San Francisco Bay, the Meg's olfactory cells had been inundated with the female's pungent scent, the odor becoming more powerful as the predator moved deeper through the Monterey Submarine Canyon. The female had been there, but her scent lingered everywhere, making it impossible for the Meg to pinpoint her presence.

The male zigzags through shadows of gray, eight hundred feet below the surface. Though it prefers to hunt at night, its last two feedings have occurred during the waning hours of day. While the indirect light still stings its nocturnal eyes, the female's hormonal perfume is more concentrated in the mid-to-shallow waters.

The male's close proximity to the ovulating female has caused its brain to secrete increased levels of testosterone, fueling the Meg's overly aggressive nature. Gliding through a kelp forest, it lashes out at anything that moves, its sensory system on overload.

Caught off-guard, a half-dozen seals become a quick snack, their skulls popping like walnuts within the male's crushing orifice.

The hunter continues its trek south, then suddenly detects something else . . . something familiar. At first it is just a distant reverberation, then it graduates to sound—a baritone echo that fills the underwater gorge for tens of miles.

Pinpointing the disturbance, the Megalodon accelerates east, racing through the submarine canyon like a mad bull.

ABOARD THE TANAKA OCEANOGRAPHIC INSTITUTE'S HELICOPTER

Terry scans the surface of the Pacific through her binoculars. The Great White sharks have disappeared.

Mac taps her on the shoulder. "Well?"

She checks her fish-finder again. Shakes her head. "She's gone."

TANAKA CANAL

David and Joshua pry off the outside panel of the junction box, exposing the bucket-size power-pac.

Removing the corroded mini-generator from its harness, David feels around, then locates a suitable female receptacle.

Plugs in the cable.

Reaching inside the top of the junction box, he dials in his access code.

Nothing.

David knee kicks the cursed machine, then stops. Thinks. Grins at Joshua through his regulator. He signals to the surface, indicating as best he can that the generator must be powered up before the junction box will work.

Joshua signals okay, then kicks away from the bottom—

—as the ghostly white demon's snout rises over the ledge of the submarine canyon.

The big male's head is as large as the front end of a C-5 cargo plane, its quivering lower jaw purple around the titanium hook still embedded in its flesh. A dark steel cable trails below the festering wound like some bizarre antenna.

Joshua's eyes widen, his heartbeat jumping. Thirty feet from the surface, he forces himself to remain motionless in the water.

His pulsating internal organs announce his presence.

The agitated male turns its cold gaze upon its overmatched prey.

Man and beast make eye contact.

And then, in one gut-wrenching spasm, it is upon him.

Abominable jaws open, the widening gullet expanding until it is beyond Joshua's field of vision, and then he realizes, in his delirium, that he is being inhaled.

Sudden darkness . . . followed by an explosive eruption of pain and blood and splintering bones as dozens of seven-inch blades skewer his shattering existence before—

Chomp.

Gone.

Twenty feet away, David vomits into his regulator, his entire being shaking uncontrollably as the monster's jowls smack open and shut, spewing shards of flesh and blood and shredded wetsuit everywhere.

The Meg shakes its head and expels the mangled, inhuman remains of Joshua Bunkofske's crushed air tank from its mouth, then turns its heart-stopping gaze toward David.

TANAKA LAGOON

Jonas climbs out of the limousine and stretches. Two vehicles are parked on the sidewalk adjacent to the main entrance of the arena. He recognizes Mac's truck, and then he registers a familiar tingling in his bones.

James Gelet emerges from the backseat. "So here's what I was thinking . . . we bring a film crew over about an hour before tonight's episode airs, then we do a live satellite feed with—"

"Quiet!" Jonas listens. Kneels by the pavement. Touches it with his palms.

Gelet waits. "What? Is it an earthquake?"

Dani exits the limo. "Dad, what is it?"

"Thumper!"

Jonas races through the tunnel leading into the arena. Hears a woman scream.

Patricia bounds down the concrete aisle of the western bleachers two steps at a time, her binoculars bouncing against her chest.

"Trish!" Jonas waves.

The blonde looks up, startled. "Jonas? Jonas, quick, there's another shark in the canal! Another Meg!"

"What?"

She hurries over, beads of sweat running down her flushed cheeks. "Jonas, David's in the canal."

The monstrous fish lurches forward.

David kicks his flippers. Tumbles backward over the junction box. Regains his balance and swims as fast as he can, scurrying around the backside of the canal door toward the shadowed crevice that harbors the door's hydraulic hinges.

Don't look, don't stop, don't look, don't stop—

The big male lunges forward, ramming its head through the gap between the open door and the northern canal wall.

David disappears into the shadows, hugging one of the hinges as the Megalodon attempts to wriggle its way deeper into the tight space, the side of the open steel door pinching tightly against its right flank.

David hyperventilates into his regulator, unable to take his eyes off the gruesome white head. The gray-blue eye is rolled back, revealing a bloodshot white sclera.

For a long moment, he remains paralyzed in fear, and then the gut-wrenching strain of metal echoes in his ears and he realizes, to his horror, that the canal door is giving way.

Jonas activates the A-frame's winch, sending the eviscerated 350-pound bovine carcass plunging into the southern end of the tank.

Reversing the line, he drags the dripping side of beef from the water, then hands the controls to Patricia. "See? Up and down, like a giant tea bag."

"Got it. Wait—what're you going to do?"

Jonas sprints toward the end of the arena. "I'm going to save my son!"

David feels for the buoyancy control valve. Presses it, inflating his vest.

Rising along the V-shaped crevice, the teen shoots toward the surface, then he reaches out and slows his ascent, remembering the last time he panicked in these same waters.

Pausing at thirty feet, he forces himself to relax and breathe.

The testosterone-laced Meg stares as its prey ascends beyond its reach. Wriggling free of the gap, the hunter searches for another way to access David, when its senses detect something else.

Surface disturbances.

Blood.

Prey.

The hungry fish moves into the canal, its sickle-shaped tail slicing up the surface.

Jonas balances precariously on top of the concrete wall, the sea to his left, a fifteen-foot drop to the beach below on his right.

Looking up, he spots the approaching ivory dorsal fin.

Dropping slowly into a squat position, he straddles the twelve-inch-wide wall with his knees and waits.

Another male, even bigger than 'Scarface. What would bring Angel and this male so far from the Pacific trenches? Think, Taylor. Something significant's happening here . . .

Grinding his teeth, he waits for the Megalodon to pass, noticing its trailing length of steel cable.

Sweet Jesus . . . the Monterey Canyon! Angel's using the gorge as a nursery site, just as her mother did, twenty-two years ago.

Jonas leaps to his feet, continuing his dash along the top of the narrow canal wall.

Moving beyond the beach, he continues another hundred yards, the canal now blending into the Pacific, the waves cresting along both sides of the concrete wall to greet him.

High tide has submerged the last third of the seawall, making the going even more treacherous. He sloshes through ankle-deep water, then holds on tenuously as an immense swell rolls over his knees and chest.

The power of the wave causes him to lose his balance, casting him into the canal.

Jonas surfaces and kicks toward the wall. Regaining his footing, he stands, the sea pulling at his calves.

His heart leaps as he sees his son's head surface at the end of the canal.

A massive wave crashes against the far end of the main tank, and then Patricia sees the approaching male, its ivory-white head plowing the olive-green waters like Moby Dick.

"Oh my God—" Dropping the controls, she backs up the steps of the bleachers.

In one motion, the male raises its upper torso out of the water and snags the dripping cow carcass from its hook. Shaking its head from side to side, it tears loose its meal, sending ten-foot waves ricocheting around the horseshoe-shaped end of the tank.

Patricia covers her ears against the screech of folding steel as the rusted A-frame is torn from its concrete base, the entire structure collapsing into the lagoon.

David treads water along the top of the submerged northern wall. He sees ripples flowing from the far end of the tank and hears the A-frame as it collapses.

He eyes the dredging platform. *Fifty yards, maybe sixty. Gotta risk it.*

Ducking his head, he swims an awkward crawl stroke toward the rig, his scuba gear restricting his movements.

Halfway there, keep going.

"David!"

David turns, startled. "Dad?"

Jonas ducks beneath another incoming swell, then waves at his son. "Go, get to the platform! Watch the barbed wire!"

David strokes and kicks. Ducks beneath the surface barrier of barbed wire. Moves beyond the orange marker buoys. Grabs onto the edge of the floating steel platform and hoists himself up and out of the water.

Pulls off his fins. Dumps his vest and tank. Sprints over the dunes of sand to the generator.

Presses the red POWER switch.

A double choke, and the machine jumps to life.

The flaccid four-foot-wide rubber suction hose coughs, inflates, then releases a steady stream of ocean and sand onto the platform.

The doors of the canal begin to close.

Devin Dietsch is exhausted and angry. Moving in forty feet of water, the underwater mine clutched to his chest, the amateur diver has been zigzagging against a strong current for twenty minutes and has already had to surface twice to regain his bearings.

I'm gonna strangle Drew, making me do all this crazy Navy SEAL bullshit . . .

Looking up, he sees the line of orange buoys dotting the surface. *Dammit. Must've overshot the southern door.*

Turning, he angles back, using the buoys to guide him. Thirty more feet and he smiles, relieved to finally see the half-open steel door as it materializes from the shadows.

Devin examines the underwater mine. There are two controls located on the explosive, the first designed to magnetize the outer steel shell, the second to activate the timer, which his brother has set to detonate in one hour.

Devin magnetizes the platter, then presses it against the inside face of the barnacle-encrusted door.

The mine adheres momentarily, then falls free, tumbling past his swim fins.

Crap! Devin ducks and swims after the sinking explosive, catching it at fifty-seven feet.

Swimming back to the door, he removes his dive knife and begins hacking away at the barnacles, attempting to clear a path to the steel.

Jonas treads water, massaging a cramp over his stomach muscles. The top of the northern concrete wall is somewhere beneath his kicking feet. Ahead—the line of barbed wire marking the canal entrance.

And suddenly he is moving, caught in a swirling eddy created by the movement of the submerged canal doors.

The moving door catches Devin off-guard, the steel wall nearly breaking his nose as it collides with his face mask. Blood flows from his left nostril into his mask as his body is swept backward by the rapidly sealing southern door.

Glancing to his left, he sees the approaching northern door, groaning on its hinges as it moves to meet its twin.

The big male lashes at the blood-stained waters in the southern end of the tank, but there is no more prey to be had.

The reverberations of the sealing canal doors draw its attention.

Leaving the lagoon, the agitated Meg finds its way back through the canal, heading for open ocean.

Jonas paddles and kicks as hard as he can, but the swift current continues dragging him backward toward the middle of the canal entrance, straight for the coils of barbed wire.

Lunging for the nearest orange warning buoy, he hangs on.
"Dad, the Meg!"

Jonas looks over his shoulder and down the canal's long stretch of waterway. *Oh, hell . . . not again.*

The ivory wake plows the surface, the big male heading straight for him.

Jonas feels the northern canal door grind to a halt eight feet beneath him. Ducking his head, he searches for the top of the northern door.

Sees it has stopped ten feet from closing, its companion falling seven feet short.

The gap between the two doors is wide enough to drive a car through.

Not good . . .

The current has ceased.

The dorsal fin has not.

Devin Dietsch hovers fifty feet beneath Jonas's buoy, the real estate mogul's eyes staring in disbelief at the nightmarish albino creature bearing down upon him. Dropping the mine, he swims backward through the twelve-foot gap, unable to take his eyes off the monster.

Devin screams into his regulator as the big male drives its conical snout halfway through the gap before the unyielding steel doors pinch its gill slits, forcing the enraged Meg back inside the canal.

Devin stops screaming, tears flooding his mask as he realizes he's still alive. His heart patters in his chest, his muscles quivering with adrenaline as he watches the eerie white Megalodon stalk the semi-open canal entrance like a hungry, caged tiger.

Oh, God . . . those bastards did it, they actually recaptured her. Forget Esplanade by the Sea, *this is even bigger.*

The Megalodon attacks the gap again, causing the steel doors to groan.

Devin flees—

—only to be confronted by an even bigger nightmare.

Angel appears from out of the dense blue periphery like a ghostly-white dirigible, her jaws parted slightly, her steel gray-blue eyes taking in everything.

Adrenaline courses through Devin Dietsch's being like electricity. He flutter kicks backward, as the big male attacks the gap.

Devin bounces off the male's snout, then rips off his weight belt and kicks like a madman for the surface.

Angel ignores him, her senses focused more on the presence of another Megalodon in her pen. With a flurry of tail movement, the forty-ton female bull-rushes the gate, her open jaws colliding with those of the male.

Blood, bubbles, barnacles and silt swirl amid the two jarring behemoths, the steel doors groaning with each colossal impact.

Freed of his weight belt, his vest filling with air, Devin Dietsch ascends like a beach ball, his skull smashing against the bottom of one of the orange buoys, the sudden impact knocking him senseless.

Dangling from the buoy, half out of the water, Jonas can only hold on as the surface around him becomes a maelstrom, the two Megalodons bashing and snapping and biting one another through the gap in the canal doors forty-five feet beneath him.

Whomp!

Jonas lets out a yell as something collides with his buoy. For a long second, he squeezes his eyes shut, waiting to be ravaged, then realizes the impact was caused by something else.

Opening his eyes, he sees the inert scuba diver floating facedown in the water. Jonas pulls him closer to the buoy. Verifies he is breathing.

David waves frantically from the platform. "Dad, what should I do?"

"Open the gate!"

Open the gate? How can I do that? Wait a sec . . . David stumbles over the piles of silt to the generator. Powers off the generator. Counts to thirty, then restarts the engine.

The big suction hose resumes pumping.

The canal doors reverberate within their frames, then, with a heavy groan of metal, the two barriers of steel begin reversing themselves, the gap widening.

Angel pushes through the widening gap and enters the canal.

The male Meg circles away, yielding to the larger female.

Angel remains close to the southern wall as she glides toward the lagoon.

The big male inches his snout closer to her cloaca, his gray-blue eyes rolling back against the late afternoon gray.

The two leviathans enter the main tank side by side, the male driving the larger female against the eastern seawall as the prehistoric sharks begin their mating ritual.

Jonas inflates Devin Dietsch's BCD vest, then using the unconscious diver as a raft, he paddles both of them toward the barge.

David helps his father out of the water, the two of them dragging the heavier Dietsch brother onto the platform.

Father and son embrace. "Dad, we have to get those doors to seal."

The radio buzzes, Patricia's voice bleeding through the static. "Base to rig, David, are you okay?"

"Yes, but we lost Josh."

Jonas heart skips a beat. "Josh? Who's Josh?"

David ignores him. "Trish, what about the Megs?"

"They just keep circling, the one with the hook in its mouth smashing the larger one against the seawall."

"They're getting ready to mate," Jonas says, taking the radio from his son. "Trish, there's a Coast Guard cutter approaching that cigarette boat. Contact them. Have them pick up Devin Dietsch and my son, right away."

"You got it."

"David, how much air do you have left in your tank?"

"Why? What're you going to do?"

"Hopefully, prevent an ancient species from being reintroduced into California waters."

The big male plows Angel sideways against the eastern seawall, inching its mouth forward until it clamps its jaws on her thick right pectoral fin. Securing a hold, he drives his skull into her right gill slits, forcing her to roll over so that she is upside down.

Swimming belly-up along the inside wall of the oval-shaped lagoon, Angel slows, allowing the male to mount her.

One of the male's rigid five-foot claspers inserts into the female's vent, its barbed tip embedding itself along the interior wall of Angel's orifice like a grappling hook.

From their vantage in the upper bleachers, Patricia, Dani, and James Gelet watch in amazement as the two magnificent creatures continue cruising slowly around the tank, joined at the lower torso.

Jonas loosens the straps of David's BCD vest, slips his arms inside, then checks the air supply: *Eighteen minutes.*

"David, shut down the generator again and reverse the doors so they close. I need to see just how much sand we're dealing with."

"But Dad—"

"And tell Trish to shut off that damn thumper."

"Yes, sir. Dad, please don't do this."

Jonas hugs his son. "I'll be all right, but I want you off this barge. As soon as that male finishes his business, all hell's gonna break loose as these two decide who rules the roost."

Positioning his regulator, Jonas holds his mask against his face and jumps into the sea. Releasing air from his vest, he sinks beneath the dredging platform, then swims toward the huge black suction hose, following it down.

At thirty-five feet, the generator shuts down, the hose going limp.

At sixty feet, it starts up again.

Steel groans in Jonas's ears as the two canal doors jump to life, inching toward one another as they close.

Jonas touches down on the seafloor. Grabbing the guide bar of the suction hose, he swims the end of the vacuum toward a seven-foot-high, twenty-foot-wide pyramid of silt marking the center convergence point of the two doors.

The hose begins inhaling the pile, dancing in his arms like a giant eel.

The Tanaka Oceanographic Institute's helicopter slows as it approaches the lagoon, its two passengers spellbound as they take in the scene below.

"Geez, there's two of them. And they're doing the nasty."

Terry grips the edge of her seat. "It's the big male Joshua captured. David warned me not to allow both of them into the lagoon at once."

Mac smiles. "Looks like they're getting along just fine to me."

Beneath the male's skin, forward of each five-foot-long clasper lies a bulbous siphon sac filled with a mix of sperm and seminal fluid.

Pinning Angel against the bottom of the tank, the male gyrates its lower torso, causing its claspers to flex and relax, flex and relax, the pumping action sending seawater into its siphon sac, the pressure building . . . building, until—

—the big male ejaculates twelve gallons of sperm and seminal fluid into the female's reproductive tract.

Copulation complete, the male squirms its clasper free, the organ's calcified ridges tearing at Angel's orifice as it is withdrawn.

Angel attempts to roll over, but the male refuses to release her, preventing her from attacking.

For several moments, the two combatants continue bashing and bruising one another along the bottom of the tank. And then the male releases the female's pectoral fin and breaks free, racing toward the far end of the lagoon and the access canal.

Angel rights herself, then goes after her mate.

Enveloped in a cloud of silt, Jonas continues to focus the huge hose on the diminishing pile of sand. *Give me five more minutes Angel, just five more minutes.* ·

The two steel doors move into view, reverberating as they inch closer to one another.

David climbs onto the deck of the Coast Guard cutter, a lump in his throat as he stares at the Pacific, praying for his father to resurface.

Seaman First-Class Debra Garlinghouse points to the towering dorsal fin steaming toward the canal entrance, followed by an even larger second fin. "Skipper, get us out of here!"

David holds on as the boat races away from the mouth of the man-made channel.

The gap between the canal doors shrinks to five feet.

The southern door grinds in the sand and catches.

Jonas repositions the hose, then looks up, his spine tingling.

The thirty-two-ton male's conical head strikes the closing steel doors, the collision rumbling like an avalanche in Jonas's ears. The concussion wave, magnified between the gap in the doors, flips him heels over head and around again, driving the back of his skull into a clump of coral, knocking him woozy.

Mac hovers the chopper one-hundred feet above the canal entrance, he and Terry watching breathlessly as the big male desperately attempts to squirm free of the doors.

Angel moves in to attack.

The female snaps at the big male's tail, but the younger Megalodon is too quick. Wheeling about, it plants its hyper-extended jaws against Angel's left gill slits, driving the larger, bulkier predator against the seafloor, pinning her between the southern wall of the canal and its door.

In his blurred vision Jonas focuses upon the gap between the steel doors. Through swirls of silt he sees Angel's pectoral fin, flapping upside down against the seafloor at an awkward angle.

The male's got her pinned. If she doesn't move soon, she'll drown.

And then something else captures his attention.

Snaking along the seafloor—a steel cable.

Jonas eyes the line, still attached to the hook lodged deep inside the male's lower jaw.

Go! Get out of here! Stop flirting with death.

Instead, he swims closer, the rumbling steel rattling in his ears. Body trembling, his stomach doing somersaults, he peeks between the gap.

Between clouds of blood and silt he sees the big male's jaws hyperextended around Angel's flank. The thrashing female is suffocating, unable to draw water into her mouth to breathe.

Okay, now go! Get the hell away from here! Move!

But he doesn't move. Instead Jonas slips his body between the two doors and inches his right arm closer . . . closer . . .

Snatching the steel cable.

Jonas backs away quickly, then looks up as an ominous shadow passes over him, followed by three more.

Great Whites. Males. Agitated by Angel's scent.

He sucks another breath from his regulator. Gets nothing. Checks his air pressure gauge.

Empty.

The dominant male shark, a seventeen-foot, twenty-two-hundred-pounder, banks sharply away from the southern door and bull-rushes him. The peppered snout lifts, exposing rows of horrible teeth.

Yanking off his BCD vest and air tank, Jonas shoves them at the Great White's outstretched jaws, using them as a shield.

The Great White bites the tank, then shakes it loose from his grip.

Still gripping the steel cable, Jonas dives headfirst into the four-foot-wide opening of the dredging hose. The suction inhales him, launching him upward through the darkness of the vacuum tube like a human bullet.

Jonas plows into the bend in the tube, then punches through the hose, only a few feet from the dredging pump. He then falls out of the hose, sprawling headfirst down a wet pile of silt.

Doubled over in pain, he gasps several quick breaths, then remembering Angel, hurries for the generator and presses the POWER button, shutting down the machine.

He scans the junction box. Locates a free terminal. Jams the jagged end of the steel cable into the live opening, then powers up the generator.

Sparks fly, the steel line dancing like a cobra.

Seventy-six thousand volts of electricity surge through the sea into the titanium hook, searing the big male's gums, causing its entire girth to writhe in uncontrollable spasms.

The male Megalodon bashes its body against the side of the concrete canal, then whips its head wildly back and forth, tearing the hook from its lower jaw.

No longer pinned upside down, Angel slaps her tail and rights herself, then glides back into the lagoon, the seawater rushing into her mouth as she gasps for breath.

The dazed male shakes its still-buzzing head like a horse, then swims through the door's widening gap. Still dazed, it collides with the edge of the barge, its caudal fin slapping at the rig's flotation pontoons as it swims by.

Jonas shuts down the generator, then powers it up once more.

The steel doors shudder in their tracks, then slowly move to close.

Before they can seal, Angel shoots through the gap, disappearing into the depths.

Jonas slumps back against a pile of wet sand, too bruised and exhausted to move. His lower back feels twisted like a pretzel, his entire body shaking in the cool evening air.

He closes his eyes, passing out.

The chopper's thunder rattles the barge.

Jonas opens his eyes, staring at the Tanaka helicopter, now hovering fifteen feet above the dredging platform, the fury of its whirling blades sending up a windstorm of sand.

Terry jumps from the cockpit and slides down a pile of silt.

He watches her approach, her ebony hair flying in all directions. *So beautiful.*

"You think you're twenty years old again?"

"I feel more like a hundred."

"Guess you think you're quite the Daredevil, don't you?"

"Not anymore."

Terry kneels by his side and hugs him, warming him with her body heat. "Welcome home."

"I missed you, Tee."

"Shh." She kisses him, her sunbaked lips melting against his cold, salty mouth.

Terry lays his head against her chest, wrapping her arms around him tightly. "I told you not to go on that stupid reality show."

"When you're right, you're right."

"I tried, Jonas, I really tried. First we had the male, then Angel. Did you have to open the doors? So what if Angel drowned, we'd still have the male."

Jonas closes his eyes, thinking back to the last time he and his monster had crossed paths, eighteen years ago in the Mariana Trench. Celeste Singer had died down there, but Angel had spared him and his wife, allowing them to surface.

She was *his* monster. He felt a kinship for the Megalodon. "I couldn't do it, Tee, I couldn't just let her die like that."

"I know. Of course, now we have nothing, except we're even deeper in debt, stuck with an empty lagoon nobody wants."

"Come on, Tee, we have each other, we have the kids, we have our health." He struggles to sit up, his injured ribs taking his breath away. "I've wasted enough of my life thinking about what could have been, what I could have had. It's time to start appreciating what I've got."

Terry stares at him. "Who are you and what did you do with my husband?"

Jonas pulls her tighter to his chest. "I'm right here, exactly where I belong."

LATE PLEISTOCENE

NORTHWESTERN PACIFIC OCEAN
18,000 YEARS AGO

The exhausted female leads her seven surviving pups into deeper water, the adolescent male closing in from behind.

A thousand feet and the blue ocean turns gray.

Twelve hundred feet and they are enveloped in eternal darkness, the chill of the Ice Age intensifying.

The juvenile male moves in, targeting the runt of the litter, an eight-hundred-pound male.

The newborn pup darts away, only to be seized from behind, the larger adult severing it with one devastating bite.

Mother whirls around and attacks, sinking her teeth deep into the thick layer of flesh behind the adolescent's head. The female shakes the male back and forth, the two grappling Megalodons intent on settling their territorial dispute, the pups' lives hanging in the balance.

Titanic reverberations ripple through the Pacific. The six pups flee, racing deeper into the twinkling depths. Luminescent creatures blink in and out of existence, tempting a few of the young to feed, but the gnawing cold keeps them moving, forcing their swimming muscles to work harder.

The pressure increases, but has no effect on the pups.

The surface reverberations fade, still the escaping young continue their journey deeper.

In time, the pups reach a swirling layer of minerals and debris, the water sizzling. Fighting through the maelstrom, they enter the valley of a prehistoric sea.

A balmy tropical current soothes the Megalodon young, the warmth originating from a petrified forest of volcano-shaped stacks. Plumes of superheated sulfurous water pump out of these hydrothermal vents, filling the submarine gorge, spawning an oasis of life. Clusters of ghostly white tube worms flutter in the warm stream like unfettered African grasslands. Squid dart in and around the Riftia, feeding off the chemosynthetic life forms. Schools of primitive fish move through the hydrothermal layer as one, their formation meant to ward off attacks from larger marine life.

The Megalodon young have entered a haven of existence that pre-dates the time of the dinosaurs. Warmed by the Earth's core, nourished by a food chain that has never seen the light of day, Nature's apex predators will remain within these primal waters for the rest of their reign, living and breeding, avoiding extinction, until one day in the distant future, when the vents run dry and the prey disperses—

—forcing the few surviving creatures back to the surface from which they came . . .

EPILOGUE

GOVERNOR'S MANSION
SACRAMENTO, CALIFORNIA

The governor's mansion is located on forty-three sprawling acres of riverfront property in the western section of Sacramento.

Jonas Taylor and James Mackreides enter the Victorian dwelling, then follow an aide through a high-ceilinged reception area and down a corridor to the open glass-paneled double doors of a billiards room.

Governor Aaron Byzak, pool stick in hand, watches a wide-screen projection of the 49ers–Cowboys game while he awaits his turn. A second man, Senator Brandon Money, bends over the pool table, concentrating on a tough bank shot.

The aide knocks. "Excuse me, Governor, but your noon appointment is here."

Byzak waves Jonas and Mac into the room. "Professor Taylor, appreciate you driving up on a Sunday."

"Actually, we flew up by chopper. You've met my business associate, James Mackreides?"

"Mac, right?" The Governor shakes his hand. "Make yourselves at home. Scotch and water?"

Mac glances at Jonas. "Just the water for me."

"Suit yourselves."

Senator Money curses as the cue ball follows the five into a corner pocket.

"Senator, stop grumbling over there and say hello to our guests."

Brandon Money shakes Mac's hand, then turns to Jonas. "Saw you on that *Daredevils* special last week. You got some set of cajones, my friend."

The governor slaps Mac across the shoulder. "So, how's it feel to be back in the limelight after so many years?"

"Personally, I can't stand it. Forces you to waste time exchanging bullshit with the local politicians."

"Touché." The governor circles the table, then buries the two ball in the side pocket. "You know, many years ago, back when my father was lieutenant governor, he took me to see that Megala-shark of yours. Amazing experience. Humbles the soul. Afterward, Masao Tanaka invited my father and a bunch of VIPs down to that underwater viewing chamber to see Angel up close. Must've been thirty of us down there . . . visiting governors, a few actors, even the president of some South American country, can't remember which one. Didn't matter who we were, all of us pretty much stained our boxer shorts that afternoon. Me, I couldn't get enough. Would've stayed down there all day and night just to watch that glorious creature swim by. You can imagine how disappointed I was when she escaped."

"Angel's an incredible animal," Jonas concedes.

"That big male that washed up on Half Moon Bay three days ago was a pretty incredible animal too. Nasty wounds. Looks like your Angel tore up half its lower torso. Mean fish. I take it you've seen the photos."

Jonas nods. "I'm the one who took them."

"Oh, right." Byzak taps in the six ball, then chalks up. "Any idea why Angel would want to eviscerate her own mate?"

"Maybe she didn't like California's new divorce laws," cracks Senator Money.

The governor chuckles, then misses his next shot.

"Megalodons are extremely territorial creatures, Governor. Like her mother before her, Angel selected the Monterey Submarine Canyon as her nursing site. The presence of another adult within her territory, especially an aggressive male, would be a constant threat to her pups. Of course, that maternal instinct will wear thin as her young grow larger, assuming she's pregnant."

"Sort of gives new meaning to the term 'dysfunctional family,' huh?" Byzak glances at the football game, watches a replay, then turns back to Jonas. "When my father and I left your facility, do you know what he said to me? He said, 'Aaron, this place is a diamond mine for its owners and for the state of California, but these people are doing it all wrong. The arena needs to be expanded, and there should be hotels and malls and restaurants.' In short, Professor, that Institute of yours needs to be converted into a major theme park. Can you imagine how many conventions we could lure into the area with the right facilities in place?"

"Masao always wanted that, but he never had the chance."

"Lawsuits from the victims' families crushed us," Mac adds.

"I studied that case back when I was a trial lawyer," Money says. "The Feds ramrodded you but good."

"Nevertheless," the governor says, "getting that facility up and running the right way could give California's economy a nice boost. So what do you fellas think?"

Jonas shrugs. "What do we think about what?"

"Recapturing Angel, of course. We certainly can't allow her to have her babies in California waters. Plenty of land near the lagoon. We could probably add three or four more lagoons, lay 'em out like a bunch of aquaducts."

"Probably accommodate a half-million visitors a day," the senator adds.

Jonas shakes his head. "Like I told my wife and kids, I think I'll pass. Imprisoning an animal like Angel just doesn't sit right with me anymore. I don't know what the lifespan of a Megalodon is, but I'd prefer Angel live hers outside the lagoon."

The governor eyeballs the senator. "Well, if that's your final decision, I guess you leave us little choice."

"Meaning?"

"We'll have to hunt her down," the senator answers.

"You can't hunt her down, Senator. She's a protected species, inhabiting a marine sanctuary."

"True, species are protected, but if one particular animal is a constant threat to human life, then we have an obligation to protect our own, especially when we're talking about an animal that tends to eat us alive."

"Angel's not after human prey," Jonas retorts.

"The families of those victims at Pac Bell would probably disagree with you," Governor Byzak says, as he flops down on one of the black leather recliners.

Mac picks up a pool cue. "Maybe it's a moot point, Governor. The Institute's broke and in no position to finance something like this. And even if we did recapture Angel, the lawsuits from those families would bury us all over again."

Jonas nods. "Unless . . ."

"Unless what?" The governor's eyebrows rise.

Jonas removes an envelope from his jacket pocket. "This is the autopsy report I completed on the deceased male. It documents multiple human body parts found in the Meg's stomach. Unfortunately, the acid within the shark's stomach made it impossible to identify the victims."

The governor glances at the report. Grins. "I get it. You want us to report it was the male and not Angel that attacked those people in McCovey Cove."

"And bye-bye lawsuits," Mac says.

"What about all those witnesses?"

Jonas shrugs. "One albino Megalodon looks like the

next unless you peek under its skirt. The only real witnesses that can prove it was Angel are my wife and that Bunkofske fellow."

"And he's dead," finishes Mac.

"It's a win-win," Jonas says. "California gets a major global attraction, and we'll arrange for the victims' families to share the proceeds from the sale of that dead male's teeth."

"Is that it?"

"No," Jonas says. "As you mentioned, the lagoon needs tons of work. We'll need a long-term, low-interest construction loan to complete repairs, and we want the state to contribute to doubling the size of the arena and lagoon."

"And don't forget the skyboxes," Mac says.

"Skyboxes?"

"Naturally, we'll be reserving one for you, Governor."

"And we'll be reinforcing the subterranean viewing chamber," adds Mac.

"Sounds to me like you fellas have been talking to the Dietsch Brothers."

"They'll be building the hotel."

Governor Byzak circles the pool table. Picks up the cue ball, its surface as white as the Megalodon's hide. "Okay, I'm game, but we're not there yet. See, the lawyers are gonna hound us. They'll want absolute proof it was that male and not Angel that attacked all those people at Pac Bell. Come up with a solid solution to that problem and you fellas have yourself a deal."

Jonas nods to Mac, who reaches into his pocket and tosses him an object sealed in a plastic bag. "Here's a little souvenir for you, Governor."

Byzak takes the object from him. Examines it.

It is a baseball, the rawhide mangled as if dunked in acid. "This is the home run Howard hit, isn't it? But how—"

"Amazing some of the things a shark will regurgitate while mating."

A grinning Governor Byzak extends his hand to Jonas. "Make sure my skybox faces away from the afternoon sun, I hate the glare."

TANAKA OCEANOGRAPHIC INSTITUTE

The full moon casts its lunar beacon on the dark waters of the lagoon. The bleachers are nearly empty, most of the spectators having left disappointed for a third day in a row.

The underwater speakers continue to pulsate with the baritone sounds. A worker pours fresh blood into the southern end of the tank, the elixir pooling directly beneath the side of beef suspended from the shiny new steel A-frame and winch.

Danielle Taylor, host of the pending series, *Megalodon World*, waits for her makeup artist to dab at the sweat lines running past her cheekbones.

Susan Ferraris checks her watch. "Today, please, while we're still young."

Jonas, seated across from Dani, winks at his daughter.

Dani sits back in her canvas chair and continues with the taping. "So, Jonas, I understand that, should Angel return, a portion of the gate proceeds will go directly to a research fund aimed at exploring the Mariana Trench?"

"Not just the trench, Dani, but all of the gorges surrounding the Philippine Plate. Who knows what other creatures inhabit that—"

A dozen spectators partying in the northern bleachers suddenly stand, gesturing at the dark canal.

Jonas is on his feet, two-way radio in hand, his eyes focused on the moonlit waters of the refurbished tank. "David, you awake up there? David!"

A groggy voice calls back from the control room. "Sorry, Dad. Fell asleep."

"Wake up, pal, and seal those outer doors. Angel just entered the lagoon."

"Yes!"

The seven-foot dorsal fin glides majestically into the main tank, a hundred people chasing it along either side of the bleachers. Reaching the southern end of the lagoon, Angel circles twice, then disappears.

Jonas squeezes his wife's hand, as Mac and his new bride join them, the two couples staring at the moonlit waters, waiting.

The surface erupts, the forty-ton Megalodon lifting its upper torso clear out of the water as it deftly snatches the 300-pound offering within its gruesome hyperextended jaws.

Jonas looks to the heavens, imagining Masao smiling down on them.

For a heart-stopping second the beast hovers above the water surface. And then Angel slips back into the dark waters of the lagoon to consume her meal in private—

—feeding her unborn young.

Jonas Taylor will return.

**For sneak previews of all of Steve Alten's novels,
go to www.SteveAlten.com**

Books in the MEG Series

MEG: A Novel of Deep Terror **(Bantam/Doubleday)**
The Trench **(Kensington/Pinnacle)**
MEG: Primal Waters **(Tor/Forge)**

AUTHOR'S NOTE

A very special thanks to

Vito Bertucci, a.k.a. the "Megalodon Man" for making available his Megalodon jaw during the promotion of *MEG: Primal Waters*. The jaw can be viewed at the Prehistoric Shark Museum and Gift Shop, located in Port Royal, South Carolina (843-525-1961), and at their Web site, www.megalodonman.net

graphic artist Erik Hollander, whose riveting Megalodon images can be viewed at www.MEGsite.com or www.ErikArt.com

and

Nick Nunziata, of CHUD.com, for all of his support.

Brandon Cole (cover—shark photo)
www.brandoncole.com

Andy McLeod (cover—diver photo)

ATTENTION
MIDDLE & HIGH SCHOOL TEACHERS

MEG: Primal Waters is part of Adopt-An-Author, a free, nationwide, non-profit program designed to excite young adults about reading and writing through the use of fast-paced thrillers, heroic nonfiction stories, motivational books, and direct contact with the authors via personal appearances, classroom phone calls, E-mails, and interactive Web sites.

For more information and to register for Adopt-An-Author, go to www.AdoptAnAuthor.com

Adopt-An-Author gratefully acknowledges our terrific sponsors:

The Hannah Langendorf Foundation

Ed & Tonja Davidson

The Writer's Lifeline
Your Bridge to the World of Professional Writing Services
www.TheWritersLifeline.com

The Law Offices of Cubit & Cubit
Ft. Lauderdale, Florida

Jacob Lions
@
Global Neighbors, Inc.